DEAD STOP

By

D. Nathan Hilliard

This book is a work of fiction. The characters, incidents, and dialogue are drawn from the author's imagination and are not to be construed as real. Any resemblance to actual events or persons, living or dead, is entirely coincidental.

FIRST SOFTCOVER EDITION

ISBN-13: 978-1478297611

***

First printing: August 2012

This book is dedicated to my wonderful and trusted circle of proofreaders. It is through their diligent efforts the atrocities are confined to the antagonists of this book as opposed to its text. I want to thank...

Alex and Claire (Charlie) Paul

April Rood

Santanita Grogg

Stephanie Hilliard

And even my lovely wife, Karla, who has absolutely drawn the line at reading a book with zombies in it, but has provided good scientific and practical advice on many book related matters.

TABLE OF CONTENTS

PROLOGUE

Awakening

Silence.
Nothing.
Then...

Awareness came to the thing that had once been Victoria Valdez.

Only awareness, nothing more as it lay there in the darkness. Not awareness of anything in particular, not even awareness of self...just the simple reception of stimuli without any form of interpretation.

It ignored the blackness and silence, since they were nothing but the absence of light and sound and therefore unrecognized. And with no history of movement, all sensation such as the wetness of the bottom of the casket remained the same as when awareness first ignited, giving nothing to differentiate any of it. The thing merely lay there, not even aware of the simple fact of its own existence.

It just was.

Things continued in this state for an unknown duration, because even time has no meaning in a world without thought.

Then it came...something new.

Something providing the first "newness" to the timeless existence of unrecognized stimuli. That "something" faded to life like the faintest of sparks in the eternal blackness, hovering within the awareness yet providing the first thing for the awareness to turn to. It hung in the dark like a dim ember, slowly filling the empty universe of the former Miss Valdez with itself.

That "something" was called NEED.

DEAD STOP

It brought focus, and provided a point for the awareness to latch onto. Something tangible. And once this had been done, the most rudimentary form of self awareness came into being. Not much. Not anything normally thought of as such. There was no concept of "I" in the usual sense...the hardened lump resting against the back of its brainpan couldn't formulate anything near so complex...but there now became an awareness of "other." There now existed the knowing that NEED should be filled, and something else existed to fill it.

No true cognition had been involved in the arrival to this conclusion. It came more as a form of recognition. But even at the most primitive of levels, one thing leads to another.

Need requires filling.

Filling requires motion.

A basic reflex, nothing more. This recognition came on a level any insect, or even some lower life forms, could have matched.

But it was enough.

Synapses hardened by formaldehyde sparked for the first time in over two years. Shrunken muscles twitched, and joints brittle from disuse cracked. Victoria's body began to jerk in its confined space...slowly at first, then with more violence as larger muscles were brought into play. The corpse started to buck and flop, filling the confined space with muffled thumps and wet squelches.

In reality, a casket is not the dry place of bones and cobwebs so often depicted in the horror movies. Over time, fluids settle and moisture from the surrounding soil finds its way in as well. Many bodies lie on a layer of quilted cloth soaked in a stew of embalming fluid, water, and bodily secretions. The humidity inside often reaches a hundred percent.

The body thrashed in wild seizures, ripping the soggy linens in its dank cocoon. The crackle of its spine, as it flexed for the first time in years, mingled with the smack of damp meat against wood. The coffin had become a noisy place, a new stimuli now being recognized by the primitive awareness while its body convulsed.

2

Even the smell, stirred alive again by the thrashing in the mortician's soup of formaldehyde and decay, registered in the dim awareness.

The seizure-like flailings continued for a few more minutes, as signals randomly flitted down disused pathways then returned with the effect of their transmission. Once again, recognition began to seep in. The most primal patterns stamped indelibly in the wasted nervous system began to assert themselves. Movements became less spasmodic, less random, and muscles began to act in conjunction as opposed to fighting each other.

The body began to remember how to move.

Not perfectly. Not even well. But the behavior of a lifetime of motions still resided in the nervous system itself.

Toes curled. Knees bent and straightened. Hands began to clench and unclench, first together then one at a time. Even a few breaths were taken, although the lung linings and other systems needed to make use of the oxygen were long gone. The thrashing subsided as control over movement was reasserted.

Now motion existed alongside need...and the need had begun to grow.

It was time to move...

...time to move towards filling the need.

Purpose had sprung into being.

Fill the need. Go to where the need could be filled.

Rot stained hands searched the coffin. They fumbled along the corpse's sides, then gripped and pulled the shredded linens on the walls of the casket. One tangled itself in the long skirt Victoria had been buried in, but managed to tear itself free after a few clumsy attempts before resuming its mission. They explored the entire casket within easy reach.

No coherent thought guided their action, but they did move with purpose. And as they moved, the thing recognized it was *inside*. It was inside and it needed to get *out*. Out to where the need could be filled.

And outside meant going *up*.

3

Once more the hands moved with purpose. This time they attacked the top of the enclosure with a power that would have surprised the deceased Victoria if she had been able to witness it. But Victoria wasn't here...not really. The flashes of activity now happening in what remained of her nervous system had little to do with the graceful young woman who played clarinet in the marching band, wrote poetry, and dreamed of designing fashions before a bad dive off a high diving board had brought all that to an end.

The assault on the coffin lid was clumsy, but it was also strong and relentless. Neither fatigue nor despair ever entered as a factor. The hands clawed and pounded the wood with no variation in their intensity, and within an hour the first trickle of dirt fell into the fetid box. In another few minutes one of those hands tore through the lid. The earth now poured into the casket, but it meant nothing to the digger. It struggled and forced itself through the widened hole, clawing its way up through the damp packed earth.

It was tight, seemingly impossible work but now the outcome was inevitable.

The abomination that had once been Victoria Valdez pulled itself out of the ground on the afternoon of October 28th in a rural south Texas graveyard.

Armageddon had arrived.

CHAPTER ONE: AFTERNOON

Afternoon - Deke

"Deke! Wait a minute!"

Deke groaned, and the boy's wiry shoulders sagged as he pulled open the front door. His mother's shout cut like a bandsaw through the tiny house. Her timing couldn't have been worse, and he winced in the knowledge she could now probably be heard by everybody on the block.

"Aw mom," he sighed loudly and hung his head, "I gotta go. Harley's waiting."

"Harley?" Her voice floated in from the back bedroom over the chatter of an unseen TV. "Harley Daughtry? What are you doing running around with him?"

Deke gritted his teeth as he clutched the handle of the screen door. He really didn't need this on top of everything else.

Hell, Mom...who else is there to hang out with? All my friends have gone to college or got jobs in Houston or San Antonio while I'm still stuck in this shitty little dump of a town.

"Harley's okay, Mom," he pleaded. "Please don't start this."

He may as well have been asking for the earth to stop turning.

"He's a bum, Deke. He's just as shiftless as his old man, and he'll probably end up the same way, too. Besides, he's older than you."

"He's only five years older and he's back from the Army, fer Pete's sake...not prison. Give the guy a break."

"He's no good! He's going to get in trouble some day, and I don't want you around him when he does."

"Mom," the boy groaned, "he's not his Dad. You can't blame him for stuff he didn't even do."

"I worry, Deke. I worry about you."

"I'll be fine. I gotta go!" He pushed the screen door open.

"Well, where are you going? When will you be back?" The voice now carried a hint of whine, causing Deke's jaw to clench. "You know I don't like staying here alone with my back what it is."

I'm going nowhere, Mom. Nowhere at all. And it ain't much of a trip because I already live there.

"We're just going to drive around for a while, then we'll probably go hang out at the Textro. I'll be back by midnight."

"Midnight! There's a storm coming in!"

"Maybe sooner!" he called back over his shoulder as he stepped out. "I love you, Mom!"

"Deke! Don't just..."

The door slammed shut, and he hustled across the small wooden porch towards the old pickup truck. His boot heels made sharp reports on the old boards before landing with a crunch in the gravel driveway. In Masonfield, concrete driveways and sidewalks were for the people who could afford to build their houses since the nineteen seventies. They had their own side of town...and this wasn't it.

The youngster ran across in front of the beat up Chevy and around to the passenger door. He reached in through the window and pulled the inside handle to open it. There was no outside handle, but Harley had only paid seven hundred dollars for the vehicle so he seemed fine with it. Of course, Harley seemed fine with pretty much everything.

Deke pulled himself into the weathered vinyl seat and slammed the door closed behind him. Free at last. He puffed his cheeks out and pulled down his straw cowboy hat, then glanced over at Harley who grinned quizzically at him.

"Don't worry about it," the boy grunted, "Let's just get out of here."

"You got it, amigo," Harley drawled and looked over his shoulder as he backed the pickup out of the driveway and onto the cracked pavement of Terrance Street. "How far are we heading?"

"How much gas you got?"

"That bad, huh?" Harley laughed and rested his elbow on the sill of his open window as they drove down the street.

Some people said Harley Daughtry was born with a smile on his face. Tall, rangy and laid back, his white teeth were almost always cheerfully visible. Even in other than happy circumstances, his smile usually remained...yet never in an inappropriate way. His grin had different expressions the same way other people's faces wore theirs.

His flannel shirt had the sleeves ripped off, revealing long arms that were hard with lean muscle. His blue jeans and boots were staple wear for this neck of the woods, and the small felt cowboy hat perched on his head was so beat up Deke had once told him it looked like it had lost the Afghan war all by itself.

The second he said it he had bit his lip, wondering if maybe he had crossed a line, but Harley had only laughed. The man was just good natured and not prone to taking insult.

Currently that grin had a tinge of concern to it as he looked over at his younger passenger.

"You okay, buddy?"

"Yeah," Deke sighed. He watched the line of small, five-room houses go by and remembered how he thought they were the norm when he was a kid. Somehow the memories of happily chasing and playing amongst them with his childhood friends now depressed the hell out of him. "I'm fine. Just another glorious day in Hooterville."

"Uh huh. Is it the job hunting, or your mom?"

"It's just the same old thing. No big deal. How about you, any luck on a job?"

"Sort of," Harley slowed to a stop as a toddler in overalls chased a dachshund across the street in front of them, with his mom screaming bloody murder not far behind. She caught him on the other side, scooped him up, and started whaling away at his butt while glaring in all directions as if daring somebody to say anything about it.

Neither Harley nor Deke were so inclined. They drove onwards, leaving the scene behind.

"Sort of?" Deke pressed.

"Yeah. County Electric told me I can have old man Foley's job reading and installing meters when he retires. Of course that's still not for about a year. So I guess I'll just hang loose and pick up a little here and there till then."

"County Electric? Sounds pretty good. I hear working for the county can be a sweet gig."

"It suits me," Harley nodded. "I'd get to get out and drive around, not be stuck indoors all day. And the county pays benefits. I'd be pretty much set."

"Yep," Deke agreed with little conviction. "I guess you got it made."

The truck turned onto Main Street and the boy watched in silence as the row of ancient brick buildings glided past. About half were boarded shut, and the other half all owned by people in their sixties or seventies...people hanging on simply because they didn't know anything else to do. The recently opened Superstore. six miles to the north in Craigsford, now got most of the business anyway. Deke figured in ten more years the whole street would most likely be deserted.

"You betcha," Harley mused cheerfully aloud, "The house is already paid for and so is my truck." He gave the door an enthusiastic pat that reverberated through the cab. "But you know what I mean...you got the same sweet setup coming."

Deke realized it was true, as far as it went.

The little house he had been born and raised in had been paid off long ago. And the same held true for the old Ford four-door sedan his mom let him drive to go shopping or hunt work.

Yep, lucky me.

He pictured the little ramshackle house on the quarter acre lot in his head. The porch already had a bit of a droop at one corner, and the shingles were now bleached white and starting to curl with age. The paint was lumpy and flaking off in places because his Dad had simply painted it directly on top of the old paint a few years

8

back...right before he left for parts unknown. The wood revealed underneath was gray, and the whole place shook if somebody stomped their feet.

"Oh yeah, lucky me," Deke muttered half aloud. "One day all that will be mine."

Harley cast a sidelong glance at his younger passenger.

"Okay, dude," he sighed, then squinted narrowly at Deke, "I can tell this has gotten serious. You have let this whole bummed out thing take over your world and it's time for an intervention."

Suddenly Deke wished he had kept his mouth shut.

"Forget it, Harley. I'm fine."

"Nope, it's too late for that. Ol' Harl is here to help, and he has a plan."

"A plan?" The young redneck cast a nervous look at his companion.

"Yessir, a plan. It's time to get you focused on other things, and I know just how to do it. All I need from you is to make a leap of faith and agree to go along with it...right now."

"Right now? I haven't heard what the plan is yet."

"Yep, right now. I promise it ain't anything illegal, physically dangerous, and it won't even get you in trouble with your Mom. Now you can't complain about terms like that!"

Deke considered those conditions with deep suspicion. They ruled out most of his usual worries when it came to hunting something to do, but still..."

"C'mon Deke, I'm your friend. Right?"

"Right," he agreed with slow caution.

"And you trust me, right? You understand I would never have you agree to something harmful to you. Okay?"

"Okaaaayyyyy..."

"So, I'm saying it's leap of faith time. Promise me you will go along with this idea, and I promise you will be a better man for it."

Now *that* sounded ominous. Things involved in becoming a "better man" had a way of including unpleasantness.

9

"I don't know…"

"C'mon Deke. Promise me. You got my word you will be okay."

Deke tipped up his hat up and stared at his smiling friend. He didn't trust this, but at the same time didn't want to offend the only friend he currently had.

"And you promise this won't get me in trouble with either my Mom or the law?"

"Word of honor, my man. Hell, your mom might actually approve."

This pretty much eliminated anything objectionable Deke could imagine, but he hated committing himself like this. Still, if it wasn't dangerous, illegal, or going to get his mom on his ass…why the hell not? It wasn't like he was doing anything else important anyway.

"Okay, Harley," he sighed. "I can't believe I'm doing this…but okay."

"You promise?"

"Yes." He closed his eyes and swallowed. "I promise."

"Great! I'll pick us up some Cokes and we'll go up to the old water tower where I can tell you the plan."

"Swell," Deke grumbled. "Somehow I bet I'm just going to loooooveee this."

Afternoon - Rachel

"Well, Doc? Is she going to be alright?"

Rachel stood up from the injured lamb, wiping her brow in the humid Texas heat with her forearm. Her normally blonde hair lay dark and sticky against her head. She still hadn't got used to how late in the year the heat lingered down this far south.

The other ewes milled about her and their fallen companion. They filled the pen with their woolly bodies and made the hot day seem even worse. Their proximity, their combined body heat, and the smell of lanolin that came with it, threatened to make her head swim. The approaching storm with its cooler weather couldn't come fast enough for her.

She looked over and grimaced at the old man asking the question. Normally, she would have composed an optimistic but professionally guarded response to the query, however Clinton Hollis was one of her best clients and about as good a friend as a professional relationship would allow.

"Well, I've sewn her up." She indicated the bloody mass of wool on the ground in front of her. "Which is pretty much all I can do. And you know how it is with sheep. When you've got one down for pretty much any reason, things don't look promising...and this one has been chewed up pretty good. Did you see what did it?"

"Yeah." The old man leaned rested his arms on the top board of the fence and watched as she started to pack her equipment. "It was a dog. Black and white. Looked like one of those collie type dogs. Kind of sad and ironic, if you know what I mean."

Rachel nodded in understanding.

Sometimes people didn't want an animal anymore, and for some reason they thought turning them loose out in the countryside was the best way to deal with the situation. Or as far as she knew, maybe it was their way of not dealing with the situation at all. Either way, the result was the same. Cold, starving, and with none of the experience or instincts necessary to successfully hunt for wild game, they invariably turned to attacking livestock...even the ones who had originally been bred to protect sheep.

"Did you get it?"

"Yeah."

There was no hint of braggadocio in the farmer's voice, the type she had so often seen in men who successfully fired a bullet into something and caused it to die...which counted as another of the things she liked about Clinton. He didn't think compassion and manliness were mutually exclusive. He had an old fashioned courtliness to him which ran deeper than mere manners.

After Matt had died, he had found reasons to do business with her going above and beyond the call of good animal husbandry. She had been new to Masonfield at the time, and most folks didn't quite know how to approach their new veterinarian whose husband had been killed only three weeks after their arrival. Both grief stricken and financially locked into a new clinic she had borrowed heavily to build, it looked at the time like both her personal and professional lives were about to implode before they ever got truly started.

But then Clinton Hollis saved the day.

When everybody else had drawn back in consternation, not knowing how to deal with this tragic stranger in their midst, Clinton stepped forward and started sending her business. One week after the funeral he had showed up in her driveway with a horse needing its teeth floated. Three days later, he called her out to palpate his entire herd of cows in order to see which were pregnant and which needed to be rebred...a practice few farmers bothered with anymore. Then it started to become obvious something was up when he called her out again and probably became the first farmer in the entire United States to get all his barn cats caught up on their vaccinations. But by that time other farmers and clients caught the message and started sending her work too.

Suddenly, so many sick animals descended on her office it seemed like the entire town had either a farm animal or pet needing something done for it.

For a while there, Rachel had been so busy and tired she hadn't known what to do with herself. All of her kennels had been full, and she had been run ragged with farm calls. In hindsight, she knew the deluge of business was what got her through the worst of the grief and despair. At the same time it also broke through the discomfort a lot of people had in dealing with her. Over the course of the next eighteen months she found a community she could be part of, and it embraced its new veterinarian with open arms.

As far as Rachel Sutherland was concerned, Clinton Hollis had saved her life.

"The body is around back of the barn, if you want to see it." The farmer gestured with his thumb. "I don't think it was sick though. Just hungry."

"I'll pass." She peeled the bloodstained gloves from her hands and dropped them into a little baggie to throw away later. "Unless you want me to dispose of it for you, that is."

"Naw. I'll take care of it, Doc. I just put it back there in case you needed it for testing or something along those lines."

She pursed her lips in thought, then shook her head.

"No, I don't think so. From the way you said it behaved, and from the looks of this, there aren't any signs of something neurological going on. Like you said, it was just hungry."

She picked up her bag from the packed ground of the animal pen, and headed for the gate Clinton had already pulled open for her. He was dressed to leave for a dinner at the Knights of Columbus Hall. She knew if that hadn't been the case he would have been right down on the ground with her in the pen beside the ewe. As it was, she was well aware Kirstin Hollis was waiting for him, and figured she could do him a favor by wrapping this up and getting him on his way.

"Speaking of hungry, Clint, you might want to feed poor Kirstin before she takes off without you. There isn't anything else we can do here."

"You sure?" He closed the gate after she walked through and peered over the top at the wounded animal.

"If it gets back on its feet by the time you return tonight, it will probably make it. If not, it most likely won't make it through the night." She glanced over at Clinton's truck where she could see Kirstin's silhouette in the window. "On the other hand, *you* might not make it through the night if you keep your wife sitting in that truck much longer."

"Well, if you're sure..."

"Go!" she urged and pointed firmly at his truck. "I'll follow you two out and close the gate behind you since I'm already dirty."

"Okay, okay, young Missy," he huffed in mock indignation as they walked towards their vehicles "I'm going. It's a sad state the world has come to when a young lady insists on closing the gate for *me*."

"It's the twenty-first century," she chuckled back. "You have to let us 'young ladies' practice a little chivalry now and then too. It's good for us."

"Oh, well if it's good for you..." He rolled his eyes then grinned at her as he opened the door to his truck. "So, are we going to see you tonight at the dinner? Kirstin and I can see to it you have a place."

"Not tonight, Clint," Rachel called back as she rounded his truck to get to her own. "I've still got a dental cleaning on Miss Tatum's cat waiting for me back at the clinic. After that I think I'll just go out to the truck stop and grab a bite before hitting the bed. I won't be fit for anything but the Textro tonight anyway. You two have a good time, and let me know how it works out with the ewe."

"Will do."

She waved and got into her own truck.

The offer to have dinner with them had been attractive. Clint and Kirsten were good company and it had been forever since she went out and had a nice dinner with people she liked. But she really did have the dental to do, and there just wasn't time to clean up and change into a nice outfit afterwards.

Besides, the Knights of Columbus dinner would be filled with a lot of her clients, many of whom would be eager to corner her and ask questions about their pets and their various ailments. Most didn't realize it was hard for her to remember all of their pet's different needs and conditions without her charts for reference. On the other hand, the Textro mainly served out-of-towners, truckers and kids hunting a place to eat out late, meaning the likelihood of her getting to eat her meal in peace would be much higher.

And with half of Masonfield at the KofC dinner and the other half at tonight's High School football game, the truck stop ought to be pretty much local free. Also, the idea of staying out late, watching the storm's fireworks, and reading a book with a never ending supply of coffee at her disposal had a certain appeal.

"Woohoo," Rachel sighed as she followed the Hollis' truck down their long driveway. "The things I do for excitement nowadays."

###

Afternoon - Amos

Amos Godfrey disengaged the clutch on the attached mower and pulled his tractor to a stop in the shallow ditch alongside County Road 498.

His back ached from the long hours in the tractor and his hands were almost numb from the vibration of the steering wheel. It had been a long day. But it was nearly over and only one chore remained.

The gates of the Mazon County Cemetery stood just ahead, representing his last job for the day.

"Amos, old man...you're getting too long in the tooth for this." He was already a couple of years past retirement age but the economy, being what it was, made leaving an option best put off a little while longer.

The man reached down and grabbed a plastic milk jug half full of water sitting next to the tractor's seat. He took a long slug of the lukewarm liquid then poured some over his head. It didn't cool him much, but at least if felt good to get the sweat off his face. The air today hung thick with moisture, despite the absence of rain. That would be coming later. Somewhere nearby, a locust unaware the summer had passed still buzzed its lazy drone in the heavy atmosphere. Even on a late October afternoon, mowing the roadsides was hot work in this part of Texas.

Amos capped the water jug and surveyed the area.

The cemetery sat alongside the back country road, bordered on two sides by brown rows of corn stalks and large piles of dirt on the third. The dirt had recently been brought in by the county, after making a deal to get it on the cheap from some wildcat copper mine reopened a few counties over. They had dumped it in great raw piles in the space between the cemetery and Clark Creek, to be used on future roadwork projects.

The old man shook his head in disgust at the eyesore.

When a couple of locals objected, the county commissioners had replied the piles would provide extra protection against Clark Creek eroding its way into the cemetery. Amos knew it was a ridiculous argument...the creek flowed too slowly and lay too far away to be a threat. But it silenced the objections. Now people visiting their deceased loved ones got treated to large piles of dirt for background scenery, to go along with the corn.

The county road worker dismounted the tractor and headed for the gates. His job was to cut the grass of the cemetery every month when his route of mowing roadsides brought him back around to it. The tractor pulled mower was not feasible for this job, but the county had an old riding mower stowed in a tool shed hidden in the trees at the back of the graveyard.

A quick peek at his watch told him he had about an hour before it started getting dark, so Amos picked up his pace. It left just enough daylight to get the job done if he wasn't too picky, and get out of here before the rain started falling. A quick glance to the northwest revealed the heavy clouds marching in, and a distant rumble promised atmospheric mayhem in the future.

He needed to move, and get this over with.

Then he would be finished for the week, and could get home in time to change and go watch his grandson play football at the high school. The Masonfield Pirates had a good team this year. They were only two wins away from getting themselves a place in the state tournament. And with their running game, the rain tonight would favor them over the visiting Bulldog's vaunted passing attack.

Amos strode with hurried purpose through the tombstones, intent on the little aluminum shed under the trees in the back. The sun already hung low in the sky. This resulted in much of the place being cast in shadow, both from the dirt piles and the tree line of Clark Creek. At least this took the edge off the heat, but it still counted as a stark reminder he needed to hurry if he didn't want to be mowing a cemetery alone after dark.

His eyes fixed on the door to the little shed and he hustled straight to it. A few seconds of fumbling in his pocket produced the key ring he used to hold all his county keys. As he flipped through the keys, Amos noted how much darker it was here under the trees and wondered if perhaps it was already too late to be starting this.

For a brief moment he paused and considered the idea of putting it off till next week. Then he remembered Monday would be the last day of the month and he had to finish the rest of his route by then.

It must be done now.

With a sigh, he found the right key and inserted it into the padlock. It opened with a satisfying click and the chain rattled in a loud, metallic staccato as Amos pulled it free from the door handles. He wasted no time in opening the doors and stepping inside.

The mower squatted in the center of the gloom under a black plastic tarp. Amos yanked the tarp off and threw it into the corner before moving over to the shelves loaded with containers of different shapes and sizes. Most were fertilizers, pesticides, and other chemicals necessary for the maintenance of a green graveyard, but he found what he sought on the bottom shelf next to a coil of rubber hose.

The county worker pulled the gas can out, and gave it a quick shake. Satisfied with the weight and slosh of liquid within, he set it next to the mower. Amos wished the shed came with electricity so he could have better light for this. Kneeling by the mower, he fumbled in the murk for the gas cap and started unscrewing it.

Thoom!

He had just pulled it free when a loud thump against the side of the shed almost made him jump out of his skin.

"What the hell?!"

Amos dropped the gas cap in surprise, and nearly kicked over the fuel can while stumbling to his feet. The confined area made sudden movement difficult, and he almost fell before reaching out and grabbing the shelves to keep from going down. The rickety apparatus shook under his weight. A jug of weed killer started to topple from the top shelf but he managed to turn and steady it before getting himself drenched in herbicide.

Finally catching both his breath and his balance, Amos straightened to his feet and stared wide-eyed at the walls of the shed.

What the hell was *that*? He was supposed to be alone out here.

Wasn't he?

Once again, a thump sounded against the thin walls...but this time it sounded softer, and he could tell it was coming from the side of the shed opposite the doors. It was followed by a dragging sound, like somebody or something was leaning against the outside and moving slightly. Whatever it was, it definitely didn't come from a low tree branch or something along those lines. This had the quality of something alive.

A cow maybe?

Amos frowned at the wall and started a slow retreat away from it and towards the door. Something *was* out there, and it wasn't supposed to be.

He thought about calling out and demanding whoever it was to identify themselves, but the mental image of him yelling at a cow like a scared old fool squelched the impulse. Besides, if it turned out to be one of his idiot coworkers out here trying to scare him, he damn sure didn't intend to give them something to laugh about for the next two weeks.

And as soon as he thought of them he realized the bang had almost certainly been somebody slapping their hand against the shed before dragging it down the wall.

Either the other tractor operater, Manny, or his buddy Curtis in Sanitation, must have known this was the day he mowed the county graveyard and had been waiting here in hopes of scaring him. They were both jerkoffs and prone to pulling this type of crap.

Well it wasn't going to work.

"Nice try, you jackasses!" He stepped out of the doorway then headed around the corner of the shed. "But next time you might want to think about waiting until..."

He came to a stop as he rounded the second corner, bringing the back of the shed and what leaned against it into view.

It wasn't Manny or Curtis.

Amos stared in shocked astonishment at the dim figure only a few feet away in the shadows.

It was a girl...and she was filthy.

She was leaning forward with both hands placed against the back wall of the shed as if for support. Her head drooped, and long black hair hung down obscuring her face from view. What looked to have once been a cream colored dress was coated with streaks of dirt and filth, and its entire back was covered with a large, mossy black stain.

And she stank.

He started towards her, then came to an abrupt stopped as she reacted to his presence.

"Holy shit! Oh, holy shit!" the old man gasped and stumbled back as the girl straightened and turned her head to face him.

Her skin was dark gray and cracked like old paint. It had a certain inert quality more associated with things than people, like the skin of a mummy only not quite as desiccated. Her eyes and mouth were tightly closed, and her face as immobile as a mask. It also had a sunken appearance that convinced him more than anything else this could be no joke.

This was real.

He was alone in a graveyard, with a dead woman standing only a few feet away.

"This is bullshit..." he whispered in weak disbelief. He could hear a slight crackling sound, like knuckles popping, as she tilted her head and seemed to be trying to locate him by his voice.

The apparition had a disturbing blend of animate and inanimate qualities, suggestive of both a person and a thing...and yet neither.

Amos watched in horrified fascination as the dead woman removed one hand from the wall and stretched it awkwardly in his direction. She groped about with it blindly, her eyes still tightly shut. Her slender fingers were blackened with dirt and corruption, and pale points of bone showed at the end of them as if they had been worn or chewed off.

The man took another step backwards, just to put a little more distance between him and the thing. The sound of his step must have helped her locate him, for the corpse took a tottering step away from the wall in his direction. Then it stumbled to a stop, now flailing sightlessly in the air with both hands.

The effort looked almost comical, despite the fact it came from something that shouldn't exist. It wobbled before him like a bad performer on a tightrope, and was forced to take a step backwards to widen its stance and keep from falling. Then the wretched thing just stood there, its arms out in front of it like a sleepwalker, slowly feeling the air in front of it.

Apparently it couldn't open its eyes.

That's right, the old man realized, *they sew their eyes and mouths shut! Or glue'em or something.*

His initial terror started to fade as he watched the shape stand there in the shadows, weaving back and forth in blind disorientation. Despite its ghastly appearance, the thing also possessed a certain pitiful quality...more like something lost than something resurrected. As the shock of its appearance faded, he realized it seemed less threatening by the minute.

It's clumsy. It's slow. Hell, it's a girl for God's sake! It can't weigh more than a hundred pounds...a hundred and ten tops. I'm almost twice its size.

Amos squinted at it in narrow concentration and took a slow step to his right, taking care not to make any noise as he did. As he expected, the few times the thing grabbed outwards it reached for where he had been standing before instead of his new position. And as he watched it grasp in futile desperation at the air, the old man started to think of it more as a "she" than a thing.

Whatever it was now, this had once been a woman who had walked this earth alive. She had lived, loved, hurt, and hoped before death had come and taken all that away from her. She must have had a family and friends, for somebody had loved her enough to see she had been buried in what must have once been a nice gown...a gown he now realized had most likely been a prom dress.

This had been a young woman, hardly more than a girl.

He could even make out a withered sprig of a flower lovingly pinned on the front of the garment.

Now horrors of a different kind rose in his thoughts.

Was this still her? Did she know what had happened to her? Did she understand where she was and what state she was in? As unbelievable as it sounded, was this an alone and confused girl who somehow awakened in her coffin? Trapped alive in a blinded corpse?

Compassion began to war with fear, as he watched the wretched thing waver in what looked to be silent misery. Amos was a kind man, and even though he didn't understand how this had happened, or how it was even possible, he realized what stood before him might be a tragedy of the most monstrous type. And while there was nothing he could imagine doing for somebody in her plight, the thought of abandoning her to a fate like this felt monstrous as well.

He had to know if she was in there.

"Miss?" he called softly, taking a careful step back as the figure immediately zeroed in on his voice and started reaching his direction. "Miss, can you understand me?"

She took a halting step in his direction, then stopped as she nearly stumbled and fell again.

Amos took another step to the side, eyeing her with both pity and caution.

"Miss? I need you to think? I need to know if you're...you're..." he held up his hands and shook his head helplessly, trying to figure out how to finish the sentence.

The dead girl started then stopped once more, obviously trying to reorient to the new location of his voice. This time she only made a half hearted reach in his direction before letting her arm fall limp at her side.

The gesture contained a certain sense of defeat, as if she understood its futility.

"I want to help you," he swallowed, and moved sideways again as he spoke. "But I need some sign you're...you."

She just stood there, blindly turning to track his voice. No expression crossed her masklike features, and he wondered if it were even possible for her face to show any emotion she might have.

"Miss?"

He frowned as the girl slowly started to shake her head.

"Miss? What are you trying to do?"

He stopped moving, trying to understand this new development. What was she doing? Could she understand him after all?

The dead young woman continued to shake her head in what appeared to be some form of denial. Her hands flexed, curling and uncurling with small, sickening crackles of disused joints. Strands of hair started to drift from her scalp as the shaking began to increase in tempo.

"Miss?" he stared in both dismay and concern. Was this emotion? Could she actually be aware of her state, and suffering from the horror even worse than him?

She now shook her head violently, her hair whipping about in a shedding black cloud that settled about her. The force of the motion caused the bones in her neck to pop and snap even louder, and the effort even threatened to upset her precarious balance. The effect was somewhere between hysterical negation and an animal shaking its head in distress.

Then she stopped and buried her face into her hands.

"Aw hell," Amos groaned, both moved and repulsed by the obviously grief stricken figure.

This was completely insane. Over the years, and even serving in two wars, Amos thought he had seen the worst the world had to offer. But this was sick beyond belief. He was as scared of death as any man, yet he could only wonder what kind of loving God would ever allow something like this to happen to a human being? Especially a young woman!

A second later, he got his answer.

The dead girl's fingers tightened into bony claws and with one deliberate, downward motion, she ripped her own face off.

The cracked, grey skin tore with a gristly rip and slid off in a single rotten sheet, revealing the stained skull underneath. Withered and blackened muscles twitched like oily worms across the thing's ghastly visage. Many no longer had a purpose and writhed uselessly, the features they were intended to manipulate having been removed. On the other hand, the jaw muscles were still attached and now could move freely, causing the exposed mandible to work in a disturbingly experimental chewing motion.

But even worse were the eyes.

Shrunken lumps set deep in black sockets, they now fixed on the old man with insane intensity. Nothing even remotely human showed in those glaring orbs, and Amos came to the sudden realization God had nothing to do with this. Not one little bit.

Its jaw gaped open and the monstrosity lurched for him. Both of its claw-like hands now extended towards him with ferocious intent. Amos stumbled backwards, caught off guard by the sudden transformation, and the thing closed the space between them in three swift, awkward steps. One of those raptor-like talons closed on his bicep as he turned to run. Its grip was painful with surprising force.

Amos had just enough time to realize he had been drastically wrong about this creature.

It wasn't slow.

It wasn't weak...

...and it was hungry.

He screamed and tried to flee as the dead woman pulled herself up on his back and sank her teeth in the place where his neck joined his shoulder. Her weight on his back overbalanced him, interfering with his ability to run, and the intense flare of pain in his shoulder disoriented him. He could feel the yellowed teeth slice into muscle. Its legs wrapped around him and its other arm now embraced him from behind. The stricken man spun in desperate gyrations, attempting to throw the stinking horror off him while it tried at the same time to shift its grip from his arm to his head.

The two engaged in a frenetic dance any antelope and leopard down through the ages would have recognized.

In an adrenaline laced burst, he rammed into a tree at an angle calculated to drag her off. The impact was painful and jarring, but it nearly succeeded. The grasping hand fell away, and white hot agony erupted as the monsters teeth tore free of his shoulder...along with a mouthful of red dripping flesh. Amos cried out and spun again in an effort to twist free of the remaining arm and make a run for the tractor.

He almost made it.

The dead woman's embrace started to slip, and he surged forward in the direction of the gates...when another powerful grip closed around his ankle. The wounded man fell, thrashing wildly to the ground.

He twisted and looked down at his foot to discover it in the grasp of another corpse. This one, for some unknown reason, was dragging itself along the ground. But it had already solved its blindness problem as well, for another skeletal visage grinned back up at him. Its freshly exposed skull leered at the man for a horror prolonged second before turning and closing its jaws around his ankle.

Amos shrieked anew as he felt bone splinter and snap under the pressure.

He tried to kick free, but the pain and blood loss were starting to take their toll. A second later the dead woman fell back upon him, hands clawing like iron talons. That's when Amos Godfrey finally understood he was going to die. But even worse, right before her form blotted out the world he saw more forms lurching in his direction from the shadows, some still dripping dirt from the graves they had just vacated.

Other hands grabbed his twisting body, and he gave one last wailing scream as more rotten toothed mouths closed on various parts of his anatomy.

Then the woman's jaws found his throat and his pain came to a quick and merciful end.

DEAD STOP

CHAPTER TWO: TWILIGHT

As the sun set, now unseen behind the encroaching clouds, twilight fell over the Mazon County Cemetery like a blanket.

A swift drop in temperature heralded the leading edge of the storm as it moved in. The first stirrings of wind began to whisper through the dry stalks of corn in the surrounding fields. Along with it came the smell of rain.

Darkness formed in pools beneath the trees at the rear of the graveyard, masking the carnage from the attack of an hour earlier.

A dry flash of lightning revealed the ground to be carpeted with crows. They covered the area of Amos Godfrey's demise like a large black amoeba, strutting and crowding against each other, while picking at the blood covered grass and shreds of flesh left behind. Others filled the tree limbs overhead, and all the nearby tombstones were crowned with their black bodies.

There hadn't been much left to go around.

What had once been the old caretaker now consisted of a large blood soaked patch of earth strewn with gnawed bones and ragged bits of cloth. Only his feet remained intact, tossed aside as they were protected by boots with laces far beyond the feasters ability to fathom and untie.

The same flash of lightning also revealed the crows were not alone. The blackness under the trees concealed figures standing still and silent in the approaching night.

No speech, groans, or any other form of utterance issued from the motionless shapes. A slight breeze picked up and stirred wisps of hair and strips of clothing hanging from their desiccated frames, but otherwise they may as well have been the statues posted over some of the older graves.

Their blank, skullish visages faced whichever direction they had been when the bloody feast had come to an end. No hint of purpose, or even the former ghoulish life, showed in their eyes.

Then, as twilight deepened...something changed.

To the east, a light flickered, then came to life against the darkening horizon. It shone bright and steady, an almost actinic white, just barely visible over the tall rows of corn.

The darkness under the trees filled with the beating of wings as their owners took flight to the branches above. A brief chorus of harsh caws filled the murk, then the birds fell silent to monitor further developments. One of their deathly companions had stirred, and caution dictated they remain a safe distance. Now they waited to see if it would happen again.

They didn't have long to wait.

Withered necks twisted with the creak of old leather as the distant beacon trickled into the empty awareness of the lurkers. Some of the forms shifted to allow themselves to look in the same direction as their companions, ignoring the consternation their movement caused amongst the crows. In about thirty seconds, more than four dozen sets of black sockets and grinning jaws faced east.

A man with sharp eyes could have discerned the light was a tall, illuminated sign. If he had binoculars, he would have been able to read the word "TEXTRO," and "Food, Diesel, Gas," in smaller letters underneath. It glowed like a bright beacon against the evening sky, a little over a mile away.

These onlookers understood none of that.

The light simply drew their gaze as a new stimulus after the past hour of inaction. Their reduced eyesight could make out no details of this phenomenon, only that it was new and it shined bright in the gathering darkness.

Ruined synaptic pathways sputtered and flickered.

Recognition started to filter into the collective awareness.

This was light.

They didn't recognize it by name, or even as much of a concept. They simply understood it as a brightness against the otherwise darkening landscape. But as they remained fixed on it, one pair of sunken eyes...and then more....started to come to life with another recognition as well.

This was light...

...and light meant life.

Need.

Once more unholy vitality sprang to being in the eyes of all the watchers, and they moved in unison towards the east.

Some lurched, some stumbled, and some even crawled as their legs had decayed at a greater rate due to the realities of the preservation process. Embalming fluid is injected into the veins at the neck, and in some it hadn't spread as far into the legs as it should. Yet this wasn't the slow shuffle of the movies of yore. They moved at a steady, inexorable rate varying from individual to individual.

It didn't take very long for them to make their way through the tombstones and across the small cemetery. And it was there they came to their first obstacle. A low chain-link fence surrounded the graveyard and separated it from the corn field.

At first they simply walked up against it and stopped, temporarily confused by this new development. They lined along its length and in some places piled up against it. Then old patterns emerged and the bodies remembered other movements.

Gray hands closed on the waist high top rail, and spines crackled as the motions of climbing were attempted. Some merely leaned over the rail, resulting in them falling into the field on the other side. Others caused the wire fencing to shake and rattle as they clambered over with awkward fervor. In one place the small barrier bent and collapsed under the pressure where a group had piled up against it.

It was ungraceful and clumsy, but the obstacle was overcome with the same silent intensity characteristic of their attack earlier. And with the barrier behind them, the grisly mob surged onward. Withered forms plunged into the tall corn; the dry brown stalks and leaves rustling like rain as they pushed their way through.

At no time did they lose their fixation on the light in the distance. The beacon drew them onwards, their feral eyes now shining with need. Leathery hands flexed and skeletal jaws parted as their owners strode down the dark rows toward their distant destination.

Death was coming to the Textro for dinner.

Twilight - Rachel

Never forget...any time you poison an animal to the point of unconsciousness, you are taking a risk.

Rachel threw her lab coat against the wall of her back office and swore as the words of her old anesthesiology professor rose in her mind.

"That's a great line, Prof," she snarled at the tile ceiling, "A real pithy truism! But it doesn't help me explain to kindly old Miss Tatum why her precious Prissy is dead when all she came in for was to have her goddamned teeth cleaned!"

Realizing those last few words had come out uncomfortably close to a screech, the young veterinarian slumped into the padded chair, buried her face into her palm and rubbed her temples with thumb and fingers.

She knew any procedure involving anesthesia ran the risk, no matter how small, of this happening. Sometimes the animal just doesn't wake up. It could be because of an unknown heart problem or a number of other hidden conditions making an otherwise healthy appearing animal susceptible to death by anesthesia.

And sometimes the cause is never known.

She had sent her tech/receptionist, Arlene, home for the evening after all attempts to resuscitate the cat had failed. Then Rachel had steeled herself and dialed Miss

Tatum's number to deliver the bad news. She only got the answering machine. Miss Tatum had probably gone to the same Knights of Columbus dinner the Hollises had attended.

Lovely.

All she could do was leave a message to call her office in the morning, and hate what a formal and unfeeling bitch it made her sound like.

She really wished she had permission to start in on a necropsy. She wanted something...anything...to tell Miss Tatum that would explain how this could have happened. Some defect she could point at to help make sense of the treasured pet's death.

From all appearances Prissy had been a perfectly healthy eight year old cat. Now she lay stiffening in the freezer while Rachel slouched in her office, hating the world.

Life was supposed to make sense. Things were supposed to happen for a reason. Those two central tenets of her life had propelled her into science with the firm confidence all the answers were out there, just waiting for somebody with her type of determination to find them.

Rachel found comfort in the immutable laws of physics, math, and chemistry. Matter is neither created nor destroyed, two plus two invariably equals four, and multiplying the squared radius of a circle by pi would always give you its area. The universe had rules. Deep down she nurtured the unspoken conviction that "mystery" simply arose from the absence of data and there were no truly unpredictable events in the world.

Her physics professor had once stated that God was found in the places where the outcomes couldn't be predicted.

The only thing Rachel had ever found there was disaster.

People's cats weren't supposed to die just because you sedated them, and husbands weren't supposed to get killed just because they agreed to come out with you on a house call at night and help you with a sick horse. If God liked hanging out in those kinds of places then he could damn well do it without her.

A brief flicker of distant lightning lit the room, causing her to look up and glance at the clock.

"Crap," she muttered, "Looks like the rain is almost here. If there's going to be any supper for Dr. Killjoy, I guess I better get moving."

Rachel grabbed her jacket off the hook, started for the door, then came back to her desk to grab her Kindle and notebook as well. She decided she might as well have a book to read if the storm got bad and she stayed late. And who knows, maybe she could also write Mrs. Tatum something while she sat out there.

A distant rumble of thunder mirrored her thoughts on the subject, and she turned and headed for the door.

Twilight – Deke

"You want me to *what*?!" Deke choked on his Coke and sputtered at his grinning companion. "Are you out of your mind?"

The two sat parked beside the water tower on the low hill overlooking Masonfield, drinking sodas and watching the storm front roll in. The line of clouds towered over the little town. They rumbled with internal flashes of light that ricocheted back and forth throughout the approaching mass. Tiny street lights started to flicker on, a good half hour earlier than normal as the great shadow moved across the streets and houses. The distant lights of the football field already blazed with the game well under way.

"Calm down," Harley laughed. "You act like I just asked you to jump off a roof or something."

"Yeah? Well that might hurt too but it would be a lot less humiliating!"

"Aw c'mon, Deke. You've asked out girls before. Hell, you were running around with that Harper girl when I first got back."

"Yeah, but that was Molly Harper. This is a whole different ballgame!"

"How?" Harley took a long swig of his drink then crumpled the can. "Did Molly have webbed feet or something?"

"No! Jeez, Harley!"

"Okay, just checking. You never know. So what's the big problem here? I don't see it."

"The problem is, we're talking about Stacey Collins."

"So?"

"So?" Deke looked at Harley as if he had grown a second head. "We're talking about me asking out *Stacey Collins*! Do you realize who she is?"

Harley squinted at Deke, tossed the can into the back of the truck, and started the engine. Then he tilted back his hat and made a big show of scratching his head.

"Let me think...works at the Textro, pretty face, sexy smile, sunny disposition, and ginormous ta-tas. That Stacey Collins?"

"Harley," Deke shook his head, "you just don't get it. I went to school with Stacey. She was a pom-pom girl...hell, she was THE pom-pom girl. She was runner up for both Homecoming Queen and Prom Queen. She dated the quarterback, fer God's sake. She was way up there on her end of the social ladder...and let's just say I was a few rungs down."

He wasn't about to go into just how many rungs those were.

"Really?" Harley shrugged and pulled the truck out onto the roadway. "Well, high school is over and now she's a waitress at the Textro, trying to keep her ass from getting grabbed by every horny trucker who drops in. She might not look down on you from as high as you might think. Besides, the worse that can happen is she says 'no.'"

Deke wasn't so sure about that. He had a pretty vivid mental image of the gorgeous waitress dissolving into

33

a fit of hysterical laughter so full of feminine scorn the mere sound of it would melt him into a puddle of pure humiliation.

"So this is why you wanted to go hang out at the Textro tonight, isn't it."

"Well, I had noticed you looking at her before, and I just thought..."

"Of course I was looking at her, Harley! I'm male and I'm human! I've noticed the other hot number they have waitressing there too, you know."

"I just thought," Harley persisted, "that you have been pretty down in the dumps lately and needed to do something to shake things up. I hear she's available right now, and I think it would be good for you to take a risk and ask her out."

"Getting my pride squashed and used as toilet paper ain't exactly what I call shaking things up, Harley."

"Oh come *on*," the older redneck laughed again. "Now I know you're bullshittin' me. You've been turned down before, and you survived."

"Yeah, but those were surprises. At least I thought I had a chance with those girls. Besides, what would I say? Hey Stacey, how's it going? You want to come hang out over at my house with me and Mom?"

Harley didn't answer right away.

The two sped down the hill in the rattle trap truck, neither speaking for a moment. Harley reached over and popped open the glove box with a sharp blow and pulled out a cd case. He fished out the disc and pushed it into a dusty cd player he had duct taped on top of the dashboard.

"Oh no," Deke groaned. "Not this."

"It's time for some man-up music, Deke. You need this, son."

The deep twang of a steel guitar rang through the truck to the tune of *Ghost Riders in the Sky*. Deke rolled his eyes as Harley started beating the steering wheel to the rhythm of the song with his hands.

"Harley," he raised his voice to be heard over the music, "this ain't the answer to everything, y'know."

"It is for what ails *you*."

34

"Aw c'mon. What's that supposed to mean?"

Harley didn't answer right away, but chose to sing along with the song instead. It didn't end until the truck chugged to an intersection where they turned off the road and onto the highway heading away from town. The shadow of the great line of clouds fell across them as they accelerated down the roadway towards a distant white sign glowing on the horizon.

"Your problem," Harley nodded towards him, "isn't that you're afraid she'll turn you down."

"Oh no?"

"Nope. You're scared to death she is going to say yes."

"What do you mean, 'is going to'? I'm not sure I'm doing this."

"You will."

"Oh, you think so? I'm just gonna march up to the hottest living female in Mazon County and say 'Hey babe, how about you and me gettin' together and startin' something special,' huh?"

"I don't know how you're gonna do it...and I sure don't recommend that approach...but you will. You promised, remember? Besides, you *need* to."

"I do?"

"Yep. You need to start doing something to feel good about...even if it means getting shot down. Remember, it ain't about whether or not you win every battle but whether or not you fought them. There's the way you win the war of life."

"That's deep, Harley." Deke rolled his eyes. "Maybe I ought to just walk in and shoot the girl. It'll save us both a bunch of embarrassment and I don't have to grow old living with my Mom."

"That's a solution too," Harley nodded sagely.

"You're not helping."

Deke felt a small pool of acid form in his stomach as the Textro sign grew larger in the windshield. Even if by some unbelievable miracle she agreed to this, what the hell was he going to do with a girl like Stacey Collins?

"You see, you *are* going to do it. Good for you!"

"I am? Oh really?"

"Yep. I can tell by the look of sheer terror on your face. You're already considering outcomes."

"You're a real pal, you know that?" Deke watched the approaching sign like it was a harbinger of doom. "If I ever get hit by a bus, at least I know who I can count on to tell me how painful it looked."

"I'm just here to help."

"Oh, yeah? So what exactly am I supposed to ask this girl out to do? Sit at home and watch Jeopardy with Mom?"

"You'll think of something."

"Dammit! If you're going to throw me to the wolves, you can at least throw me a bone to wave at them! This is your stupid idea, so how about a little help?"

"Listen to you!" Harley crowed, "Think about where you are...now you have reached a place where the idea of *succeeding* in asking out a hot girl scares you."

"I know, Harley! Maybe I ought to start smaller. What do you think?"

"I think you would only end up with 'smaller'...which is part of your whole problem. If you don't do this, you're going to end up ten years from now sitting at home with your mom and making excuses to yourself for another girlfriend with webbed feet."

"Molly didn't have webbed feet!"

"Don't you think it's time you upgraded your criteria from that?"

Deke slapped his forehead into his palm, and then dragged his hand down his face to see they were arriving at their destination.

The Textro was a medium sized truck stop. It sat near the front of a five acre square of grease-stained asphalt at the corner of the US Highway 103 and a small country road. Its bleak isolation was accented by the cornfield bordering the parking lot on the other two sides. The main building was a rectangular structure with large plate glass windows running across the front and about two thirds of the way down each side. A large row of gas pumps sat under a red and gold awning out front of the store/restaurant, and another long awning covered the diesel pumps off to the south.

At the rear of the lot, a large maintenance building housed the garage and mechanic shop. Attached to it was a smaller structure containing a restroom, showers, and a small locker room for the truckers parked nearby. Most of the trucks were parked in a line near the back of the parking lot. At the moment, only the tall Textro sign and the red and gold neon around the top of the main building was lit, leaving the trucks sitting back in the gathering gloom.

"You ready to do this, kemosabe?" Harley pulled the old pickup into a parking space between the gas pumps and the front of the building. The spaces for cars ran in a row parallel to the building, about thirty feet away from the front sidewalk.

"Just give me a minute," Deke complained, his throat suddenly tight and dry. "I need to think up an approach that at least has some chance of success here. You act like you just want me to run in there and tackle her or something."

Harley laughed.

"Now I would pay real money to see that!"

Deke shook his head and rolled his eyes.

"You're a sick man, Harley," he sighed. "Just so you know."

"But I'm in your corner, Deke. Never forget."

"Oh yeah, lucky me," Deke grumbled and opened the truck door. "Well, let's get on with it. I can figure out how to do this over some coffee."

He hopped out and met Harley in front of the truck before the two strode across the parking lot under the darkening sky. The air felt thick and electric from the approaching storm. It wasn't quite nightfall, but the windows already shined with a cheery light casting long bright rectangles on the ground outside. Still, the only hint of autumn Deke could detect was the less than usual number of bugs starting to fly around the outside lights.

He pushed open the door and stepped into the truck stop.

The entrance opened into the store side of the truck stop, with another glass door to his immediate left leading to the restaurant. The store itself featured a bright collection of knick knacks, bumper stickers, drinks, and the usual junk food that people on the road found convenient to eat on the go.

Gladys Deacon looked up from her perch behind the counter, then immediately lost interest and went back to watching the little portable TV behind her counter. A skinny, middle aged woman with a beehive hairdo, Gladys had been a fixture here as long as Deke could remember. The only concession the schoolmarmish clerk had made to the changing times was now she stepped outside to smoke her cigarettes. Otherwise, she remained the same dour woman Deke remembered when his father brought him here as a kid.

He wasted no time in turning and pushing through the side door to the restaurant beyond.

"Hey Deke! Hey Harley! I'll be right with you."

Candy Beller finished ringing up the tab of a couple of highway patrolmen then hustled around the desk to them. The little blonde was a bundle of energy in a constant motion.

"I'm going off shift here in just a minute, but I can get you drinks if you like. I'll leave the menus with you guys, and Stacey or Marisa can get your orders when they come up front." She gestured at the mostly empty diner. "Go ahead and pick your own table."

The only other diners in the place were a couple of truckers sitting at the bar, a pair of young out-of-towners at a table beside the window, and a woman he vaguely recognized as the veterinarian, Doc Sutherland, who sat reading one of those new e-readers in a booth against the inside wall.

Deke gave a brief thought of asking which tables were served by which waitress, then came up with a more elegant and less embarrassing solution. He headed for an outside booth by the windows. Whichever girl had the inside tables would also have the bar, and if it turned out to be Stacey he could easily move there later to talk to her without raising a spectacle.

Pleased with solving his first problem in this evening's little exercise, he took his seat and smiled up at Candy as she brought them their coffee.

"Not much happening tonight, huh?"

"Not yet." The waitress set their coffees in front of them and added a pair of menus. "This place don't see much action on Friday nights until the football game lets out...then it's a madhouse."

"Pretty crazy, huh?"

"Yep." She leaned in close and lowered her voice. "That's why I'm in a hurry to clock out and get out of here, before Big Earl calls in and wants me to work a double shift. It's still a couple of hours till the game lets out though, and until then this place will be dead as a graveyard.

Twilight - Benny

"Hey girls, come check this out!"

Benny Trujillo held the back door of the truck stop open and motioned to the pair of girls who were just putting on their aprons to go on shift. He waited patiently as Marisa and Stacy glanced at him, and then at each other. The look conveyed their shared opinion of men and the often dubious outcomes that particular line led to.

In his case, the portly little janitor knew it was just habit on their part. In truth, both of them considered him a safe, older, and married man who was fun to tease yet trustable enough to confide in. Still, he found it slightly humorous and flattering the habit extended towards him too.

Not that he blamed them.

It only took one glance for anybody to understand their job history hadn't been the first thing Big Earl Anderson looked at when he hired this pair. They were as different as night and day, and quite possibly the two most smoking hot women within a hundred miles. Both were sharp as tacks, and had turned out to be surprisingly good workers, but there the similarities ended.

Marisa Valdez was a tall and graceful Latina with a full mane of lustrous black hair, expressive brown eyes, and legs seeming to stretch for miles. She moved like a dancer through the tables, drawing admiring looks from most of the patrons...especially after she passed. As Big Earl had once so eloquently put it, "If eyes were lasers, that girls butt would have caught fire after only a few seconds on the job."

Benny had laughed at the time, and pointed out if that had been the case then poor Stacey would have gone up in flames as soon as she stepped into the room.

Stacey Collins was not near as tall as Marisa and built along completely different lines. She had short brown hair, perky features, and a bright elfish smile that lit up any room she entered. The girl possessed an earthy, slightly redneck charm combined with a vivacious good cheer which tended to infect the people she interacted with. She also had what Earl once poetically described as "the most magnificent pair of huge, natural born hooters this side of the Rocky Mountains."

Benny had warned Earl that hiring these two beauties and putting them on the same shift (hell, even the same crew) was asking for trouble. He pictured the Textro turning into a battlefield of feminine egos and seething rivalry, with the rest of the crew caught in the middle.

As it turned out, he couldn't have been more wrong.

After a couple of days of quietly sizing each other up, the two astonished everybody by forming a tight working friendship that at times seemed to pit them against the world. Despite their vastly different backgrounds they became a two girl team, supporting each other with both customers and coworkers alike. After his initial surprise—and a big helping of crow—Benny came to understand that despite their differences the two girls realized they had a lot in common in a world prone to dealing with them primarily on their looks.

Now they regarded him with matched smiles of mock suspicion as he gestured towards the door.

"You see?" Marisa addressed Stacy while nodding towards him. "I told you he was a dirty old man. 'I want to show you something,'" she made little quote marks with her fingers. "You know how that always works out. Like we've never seen one of those before."

"Maybe he meant it like 'Hey girls, watch this," Stacey responded. "But those are usually more funny than bad...especially when they wipe out and break bones."

They both giggled, eyes twinkling in merriment.

"Ay yi yi!" Benny groaned aloud, "You two are exactly like the awful daughters I was afraid I would get, way back before I got lucky and had boys! When you're through giving a poor old man a hard time, you should at least come over and see what he was trying to show you."

"Sorry, Benny!" the pair sing-songed together with exaggerated looks of contrition on their faces. "We'll be good!" They made a big show of shuffling over to him with their heads down and hands clasped in front of them like chastened school girls.

"Augh!" He rolled his eyes and pointed through the open back door into the twilight. The girls peered out in the direction he gestured,

"*Que?*" Marisa frowned out into the gloom. The sodium vapor lamps were just beginning to flicker on and illuminate the back parking lot under their yellow glare. "I see the maintenance garage. And I see some trucks lined up along the back of the lot. Aaaannnnnd I see a cornfield."

"Oh look!" Stacey pointed off to the south at a female figure wearing tall hair, a tube top and hot pants, who was slowly making her way towards the line of trucks. "It's Libby the Lot Lizard, starting her rounds."

"Hi Lizzie!" the two girls sang out loudly, waving furiously at the truck stop prostitute.

Benny groaned as the older woman stopped and glared. She snatched the cigarette out of her mouth and snarled something incomprehensible at the waving pair before shooting them the finger and resuming her slow walk towards the garage. The waitresses almost collapsed in laughter, and the little janitor could only shake his head at the strange politics of women.

"So that's it?" Marisa dabbed her eyes as she recovered. "You wanted to show us Libby? We've seen Libby before, you know."

"All of her," Stacey chimed in, "If you count those two times she got thrown out of trucks without her clothes."

Benny winced at the memory, but stayed on topic...a real challenge when dealing with these two.

"No, you gooses! I was pointing at the sky back there above the cornfield."

"Ohhhhhhhhh...."

Both girls looked back out the door at the western sky.

"Well, it's dark," Marisa offered.

"Wait for it..."

"And it's getting windy."

"Wait for the lightning."

"Okay, but we need to..."

Fortunately, right then nature decided to be kind and produced the desired illumination. Lightning flashed and the girls both "oohed" at the scene revealed under the brooding clouds.

The western sky was full of birds.

Hundreds of black silhouettes flickered as if in a strobe light as they whirled in a great circle beneath the thundercloud. It was like a cyclone of crows, all sailing in the dark, windy sky.

"*Hijole!*" Marisa gasped. "What are they doing, Benny?"

"I don't know, *chica*," the little janitor frowned at the sky. "I saw them earlier, before you two came in, but they were circling way out there over the corn field. Now they're almost here."

"Awesome!" Stacey enthused. "And weird! I bet they are coming in ahead of the storm."

Benny studied the aerial whirlpool for a second, then gave it a bemused grimace.

"Could be," he shrugged. "You'd think they would go hide out in the trees at the Clark Creek, but maybe they got other ideas."

The two girls watched for a few seconds longer, then glanced at each other again and then their watches.

"Yeah, you would think," Marisa agreed, "but *we'll* have to go hide out in Clark Creek if we don't get a move on and get to our tables."

"Go ahead," Benny waved the girls back to their duties. "I've got to get a move on too. Tomas wants me to hold down the kitchen for him while he goes on break and runs some food back to Arnold and Leon."

Marisa snorted.

"You know the only reason he does that is so he and Leon can share a joint behind the shop, right?"

"Not my business," Benny shrugged. "He just needs to work on being a little quicker about it."

"You're too nice, Benny," the black haired girl frowned. "You need to stand up for yourself. Don't let him run all over you."

"Yeah, that's our job!" Stacey piped in.

"Will you two go to work?!" the older man groaned and shooed the girls away.

After they left, he spent a moment longer at the back door and watched the skies. Lightening flickered within the clouds again, once more revealing the frantic aerial whirlpool of crows. Their winged bodies swooped and swerved high overhead. Then the lightning faded, causing the vast flock to disappear once more against the blackening sky.

Benny frowned up at the blackness.

Stacey was right. It really did seem odd for birds to be cavorting out here in front of an oncoming storm like this. He figured they should be hunting for trees to shelter in by now. There certainly weren't any around here.

"Then again," he shrugged philosophically, "what the hell do I know about birds?"

What he did know was there was work to be done. The football game would let out soon and he had things to get ready. So Benny decided to leave the storm and crows to sort themselves out, and pulled the door closed behind him.

###

Twilight - Libby

Those smart ass little sluts!

Libby Darnell seethed as she resumed her course towards the distant trucks at the back of the parking lot.

Well they could call her "Lizzie" and have their little laugh, but as far as she was concerned those two little tramps didn't have any damn right to look down on her. If they thought for one minute they had been hired for their waitressing skills then they were even dumber than they acted. They already had their feet well down the road she had travelled and were too damn stupid to see it.

She would have loved nothing better than to get in their snotty little faces and explain the facts of life to them...with a little fist action involved...but she knew Big Earl wouldn't tolerate her laying a finger on them. And the last thing Libby wanted to do was get crosswise with Big Earl Anderson. What she called a living nowadays depended on having access to the Textro Truck Stop, and he could wreck it just by forbidding her from setting foot on the place.

She didn't dare let that happen.

The next truck stop this size was two counties over, and the owner there took a sizeable cut of a working girls income...as opposed to just being willing to look the other way in exchange for the occasional favor like Big Earl. She couldn't afford to relocate, and she damn sure didn't want to be giving up any of her hard earned money to some pimp. Not to mention, she had certain habits. And moving would mean having to learn a whole new group of contacts so she could get what she needed.

So, at least for now, the two little shitheads were safe.

For now.

Lightning flashed, and Libby looked up to see the crows wheeling overhead. She squinted briefly at the flying air-show before hunching her shoulders and continuing on her way.

There had once been a time in her life where she might have indulged in a little wonder at the sight, but that girl was long gone. Right now her main goal was to get together a little scratch so she could get to Conner's Liquor to set herself up for the weekend. And getting shit on by some stupid crow would not help her chances.

The prostitute stopped at the corner of the maintenance garage to finish her cigarette and pat her hairdo to make sure it remained bird shit free. Thankfully her hair was still clean. The rest of her would just have to do, since she hadn't had money to run down to the Laundromat lately. She had chosen the little tube top and hot pants primarily because they were small and therefore in her mind less obviously dirty than her other clothes.

Now she wished she had picked something else.

Libby wasn't terribly happy with the figure the little outfit revealed. She knew she had put on a few pounds over the years, but tonight's encounter with those teenage trollops with their ridiculous young figures had served as a reminder of how things were starting to slip. She knew her hot pants were causing her to sport a serious muffin top these days, with a pale stomach threatening to overhang her belt in a way she didn't want to think about.

She didn't dwell on it though because that would lead to thoughts of possible future remedies, and Libby preferred not to think more than a couple of days ahead. The future was a place best left unconsidered...at least until her winning lottery number arrived someday and changed everything.

The blast of an impact wrench sounded through the thin metal bay doors of the garage, causing Libby to jump.

Damn! Arnold was still here, and must be working late! The Textro's mechanic was a mean-hearted old shit who didn't like her hanging around "his" building. The last time he had caught her out here he had cussed her out royally. And of course she had to take it or he would run to Big Earl and start trouble.

Growling a curse, the woman threw away her cigarette and left the slight shelter of the buildings corner. It was time to get to work anyway, so she headed towards the row of trucks. She didn't even bother to look at the showers and bathroom as she walked by, other than to note the light was on inside, since it was another area forbidden to her. Big Earl had restricted her hooking to the side of the lot near the diesel pumps, and the rows of trucks themselves. He said it cut down on complaints.

She had her own ideas about the complainants and what they could do with their whiny bitching. She had to make a living, dammit.

At least she recognized a couple of trucks.

There was a rough old Peterbilt belonging to "Leaping Larry" Brown, which counted as a minor bit of good news. Larry always had twenty bucks for a blowjob, which meant he was a reliable client and quick and easy to please. At least she would be able to pick up a couple of cheap bottles at the liquor store tonight.

There was also a big new International ProStar owned by Gary "Buddha Boy" Norville. On the bright side he was actually semi-polite to her, and also willing to pay well for the full deal. On the downside, he was completely hairless and weighed well north of three hundred pounds...and he insisted on being on top. Doing business in his sleeper cab was kind of like having Moby Dick repeatedly land on you while you were both stuffed in a sardine can.

"Beggars can't be choosers," Libby opined philosophically, but relegated Buddha Boy's truck to the end of her list of intended stops.

Lightning flashed again, dotting the parking lot with the shadows of the gyrating birds overhead, and she quickened her pace towards the trucks while holding her purse above her head. She could smell the rain in the wind as it picked up. The storm was almost here, and getting caught in a downpour was almost as bad as getting plastered in a mass crap attack by a flock of birds.

Libby reached the first truck in the row and wasted no time in pulling herself up on the passenger side step and hammering on the door. Being coy didn't pay in this business. It wasn't expected of her, anyway. After waiting for about ten seconds, she knocked again on the truck.

Still nothing.

When no lights came on, she assumed the trucker was either in the restaurant or ignoring her and waiting for her to go away. Nice way to treat a lady with it being about to rain. Bastard. The prostitute gave the door a third good banging, just to be sure, then climbed down from the side of the vehicle.

The first try seldom got results anyway, but one had to start somewhere. She slouched her way around the front of the big semi, and winced at the rumble of thunder. A glance at the distant store and restaurant reminded her that if it started raining now, there would be no way to avoid getting drenched. Her best hope lay in getting admitted into one of the cabs, and catching a ride up to the store later.

Coming to the other side of the semi, she paused briefly at the blackness filling the gap between the large rigs.

A tiny flash of instinctual caution tried to assert itself, but another growl of thunder intruded. This time a brief spatter of drops accompanied the rumble, and Libby realized her time to find shelter might be measured in seconds rather than minutes. Fortunately, the next semi belonged to Larry.

She hopped up onto the step and knocked.

No answer.

"Oh c'mon, Larry!" She now banged on the door with enthusiasm. "It's starting to rain!"

Nothing.

Either Larry was up at the restaurant having a cup of coffee, or he just wasn't in the mood.

"God dammit!" she yelled and tried to kick the door. Being too close to do it with any force, she settled for banging her knee against it instead. That didn't satisfy very much either. "Screw you, Larry! I would have done you for free if you had let me in!"

This wasn't getting her any closer to shelter, and Libby could now hear the rain falling in the corn field behind the big rigs. She was about to get wet. Grumbling in frustration, the woman turned to get off the truck and stopped...

Somebody now stood on the ground in the darkness directly behind her.

And he stank.

"Sweet Jesus, Larry!" She wrinkled her nose and tried not to gag. "What the hell have you been rolling in? Look, I'm sorry for losing my temper but don't start giving me shit about kicking your truck till we're inside. Okay?"

The figure didn't answer.

"Okay?" she repeated, then thought better of it. "Hey, don't paw at me. You know, on second thought just forget it. You smell awful and I would rather get wet than be stuck inside with y..."

That's when fate chose to have another flash of lightning illuminate the area, and the face of the figure in front of her.

It wasn't Larry.

The skeletal face grinning up at her parted its jaws in wolfish anticipation, and Libby's mind screamed while her body struggled to catch up and join in. She never got the chance.

Just as she inhaled to shriek the thing struck.

It drove a powerful open palm into her bare midsection, pancaking her pudgy belly against her back and pinning her to the side of the truck. Libby's air exploded out of her before she could make a sound. Bile rose in her throat and she doubled over in nauseous pain. Even worse, her head came to rest on the bony shoulder of her assailant, causing its stench to envelope her head like a fog.

Then the immobilizing pain in her gut blossomed into molten anguish as the monster closed its hand, driving spike-like fingers through the skin and muscle of her abdomen and hooking them into her viscera. It hurt...it hurt really bad...and Libby gagged from both the pain and the horrific smell while fighting to draw in breath to cry out. Then, just as she thought it couldn't possibly hurt her any worse, it yanked back just as hard and she could feel skin and muscle rip free in a white hot explosion of tearing agony.

She had been torn open!

No longer pinned to the truck, the wounded prostitute rolled off the shoulder of her attacker and fell to the asphalt below. She managed to twist as she fell, landing on her back and shoulder. Loose pebbles drove into her back and side, and the asphalt grated a good slice of skin off her bare shoulder as well. The stricken woman writhed on the pavement, battling to maintain consciousness.

Instinct told her she needed to get a handle on things fast.

Looking up from the ground, Libby could see the silhouette of the thing shoving the chunk it ripped out of her into its jaws. It was eating her! Yet she had no time to try and wrap her head around that right now. She gripped her gut in agony, feeling wet insides trying to slither out of what felt like an enormous hole. The woman realized she had to get help fast or she was going to die.

The problem was the monster stood between her and the way out between the trucks.

Regardless, it was move now or die.

Using one hand to hold her intestines in her body, she pulled her knees under her in an effort to start climbing to her feet. She didn't know how she intended to get around the creature, as the trucks were rather close together and it could probably reach to either side just by taking a step or two. The idea of going out the back way occurred to her, since it would be going away from the monstrosity anyway. But it would also mean going all the way down the length of the trailer and coming back up the other side...and Libby didn't know how many steps she had left in her before she dropped. Then she realized there was a better way.

Keeping a tight grip on her ravaged stomach, she rolled underneath the cab of Larry's rig. Behind her, she could hear the thing shuffling back and forth. She had no idea if it was looking for her or had lost interest and still focused on chewing the piece of her it had. She thought about crawling, then figured out it would be easier just to keep rolling.

That would allow her to protect her stomach with both hands, and probably get to the other side faster. Besides, she didn't want to come out from under the front of the truck because her attacker would be able to see her before she could get to her feet and get moving. No, it would be better to keep rolling and come out the other side of the truck...or maybe even the next truck over.

Still, she was bleeding badly and time was running out.

Clutching her middle, Libby started to roll away from the dead thing and towards the other side. She didn't know if it understood where she had gone, but tried to move quietly just in case it lost track of her. The effort nearly made her pass out from pain. Every turn onto her stomach hurt like the fires of hell itself, and the act of rolling must have involved abdominal muscles because every effort brought screaming anguish to her midsection.

The woman choked back a whimper with each move. She was a self contained universe of misery. It took a supreme act of will just to keep going through the motions required to keep her moving. She didn't even realize she had rolled out from under the truck...

...until she struck the thicket of legs standing on the other side.

This time Libby managed to scream as she was hauled to her feet by viselike grips and pushed up against the side of cab. Teeth sank into her arms and shoulder, and several more withered hands plunged like gnarled spears into the gaping hole in her stomach. Now her whole body became a mindless blossom of agony. The pain before had been nothing compared to this. She could feel their claw like fingers close around the vitals inside her before twisting and tearing them free.

Yet despite the hopelessness, the all encompassing pain, and the knowledge she couldn't hope to survive the damage now done to her, Libby still writhed in ever more feeble attempts to jerk free. She still didn't want to die.

Not now.

Not like this.

Above her, the sky erupted with a harsh cacophony as a thousand crows started calling at once. Lightning flared again, and Libby got one last look at the world. She couldn't see the faces of her assailants, as they were all pressed up against her arms, body, and legs while eating her alive...but that meant she had a clear view over them.

Libby's last vision on earth was of even more of the skull-faced horrors pouring out of the cornfield before the darkness closed back around her forever.

DEAD STOP

CHAPTER THREE: NIGHTFALL

Nightfall - Holly

"You see, Holly?" Gerald gestured out the window of the Textro's diner after a flash of lightning. "It's going to rain. Those idiots at the game are going to get soaked while we can enjoy the weather from in here."

"I suppose," Holly sighed and picked up the menu. She really didn't feel like going into this. Disagreeing with him would only make him get defensive and loud, and his nasal voice carried enough as it was.

"You suppose?" The plump redhead waved his hand in exasperation. "Come *on*, Holly. I know this is your home state and you feel obligated to defend its honor and all, but at least you're a city girl...this is knuckle dragger territory."

Holly kept her face blank and started perusing the menu. As a suburbanite from South Houston, she did qualify as a city girl. But she had still looked forward to spending a long weekend home from the University of Texas in Austin, getting together with her old high school friends and cheering on her Bulldogs against the hated Pirates.

But it wasn't to be.

At the last minute, Gerald had showed an uncharacteristic interest in her origins and insisted on accompanying her on this get together. She had initially been taken aback. The little dilettante seldom liked travelling outside his circle of coffee shop friends, or wandering far from an internet connection. Then a flare of hope had occurred along with the idea of him finally starting to take a healthier interest in her as a person.

Just maybe her long suffering patience was beginning to get through the wealthy little nerd's shell of narcissism and awful social skills.

She should have known better.

Gerald had demanded they take his BMW as opposed to her old Toyota Scion. That should have been her first clue of trouble brewing.

Usually he preferred her to drive, especially if they were going to unfamiliar territory for him, but this time insisted he needed to road test "the beamer" since it was fresh back from an overhaul and detailing. But once underway he had fussed about the dust and dirt from driving the three hours over rural highways he assured her only the most desperate of Neanderthals would ever dream of living along. Then he insisted on stopping at a carwash before meeting her friends.

By that time she had already begun to smell the disaster coming.

Sure enough, what she had hoped would be an occasion to show off her boyfriend on his best behavior had turned into a debacle.

He had strutted around in his little suede beret and didn't miss a chance to flaunt his car, expensive cell phone, and pretty much act a general ass...and all the while probably thinking they were impressed. Then, when they had caravanned to Masonfield to watch the football game, he had checked the weather on the radio and rebelled at the thought he might get caught out on some "grubby, three mule school's bleachers in the middle of a typhoon."

So now her friends were likely huddled under tarps and having a great time at the game, while she sat here listening to Gerald congratulate himself on how smart he was.

She couldn't decide if the fact it never occurred to him to consult with her on this decision was more irritating or depressing. She had grown used to it in Austin, and honestly didn't care since most of the different things Gerald did there had about equal appeal to her. But this was supposed to have been her weekend...

Her weekend.

But he was connected, and his father was a lot more connected, and when your major is theater one of the first things you learned was who you knew mattered. And she honestly liked his father. Connor Plimpton was thoughtful, generous, and treated her nicely. He even once said she deserved a medal for her patience with his self-absorbed son. Holly liked to think that one day, with patience and understanding, she would be able to bring out some of Connor's qualities in Gerald. She knew they had to be in there somewhere.

It would just take time to reach him.

Until then, she would console herself with the decent roles she was getting via Connor's influence in the theater department. Not leading roles, of course, but still enough stage time to build a list of credits for her resume. It was still up to her to master the roles given and do them credit. Holly took care never to forget that and worked hard to take advantage of her opportunities. This helped negate any residual guilt she felt over the advantages she had received, and it gave her a greater sense of control over her own situation...

...and next time she decided to come visit her old friends, she would just leave Gerald an email after she left.

He would panic, and suspect she was seeing somebody else, but that was old territory for her. She knew how to let those little tempests blow over. For now, her only wish was to get him back to Austin, to the crowd who knew him, before he caused her any more grief or embarrassment.

Which was impossible, naturally.

"Hey Senora!" Gerald waved his little beret at the tall Hispanic waitress as she walked by. "Uno momento, por favor."

Holly fought the urge to slide under the table as the young woman stopped and fixed them both with a blank stare. Oh yes, she definitely intended to get out of here as soon as possible. She would just order a drink and start texting goodbyes to her friends at the game. She would see them next time. Getting back to Austin couldn't come soon enough.

"Yes, sir?" The waitress pulled out her ordering pad and walked back to their table. She spoke with a controlled courtesy that made Holly wince.

If Gerald noticed the tone, he gave no indication.

"Ah yes, my good woman," he expanded and held up the menu, "I was just perusing your selection of culinary choices and I noticed a certain running theme in the collection. So I was wondering...do you perchance have anything on this menu that isn't fried, or even worse, deep fried?"

The waitress blinked as if confused by the question. Then she regarded Gerald with an expression one would favor on a slow child.

"No sir. This is a truck stop. Everything here is fried. Even the coffee is fried...sometimes."

Gerald, perhaps sensing the sarcasm despite his usual lack of social cues, started to look unamused.

"Oh really. Perhaps a salad?"

"A salad? You want a salad?"

"Please." His voice didn't have a hint of "please" in it.

The waitress tapped her finger on her pencil for a few seconds, then favored him with a bright smile.

"Okay, here's what we will do. We'll order you a hamburger, and leave off the meat and bun. Instant salad!"

"Are you serious?"

"It's a solution," the girl stated primly, putting pencil to her order pad. "Do you want regular or curly fries with your 'salad', sir?"

Holly could sense this would be heading south fast.

Gerald didn't have the sense to know when to quit, and she was already picking up on the vibe this waitress had a problem with him. Any second now Gerald would go into a huff and demand to see her boss...and if he employed his usual grace and social skills in that encounter then it would probably result in the two of them getting tossed out and the waitress getting a bonus for having to put up with such an obnoxious idiot.

"We'll just both have a slice of that silk pie in the display," Holly interrupted, "and a couple of cokes."

She forced herself not to bite her lip as two pair of eyes settled on her. Gerald glared in obvious dismay at her interruption, and she knew she would be hearing about this later. He hated it when she smoothed things over for him, and almost always took it as some kind of affront to his competence as a man.

On the other hand, the look of pity the waitress favored on her almost made Holly cringe.

"Yes, ma'am. Coming right up." The tall girl snapped the order pad shut and walked smartly away from the table.

Holly sighed in relief, and ignored the wounded glower now focused on her from across the table. She would have a little peace while he pouted, then it would be time to patch things up. The best approach would probably be to insist such a squabble would have been beneath him. An appeal to his ego usually had the best rate of success.

Until then, she could start texting apologies to her friends.

Nightfall - Deke

"Hey, Harley? Is your dad's boat still parked behind your house?"

Deke addressed his companion while casting a calculating eye across the restaurant where Stacey Collins poured coffee for a white haired trucker at the bar. She laughed at something the customer said and flashed a smile that seemed to illuminate the entire bar area. His nerves were on high, but oddly enough the pressure now had an almost calming effect as he realized he was committed to taking action.

"Sure." Harley stirred sugar into his coffee and looked at him with interest. "Whatcha got in mind?"

"An alternative to watching Jeopardy with my mom. Let's find out if the sucker still floats. How does Sunday work for you?"

"Not bad!" Harley mused, "If you go down in flames tonight, at least we still got something to do."

"Thanks for that enthusiastic vote of confidence."

"You're welcome, but make it Wednesday."

"Why Wednesday?"

"Because," Harley gave a mild look over his coffee at Deke, "Stacey works on Sunday, and her next day off isn't till Wednesday."

"Oh, well I guess that makes se..." He stopped and narrowed his eyes at his bigger friend. "Now how the hell do you know that? How long have you been planning this, anyway?"

"Son, if you're going to get out of the webbed-foot bracket and start playing in the bigger leagues, you have to do the simple homework like this. Women expect you to have your shit together."

"Molly Harper doesn't have webbed feet! Sheesh, did she kick your dog or something?"

"Stay on target, young jedi." Harley winked and nodded back towards the bar area.

Deke took a deep breath and glared.

"Okay, oh wise one, just how do I pull this off without appearing to come out of nowhere with only one thing on my mind."

"What are you talking about? She knows you. You went to school with her, and you've been coming here just about every week since before she started working here. You know, if this was some other girl, you wouldn't be coming up with half these problems."

"It ain't that simple."

"It is exactly that simple," Harley took a drink of his coffee than set it back down, "and you need to quit stalling and get your butt over there. The way that skinny trucker at the end of the bar is eyeballing her, he's going to make a pass at her soon. And if he does, she won't be in the mood to hear anything on that topic from anybody else for a while."

Deke looked over to where his partner indicated. A thin, man with greasy hair and the words "Leaping Larry" printed on the back of his wide, western style belt, stared at Stacey with almost open lust.

"Aw crap."

"On the other hand," the larger young man continued, "he's got to be making her uncomfortable, leering at her like that, so you would be a pleasant change if you act now."

"I'm on it."

Deke was up and moving before he had time to consider any further contingencies.

As much as Harley could irritate him on topics like this, he never doubted for one second his friend knew exactly what he was talking about. He secretly thanked heaven he had the other man's advice to rely on. Of course, it would be a lot easier if he also had Harley's looks...and his muscles...and his easy manner...and his almost scary ability to be so much where he was at any given moment that the right move always seemed obvious. Hell, if he had all those things going for him he would be in a good mood all the time too.

Focus, stupid! You only get one shot at this!

"Hi, Deke! What's up?"

Stacey's smile lit up her elfish face as he reached the bar, and Deke's stomach threatened to turn into water. Her blue eyes sparkled with a cheerful life that infected the world around her, reminding the young man it wasn't only her looks putting her in a league of her own. She possessed a bright disposition coupled with an exuberant blend of mischievousness and honest warmth most men could only dream of finding in one girl.

Men with a lot more going on for them than he did.

Stop it, Deke! Stop it! Just talk to her!

"Hey, Stacey," Deke shrugged and slid into a nearby stool. "I'm just hanging out, drinking coffee and talking to Harley."

"Ah, I see."

He found himself staring stupidly at the empty bar in front of him and realized he had left his coffee cup back at his booth.

A quick glance back at his table showed his cup sitting where he had left it. It also revealed Harley had left the table as well, and had just seated himself by "Leaping Larry" and engaged him in conversation. It looked like his friend intended on running interference to make sure his attempt at asking Stacey out wouldn't be interrupted.

Okay, Harley. I take back every mean thing I ever thought about you. You're alright.

Then he also realized the other result of Harley's intervention.

The lack of a cup meant Deke hadn't come over here to get a refill, and his friend's simultaneous move made it look like they had a coordinated plan. His intentions couldn't have been more painfully obvious if he had been wearing a sign around his neck with large block letters reading "Get ready, Stacy! Here it comes!"

He fought the urge to swallow and returned his gaze to the girl in front of him. She still smiled and looked at him inquisitively.

Well, she ain't running for the back, and she hasn't already started laughing, so I guess that's something. At least she's going to be polite about this.

"Yeah," he sort of half laughed, "Okay, I guess I actually wanted to ask you something."

"Sure." She tilted her head with a curious glint in her eye. "What is it, Deke?"

Okay, you can do this.

"Well," he gathered his will and pressed onward, "Harley and I are going out to the lake next week to try out his old boat. I was just wondering...if...if you would like to come hang out with us at the lake."

He sincerely hoped that hadn't sounded one tenth as lame in her ears as it did in his.

"Hmmm..." Stacey stroked her chin and glanced back down the bar where Harley and Leaping Larry talked. They had a napkin on the bar in front of them, and Larry was pontificating about something he had drawn on it. The girl studied the pair for a couple of seconds before returning her attention to Deke.

"Soooo...." she fixed him with an evaluating eye, "we're talking about just you, me, and Harley out at the lake?"

Doh! Deke, you idiot! What girl is going to feel comfortable with a setup like that! Think fast, you moron!

"Oh! Harley would bring somebody too...of course. Heck, I should have said that up front...I mean...sure...it would be...." His mouth had already started trying to salvage the situation while the rest of him still tried to catch up. "That is...if it's cool with you."

He wasn't exactly thrilled with the job it was doing.

"Ah," Stacey rested her elbows on the bar and nodded in satisfaction. "So we're talking a double date, then."

Deke noted with disbelieving hope the idea seemed to appeal to her. Was he actually going to pull this off?

"Uh, yeah." At this point, the only thing he could think of was to just go with it. "Exactly!"

She considered him with a half smile for a second or two longer, then it spread to its full brightness.

Holy shit! She's going to say yes!

"That sounds like it could be fun..."

It was all he could do to keep his jaw from hitting the floor. Stacey Collins...yes, *that* Stacey Collins...was about to agree to go out on a date with *him*.

"...so who is Harley's date?"

Once again the mental train lurched to a stop, and Deke spent a frozen moment staring at the girl.

"Huh?"

"The other girl?

"Oh...uh...Harley's date?"

"Yes."

"Oh...uh..."

Stacey rested her chin in her hand and raised her eyebrows at him.

"Doesn't Harley have a date?"

"Well...actually...not yet."

"Hmmm..." She looked down the bar to where his friend still had the trucker occupied. "I wouldn't have thought Harley to be the type to have trouble finding a date."

"Oh...well..." He thought fast. "He's only been back from the army a few months. He's just been kind of settling in. You know how it is."

"Ah, I suppose that makes sense."

Deke held his breath, trying to figure out if Stacey was buying any of this and whether he had a date with her or not. She continued to look down the bar, apparently deep in thought. Then a certain calculating gleam came into her eyes.

"Okay, Deke," She turned back to him with a warm smile. "A day at the lake sounds like fun. But we do need to get poor Harley a date so he won't feel weird...and I'll have another girl to talk to."

"We?" Deke queried, now torn between joy over Stacey's acceptance and dismay over the twist of events it led to.

"Yep. But that's okay. I know just the girl."

"You do?"

"Uh huh. I'm thinking Marisa." Stacey looked inordinately pleased with herself about something.

"Marisa? That Marisa?" He gestured over to where the other waitress was bringing Doc Sutherland another coffee.

Marisa must have heard something because she looked back over at him sharply. Stacey flashed the other waitress a brilliant smile and wriggled her fingers at her, causing the raven haired beauty to give her a puzzled look before going back towards the kitchen.

"Sure. Marisa would enjoy a day at the lake. If Harley will take her with him, I'd be happy to hang out with you guys."

"Really?"

"Sure! You don't think Harley will mind, do you?"

Not if he knows what's good for him.

"Nah. I can't see Harley objecting to something like that."

"Great!" she chirped and stood back up. "Your job is to see to it Harley asks her out tonight...and I'll see to it she says yes. This is going to be fun!"

Deke could only stare at her for a second in helpless wonder.

Then a smile of his own slowly grew to answer hers.

Oh crap! I love this girl! Okay Mr. "Trust me". You're now in this with me, so you can just put your money where your mouth is.

#

Nightfall – Buddha Boy

"How deep is your love...How deeeep is your love. I really need to leeeearn... "

Gary "Buddha Boy" Norville's high pitched voice rang off the white painted cinder block walls of the Textro's shower. In the steamy confines of the room, his huge white body glowed like a pale moon in the mist.

"Okay, Buddha Boy," a voice drawled from the other end of the room. "That's the last song I want to hear a fat guy singing while I'm sharing a shower room with him. I'm out of here."

Gary giggled like a school girl.

"You ain't my type, Red! Besides, I got a date planned for tonight anyway."

"Lizzie ain't a date, Gary," Red Tex noted, "She's a transaction."

"Ha! You're just mad because she charged you the same for those two minutes as she does for half an hour."

Gary laughed again as Red Tex Collier turned off his shower and wrapped a towel around his waist. The lanky redhead pulled his hat from where he had hung it on a protruding soap dish and squashed it down on his wet locks before walking out with all the bow legged dignity he could muster.

"Hey!" he yelled after the departing figure, "Don't forget to leave that cologne on the bench. I'll get it back to you later!"

Buddha Boy couldn't hear Red Tex's mumbled reply over the sound of the shower, but knew the guy was good for it. Red Tex was good people. The big trucker giggled happily and returned to the business of methodically cleaning every inch of his massive, fish-white body.

He had no illusions about his appearance, and had long ago accepted his fate to be forever single. But while his options were reduced to the women who worked the asphalt at truck stops across the US, he still approached each encounter with all the hygienic care of a first date. Gary figured if a lady was willing to endure his gargantuan bulk, the least he could do was smell nice for her.

So, before each encounter he went through his ritual cleansing.

He always brought a little stool into the shower with him so he could sit down and start with his toes. The large trucker would then clean toe by toe, the tops and bottoms of each foot, the ankle, and then work his way up inch by inch from there. Each crease of fat was lifted and scoured clean, and every nook and cranny sponged with care. His head and nether regions got the same treatment. He had long ago undergone a procedure to remove all the hair on his head and body, unwilling to tolerate even the moderate amount of dirt that could hide in such growth.

And he always sang through the entire procedure.

His voice made him a natural for songs by Andy Gibb and the Bee Gees...and he occasionally mixed those in...but his true favorites were those by Hank Williams Jr, Johnny Cash, and Marty Robbins. The only problem was him singing any songs by those artists was guaranteed to send an entire locker room into hysterical laughter, so Gary always kept his song selection tailored to the circumstances at hand.

The singing got him through what was otherwise a slow and painstaking process, but in fifteen to twenty minutes Buddha Boy was the cleanest human being within a fifty mile radius. Satisfied that no possible odor remained to offend even his own delicate sensibilities, he turned off the shower...and stopped in mid-reach for the towel at the sounds coming through the wall.

He had chosen to bathe near the wall seperating the shower room from the mechanics garage because it featured a long steel bar at waist height to make it handicapped friendly. And while he didn't exactly count as handicapped, he figured he was close enough not to get too picky about it.

Now he stared at the wall in surprise.

Just over the clatter of an automatic air compressor, he could make out a scream.

It was faint, and whoever was doing it was drawing in short lungfuls of air between each one...but there could be no mistaking the sound. A rattle and a couple of thuds sounded through the wall as well, giving the impression of somebody thrashing in distress. Images of somebody with his arm caught in a fan belt pulley flashed across Buddha Boys mind, or maybe wounded by a power tool. There were a lot of ways to get hurt in a mechanics garage. Whatever was happening over there...somebody was in trouble.

"Hey, Red!" Gary called out, "Do you hear that?"

The other trucker didn't answer.

"Red! Can you run over to the garage? I think somebody is hurt over there, and needs help!"

Further silence indicated Red must have already gotten dressed and headed up to the truck stop. That left it up to Buddha Boy to deal with the emergency.

Gary grabbed his towel and did a fast waddle towards the shower room exit, leaving his stool behind. If somebody was really in trouble over there, then he couldn't afford to take the time to dry off and get dressed. A far better solution would be to get to his cell phone in the locker and call Red Tex back to the building. The other man could size up the situation and either render aid or get help long before Buddha Boy could get dressed.

He wasted no time in pushing aside the little curtain and stepping out into the small hall leading to the locker room. The fat man wiped the water out of his face as he hustled down the hall, then came to a horrified stop as he stepped into the locker room proper.

Red Tex hadn't left the building after all...at least not in body.

The filthy crowd surrounding him parted to turn their attention to Gary, revealing the wreckage that had just moments before been the man sharing a shower with him. Red stared at the ceiling, mouth open in a scream he must have never gotten the chance to utter. His throat had been ripped out, windpipe and esophagus protruding like twisted tubing in a car wreck. Blood covered his naked body and somehow the flesh on the front of his entire torso had been torn downward in one large dripping sheet...revealing now chewed muscle and the pale rib cage beneath.

His killers appeared just as horrid.

Their ruined faces drenched in blood, they grinned back at Gary like a bunch of crimson skulls under matted, dirt-caked wigs. Strips of dripping skin, probably what remained of their faces, hung below their chins like stringy beards. He stepped back with a thin wail of fear as their small eyes fixed on him with laser-like intensity. Their fingers spread like claws, and the horrors lurched for him in one unnerving motion as if operating by a single mind.

They outnumbered him more than ten to one.

Even worse, they were between him and the exit.

Buddha Boy shrieked and turned to flee. Even as he did, he realized there was nowhere to run. But understanding that meant nothing compared to the tearing pain of his skin parting as skeletal fingers sliced down his back and laid him open from shoulder to hip. Blood ran down his pale legs in rivulets as the fat man tried to get away. He floundered back into the steamy shower with the silent scrabbling horde on his heels.

They caught him in the corner...

...and his shrieks hit higher notes than ever before.

Nightfall - Grandpa Tom

Not bad kid. Thomas "Grandpa Tom" Burns chuckled to himself as he watched the young local boy walk back towards his booth with a bemused expression on his face. *But I hope you're ready for a wild ride because that girl is definitely in the driver's seat.*

The white-haired trucker had been sitting closest to the waitress when Deke had approached. He had just come in for a cup of coffee after filling his truck at the diesel pump outside. Then he would be hitting the road again and making his way to Houston. The old hauler had hoped to finish his coffee and get out of here before the rain started, but saw from the drops starting to hit the big windows it wasn't likely to happen.

So Grandpa Tom had sat and sipped his cup in a posture of minding his own business, while the two youngsters arranged their tryst at the lake. It had taken a supreme act of self control not to spit his coffee out in laughter at Deke's floundering approach. But he could tell by the fond look the girl gave the boy's retreating figure that as long as he hadn't done something stupid, his success had already been pretty much in the bag.

"And what are you looking so smug about, Grandpa Tom?"

He looked up from his cup to see the young waitress regarding him with mock haughtiness. It was a look she only partially succeeded at, as the twinkle in her eyes betrayed her good mood.

"Oh nothing," his own eyes crinkled in amusement, "but you're going to need to show that boy encouragement till he gets his confidence up. He knows he's way out of his league with you."

"Ugh." She managed to both grimace and look secretly flattered while she poured him more coffee, "You men and your 'leagues.' Deke is nice...and sometimes a girl just likes nice."

"Ah," he nodded, "Nice is good."

"Yes it is," she now grinned broadly, "and you were eavesdropping, you old snooper. You should be ashamed of yourself."

He spread his hands in a gesture of profound innocence.

"I couldn't help it! I was sitting right here!"

"Uh huh."

Stacey laughed and started refilling a glass sugar canister while the old trucker furthered his case for the defense. She worked with a look of skeptical amusement while he made claims that a man his age was well past such foolishness.

"Besides," he concluded, "if I wanted to eavesdrop, then it wouldn't be on you and your new boyfriend."

"Oh reeeallllly," she responded with a saucy smirk, "and just who would you want to spy on me with, Grandpa? Is he cute?"

He shook his head and rolled his eyes.

"Ohhhhh...maybe it's a she then. Is *she* cute?"

This girl was impossible.

"Actually," Grandpa Tom laughed and stirred his coffee, "if I were to be a fly on the wall, then I would want it to be when you tell Marisa about her new date. Now that is sure to get interesting."

"Ohhh...that."

"Yesssss...that." He pointed his spoon at the girl, "Your job comes with health insurance, right?"

"Oh pshaw!" The girl waved dismissively. "Marisa is a sweetheart. She's just ser..."

The girl stopped in midsentence and suddenly leaned forward as if to get a better view down the counter.

Tom turned to see what she was looking at, and saw the flashing lights of a police cruiser out on the highway as it sped by. A second later two more raced past, soon to be followed by yet another pair. They all flew past in silence, although their roof flashers cast brilliant blue and red beams that pierced the falling night drizzle.

"Whoa," the waitress murmured softly, "Was that the Sheriff's Department? They were all heading into town."

"The first three were," Grandpa Tom replied, "but those last two were state troopers. It looked like they were acting as backup or something."

"They were certainly in a hurry," Stacey continued to watch the front window.

"Anything going on in Masonfield tonight?"

"Just the football game," the girl shrugged. "But it's us against the Bulldogs, and it's supposed to be a big game. Maybe they had a big fight break out?"

"That's probably it," the old trucker nodded. "You small town Texans do take your high school football seriously."

"Try growing up around here, you would understand why."

"That bad, huh."

"I didn't say it was *bad*," the girl laughed, "It's just kind of...limited."

"Ah, well I guess I can see..."

A muffled outburst came from the direction of the kitchen, causing the pair to stop and look towards the swinging door. A male voice said something indecipherable, followed by another sharp retort from a female speaker. It sounded like Marisa was definitely unhappy about something.

"I believe that's your friend, the 'sweetheart', isn't it?" Grandpa Tom raised his eyebrows at Stacey.

The girl cocked her head, and listened to the kitchen for a moment longer before answering.

"Yep," she chirped brightly and snatched up a towel hanging next to the coffee machine. "She *is* a sweetie. Now I have to go stop her from murdering Tomas!"

Nightfall - Benny

"No Benny! I don't do the kitchen, you know that!"

"*Chica*, please!" The little janitor tried to soothe the angry waitress. "I'll just be gone a minute. Tomas has been gone for half an hour now, and I need to get him back here so I can catch up on my work."

Truthfully, he felt a little irritated himself at how the young cook took his good nature for granted. But there were worse things than standing in a kitchen when he needed to be somewhere else. For instance, the situation developing right now...

"Oh no!" Marisa's dark eyes flashed. "*I'll* go get Tomas. And when I get hold of that little *pendejo* we'll have a chat about wandering off and leaving his job for other people. It's time this crap came to a stop."

"I don't think that's such a good idea."

"Oh I think it's a great idea," she snarled. "Me and that clown definitely need to talk."

Benny had a pretty good idea how such a "talk" would go down.

Knowing Marisa, it would be heard all the way into Masonfield, and anybody who spoke Spanish would get a real education in profanity. She usually refrained from bad language, as he knew she considered its casual use a sign of ignorance and low class. But when her temper was up...like it threatened to be now...she commanded a vocabulary of obscenities that was breathtaking in its scope.

"No, you won't," he stated with gentle finality. "*I* will deal with Tomas."

"Hmph!" she snorted and frowned at him with folded arms. "I know you. You will give him a gentle lecture and ask him to be more 'considerate' in the future."

"You catch more bees with honey than vinegar, *chica.*"

"Tomas isn't a bee!" She rolled her eyes. "For one thing, he's too lazy to be a bee. Honey is wasted on him...unless you're drowning him in it. Now *that* would be a good use of honey."

She made motions with her hands of clenching a neck and holding a head underwater.

"You are such a sweet flower," Benny laughed.

"Benny, I mean it! This is getting old. Big Earl is paying him by the hour, not by the joint. He's going to get you in trouble, and you're not the one doing anything wrong."

"Okay, okay," he assured her. "I'll talk to him...I promise."

He was a little annoyed about having to deal with her as well as the recalcitrant cook. But at the same time he felt relieved to see her acerbic wit replacing the fury that had threatened to manifest a minute earlier. She had now settled for folding her arms and giving him a black look, before conceding the issue with a resigned grimace.

Tomas, I just saved your butt from a world class scorching. You better appreciate this. But if you do this again, I swear I'll let her rip your ass to ribbons.

On a more honest level he knew this would most likely happen again, and he would once again intervene to keep the peace then as well. But it still made him feel good to indulge in the thought.

"And you are too nice for your own good," the waitress sighed, and shook her head despairingly. "There is just no hope for you."

Benny braced himself for another lecture on the evils of being too nice. He had heard those before too. Fortunately, right then Stacey bounced into the kitchen... much to the man's relief.

"Hi guys!" she chirped with a high wattage smile. "Guess what!" She did a skip and pirouette while waving a towel over her head before coming to a stop and beaming at the pair of them like a kid on Christmas morning.

"What's up?" Benny laughed at her exuberance, while welcoming the distraction she provided.

"I got asked out on a date!"

"Again?" Marisa intoned with exaggerated weariness. "So that makes four for you this week? Hah! I'm still up on you by one, and remember midnight starts the new week."

Sometimes Benny really wondered about the world these two lived in.

"For your information," Stacey stuck her tongue out at her partner, "I accepted this one."

"Ohhhhhh!" now Marisa's face lit with interest. "In that case, spill it, girl! I want details!"

"It was Deke!" Stacey squeaked with glee.

"Deke?" the taller waitress looked puzzled.

"Deke," the shorter girl beamed. "He and Harley are taking Harley's old boat out to Lake Cowell to test it out, and Deke invited me to come hang out."

Marisa stared at her for a second longer before turning back to Benny with an exasperated groan.

"You see, Benny?" She waved in the other girl's direction, "She's as bad as you are! There are two available rednecks out there. One is tall, hot, with muscles and a great butt...and she's excited because the *other* one asked her out!"

71

DEAD STOP

"Ha...ha..." Stacey grinned in return. "So I see you've noticed Harley, even if you wouldn't admit it."

"So?" Marisa shrugged dismissively. "Just because he's a yahoo doesn't mean I can't see he's a fine specimen of one. Of course I guess you thought he's a little too old for you, huh."

"I just really like Deke," Stacey shrugged with a pleased smile. "He's nice...if a bit timid. But I can work on that."

"Nice *and* timid," the raven haired waitress groaned. "See, this is what I'm talking about. Girl, you need to reexamine your criteria."

"On the other hand," Stacey continued, now checking her lipstick in the reflective surface of the wall mounted paper towel dispenser, "I doubt Harley has a timid bone in his body. So now that Deke is filling him in on what's up, I imagine he'll be asking you out in the next fifteen minutes or so."

"I figured he wasn't...wait...WHAT!?"

"Well," Stacey murmured as she examined the corner of her mouth critically in the reflection. "You didn't expect me to go out there on the lake alone with both of them, did you?"

Marisa stared at the other girl, eyes and mouth wide with shock. For a moment, it appeared she had lost the capacity of speech. She stood there in obvious dumbfounded silence as the smaller waitress smacked her lips at the dispenser, then finally managed to rally back to the world of the speaking.

"Oh...oh...oh no, you *didn't*!"

"You owe meeeee." The pert brunette glanced slyly back at her friend. She had the smug look of somebody who was playing a trump card. "And you knooow it!"

"Oh don't you dare! Not this! Do I look like the type of girl who dates guys named Harley to you?"

"Youuuu oowwwweee meeeee!" Stacey sing-songed in a triumphal tone. "Or need I remind you of your cousin Rueben?"

"That's not fair!" A note of desperation entered the dark beauty's voice. "At least I mentioned Rueben to you before setting you up with him!"

"Yeah, suuuurrre you did...but I notice you forgot to mention the glass eye while you were at it."

"You would have never noticed," Marisa responded with an air of injured innocence, "if he hadn't taken it out and shown it to you."

"Which he did on three different occasions during the picnic. By the way...Ew!"

Now Benny really wondered about the world these two lived in. He started to be truly glad he didn't have daughters. His poor old heart couldn't take drama like this...especially not with his wife involved. She had hysterics over the boys as it was. This would push her to the point of homicide.

"Augh!" The Latina threw up her arms in dismay, "You're really going to do this to me, aren't you. I can't believe you!"

"Why not?"

"Seriously? You don't see the problem here?"

"You'll have fun."

"Fun?" Marisa exclaimed. "Fun? Do you hear this Benny? I'm going to have fun! They're going to drag me out on the USS Yeehaw and sink us all in the middle of Lake Cowell! And I'm going to end up in Hell because they only allow rednecks into Heaven after dying in stupid ways like that! But I'll have 'fun!'"

"You'll be fine." Stacey laughed. "Besides, I'm sure if we did sink Harley would rescue you...and do whatever was necessary to revive you too. But be sure and bring a swim suit, just in case."

"In case?"

"Well, it *is* an old boat."

"I don't believe this!" The tall waitress smacked her palm to her face. "Now *I'm* letting people walk all over *me*." With her other hand she stabbed an accusing finger in the direction of the little janitor. "This is all *your* fault Benny! You've been a bad influence on me! Now look at the mess I'm in. You see what happens?!"

Benny could only shrug in dazed confusion. Since he was the only male here, he figured something would end up being all his fault sooner or later. Forty five years of marriage had taught him that much. He would work it out later.

"You'll be fine," Stacy soothed, "but I'm sure he'll be asking soon and I think you just smudged your eyeliner here." She pointed to the corner of her right eye.

Marisa gasped and hurried over to the paper towel dispenser to peer into the mirrored surface.

"Oh crap!" she blurted out over some microscopic flaw Benny couldn't even make out. "I've got to fix this! I'll be in the little girl's room!"

She hustled down the back hallway, and disappeared through the employee's door leading to the bathrooms in the store side of the truck stop.

"Waitaminute..." the man called after her, then let his arm fall in resignation after realizing she was gone.

"And that," Stacey brushed her hands off against each other with an air of immense satisfaction, "takes care of that."

"But..." Benny gestured after the departed waitress.

"Oh don't worry," The elfish girl reassured him. "I heard you trying to talk her out of going after Tomas before I came in."

"You did?"

"Yep. I'll go get him instead, and you don't have to worry about any scenes." She pushed open the back door and stared out into rear parking lot where the rain was just beginning. "You just stay near the door and open it when I knock. I don't want to get wetter than I have to."

"But..." Benny watched helplessly as the girl snatched a folded piece of cardboard leaning against the wall and held it over her head as a makeshift umbrella. Without further ado she stepped outside.

"But..." the little janitor said to nobody in particular.

The door slammed shut, leaving the man alone.

He stared at the door, and struggled to catch up on this latest whirlwind of events. Nothing was ever boring with these two. Confusing maybe, but never boring. This pair of girls had encounters and escapades that would do any TV sitcom proud. And it was while shaking his head over that analogy that the end result of this little episode of the 'Marisa and Stacey Show' finally dawned on him.

Now he had to run the kitchen *and* the dining room all by himself.

Stacey Collins – Nightfall

The door fell shut behind her, leaving Stacey alone in the nighttime expanse of the rear parking lot.

She did a quick glance left and right.

The sodium vapor lamps wore yellow halos against the black sky, and highlighted the streaks of early raindrops. The asphalt had already started to acquire a shine from the moisture. It wasn't quite wet yet, but it soon would be...as evidenced by the strengthening patter of drops against the cardboard she held over her head.

The storm would be here any minute.

Still, she took a few seconds to indulge in a gleeful happy dance.

What had started to look like another lousy night of fending off complaining customers and leering truckers had just taken an amazing turn for the awesome. She had just about given up on Deke working up the nerve to ask her out, so when he came over and started his awkward little approach it had come as a pleasant surprise. Despite Harley's smooth move in distracting Larry, it didn't take her long to realize their actions were uncoordinated and this had been practically a spur of the moment decision.

Which meant Harley didn't have a date...

...which meant it was time for some friendly payback regarding a certain glass eye.

Not that she had been terribly upset about the Rueben fiasco. In truth, he had been a fairly nice guy. Besides, her Uncle Tony also had a glass eye and she was

75

already well immune to that particular stunt. But it was still a little unsporting of Marisa not to mention it.

And the other waitress knew damn well she was getting the better end of this deal, even if she would never admit it.

Stacey had seen Marisa surreptitiously checking Harley out, even if social boundaries and the fear of what her family would say prevented her from ever showing even a hint of availability. Now she had the excuse of claiming she was forced into it by her friend, and Stacey chuckled at how despite her protestations she had wasted no time in getting to the bathroom to make sure everything was perfect.

"I done good," the impish brunette gloated.

Besides, it would do the other girl good to spend some time with a guy who wasn't in total awe of her.

Of course, Stacey realized her own problem was just the opposite.

Her job would be to coax Deke out of his current awestruck stage without him losing respect at the same time. She had no illusions that he wasn't going to be a project, in more ways than one, but it wasn't like she was doing anything else this autumn. The boy needed to find motivation, and a little ambition, but Stacey figured she was just the girl to help him discover it. Besides, she knew he was a fundamentally decent guy which gave her a good starting spot to work with. And he was nice.

As far as Stacey was concerned...not being nice was a deal breaker.

And speaking of not nice...

Stacey gave the rear lot another careful scan before heading for the distant building in the back. The young waitress knew Libby was back here somewhere, and the last thing she needed was an encounter with the prostitute while she was alone. The woman had taken a special dislike to her and Marisa as soon as they had hired on, and the feeling had been immediately mutual.

Which suited her just fine.

It had been the sight of Libby crawling into a rather hideous old trucker's cab on their third day here that provided the first common ground she and Marisa had built their unlikely friendship on. Therefore Libby had done at least one good thing, even if she were completely unaware of it.

But be that as it may, right now she just wanted to find Tomas so he could walk her back to the main building. She wouldn't tear him a new asshole like Marisa would, but she wasn't in the mood for any attitude from him either. The rain was picking up, and she had always been a little nervous about being outdoors when lightning was about. Not to mention, she wanted to get back in time to spy on Marisa and Harley in hopes of catching the big moment.

So as Stacey walked she kept a cautious eye on the distant row of trucks off to the right of the garage and locker room. Out there would be where Libby would most likely emerge if she showed herself. She put a little quickness into her step as the patter on the cardboard over her head increased. The raindrops started hitting the asphalt with audible force. It occurred to her she was probably being silly and Libby had probably holed up in a cab, taking her time with a guy so she could stay inside and dry while Stacey was out here in danger of getting soaked.

So get a move on, girl. Or you're going to end up making Libby look like the one with all the sense tonight.

The waitress now hurried towards the bright rectangle at the right corner of the garage building, where the smaller metal door stood open. The two large bay doors were closed, probably in anticipation of the rain, but it was common practice to leave the "walk-in" door open to allow extra air into the building. So on the nights Arnold and Leon had reason to stay here late, the appearance of the bright fluorescent light from within spilling out the door was an expected sight.

The crows were a new touch, though.

Stacey slowed her walk again as she noticed the group of large ebony birds milling about on the asphalt in front of the door. They strutted and crowded each other like an inky pool of darkness in front of the entrance to the shop. As she closed the distance, she could even see a couple on the chair and workbench immediately inside the door. Then a couple more hopped across the threshold before flying up and out of sight into the building.

What the hell?

The waitress paused a second, and fixed a narrow eye on the door.

Were the birds that desperate to get out of the rain? And if so, why not just get under the awnings over the rows of fuel pumps? Or under the parked semis? Choosing a building with three men working in it struck her as a far more unlikely choice.

And where were the guys anyway?

Stacey could picture the young Leon and Tomas getting a kick out of birds hopping into the building, but doubted old Arnold would permit such foolishness. Maybe he was under a car and the other two were encouraging the birds to come in with pieces of bread?

A quick glance to her right showed another dark circle of birds in front of the locker room door as well. And several of them were likewise making cautious hops into the building. More of the ebony birds lined the roofline, ignoring the falling water from the sky. A flash of lightning revealed a third and fourth group also standing down in front of the trucks. Stacey blinked and tried to make sense of the odd sight.

What in the hell was going on here?

An instinctual unease rose within her at the strange behavior of the birds...and her solitude in witnessing this weird phenomenon didn't sit well with her at all. Stacey had firm opinions about the girls who wandered off alone in horror movies, and this situation began to uncomfortably remind her of several of them. It was generally at this point in the film that bodies started turning up, and the big man with the mask and machete came strolling around the corner of the building looking for a little "alone time" with the lead actress.

Not funny, girl. Knock it off.

Stacey snorted in annoyance at her self induced case of the willies. She liked to think of herself as more practical than this. Still, the only reason she didn't turn around right now and head back for the main building was she didn't want deal with the embarrassment of returning without Tomas in tow.

Benny would be both sympathetic and understanding, of course, but when Marisa found out she would give her gleeful hell about it for the next two days. Especially after fixing her up by surprise like she did tonight.

Taking a deep breath and setting her jaw, Stacey marched in the increasing downpour towards the door. Enough was enough, and she needed to get Tomas back to the kitchen so Benny could get back to work and she could get the juicy details on Harley's approach to Marisa when it happened. The birds scattered but didn't fly off as she walked through them and stepped up to the door. She leaned in to the building to call out to the men...

...and slapped her hand to her mouth to keep the call from going out.

DEAD STOP

CHAPTER FOUR: THE STORM

The Storm - Stacey

The garage was a slaughterhouse.

And the slaughter was still in progress.

Ten feet away, Leon's lifeless eyes stared back at Stacey from where the assistant mechanic's severed head rested next to a toolbox. The concrete floor was literally covered in blood, and crows dotted all the work benches and shelves, picking at pieces of flesh they would fly down and snatch back up to their roosts.

A large knot of figures were clustered into the far corner with their collective backs towards her. They struggled and pulled at something, while bending as if to take a closer look at whatever it was. Their skin was gray, and from this distance looked to be cracked and flaking like old paint. At least what she could see from the rear. They were covered in filth, and their clothes looked torn and ragged...although they were comprised of suits and dresses.

Almost half of these "people" were women.

Stacey froze as motion caught her attention near the front of the garage. She swiveled her eyes in time to see another figure come shambling around the end of the car the men must have been working on.

It was a woman in what had once been some kind of pale dress. Long black hair hung down, obscuring most of her face...a fact for which the young waitress was grateful. She had a severed arm in her grip, and tore at it with crimson dripping teeth that were far too visible for Stacey's imagination not to put the rest of the picture together. Fortunately, the thing's attention remained focused on its grisly meal and it didn't appear to have seen her yet.

But now with her prize in hand, the horror seemed content to wander away from the feeding pack and back into the area closer to the door. A couple of crows flew to the rafters at her approach. All she had to do was look up from her meal and she would be looking straight at the wide-eyed waitress from only fifteen feet away.

Stacey had definitely seen this movie before, and had no illusions about what happened to solitary women in this situation unless they did precisely the right thing.

She was one wrong move away from dying horribly.

No fast moves, girl. You just slowly pull your head back out of this building. Then you take a good look around to make sure there ain't nothing sneaking up on you...then you run like hell. And whatever the hell you do, don't you dare scream.

Unfortunately, things never had a chance to work out that way.

The dead woman tore a chunk off the arm with her teeth and raised her blood drenched skull to full view while she chewed the meat. The waitress stopped breathing as the thing stared in her general direction while it lifted a hand to push more meat into its lipless maw. Its jaw worked in a ghastly rhythm as the blackened muscles still attaching it to the skull flexed in oily contractions.

For one brief second Stacey thought the thing may have failed to see her, then it stopped chewing as its shriveled eyes locked with hers.

The two women...one dead and drenched in blood, and the other wide eyed in shock...stared at each other across the small distance of gore spattered concrete. Stacey swallowed as the grinning horror lowered the severed arm and tilted its head as if puzzled by her sudden appearance. It made no noise as it regarded her, other than a faint gristle-popping creak as its head now leaned the other way like it was trying to figure out what to do about this new development.

The crows rustled in the metal rafters above, eager to see the outcome of this meeting.

Stacey fought the urge to whimper and held her breath...waiting for the one small move that would dictate her next action. She tensed, eyes still locked with the monster in the pale dress.

Time seemed to slow to a stop.

Then the thing lifted the arm back to its face and tore away another chunk of meat.

It didn't walk off, or even turn away. It just appeared content to watch her while it fed on the arm of one of her coworkers. Stacey struggled not to gag, and kept her gaze focused on the feeding corpse.

Now what?

She hadn't had time to adapt to this new reality...as if it were even possible...and didn't know what to do.

The young waitress wanted nothing more than to turn and put as much distance between her and this horror show as possible. She wanted Benny...and Marisa...and yes, Deke too. The realization that all this gore had once been Arnold, Leon, and Tomas was just beginning to sink in and she knew if she didn't do something quick she would break down right here...and that would be fatal.

But she was just as afraid any sudden moves on her part would cause the rotten abomination in front of her to attack. For the moment it remained satisfied with its current meal, but the fact it continued to watch her had unsettling implications. She felt like a fly that had caught the attention of a spider, but hadn't jerked the web hard enough to provoke it.

She didn't dare move, and she damn sure couldn't stay here.

She was trapped.

And of course, that's when all hell broke loose.

Behind her—actually, outside and somewhere to her right—a raucous storm of caws and flapping wings erupted.

Her nerves tight as a high tension wire, Stacey jerked her head out the door and whirled to her right before thinking...and she knew as she did it things were about to start happening very fast.

To her right, the puddle of crows in front of the locker room door had launched into a cloud of whirling night shadows as a hideous pale form lumbered into their midst. It plodded and mewled, and it took a brief instant for the young woman to realize what she saw.

83

It was a huge, naked man...with three different horrors like the one she had just faced clinging to him...and they were tearing him to pieces as they rode upon him. Deep bloody gashes flapped open and closed along his back and sides as he waded out the door and into the rain. Blood poured down him in streaming rivers, and great gobbets of meat hung from places where they had been half gouged out of his flesh. He sobbed and flailed at the things hanging on him, and even during the split second she watched several more of the dead things clambered out the door in pursuit.

In the next instant she remembered her own peril and tore her gaze from the ongoing carnage to look back into the garage. The dead woman had already dropped the severed arm and was halfway to her...hands outstretched and mouth agape like some kind of attacking animal.

This thing could move!

Stacey shrieked and turned to run. There was no time for considering options or even thoughts of helping the nearby man as he floundered to his knees under the weight of his attackers. As a matter of fact, one last glance at him revealed a couple of his tormenters had broken off the attack on him and were now doing a fast lurching lope in her direction instead.

Shit!

Stacey threw aside the cardboard and sprinted for the distant main building. While she didn't possess the long legs of her fellow waitress, the former pom-pom girl was in excellent shape and now put the conditioning from practicing all those dance routines to good use. Her legs pumped like pistons as she shot away from the garage in a standing start that would have done any of the girls on the track team proud. She wasted no time in hitting her stride while taking in gulping lungfuls of air.

"BEEEENNNNNNNNNNNNIIIIEEEEEEEEEEEE!!!!!!"

She screamed at the top of her lungs as she ran. At this point the girl operated on terror and adrenaline, instinctually understanding her role as the deer in this scenario and the need to get back to her herd. And the pack of nightmares on her heels grew by the second. A glance to her left showed even more black figures loping in their strange lurching motion from the row of trucks...although those looked like they were heading for the store side of the main building, and were too far behind her to pose a threat.

But it was the ones to the rear that concerned her at the moment, for she had no idea how she fared in her race with them. Would there be time to reach the back door and pound for assistance, or did she need to change course and attempt a longer run for the front of the truck stop instead? The girl knew her life depended on that decision, and the wrong choice would have her go down under the teeth and claws of the ghoulish pack pursuing her...but she couldn't make it without knowing how close they were.

And that was when she made her first mistake.

A desperate look back revealed she had actually put distance between her and her pursuers, with them strung out in a line behind her due to their varying speeds. A couple of the predators who had been savaging the doomed man back at the locker room had passed the dead woman from the garage and now led the chase. They lunged after her with outstretched arms and jaws agape as if in silent screams. Framed in the now pouring rain, it was a vision straight out of hell.

But at the same time, even though they were far from slow, she now realized she could outpace these things. These monsters were deadly in close spaces, and could probably chase down the average trucker or middle aged person as well. But a healthy young adult could outrun them...at least for a while. She was going to win this race.

And just as she came to that conclusion her ankles clipped against each other...

...and exactly like those girls in horror movies, she fell.

Pain flared in her ankle and despair threatened to overwhelm the panicked girl.

No dammit! Not like this! Please God, not like this!

She half rolled to her feet almost in the same motion as she went down and stumbled desperately onward towards the back door, now slowed by a noticeable limp.

"BEEEEENNNNNNNNIEEEEEEEEEEEEE!!!! HELP MEEEEE!!!"

At this point, the janitor remained her only hope. Injured, and having lost ground, the girl knew the things would catch her before she could ever make the longer run for the front door.

"BEEEENNNNIIIEEEEE PLEEEASSEEEE!!!!"

The door grew closer, but she could feel her pursuers closing in at the same time. They didn't breathe or pant, but the slap of their shoes on the wet asphalt came from almost directly behind her.

"BENNNIEEEEEEE!!!"

Ahead, the door cracked open like the gates of heaven, spilling the blue white light of the kitchen area out into the strengthening storm. Benny stood in the doorway, a look of horror frozen on his face.

Stacey could only imagine what he was seeing...a drenched and screaming girl being pursued by a bunch of skull faced demons...and the shock it must have been.

Please Benny, don't slam the door on me. Oh please don't do that..."

She wouldn't have blamed him if he did, knowing full well it would have been her first instinct if faced with the same scene. Any human would have been hard pressed not to.

Oh please, Benny! Just give me a few more seconds...."

Instead, the little janitor did the last thing she ever expected.

He charged.

In an act of seeming insanity, the older man leaped out the door towards her and ran in her direction.

"*Niña*, get inside!" he yelled as he flew past, and she heard him collide with the monsters right behind her.

She staggered the remaining feet to the doorway and wheeled to see what had become of her unlikely savior. Benny and the two creatures were all on the ground, and they fought to regain their feet as the rest of the horde closed in from behind.

"Benny. Come on! RUN!!"

Stacey gripped the doorknob so tight the whites of her knuckles stood out. Time was running out and the monsters would be upon them in seconds. They would both be overwhelmed by the vicious pack.

I won't do it, her mind screamed at the internal voice begging her to close the door, *I won't leave Benny out there!*

"BENNY! COME ON!"

The little man struggled to his feet and made for the open door as the pursuing horrors closed the distance. He staggered as one of the things still on the ground made a swipe at his ankle The blow connected and he lost his balance for a second, then righted himself with two more stumbling steps.

"BENNY!"

Stacey released her hold on the doorframe with her other hand and reached out for her friend instead. His face pale with exertion and fear, the man made one final lunge for the doorway...his arm outstretched for hers.

The horde fell upon him just as he reached the door.

The Storm - Rachel

"SOMEBODY HELP MEEEEE!!!"

The ragged scream tore through the restaurant, bringing all conversation to a stop. It carried a raw edge of primal anguish so intense that Rachel had no doubt somebody was being murdered.

She dropped her e-reader and looked around to see the rest of the patrons staring at the door to the kitchen in wide-eyed shock. For a frozen second in time nobody moved, and then another agonized shriek ripped through the air.

Somebody was getting hurt...bad...and it sounded like one of the waitresses.

It was the second scream that jolted people into motion.

The two truckers at the bar were closest to the kitchen, and both leapt to their feet and charged through the door. The younger of the two rednecks at the window table shot after them, while the bigger one fought to scoot himself out of the booth so he could join in. Rachel ran after the younger man, wondering what in the hell she was going to do when she got there.

Help whoever's hurt, you idiot! You're a doctor, remember?

An enormous pool of acid filled her stomach at the thought.

The last time she had told herself that was when staring down at Matt's crushed skull, from where the horse had kicked him.

A person should never, ever, walk behind a horse... especially one in distress. It was such a basic tenet of animal husbandry she had never thought to warn her city bred husband, or consider the possibility he didn't know better. So when she asked him to run to her bag to fetch some tubing, she didn't even bother to notice the route he took to do so.

A second later the horse had bucked and lashed out, and she heard a sickening crunch from the behind the large animal. She had looked up just in time to see his body hit the ground like a rag doll.

And just like that, she had been a widow.

You're a doctor! Do something!

All she could think to do was cradle his ruined head, and scream at him to not to die.

Do something! You're a doctor! Do something, God Damn It!

And she hadn't.

She had just held him and cried his name over and over again.

Matt died within a minute...and then the world quit making sense.

The coroner had later assured her it was over before she ever reached him. The man swore to her there had been nothing she could have done even if she had been a fully qualified neurosurgeon for humans and had all her equipment on the spot. And her medical side agreed as it read the autopsy report with its usual clinical detachment...the damage had been immediately fatal.

But the part that had driven her into medicine, the same part that demanded the world make sense, railed back that she should have done something...anything...to see to it Matt would be there in the morning to greet her instead of being prepared for burial on a stainless steel table. If she couldn't have done anything, then it had to be because the thing to be done hadn't been discovered yet. But it had to be out there and she had failed to come up with it when it mattered.

Another scream brought Rachel back to the present as she pushed through the door. She snatched a towel off a counter as she ran past, both for the comfort of having something in hand and to be ready to staunch bleeding if necessary. She turned the corner and came to a stop, staring in shock at the scene before here.

The two truckers were just reaching the back door where the commotion seemed to be centered.

It was the short haired waitress...the one she had seen the young redneck talking to earlier.

The girl was on the floor with one foot braced against the wall, the other one against the back door, and she seemed to be fighting with all her might to keep the door from opening further while trying to pull somebody into the building with her. Rachel couldn't make out who the girl was trying to help as he was both obscured by the waitress's body, and the forest of arms reaching in through the opening of the door to grab both him and the girl.

The waitress screamed again as one of the strangely clawlike hands sank into her upper arm, drawing blood where the tips of the fingers buried into her flesh. A second later the first trucker, the paunchy man with white hair, reached her and grabbed her by the shoulders to pull her back.

"No! Not me!" the girl shrieked even as she cried out in pain over the damage being done to her arm, "Grab Benny! They're killing him!"

The young redneck tried to grab the man in her arms as directed, while the older trucker turned his attention to the hand ripping up the girls arm. At the same time, the skinny trucker started kicking at the head of one of the attackers who had forced himself partway in and was laying on top of the man the girl held. On the third kick he managed to dislodge the man from where it looked like he had been biting the shoulder of whoever the girl was trying to protect...and for the first time he saw the face of her attackers.

Apparently, he didn't like what he saw.

"Holy shit!" the thin man screamed and unbalanced himself trying to jerk away while being crowded in between the young redneck and older trucker at the same time. The result was him overbalancing and bending over, whereupon another grasping hand caught him by the hair and jerked him down on top of the girl and her charge.

In another second he was pulled headfirst and screaming halfway out the door.

Rachel could think of nothing else to do but run up and grab the skinny trucker's legs. It wasn't easy because he thrashed wildly, making grabbing him without getting kicked almost impossible. Even worse, the white tiled floor around the door was now red with great smears of blood, causing people to slip and slide as they fought to accomplish whatever each of them were trying to do.

"Let me in!"

The bigger redneck had arrived on the scene and was attempting to find a way through the melee to get where he could do some good.

"Harley!" the waitress screamed, "Harley! There's more coming around on the store side where Gladys is! You got to go get that door closed!"

"But..."

"Go!" the girl cried out as the older trucker pried the withered hand out of her arm. "Please! Help Marisa and Gladys! Don't let them get in here!"

The big man hesitated a second more, then turned and ran from the kitchen.

The battle at the back door continued...limbs thrashing wildly and people yelling and straining against a mostly unseen enemy.

Rachel didn't have time to make sense of the melee, and fought to hold on to the skinny trucker while slapping ineffectually at a wizened hand gripping her charges belt, right between the "Leaping" and the "Larry." Whoever owned that hand had serious health problems, but it didn't seem to be slowing him down. What the hell were they fighting against? Hobos? Some kind of gang of diseased vagrants? Lepers?

And then the older trucker shifted his position, allowing her to look down the length of the man she held, and straight into the face of the thing she was pulling against.

The woman didn't scream, or even recoil at the sight of the horrid monster staring back at her. That would have required believing her eyes. She just gaped in numb shock at the ghastly visage as it leered its deathly grin over the trucker's shoulder. At this distance, there could be no kidding herself into believing it was somebody in a mask or well crafted makeup.

This was the real thing. That was a real, blood drenched skull snarling back at her.

Somebody...some absolute maniac...had cut their own face off.

And as she watched, she could see its bare muscles flex as its jaws opened wide and it turned its face towards the trucker's neck.

"Nooooo!!!" Rachel cried out for the first time, redoubling her efforts to save the man even as she knew what was about to happen.

The horror's teeth sunk into the side of the thrashing man's neck as he attempted to twist away from it. Leaping Larry Brown screamed in a way Rachel would never forget. It was a cry of both pain and denial, a last agonized rejection of the reality that his time had come and this was how it would end. The rotten teeth sliced into his

91

jugular and carotid artery, causing blood to fountain into and around the monsters jaws, and drenching the people underneath.

The trucker kicked and thrashed, but his struggles grew weaker by the second. Rachel held on for as for as long as he moved. She knew he was dying...and she could do nothing to save him...but still the woman clung to his legs for all she was worth. All she could think of was refusing to let him go to the animals out there in the dark until he was too far gone to ever know.

After another minute, Leaping Larry stopped moving.

She knew it hadn't been much, but at least the man had died knowing somebody had held on till the very end.

Now she changed tactics.

Gathering her feet under her, and trying not to slip in the amazing amount of blood now covering the tiles, she started pushing the trucker's corpse out the door.

"What are you doing?" the young redneck cried in horror, still pulling for all he was worth on the man the waitress still clung to.

"He's dead!" Rachel yelled. "I'm giving him to them!"

"WHAT!?"

"I'm giving them his body," she gasped with exertion and pushed harder on the corpse. To her relief she saw more hands snag on to it. "The more of them that grab it means the less that are pulling against you!"

A second later the older trucker released the girl and helped her push the corpse forward through the opening. Even more arms grabbed it, and Rachel let go as it started to move of its own volition through the gap. Then the veterinarian and the older man grabbed the girl and the man she protected and pulled for all they were worth.

The things outside held for a moment longer, then the injured man's body and legs slid in through the door and into the back hall. The waitress tried to slam the door shut with her foot but a couple of intruding hands pushed back.

"We're not done!" she yelled, "We've got to close the door!"

But even as she said it, the young man and the older trucker slammed their bodies into the door. Two hands were still inside, and bone crunched as the metal door closed on the wrists. For a moment, Rachel wondered how they were going to free the doorway but the matter took care of itself.

The owners of the appendages must have been more interested in the corpse outside than getting in through the door. One of them managed to somehow pull its damaged hand back through the narrow crack in the door...peeling the skin off like a fleshy glove as it did. The other simply tore itself free from the trapped extremity, leaving it to tilt and fall to the floor as the door finally slammed shut.

The trucker and the young redneck looked at the severed hand, then at each other in disbelief. For a moment they continued to push against the door, as if not sure what else to do, then exhaled together and eased the pressure.

It was over.

The two men slid down to the floor, their backs against the door. The younger scrunched his face in distaste at the two pieces of human debris left behind and kicked out with his foot until he had knocked them both under the big stainless steel sink nearby. The older man just panted and stared at the ceiling above.

Blood smeared the floor and walls, and covered all of them from where they had been squirming and thrashing in the stuff. The smell of it mingled with the cloying scent of rot and formaldehyde remaining after the door closed on their attackers.

The odor reminded Rachel of the necropsy lab back in school.

But that observation was merely tangential because her ears still rang from the dead trucker's last cry. It had been the worst sound she ever heard in her life and it now echoed in her mind like a mental banshee.

93

So that's what it sounds like when people die and know it's happening.

She closed her eyes and buried her face into her hands. The shaken woman knew she would be hearing that scream for a long time to come.

"Benny?" a nearby voice intruded into Rachel's awareness. "Benny, answer me!"

It was the waitress' voice...but also one she had heard eighteen months ago.

"Benny! Answer me! Oh God, please don't die! Don't you dare die!

Do something.

"No, Benny! Don't you dare die on me! Do you hear me!" the voice was growing shrill, and heading for a very bad place...a place Rachel knew all too well. "BENNY!!! DON'T YOU DARE DIE!"

Do something, Rachel! You're a doctor, dammit! Do something...right now!

But I'm not a human doctor.

You'll have to do.

But I'm not qualified!

You're what she's got, dammit! Now do something! Anything! But do it!

Rachel squeezed back the tears and opened her eyes. She got to her hands and knees and crawled over to the where the young woman was screaming and shaking her fallen friend. Blood covered the man from the waist down, and she couldn't even tell where the wounds were due to the blood-soaked clothes.

Good! Start with that. Find the wounds and assess them. This is about a hundred and eighty pound mammal with multiple wounds of unknown severity. There is evidence of major blood loss accompanied by the large probability of shock. Now move!

The clinical side of her mind asserted itself and Rachel felt the first harbingers of control return. She was a doctor. She had a patient. And she had a client who was approaching hysterics. She had a job to do, and she needed to act.

Now.

"Easy," Rachel Sutherland, DVM, laid a hand on the girl's shoulder and moved next to her beside the stricken man. "I'm something of a doctor. Let me help."

The Storm - Marisa

Marisa inspected the repaired section of eyeliner with a critical eye that would have done any makeup artist proud.

Not that there had been much wrong with it in the first place.

The damage had been minor, although she did prefer her makeup to be flawless. But she now suspected Stacey had used the tiny smudge for her own nefarious purposes. For one thing, the little minx knew quite well the art of applying makeup was like a zen exercise to Marisa, who found the concentration of the process to be calming, and the tall waitress now harbored no doubt it been brought up for just such a purpose.

And like most of Stacey's little schemes...it worked.

"Okay, you stinker," she chuckled. "You win this one, but don't think I will forget this."

She straightened and stepped back to survey the rest of herself in the bathroom mirror. Her lustrous black hair still lay thick and almost straight from its earlier brushing, with just the perfect hint of wave to frame her face without looking the least bit styled. Her uniform hugged her long form without being tight enough to be tacky, and she wore the little waist apron at the perfect level to both accent her figure and have the desired effect on the length of torso.

Marisa favored her reflection with a smile so catlike in satisfaction one would almost expect her to purr.

This would do.

This would do just fine.

Mr. Harley Whatshisname was now officially the luckiest redneck on the planet.

The young woman popped a hair brush from her apron, deciding a few more strokes might be in order. Marisa would be damned if she was going to appear to hurry back out there just to be available for this escapade. Appearances mattered. Girls of her caliber were worth waiting for, and it never hurt to drive that point home early. Besides, it would serve her conniving little friend right to have to watch the whole restaurant for a few more minutes.

"Hmph! The place is dead anyway," she smirked. "And one should always do at least a hundred strokes."

She was only into the third stroke when she paused and frowned at the bathroom wall.

What was that?

She thought she had heard something...a yell, or some kind of commotion.

The fan in the women's bathroom was loud, and the fact the restrooms were on the store side of the truck stop building meant there was a brick firewall between them and the restaurant side. Still, however faint, she felt pretty sure she had heard something. And that something hadn't sounded good.

Her brow furrowed with both curiosity and concern, and she moved towards the back wall of the restroom and away from the noisy ceiling fan. As she did, the faint noises of thumping and the metallic thud like the back door being kicked reached her ears. What the hell was going on over there? The waitress tilted her head in confusion at the faint din.

Then a second later, the unmistakable sound of a scream pierced the thick wall.

Marisa stood up straight and whirled towards the door. The brush fell forgotten from her hand as she hurried towards the exit.

That had been Stacey, and she sounded like she was in trouble...bad trouble.

Her mind raced as she moved. If Stacey were in some kind of struggle at the back door, then she must have gone outside after Tomas instead of Benny. Which was probably another reason she distracted her with the eyeliner ruse, to keep Benny in the kitchen and yet spare Tomas a well deserved ass shredding at the same time. Only she must have run into some kind of trouble while out there...and Marisa had a good idea what that trouble was.

"Libby," she snarled and fished her car keys out of her pocket as she moved. Her fist closed around the ring, leaving a key protruding like a metal spike between each finger.

It sounded like the hooker had decided to take their little feud to a new, more violent level and chose to go after Stacey when she saw the opportunity. The smaller girl, out in the parking lot alone, must have made a target the mangy prostitute just couldn't resist. Well, if that was the case then Marisa intended to dish out an education the sorry whore would never forget on the subject of what happened when she messed with her friends.

"You should have come after me first, *puta*," she growled as her hand reached for the bathroom door, "because then I would have gone a lot easier on you. Now I'm going to wreck your ass!"

The bathrooms faced each other across a short hall in the back of the store side of the truck stop, with the employee's entrance at the back of the hall. The only problem was the employee's door could only be opened from the other side without a key, so when the waitresses had to use the restrooms they were forced to return to their stations by walking through the store and coming in the front door of the diner.

Only a minute longer, amiga. I'll be right there.

Then, as her fingers closed around the handle...

...all hell broke loose on the other side of the door.

Marisa froze at the explosion of crashing and screaming that erupted all at once. It sounded like a full blown riot had broken out in the store.

She recognized the shrieks as coming from Gladys, who must have been either at the side door smoking a cigarette or behind the nearby counter. Somebody else was screaming as well, as if Gladys had a customer at the time and they were being murdered together. A mighty crash and clatter shook the place, and Marisa realized it could have only come from the big cigarette rack suspended over the counter being yanked down.

What in the hell was going on out there?

Marisa stopped and reconsidered her options.

Nobody who knew her could have ever confused the raven haired waitress for a coward, but she wasn't a fool either. Whatever the heck was going on out there, it was a lot worse than some truck stop hooker with a grudge. It sounded more like a gang of some kind had broken into the store and was wrecking the place. Wading out into the middle of something like that didn't make sense to her in the least.

At the same time, she knew hiding out in the bathroom didn't count as an option either. She couldn't risk getting caught alone in here by this gang of mystery marauders with nowhere to run. She needed to go out there, but she needed to do it smart.

The girl reached over and snapped off the bathroom light and fan. Now the noise of the fan wouldn't herald the opening of the bathroom door to any listeners nearby. Then she checked herself to make sure she had nothing likely to fall out of her apron or pocket that might make a sound and give her away.

She knew she was only going to get one chance to do this, and it had to be right.

Marisa waited until the fan quit whining, then crouched and slowly pulled the bathroom door open. Once she had it wide enough, she slipped through into little hallway. The girl stayed low, which meant she couldn't see over the shelves into the store, but it also meant she wouldn't be visible to whoever was doing the thrashing and crashing on the other side of the room.

A loud rumble of thunder, along with the distinct hiss of rain, told her the side door must be wide open. That, combined with the current location of the thrashing sounds, meant her exit options were now either the front entrance or the door to the restaurant. Each had its merits, but she wouldn't be able to make the final decision until she got there.

Reaching the front of the little hall, Marisa stayed in her crouch and did a quick look left and right down the length of the back wall and the cooler doors. Nobody lurked in either direction, so she made a quick dash straight ahead into the aisle of automotive products. The waitress stopped to catch her breath, and listen for more clues on what to do next.

Gladys had stopped screaming, but Marisa didn't know if it counted as a good or bad thing. A male voice still made a guttural "ungh ungh" sound she found deeply disturbing, as if it were made by a dying animal that was pinned and too weak to struggle further. There was still enough rustling and thrashing for her to know there must be several people moving around near the counter. What the hell was going on over there?

Part of her really didn't want to know.

Then things got worse.

A second later she heard the door to either the restaurant or the entrance jerk open, and realized she was only ten feet from that end of the aisle. If this was one of the maniacs attacking people then he would be on top of her in just a matter of seconds, and there would be almost no way she could avoid being seen by him. Retreat was the only option.

Marisa remained crouched and crabbed her way backwards for a few feet. Eyes fixed on the front of the aisle, she kept her keys clenched in her fist. Right now she would have preferred a weapon with more reach...like an assault rifle, perhaps...but this was what she had and she had it ready for use. Still, this scenario demanded avoidance, if at all possible, so the young woman took a few more crouching steps rearwards before turning to make a hurried dash back to the restroom hallway.

That brought her almost face to face with the nightmare coming around the back end of the aisle.

"*Madre de Dios!*" Marisa choked back a scream, and crossed herself at the same time.

Suddenly she was a little girl again...the one who listened to her Aunt Estelle's litany of horrors who licked their lips and waited in Hell for the bad women who didn't go to church and behaved without shame. Aunt Estelle must have had a rogue's gallery of demons somewhere, for she could go into great and gory detail of what awaited each naughty brat who got too full of herself and fell away from the protections of Heaven. Several of them bore a remarkable resemblance to this monstrosity...only this thing must have decided it had waited long enough and crawled its way out of Hell to come looking for her instead.

The young woman instinctively reached for the little cross she no longer wore around her neck, and felt the little girl inside wail when her hand closed on air. She had put it away her last year of high school, unwilling to endure the scorn from the more "modern" girls in her class. She wondered if Aunt Estelle was looking down on her from Heaven right this moment, and if so was she pleading to the saints nearby for intervention...

...or shaking her head in righteous finality at the niece who had brought damnation on herself.

Marisa could only lift the fistful of keys between the horror and her in warning as she backed away; while keenly aware of what a puny threat it was in the face of such a demon.

Its tiny eyes glared with mad lust from their dark sockets as it approached, picking up the pace with each step. It closed with her rapidly, and the woman knew it was going to be on her in a second whether she faced it or turned to run. She did the only thing she could and lashed out with her key spiked fist as the stinking creature reached for her.

The blow landed at a solid angle, and actually snapped the things head to the side. Marisa was not a tiny girl and could throw a soft ball from her position in center field all the way to second base without a relay man. On top of that, she had been raised on the side of town where a girl had to step up for herself from time to time, even if she usually found such activity classless and shameful.

Usually.

Right now she was scared out of her mind and ready to throw down with the devil himself.

Unfortunately, this thing gave no sign of being impressed by her resolve...or her makeshift weapon. The horror turned its nearly fleshless face back towards her, its grin seeming to mock her attempt at self defense. It showed no sign the blow had even fazed it.

Marisa screamed and drew back her fist to strike again as the thing's jaws parted in anticipation of its final lunge.

But the fist that landed next didn't come from her...and it impacted with power enough to spin the monstrosity around and knock it to the ground.

Marisa squeaked as the fist drew back past her and twisted to see the tightly smiling face of Harley as he put a hand on her shoulder and pulled her behind him.

"There's more of these things outside," the tall redneck gritted in a weirdly calm voice as he stepped past. "So go back through the restaurant door, but be ready to let me through."

Marisa didn't move, standing like a deer in the headlights, and could only bring herself to point at the monster behind the man as it started to climb to its feet.

It never got the chance.

Harley turned and caught it by the back of the neck with one hand and its outstretched arm with the other. He shifted his weight and brought the thing to its feet in one smooth motion before spinning around with it and smashing it face first into the cooler doors with enough force to shatter the glass. The man didn't hesitate to see the effect of the move, but adjusted his grip and yanked the flailing monster back out of the glass. He turned with it and smashed it face first on a steel shelf three times, just like a professional wrestler would put his opponents head into a turnbuckle, before spinning once again to throw the creature into a nearby pyramid of oil cans.

Marisa knew martial arts when she saw them, and apparently they had been trained to the point of reflex with this guy. And at his size, with those muscles, his moves had all the power and authority of a tiger. To say the man was devastating was an understatement. The fact he was ridiculously good looking on top of it was almost taking things to the absurd.

The thing he was fighting wasn't so impressed.

The demon floundered straight back to its feet in the cans, seemingly unbothered by the beating it had just taken.

"Holy shit! You're a *tough* bastard," the rangy young man sounded surprised.

The monster's sunken eyes fixed on Harley with the same look of intense ferocity it had only seconds ago regarded Marisa with.

It attacked without hesitation, only to have a stepping over side kick drive into its chest and slam it back against the wall. It still didn't go down. Clearly pain meant nothing to this thing. The horror rebounded from the wall and started straight back towards the man...

...just in time to take a roundhouse kick to the side of the head that smacked it's skull off its shoulder with an audible snap.

This time it went down for good.

It fell at the man's feet, who stared at it with wide-eyed suspicion from a fighting stance as it twitched on the floor. Marisa watched as Harley prodded the now obvious corpse with the toe of his boot a couple of times. The hateful skull snapped in blind hunger, but the body just twitched in uncoordinated jerks. It still lived, but acted like it had lost all control of its body below the neck.

Harley knelt down beside the thing for a second, then stood as if satisfied the fight was over.

Marisa stared in shock as he straightened his hat and looked back in her direction.

"Door," he reminded the girl gently.

"Right!" The waitress turned and made a dash for the restaurant entrance.

What the hell were you doing, you idiot! She berated herself internally. *The world is going to hell around you and you're staring at some yahoo like a moonstruck cow! Snap out of it!*

Marisa bolted out of the aisle and made the mistake of looking to her left, towards the cash register as she did.

What she saw there would give her nightmares for the rest of her life.

Four more of the skull faced demons were rising to their feet in front of the wreckage that had once been the store counter. Several others ripped and tore at something behind the debris, and she saw one leg protruding on the floor from the feeding tangle. It wore one of Gladys' orthopedic shoes.

But even worse was the bloody mass of meat at the feet of the four monsters in front of the ruined counter. She could barely recognize it as human, it was so torn and shredded. But even as she stared in horror, it made a mewling whimper and a hand with missing fingers jerked up and reached towards her in a desperate appeal for help.

She cried out and kept running, trying to ignore the renewed screaming when two of the monsters reacted to their meals movement with fresh attacks. Unfortunately, the other two must have decided they were more interested in the movement on her end of the store.

In what she was starting to recognize as some kind of attack posture, the blood-soaked creatures spread their talon like hands and gaped their jaws before heading her direction.

"Harley!" she screamed a warning as she pushed through the restaurant entrance and turned to hold the door. "They're coming!"

She gripped the door, wondering where the man had disappeared to. The two monsters had now picked up speed and would be at the doorway in another second or two.

"Harley!"

The man erupted from the aisle he must have been crouching in just as her pursuers reached it and shoulder blocked them into each other and the post card display by the front window. They went down in a thrashing heap while he bounced off and used his changed momentum to run towards the door.

Marisa started to make a sharp comment on stupid moves as he reached the entrance, then bit it off.

It dawned on her that he had actually put himself in danger and waited back in the aisle, just to make sure those things wouldn't catch her before she made it to safety. The man must have seen them when he came in the store in the first place, so he already knew the threat they posed.

Harley slid through the door and both of them pushed it closed and put their backs to it.

A second later the sounds of withered hands slapping and sliding on glass came from behind them. Marisa braced herself and helped the tall redneck hold the door as the pressure from the other side increased. She knew her contribution probably amounted to a quarter of his, but silently swore this "dumb, helpless female" role she had stumbled into the past couple of minutes was going to end...right now.

The pressure on the other side of the door steadily increased, causing the two to put their feet far out in front of them in an attempt to brace better.

"Keys..." Harley gritted as he strained against the door, "Are there keys to this door?"

Marisa fought to remember for a second, then the answer came.

"Yeah," she gasped, "the night manager has them."

"Who's the night manager?"

"Gladys."

"Crap."

"Yeah..."

"Well, we're gonna have to think of something pretty quick," the man panted, "because I've got a feeling these things don't tire out as fast as we do."

She had a feeling he was right.

"Okay, okay, just let me think..."

Marisa found it hard to concentrate while exerting so hard. And there also remained the matter of still being scared half out of her mind to contend with as well. She cast her gaze around for something to brace against the door, but instead found herself staring at the frightened faces of those who remained in the booths of the restaurant. Two out-of-towners...which included a certain jackass who thought truck stops should have salad bars...

"Hey! *Señor!*" she yelled at the pudgy out-of-towner in the red beret who was staring at them in open mouthed shock. "You want to come help us hold this door?!"

"I – I" the young man gawped and shook his head in negation, "I'm not – not involved in this!"

The waitress couldn't believe her ears.

"Oh, believe me, "Marisa snarled, "if these things get in here you are going to be involved! They're going to involve you in your own slaughter! *Now get over here and help us with this damn door!*"

The young man flushed red, and sputtered in indignation, but exited the booth and took a few noncommittal steps in their direction. He stopped when he got a better look at the bloody visages pressed up against the glass behind them.

"Now dammit! Or we're all going to DIE!"

He hustled forward again, but stopped in front of her in irritated confusion.

"There's only room for two against that door," he complained. "Where am I supposed to fit?"

"You're going to be taking my place," Marisa winced in effort. "So get ready. We've got to make this switch fast."

"Wait," he objected. "Why do I have to take *your* place?"

"Because, Galahad," Marisa snapped, "I've got to go get the spare set of keys to this lock, and I can't do it with my butt against this door! "

"My name is Gerald," the redhead huffed.

"Spare keys?" Harley queried through effort clenched teeth. "Hey, I like the sound of that!"

The cords of the tall man's neck stood out as he strained backwards against the door. The muscles of his arms and shoulders knotted with exertion and Marisa started to suspect her contribution to this effort was probably a lot less than the quarter she originally thought. She also realized time was of the essence here.

"Okay...Gerald..." she fought down the urge to call him something a lot more colorful, "I'm going to count to three. When I hit three, I'm going to roll away from the door and you just step up and put your back against it. Got it?"

"Wait," he protested, "Do you mean 'one, two, three and then move...or one, two, and move at the same time you're saying three?"

If I live through this, I'm going to kill this man.

"On three," she growled. "Got it?"

Gerald nodded, managing to look both irritated and unsure.

"Okay...one...two...THREE!"

Marisa rolled sideways away from the door, and came up on her knees to see the man looking at her in surprise, before making an awkward lunge for the door. She didn't want to take the time to curse at him, so satisfied herself with glaring at his girlfriend still in the booth as she came to her feet and started running towards the kitchen door. The girl looked away in obvious embarrassment. Marisa couldn't help but wonder what any woman could even see in a useless and abrasive little troll like Gerald, but had more important matters to attend to at the moment.

She sprinted for the kitchen, and prayed Harley and the snotty little dork could hold the door long enough for what had to be done. The waitress remembered Big Earl had a spare set of keys in his office. She also remembered Gladys was the only one to have a key to Big Earl's office as well, but a past exploit of that idiot Tomas reminded her there was another way into there.

Now if she could get one of the guys back there to step up.

"Benny!" she yelled as she pushed her way through the door, "I need you to...HOLY SHIT!"

Marisa came to a stop and gaped at the rear wall of the kitchen near the back door and hallway.

The entire area was drenched in blood.

CHAPTER FIVE: DOWNPOUR

Downpour - Deke

"Holy Shit!"

Deke looked up from tying the makeshift bandage on Stacey's arm to see Marisa standing in the doorway of the kitchen with a shocked look on her face. He could only imagine what she was seeing.

The group of them all sat on the floor around the janitor, Benny, bandaging him as fast as they could under the veterinarian's direction. Stacey had run and grabbed an armful of rags from a storeroom, and now they were tearing them and tying them around the little man's legs under Rachel's watchful eyes. They were all covered in blood from both the janitor and the trucker who died to save him, and the floor and walls were smeared in crimson from their former struggle with the monsters at the door in the stuff.

"B-Benny?" The tall waitress took a hesitant step further into the room.

"Oh, Marisa!" Stacey cried, "They got Benny! He's hurt bad! Real bad!"

"Oh shit," Marisa gulped weakly, and took another two steps closer. "W-what about Tomas? I need him right now."

"He's dead!" The little waitress got up and rushed over to grab the taller girls arm. "They're all dead back there, 'Risa! Tomas. Arnold. All of them! These things were EATING them!"

Marisa stared at the smaller girl in horror for a second, then seemed to collect herself.

"Easy, *amiga*," she put her hands on Stacey's shoulders and looked her in the eyes. "I know it must have been bad, but we're not out of trouble yet. Those bastards are in the store, and they're trying to get into the restaurant. Harley is holding the door shut, but he can't keep it up for long. I need to get into Big Earl's office to get the spare keys, *comprende*?"

Stacey gulped and stared at her for a second. She looked half hysterical, and Deke realized she had probably run to the other waitress for comforting. Instead, the smaller girl swallowed hard and nodded.

Marisa started to pat her on the shoulders then decided not to when she noticed the gashes on the girl's upper arm. Failing that, she turned to Deke with a look of urgency on her face.

"It's Deke, right?" She used the hand she had originally intended to put on Stacey's shoulder to grab his arm instead. "I need your help with something. I know you want to stay with Stacey, but I need you right now. Okay?"

"Uh..."

"You need him to climb like Tomas did?" Stacey interrupted. Deke thought she appeared to be recollecting herself with admirable speed, although she had a certain wide-eyed, frail look that worried him.

"Yes. And we need to hurry. Harley can't hold that door much longer."

"Okay," the smaller girl nodded again. She didn't sound terribly happy about it, and Deke didn't want to leave her. But if those things were about get in here, then he needed to do everything in his power to stop them...right now.

The young redneck looked back at her as he let Marisa pull him down the back hallway.

"Come *on*," Marisa urged. "Once you've gotten these keys for me, you can get back to taking care of her. But she needs you to do this, too. All of us do."

"Right!" Deke refocused ahead as the tall waitress pulled him past a couple of doors in the rear hallway and stopped at the third one. "Let's get on with it. What do you need me to do?"

"That," she pointed at a fourth door set into the wall at the end of the hallway, "is Big Earl's office. There is a spare set of keys in the lap drawer of his desk."

"So let's get them." He headed for the door but Marisa caught his arm again.

"Wait," she ordered. "It's locked and we don't have the keys to it. It's metal and set in a concrete and cinder brick wall, so you aren't going to be able to bust it open either."

"Okay." He could see she was telling it like it was. "So what do we do?"

"You," she emphasized, "are going to go through the ceiling and over the wall and drop into the office."

"Got it." Deke began an immediate scan of the area for something to stand on so he could reach the ceiling and do as instructed. He spied some plastic crates for carrying large jugs of salad dressing and started for them.

"No, Deke." Marisa tightened her grip on his arm, and he turned to look at her in confusion.

Her face was tight, and he suddenly got the feeling she was about to tell him something he really didn't want to hear.

"What?"

"Now for the bad news," the waitress continued. "You can't get there from here. The wall all these doors are set in is a firewall. If you go up into the ceiling here in the hallway, you can only get to places inside the restaurant. The office is on the store side of the wall, so to get in there you're going to have to go up into the ceiling from the store side."

His urge for decisive action faded as he considered the ramifications of that.

"Wait," he swallowed, "You mean where those..."

"Yeah."

"But how? If those things are in there, how am I supposed to do this? It would be suicide!"

This changed everything. Deke didn't want to let everybody down, but getting ripped to pieces didn't appeal to him either. He had seen the damage these monsters could do to a man in a very short time while fighting at the door.

"By sneaking past them." Marisa's grip tightened on his arm. "You can do this."

"Are you serious?" He eyed the girl warily. "How?"

"I saw seven of them in there. Four were eating Gladys and some other guy at the counter, and two were at the door trying to push their way in. I think a couple of them moved to join the ones at the door while Harley and I were trying to hold it closed. But that still means they're all up front of the store. If you go through this door, you should be able to duck right into the men's room on the other side without being seen.

"That makes six." Deke really didn't like this. "You said there were seven."

"Harley killed the other one. By the way, what is he...some kind of redneck ninja or something?"

"Huh?"

"No, nevermind that," she shook her head as if irritated with herself. "The point is it's down, and you should be able to do this without getting caught. Just duck into the men's room and go to the last stall. Climb up through the ceiling there and you should be able to go right over the wall into Big Earl's office. Got it?"

"Yeah," he shrugged without enthusiasm. "Okay."

"Deke, you have to do this. If you don't...we're all dead. Stacey, too."

"I know," he set his jaw. "I know. I'll do it. I'm just trying to figure out how this could suck any worse than it does."

"You could be on fire," she suggested as she gripped the doorknob to the employee's entrance to the store.

"Oh ha-ha, and here I thought Stacey was the comedian of you two."

"Oh, trust me," Marisa rolled her eyes and glanced back up the hallway. "She has her moments. Now, I'm going to open the door on three. Are you ready? On three...One..."

"Wait a minute. Do you mean..."

"Oh, nevermind!" she hissed and pulled the door open a bit to take a peek out. "You're clear. Just go! And stay low until you're in the bathroom."

"Right."

"And hurry!"

D. NATHAN HILLIARD

"Right!"

Deke took a deep breath and slid around the door into the short rear hallway of the store. He crouched low, one hand on the floor and located the bathroom door only six feet away. Behind him, the door to the back hallway closed with a soft click.

He was now in enemy territory...and scared half out of his mind.

But so far, still alive.

The killers must have been at the front of the store like Marisa had predicted. Deke had an unobstructed view down one aisle and to his relief it stood completely empty. But something had definitely happened there. The floor was littered with broken glass and cans, and the steel shelf on the end was bent down into a shallow "U" from some kind of impact.

He could also hear things.

From somewhere in the front corner of the store, where the cash register ought to be, he could hear a strange, soft whimpering punctuated by the tear of cloth and rustle of movement. His mind rebelled at the image the sound conjured and focused more on the scrabbling noise emanating from the direction of the door to the restaurant. There was an occasional squeak, like the sound of a hand sliding on glass, consistent with Marisa's tale of the things trying to push their way in to get to the rest of them...

...a reminder that time was of the essence here.

Deke ghosted over to the entrance to the men's restroom. He pushed the door open with slow care, trying not to make either noise or a sudden motion that might catch the attention of the monsters, and slipped inside. Once in, he eased the door closed while holding his breath...expecting it to be slammed open again by some skull-faced horror any second. When that didn't happen, he wasted no time in hurrying over to the far toilet stall.

Step one had been accomplished.

This was an industrial style toilet, without a tank on back. It only had a pipe leading up from the toilet itself featuring a valve handle on its side. Deke stepped up onto

111

the bowl and then the top of the pipe in two quick strides and examined the ceiling. A rectangular fluorescent fixture hung over the center of the stall, but in the back corner a large ceiling tile provided exactly the exit he was searching for.

He pushed up the tile with alacrity, did a quick check of the top of the wall for spiders or other vermin he had no wish to put his hands on, then grabbed the wall top. The young man pulled himself up into the ceiling with limber ease and found himself crouching in the dark recesses of the ceiling, on top of an eight inch wide strip of concrete wall. A stray part of his mind noted he was getting filthy, but it barely pinged on his consciousness at the moment.

"Okay," he muttered while reaching for a tile on the opposite side of the wall from the bathroom. "If Marisa is right, then this should be the ceiling to the office."

He pulled up the tile to reveal a square of blackness below.

"Naturally, the lights are out," he grumped. "Oh well, here goes the dashing Deke leaping blind into the jaws of...uh...whatever."

The boy grabbed the top of the wall, and slid his lower body down through the hole as fast as he could and still maintain control. He worried he might end up hanging down the side of the wall, and have to let go and drop in the darkness without being able to gauge where the floor was beneath him. As it turned out, the exact opposite became the problem.

His feet hit an obstruction just as he had the top of the wall at chest level.

The fact he was allowing himself to descend rapidly meant he essentially landed on whatever it was, with his legs now absorbing the brunt of his weight as opposed to arms. The result of this was his arms suddenly ceased to support him and he reflexively relaxed them, and then a second later he flailed in the darkness as the surface starting slipping out from under his feet. Instinct told him he must have landed on the desk, and on a large stack of papers, because now he was slipping and kicking them all over the darkness in a desperate dance to keep his balance.

"Aw shit!" he yelled as one leg kicked a tad too far and he went down in a crash of plastic, glass, and papers.

"Deke?" A worried voice came through what had to be the door to his right. "Are you okay? What are you doing?"

"Nothing!" he retorted while flailing on the floor to get his feet under him. "Where are the lights in here?"

"On the wall, near the door."

Her tone left "where they always are" unspoken but not unsaid.

"Right."

Fumbling his way up the wall, he found the switch and turned it on. As he expected, the office now qualified as a wreck. Papers, pens, and plastic desk trays covered the floor. And the desk... he hoped Big Earl was in a forgiving mood when he saw this, because the desk was going to have to be replaced. It had broken in the middle when he had fallen and landed on it.

"I did that?" he muttered, astonished at the destruction.

On the bright side, the lap drawer had been forced open, and now revealed the object of his quest.

"I got it!"

Deke snatched the large key ring from the broken drawer and held it aloft like a prize.

"Well," the girl retorted from the other side of the door, "then hurry up and get out here with it!"

"Right," the youngster sighed and turned towards the door. He twisted the little knob in the handle to unlock the door, then turned his attention to the dead bolt above.

"Aw crap!"

"What now?"

"The dead bolt takes a key on this side too! There has to be forty keys on this thing!"

Marisa said something in Spanish that Deke suspected wasn't very nice...and probably had something to do with him. He was beginning to get irritated with her attitude, but understood it probably had a lot to do with the fact their time was running out. Besides, she was Stacey's best friend so he figured it wise to stay on her good side.

"Okay, look," he said, "I'm not going to waste time trying all these keys on this lock. I'm just going to go back the way I came. Be there in a minute."

"Good thinking!" the voice sounded relieved. "Be careful."

"You just be ready to open that door for me, okay?"

"I'll be there."

Since the desk was a collapsed heap, he couldn't use it to get back into the ceiling. He cast around for something else, and settled for the file cabinet in the corner. Rushing over, Deke grabbed the metal cabinet and pulled with all his might. The thing was heavy, but he was now desperate and in a hurry. Redoubling his efforts, he dragged the thing close enough to the ceiling hole for him to use, before clambering on top and grabbing the top of the wall.

Deke jammed the big key-ring into his front pocket and grabbed the top of the wall again. This time he knew where he was going, so he practically vaulted himself up over the wall and started lowering himself down the other side. This had already taken longer than he intended, and the pressure to get the key back to Marisa spurred him to greater effort. Not to mention, he wanted to get through the bathroom and hallway and back behind the safety of the employees entrance door as fast as possible...

...which was why he wasn't paying attention and stepped on the handle of the toilet on the way down the other side.

The toilet thundered with a roar Deke knew from prior experience could be heard all the way to the front door.

"Oh shit!" he groaned. "Nobody in here but us dead guys taking a crap. Seriously!"

Fearing the worst, the young redneck dropped the rest of the way to the floor and scrambled out of the stall. He clutched his hat to his head as he raced across the bathroom to the door, his boot heels echoing on the tile floor. Behind him, the stall door banged shut with all the subtlety of a shotgun blast.

"Oh shit ohshitohshitohshit..."

He reached the door and ripped it open, fully expecting to be greeted by a carnivorous horde of death faced killers.

He was almost right.

The hallway still stood empty, but when Deke came out of the bathroom a motion caught the corner of his eye and he turned to face a nightmare coming down the aisle towards him.

She must have been old.

Curly white hair hung in wet mats down the sides of her head, and she wore a filthy white dress that looked more like a nightdress than the usual formal wear women were buried in. Half of her skull still boasted the grey cracked skin it wore in the coffin, leaving just one eye to glare at Deke with insane hunger. The partial death mask split at the cheek, allowing the teeth on that side of her face to continue the skeletal grin started on the other side.

She flew down the aisle towards him, jaws wide in a silent scream of bloodlust.

Deke gave a terrified squawk and raced to the door in the back hallway. In his panic he tried to open it himself, then remembered it was locked from this side. Oh well, there certainly wasn't any point in silence now.

"MARISA!" he screamed and hammered on the door with his other hand. "Open the door!"

"I'm trying! Let go of the knob!" came the muffled reply.

He felt the doorknob try to twist in his hand and realized he was keeping the girl from being able to open it from the other side. Crap! Even as he released the handle, he knew time had run out. He turned to face his attacker, arms instinctively raised as a shield.

"Aw shit," Deke groaned.

The horror landed on him like a rotting nightmare.

###

Downpour - Holly

"What do you mean 'a line will come open shortly!?'
This is 911 goddammit! You can't put me on hold!"

Holly stared in disbelief at her cell phone. She knew
she was running on borderline hysterics and fought to keep
from screaming at the little piece of technology in her
hand. The girl figured she was holding it together pretty
well considering only three minutes earlier her biggest
concern was wondering when Gerald's lecture on not
clinging to provincial old ways and friendships would end.

Then the screaming had started.

Something bad had started somewhere in rear of
the building, and almost everybody in the place had run
back there. After a few seconds, the tall redneck, Harley,
came rushing back out and ran out the door to the store on
the other side of the wall. There had been more screaming
from the back, and crashing coming from the direction of
the store. She started to get up herself, but Gerald caught
her hand and pulled her back down.

Then, almost simultaneously, the screaming in back
had stopped and the dark haired waitress came flying in
the door from the store with the man in the beat up cowboy
hat not far behind. The obvious fear in their faces when
they braced themselves against the door unnerved her, but
when she saw what piled up on the door behind them she
thought she was losing her mind.

It was like something out of a bad horror movie.

Now Holly frantically tried to call for help while
Gerald and the other man struggled to keep the monsters
out. So far, her efforts were getting her nowhere. For the
second time an answering machine at the Masonfield PD
picked up the phone to tell her all their lines were busy but
to stay on the phone and one would come open shortly.
Her teeth clenched in panicked fury at this unheard of
development.

They were going to die and evidently the police had
better things to do than come save them.

Holly snapped the phone shut and took a deep breath before returning her gaze to where Gerald and the tall redneck, Harley, were holding the door shut. She hated looking at them because she couldn't avoid seeing the ghastly faces behind them against the glass. The semi-bare skulls pushed tight against the door, their teeth making unpleasant sounds as they dragged across the glass.

The way they all piled up against the door with mindless intensity scared her almost as bad as their ghoulish appearance. The look of strain on the bigger man's face as he fought to hold the door shut didn't reassure her either. Gerald was also red in the face from exertion, And with no police coming, she realized if they were going to live through this, it was going to be due to their own efforts.

"Is there something I can do?" she offered.

"You want to take my place?" her boyfriend panted. "I'm wearing out fast here."

"No, Gerald," she barked, surprising both him and her, "I meant maybe I can squeeze down between you guys and sit on the floor with my back against the door."

"It would help," Harley gritted, "but if we have to move fast, like retreat to the kitchen, you would be trapped behind our legs on the floor. Not good. I think you would be more use as my eyes and ears for the moment."

"What do you mean?"

"Well, first of all, ma'am," he shifted his position slightly lower and rebraced his legs, "I need a head count of how many of those things are pushing against me...err...us right now. Can you do that, please? I know they ain't pleasant to look at, but it would sure help."

"Okay, "she nodded doubtfully, "but it's awfully hard to see."

"Go ahead and stand on a booth. That will give you a better angle, and even let you see past them a little bit."

"Right."

Holly moved over to the booth directly opposite the door, and clambered up on the bench as instructed. Then, setting her jaw, she turned and faced the door and its horrors again.

117

Her turning to face them seemed to excite the creatures. They all gaped their jaws in unison and their assault on the door increased in intensity.

"What the hell?" Harley gasped.

"Holy shit!" Gerald exclaimed. "Whatever you're doing...stop it! You're pissing them off!"

"I—I'm not doing anything!" She stood like a deer in the headlights on the booth seat, almost paralyzed by the glares of sheer bloodlust being directed at her. It was hypnotic, like locking gazes with a hungry lion at a zoo.

"How many..."

"What?" she shook her head and refocused on Harley.

"How many of them?"

"Oh! Ummm...one, two, three, four...five! Five! It's hard to see because the glass is all smeared up with blood!"

"Lovely!" Gerald snarled, "I really needed to hear that. Now get your butt down from there and stop provoking them!"

"I'm not doing anything!" she protested, but dutifully started to descend from atop the booth's seat.

The last thing she wanted to do was excite the killer mob on the other side of the door into overwhelming the two men holding them out. All the pressure they were putting against the glass concerned her enough as it was. They weren't hammering on it, at least not yet, but they pushed against it constantly. And if they were pushing hard enough to make the two men strain like this to keep them out...sooner or later something was going to give.

"Ma'am, wait a minute."

"Huh?" She stopped climbing down and looked at Harley.

"I need you to do one more thing before you get down."

"What's that?" she queried.

"No shit," Gerald snapped, "What now? These things are getting more worked up!"

"I want," the larger man patiently continued, "you to try and see over their heads and give me an idea of how many are behind them in the store. We need to know what we're up against."

"Right," she nodded and stood again.

Holly could see the wisdom of this, even though the glare Gerald now fixed on her was almost as baleful as the ones on the other side of the glass. Allowing the other man to countermand his order guaranteed she would be facing a sullen and resentful boyfriend in the near future. She could already tell it was going to take some major ego stroking to unruffle his feathers later. But it would be best to worry about that later and focus on the task at hand.

"Ummm..." She squinted over the activity in the doorway. "There are a couple on the ground in front of the register...Holy crap, it looks like the whole thing came down...and there are two...no three... behind the mess in the corner. Oh god!" she covered her mouth with her hand. "They're eating...that..."

"I know," Harley soothed. "Don't think about it. Just concentrate on counting."

Holly swallowed and focused over them again.

"I think that's it. Five back there and five at the door. No...waitaminute...one of the ones at the door is leaving."

"Yeah, I can feel the difference." Gerald's sarcasm stung.

"Where's he going?" Harley ignored him. "Back to the counter?"

"She...I think...it's wearing a dress...but it just turned around and went down an aisle."

"I'm not sure I like the sound of that..."

"Maybe it got bored," Gerald puffed.

"I doubt it. They don't seem the type. Maybe she's going to go eat the one I took down earlier. But I sort of doubt that too."

"You killed one?" Holly perked up. "Then they're not what they look like!"

"Not really 'killed' it," Harley strained against the door. "Just 'broke' it. And trust me...they are *exactly* what they look like. By the way, you can go ahead and get down now."

"Oh, right,"

She clambered down from the booth seat, trying to ignore the reignited glare from Gerald.

He could pick the stupidest things to get jealous or insecure about, and part of her couldn't believe he was indulging in this kind of stupidity right now. Couldn't he see the other man was just being sensible? It should have been obvious. But she harbored no doubt she would later be accused of being secretly attracted the guy. Almost two years of being with Gerald had accustomed her to this behavior to the point it was just one more thing she planned around on a given day. She could handle it...

...assuming that getting ripped to pieces and devoured by dead people didn't get added to her itinerary.

"So you are saying those are really dead people out there?" Gerald's disbelief dripped from every word.

"Yeah," Harley grimaced as the door shifted a little. "I know it's hard to believe, but I got up close and personal with one and it was one hundred percent, grade-A corpse...odor and all."

"You mean like a zombie?" Holly frowned, "Like in the movies?"

"Well, like the old dead ones, I guess. Only these are faster, stronger, and more vicious. Meaner looking, too."

"Great!" Gerald exclaimed, "I'm stuck in a backwoods George Romero movie with the cast from Hee Haw."

"Gerald, please..." she gave an apologetic look to Harley.

"Look," the redhead huffed, "if you're done pissing these things off, why don't you do something useful and go find out what's holding up that waitress with those keys. Tell her I said the service around here stinks."

Holly winced, and nodded.

"I guess it's been awful quiet back there anyway," she turned towards the kitchen. "I'll go see what's going on." Truthfully, she was grateful for an excuse to get away from both the door and Gerald.

120

She made three steps before the sounds of all hell breaking loose erupted from the back of the diner.

Downpour – Deke

The dead woman hit Deke with a flying lunge.

He caught one wrist in a desperate grab and barely managed to get his other forearm up under her chin as the horror forced him backwards against the door to the back hallway. Her strength caught him by surprise, and the ferocity of the attack stunned him. She thrashed wildly in her attempt to close the final inches between the two of them and it was all he could do to hold on. Pain lanced in his shoulder where her free hand grabbed and drove her fingers into his flesh like spikes.

The young man screamed in pain, and also at the sight of the yellow toothed maw snapping like a rabid wolf less than an inch from his nose. The awful smell of the thing threatened to overwhelm him and Deke gagged in an effort to keep from inhaling its stench. And the way she kept driving her face at his reminded him horribly of the prelude to a kiss...before she would stretch those jaws wide and try to bite his face off again.

I don't want to die like this, he despaired...knowing full well that several people had already done exactly that in the past few minutes.

And then he was falling.

The door Deke had been pressed back against suddenly opened, and he tumbled backwards into the hallway beyond...with his grisly assailant right on top of him.

Stars blasted across his vision as his head bounced off the concrete floor. Pain split a fiery crack in the back of his skull, leaving him temporarily blinded and confused while thrashing with the horror on the cement surface. Screams erupted around him, and he heard the doctor's voice yelling for somebody to close the door.

The boot to the side of his head didn't help either.

"Ow! Holy Shit! Kick *it*, not me!"

"Sorry!" Marisa snarled, but the rate her boot flew back and forth past his eyes didn't diminish in the least. It connected with the monsters head three straight times, knocking it sideways, but the thing didn't seem fazed in the least. Its one glaring eye continued to stare straight into his own like killing him was the only thing in the universe that mattered. Even worse, the last kick dislodged his forearm from under its chin...giving it a clear bite at his face.

This time he couldn't stop it.

"Nooooo!" Deke cried out as the things widening jaws filled his vision.

Then all the air was driven from his lungs as something landed on both of them with tremendous force.

"Get...*off*...him!" Stacey shrieked, now sitting on its back. Her teeth were bared and her face was livid with what appeared to be pure rage. The girl grabbed the horror by the hair on both sides of its head and leaned back hard in an effort to pull its snapping teeth away from him. It worked...for a second.

Then with a wet tearing sound the corpse's entire scalp and the skin on the side of its face slid free of its skull, leaving the waitress holding the dripping white curls and death mask in her hand. Stacey shrieked in disgust and threw the offending mass down the hall towards the office. It landed with a viscous plop in front of Big Earl's door. At the same time, the sudden release of tension on the monster's head caused its bony cranium to fly forward and butt Deke between the eyes.

The stars returned, and the pain made tears well.

The boy groped blindly with his free arm, trying to get it between him and the things mouth again. Any second he expected the feel of those rotten teeth sinking into the sides of his face. He tried to turn over, but the combined weight of the monster and Stacey in these confined quarters had him pinned. His vision cleared enough to see the little waitress now had the thing in a rear headlock and was straining to hold it back. The combined pressure of both his and her arms under its chin held its jaw shut and was the only reason he still featured a nose.

Things were not going well.

And the clock was still ticking...

"Marisa," he gasped at the waitress, who currently looked to be hunting an angle to get another kick in. "The keys...the keys are in my front pocket. Go get that door locked and...Aughhhh!"

Pain now lit up his shoulder.

Deke twisted his head to see that the old trucker had arrived and somehow maneuvered over to the other side of him, grabbed the nightmare's free hand, and now started pulling it free from his shoulder. But as he pulled back, the dead woman tried to clench her hand into a fist...threatening to tear a huge chunk of his muscle free. The boy cried out again, and blood welled around the monster's fingers where they penetrated his shirt.

"Okay," the old man breathed loudly, "you want to play rough? So be it."

Deke's eyes widened as the old trucker pulled a hunting knife out from behind his back. It was a deadly looking thing with an antler handle, a saw-toothed back, and a wickedly curved blade. The fact it gleamed only inches from his face made it seem enormous. But with all the thrashing going on, Deke wasn't sure if the knife's appearance counted as a good thing or not.

"Hey now," he gasped. "Be careful with that! I don't wa...ow! Owww! Fine! She's twisting it...Cut her! Do what you got to do! Oh crap, it hurts!"

The trucker wasted no time in sliding the blade in under one of the withered fingers and then turning the edge up. "Turn your head," he instructed. "I don't know how much this blade will jump when it cuts through."

"Right," Deke twisted his face away...

...only to find himself nose to nostril holes with the horror on top of him.

Stacey still straddled its back and had its head gripped tight, with one of her arms under its chin. She was breathing hard, and obviously squeezing for all she was worth. It looked odd, but Deke realized it did an effective

123

job of keeping the thing's mouth shut where it couldn't bite. At the same time, being eyeball to eyeball with this monstrosity was going to be the fuel for a lifetimes worth of nightmares.

Assuming he had enough lifetime left for nightmares.

"Got them!" Marisa stood up on his other side. She held the key ring in her hand as she pushed herself back to her feet. He hadn't even realized she had been fishing around in his pocket. "As soon as I find the right key that fits the lock, I'll have Harley back here to help!"

"You mean you don't know which key it is either?" Deke couldn't help but query.

"Hey!" she snapped. "Do I look like an assistant manager to you? I just...oh, nevermind!"

Marisa turned and raced for the front of the restaurant as fast as her long legs would carry her.

Deke hoped she got lucky and hit the right key soon.

He was hurt, and getting the hell beaten out of him by this monster.

The other problem was this thing didn't seem to tire, while Stacey was already showing signs of exhaustion. She was having to give it her all just to keep the things jaws shut, meaning her energy was depleting that much faster. Even worse, fresh blood ran in rivulets from the gashes in her arm and he knew that had to be taking its toll on her as well.

What he didn't know was how much longer he was going to be able to hold the thing's other hand out of the fight. He had it by the wrist, pinned between him and monster, and he suspected if that hadn't been the case it would have already managed to jerk free. Even under these circumstances, it still fought with unrelenting ferocity to get loose, and he knew it was only a matter of time.

Pain lanced in his shoulder again, and . Deke groaned aloud.

"Only one more, son," the old man wheezed to him, "Just hang in there. I've almost got it free."

"Hanging in there," the boy whimpered.

Deke had a feeling this would be over in the next minute or two...one way or another. Unfortunately he could see several ways this could finish badly but hadn't managed to imagine any happy endings yet.

"There!" Grandpa Tom exclaimed.

Another flare of pain lit up Deke's shoulder...

...and then things went from bad to worse.

The monster jerked its freed hand back, now missing three fingers. The move seemed reflexive, but couldn't have been more effective if the thing had calculated it. Its elbow drove into Stacey's ribs with a thunderous impact Deke could feel through his contact with their bodies atop him.

"Ouff!" The girl grabbed her side as she tumbled off the creature's back.

The dead woman twisted with undiminished strength and jerked its other hand free of Deke's grasp. It now fixed its baleful glare on the young waitress gasping on the floor beside them.

"Stacey! Look out!"

Stacey's pain glazed eyes widened as she realized she had become the object of the thing's attention. The wounded girl mustered a thin scream and scrambled backwards as the horror clambered after her in pursuit.

It closed the gap with her in a second.

The monster lunged for the kill...

...only this time to be brought down by Deke from behind.

"Oh no you don't!" he grunted, snaking his arms under the creature's armpits and clasping his hands behind its neck.

Stacey scurried clear as he planted the things face into the concrete.

It still fought with wild intensity, but he had it in a full nelson and it couldn't reach him with either its talons or its teeth. On the other hand, now all he could do was hold on. It amounted to another stalemate, with its duration once again dictated by how long he could last before exhaustion caused his grip to fail.

Still, every second he held on to the thing was one more second Marisa had to get that door locked. He brought all of the strength he had left to bear on the monster, trying to force its head down into its chest. He couldn't believe how much effort it took, considering the shrunken state of the thing's neck.

"Deke! Over here!"

He looked up to see Stacey holding a large metal door open in the wall. She clutched her side with her other hand, and her breathing was short and labored.

"Try and throw her in here!" the girl repeated. "Grandpa! Grab her legs while Deke's got her like that! We can lock her in!"

"Right," the old man wheezed and crawled over to where Deke had the thing pinned. The trucker was pale, and clutched his left arm as if it hurt him, but his face was set in grim determination. "Hang on to her, boy...but roll off and over to your side. Once I get her legs off the ground, that should take away a lot of her leverage."

"Whatever you say," Deke panted.

At this point the boy was ready to try anything.

He rolled over to his side, pulling the thrashing corpse over onto its side as well.

"Got her," the trucker grunted. "Now see if you can get to your knees.

To Deke's surprise, the trucker was right. Once the thing's feet were off the ground, it couldn't brace to bring much of its strength into play. Even better, he discovered the thing didn't weigh as much as he originally thought. Perhaps being dead for a while had made it lighter.

That's when he realized this plan might actually work.

Hope flared as he struggled erect, with Grandpa Tom ahead of him holding the thing's feet. Things had just gotten much better. Now that it hung completely off the ground, the monster could only twist with limited effect between them. Its arms flailed uselessly out to the sides, posing no threat to anybody.

"I like this plan!" Deke enthused "Let's do this!"

126

The two hustled the writhing corpse over to where
Stacey held the big door open. Deke could feel a blast of
cold air issue out, and realized it must be the restaurant's
walk in freezer. The irony didn't escape him.

"Oh yeah! Back to the cooler with you, Grandma!"
he exclaimed. "Okay, mister. When you get to the door, just
drop her feet and jump out of the way. Got it?"

"Got it," the trucker panted.

"You ready with that door, Stacey?"

The girl said nothing, but nodded...her face tight
and eyes wide.

"Okay, when I throw her I'm going to yell 'now' and
jump back. Got it?"

"Yeah," she half whispered. "Got it."

The two of them positioned themselves in front of
the open door, with Grandpa Tom standing with his back
to the freezer, holding her feet. They locked eyes with each
other, and the trucker cleared his throat.

"Are you ready for this, boy?"

"Yeah," Deke flashed a tired grin. "No time like the
present."

"Then, go!"

The old man dropped the things feet and lurched
out of the doorway. Deke lunged forward as its legs came
down, and used the momentum to launch the monster
through the entrance in front of them.

"Now!" he cried and jumped back.

The door almost grazed him as it went past, and
slammed shut with a reverberating crash. The noise echoed
in the concrete and cinder brick hallway. Stacey grabbed
the pin hanging from a chain attached to the door and
drove it down through a little hole in the handle. A split
second later a thud issued from the door as something
smacked into it from the other side.

The three of them backed across the hallway from
the freezer and stared wide eyed at the steel frame.

Two more thuds sounded from inside.

The heavy metal structure barely even vibrated, and
all three breathed a huge sigh of relief.

It was over.

DEAD STOP

The monster was trapped.

CHAPTER SIX: DELUGE

With a thunderous explosion of lightning, the storm finally unleashed its full wrath on the already drenched landscape below.

Old timers called storms like this a "Texas Blue Norther."

Rolling in from the Rockies out of the Northwest, it was like an advancing atmospheric wall that could cause temperatures to plunge over 25 degrees in almost no time at all. Arriving at nightfall only intensified the drop. Blue Northers almost always brought a downpour, and when they came at night they could produce spectacular storms. This one was no exception.

Water hurtled to earth from the lightning fractured sky in a titanic deluge. It descended in towering, wind driven curtains that tore through the nearby fields, and smashed against the asphalt lot of the Textro with enough force to raise a foot of spray that hung over the pavement like a fine mist. The outside lights of the truck stop became dim haloed spheres swaying like disembodied wraiths in the gale. Wind howled with the rage of all the Furies as it roared between the trucks and hammered the structures with volley after volley of liquid bullets.

Neither man nor beast ventured out in nights like this...

...but the dark figures stalking the grounds of the Textro tonight qualified as neither.

They took no notice of the rain. And if the Furies screamed around their death ravaged forms in the roaring night blast then they ignored them as well. The storm only existed as an environment through which they moved. Wet, cold, darkness, wind...all were just stimuli they uncritically accepted and disregarded. It meant nothing to any of them.

Only their need mattered.

Many clustered around the fallen prey, still ripping and tearing, but now things began to change. The feeding became less frenzied and more deliberate. Now that several full size corpses had been devoured, and their initial hunger reduced, their eating strategy began to focus more on the nutrient rich organs than just the random orgy of consumption of before. Many even walked away, attracted more by the lights from the front of the truck stop than the food at their feet.

The nature of their need had begun to morph as well.

Their hunger no longer drove them, but the desire to kill remained undiminished. Even gorged, their need to drag down and tear at prey consumed them. None of them even remotely possessed the ability of self reflection, so they made no distinction between these drives. They simply waited for the opportunity to fulfill them. It never occurred to them to doubt, or even wonder if that opportunity would come.

More wandered from the clusters of feeding dead and tramped through the deluge towards the front. The bright fluorescent lights under the awnings over the gas and diesel pumps attracted them first, but as they moved around the building their focus began to change.

A softer, more interesting light caught their attention.

As they slogged around the sides and the front, the windows of the truck stop came into their view. Yellow light from the indoor incandescent bulbs spilled out into the night, creating golden rectangles on the asphalt. And the windows themselves seemed to shimmer as they streamed with running rainwater, making this light somehow more "alive" than the cold blue illumination over the pumps. This light was warmer...more inviting.

It drew them in like death-faced moths to a flame.

And once they reached the glass, the hints of life and motion behind the distorting effects of the running windows kept them there. Nothing came close enough to the pane to trigger an attack, but just enough movement occurred to alert them that prey was near. Somewhere in the shimmering light, their need could be filled again.

Their inability to make out their victims confused them, rendering them incapable of decisive action, so they did one of the things they did best...

...they waited.

Deluge - Rachel

"Mmmph!"

Rachel paused in the process of dabbing Deke's wound with a soapy rag when the boy jerked with a suppressed cry.

She stood next to where he gripped the edge of the stainless steel sink in the truck stop's now crowded kitchen. The scene out in the diner proper had initially driven everybody but the larger of the two local boys in here. The one called Harley had elected to stay out in the diner, behind the counter, and let them know if things out there changed for the worse. At least the crowd meant she would have plenty of hands to help if she needed them.

At the moment she would have traded all those extra hands for the lidocaine she had out in her truck. Her work truck contained everything she would have needed to do this right, and it would have been a lot easier on the people she was doing it to.

Cleaning wounds was a painful business.

She knew it had to hurt, and hated every second of doing it. And with almost everybody now sitting in the kitchen and watching, Rachel figured the young man's pride was the only thing standing between him and tears. Since she couldn't get to her vehicle out in the parking lot, all she had available as a disinfectant was the industrial strength anti-bacterial soap of the Textro's kitchen, and while she didn't doubt its effectiveness she also knew it must be like pouring raw rubbing alcohol into the wounds. Stacey had cried in pain at the same treatment on her arm, and even the unconscious janitor had moaned aloud when his wounds were being cleaned.

Still, one made do with what one had.

At the moment it wasn't much...just a sink with scalding hot water, harsh soap, and all the rags that Marisa and the others could rush around and scrounge up while Rachel continued her fight to keep the janitor from bleeding to death. She had also ordered the trucker, Grandpa Tom, to take a seat on a nearby plastic crate. Something about his skin tone, and the way he kept rubbing his left arm, bothered her.

"Deke," she tried to keep her voice calm and professional, "I know it hurts and I'm sorry. Your trapezius muscle has been punctured in three places, and I'm having to clean deeper."

"How deep is that?" the boy groaned between clenched teeth.

"However deep it takes," she replied. "That monster was filthy, and I don't even want to think what some of these specks I'm cleaning out of these wounds could be."

"Which is why I said we should lock the injured people in the storeroom," Gerald's voice cut in from where he sulked at his place on a nearby countertop.

Rachel closed her eyes in an attempt to keep her temper, and could feel Deke stiffen next to her.

Gerald had indeed brought the same idea up about ten minutes ago when the veterinarian had been treating Stacey, and it had not gone over well then either. Marisa had practically exploded in a directed stream of obscenities from where she knelt on the floor next to the wounded janitor. She held a baseball bat she had retrieved from Big Earl's office that some joker had branded with the words, "Tipping Is Its Own Reward," and had leveled it at the out-of-towner in a rather meaningful way. On top of that, Rachel had thought for a second that Deke was going to physically assault the obnoxious redhead as well. She could tell he felt protective of Stacey, and it didn't take a genius to figure out the two were on their way to being a new couple.

132

But clearly such social complexities were lost on Gerald, and she wondered how he managed to get through life in one piece. Any idiot could have told him bringing up the subject again wasn't going to accomplish anything but possibly anger Deke, or get him a date with Marisa's bat. She could see he didn't use his girlfriend as an advisor on such matters either, since the pale blonde's only response was to try not to look so mortified it might embarrass him in front of others.

"In case I didn't make it plain the first time," Rachel snapped while simultaneously laying a calming hand on Deke's uninjured shoulder, "getting injured isn't contagious. Why don't you let me worry about the medical problems and you just focus on trying to get though to somebody and get us some help. There is only one cell phone tower servicing this entire area, and it's famous for going out during storms. So how about you keep trying to get through to the police before that happens."

It turned out Gerald and Holly were the only two with available cell phones left alive in the Textro. Rachel's still rested in the lab coat in her office, and Marisa had left her's in the restroom when she rushed back to help Stacey. There was a landline in Big Earl's office but it was dead, either as a result of Deke falling on it or the lines were out. Since the only other landline had been at store-side checkout, there was no way to check.

Holly dutifully began punching buttons on her cell phone again, but Gerald must not have been ready to let his point go.

"I hate to pull Hollywood on you, Your Sorta-Docterness," the dumpy redhead sneered, "but it's common knowledge that when a zombie injures somebody, they become a zombie too. I know it's 'just the movies' but this is a pretty unreal situation and I think it's only common sense to take precautions."

Rachel tightened her grip on the young redneck's shoulder while starting a mental ten count of her own. She wondered if she would really put much effort into stopping Deke if he decided to go after the little jerk. In the end, medicine decided that question for her because it simply wasn't worth the risk of him tearing his already damaged shoulder muscle. She didn't like violence, but had come to realize over the years there were some people in this world who would really benefit from a thorough butt kicking...and Gerald struck her as a prime example of one of those people.

To her surprise, Deke didn't respond with anger at all.

"Zombies?" he mused aloud, "These things don't seem much like the zombies I've seen in the movies. Those just groaned and shambled around in slow motion. These things are fast, focused, and vicious as hell."

"Hah!" Gerald scoffed with a dismissive wave of his hand, "Those were the old zombies from the black and white days. Those were due to some silly signal from outer space and never really realistic in the first place. The new zombies are faster, and are the product of a virus."

"Yeah," Deke agreed amiably, "but the zombies in those movies come from living people being infected. These guys are obviously dead from the beginning. How do you explain that?"

"So it's a virus that infects dead people," the aloof urbanite shrugged.

This was getting ridiculous.

"It's not a virus," Rachel sighed. She couldn't believe the twist this conversation had just taken. Zombies? Seriously? She consoled herself with the thought that at least it wasn't turning into a brawl.

"Oh really? Why not, Dr. Doolittle?"

Was this guy for real?

"Because," Rachel answered sweetly while wondering if things were going to end up with Deke and Marisa holding *her* back from the abrasive twerp, "a virus requires a living cell with a functioning DNA process to splice into. A corpse doesn't have those. The DNA process stops and the strands break up soon after death. That's why dead people don't catch the flu."

"Really?"

"Really. So I think you can relax and stop worrying about Stacey over there tearing her face off and trying to

134

eat your brains." She felt it was a lame attempt at levity, and regretted it as soon as she said it.

The veterinarian gave an apologetic wince at the wounded waitress.

"I don't think these things care about brains, Doc," Stacey's somber face was still tight in a haunted way that worried the veterinarian almost as much as the old truck driver's condition. "They seem more like animals or something."

Rachel had pieced together that Stacey had been the first to encounter these things and survive, and whatever scene the girl had encountered out there had shaken her badly. Unfortunately, psychology wasn't a big part of veterinary science and the doctor had no idea what to say to her. Instead, she resolved to hurry and finish up on Deke so he could get over to her and provide a shoulder to lean on.

"Okay, Deke. I think I've done all the damage I can do here, so I'm going to put a pressure bandage on you just like I did the others. Then I'm going to put you in a sling to keep you from tearing your shoulder even worse. You need stitches...hell, all three of you need stitches...but that's for the hospital guys to handle if they ever get here."

"Thanks, Doc," the young man's thanks didn't sound very enthusiastic...not that she blamed him.

"Just be glad my needles and sutures are out in my truck," Rachel quipped and handed him a folded towel. "Now hold this down against your shoulder while I try to figure out how to tie it on."

"You mean you don't know?" he looked at her in surprise.

"Well, I would if you were a Rottweiler. You aren't exactly built like most of my clients, you know."

"Oh, right."

Rachel settled for wrapping his ribs almost like she did Stacey's, then running a strip of towel over his shoulder from there to hold the pressure bandage down. The system seemed to work, which was all she cared about. She then grabbed a nearby apron off a wall and fashioned it into a sling. Deke carefully pulled his bloody shirt back on, and then let her fit him with the impromptu sling.

Rachel surveyed her handiwork then nodded in satisfaction.

"Okay, young man. I officially pronounce you 'treated.' There are to be no more heroics out of you. You are to protect that shoulder. Got it?"

"Yes, ma'am."

"Good," Rachel then leaned close, nodded towards Stacey, and whispered into his ear, "Now go over there and hold that girl. She really needs it right now. She's a tough little thing but she's hurt and she's been pushed way too far."

"But I just asked her out tonight," Deke wavered.

"Trust me on this," she hissed. "Now step up and be there for her."

The young man looked unsure, but nodded and headed over to where Stacey sat huddled next to the grill. The doctor watched him go while wiping her hands on a hot rag. He bent over and said something to the girl softly, and whatever it was must have been the right thing for she gave him a wan smile and offered the spot on the floor next to her. Rachel had a feeling he was going to have a girlfriend on his hands long before their scheduled first date took place.

Assuming any of them lived that long.

"Okay," Rachel surveyed the grim faces around the kitchen, sighed, and tossed the rag into the sink. "Is that everybody? Are there any other injuries I need to know about?"

Nobody answered.

"Anybody?" she repeated. "Bueller?"

"Well," Marisa spoke up from her place beside Benny, "I remember that Harley's hand was bleeding, but I think it was just a barked knuckle from punching the one out in the store."

"Okay," Rachel pondered for a second, "That's not critical enough for immediate attention, but I'll remember it if I get a chance at him later. Anybody else?

For a moment nobody answered, then Gerald's girlfriend raised her hand.

"You're injured?" Rachel frowned

"No," the girl blushed and shook her head in obvious embarrassment, "I'm sorry, I didn't mean to imply that. I just have a question. It's completely unrelated to injuries."

"No problem," the veterinarian shrugged...at least the girl was polite, no matter how bad her taste in boyfriends. "It looks like everybody is patched up for the moment, so what's your question?"

"Where do they come from?"

"Huh?" Rachel gave the girl a puzzled look. "What are you talking about?"

"The dead things...the zombies," Holly swallowed. "They've got to come from somewhere, right? I'm not from around here, but we passed this place on the highway before turning around and coming back, and I don't remember seeing a graveyard."

A graveyard?

Rachel gaped at the girl as her mind violently twisted away from being preoccupied with treating people and focused on the question.

A graveyard?

She had been so busy trying to help people, it had never occurred to her to question the origin of these monsters. Up until now, she hadn't had the time. She had simply considered them a hideous threat and not put much more thought into them than that. But now...

...now they were something worse.

"Oh...no..." she moaned as the only possible source for these "zombies" rose in her mind. She vaguely saw Marisa coming to her feet with a similar look of horror on her face, apparently realizing at the same time where these things must be coming from.

Only they weren't "things".

They used to be people...their people.

People who had lived, loved, and had families. People who had died and were buried at the Mazon County

Memorial Cemetery a mile up the side road beside the truck stop.

And one of those people had been Matt.

"Doc? Marisa? What's going on?"

Rachel saw Harley turn in his bar stool towards them as they crowded to a stop in the kitchen door. The door opened from behind the counter, and she had expected to have to slip past him to get into the room proper. So it came as a bit of a surprise to see him sitting out in the open on a stool in front of the counter, instead of the station he had assumed behind it when everybody first retreated to the kitchen.

The young man had tilted the scruffy hat back on his head and was lounging on the stool next to the back wall, drinking coffee that he had been serving himself from the nearby pot. For a hopeful moment Rachel wondered if things had changed out here and the big lout simply hadn't gotten around to telling them.

A quick glance at the windows revealed that not to be the case. As a matter of fact, things were worse than before.

They were surrounded.

Water sheeted down the big panes of glass, distorting the figures in the unending row grinning back in at them. The motionless forms stood side by side in a line stretching from the window closest the kitchen wall, to the glass fire door, then the windows all the way to and around the front corner...stretching across the front windows as well. The light from inside the diner shimmered out through the streaming sheets of glass, almost glowing off the bone and bare teeth of the watcher's mutilated faces. At the same time, it made their sockets look black and utterly empty of both eyes and humanity alike.

They wore dark suits and pale dresses, all drenched and hanging off their frames like overdressed scarecrows at a dinner party for the damned.

138

There was no sign the storm howling around the building discomfited them, or if they even noticed it.

They simply stood out there.

Waiting.

Rachel hesitated at the sight of them, causing Marisa to bump into her from behind before allowing herself to be slowly edged into the room. She tore her eyes from the motionless wall of dead people and fixed them back on the man at the counter.

"Harley," she whispered urgently, "We need to see something. We've got to know if something is true about these...things. It's important. Is it safe to come out here?"

The young man gave a speculative glance over his shoulder at the windows, then looked back at the two women with a fatalistic shrug. He picked up a bottle of sugar and started pouring it into his coffee as he answered.

"It's alright," he cautioned softly, "As long as you move real slow and don't get too close to the window, they don't seem to react. But stay out of sight of the ones at the door if you can. They seem to see better. I think it has something to do with the water on the glass."

"Oookaayyyy," Rachel replied doubtfully.

Part of her still insisted this had to be a trick or an illusion of some kind. Maybe some form of disease that wasted an individual and drove them to self mutilation and violence. The doctor knew what she had seen at the back door, but still felt tempted to write it off as a quick but unreliable impression in the heat of a violent confrontation. She clung to a small sliver of hope that a closer look would reveal an all too mundane nature of their attackers.

All it took was one flash of lightning to shatter that hope, once and for all.

As she reached the end of the counter, the sky flared with light and cast the line of besieging horrors into stark relief. The man looking in directly across the room from her must have had his suit torn a recent altercation, for it hung half off him and revealed the desiccated chest underneath...along with the autopsy scar. The incision must have also been torn loose in the same fight, for it hung open on one side and revealed the cracked ribcage underneath.

The woman next to him might have died in a car crash or some other violent manner, for the face of her skull was half crushed in. Only one eye glared back from its lone intact socket, and the jaw didn't hang exactly straight underneath either. She was missing an arm from the elbow down, and she stood at an odd angle that suggested hip or leg damage as well.

These people were dead.

Very dead.

And the only question left was their point of origin.

Rachel moved up to the end of the counter, and barely noticed as Marisa brushed past her and started moving down the room, peering at the ghoulish figures one at a time.

It only took Rachel one look at the window to drive home the numb certainty her own intent to search for Matt...to settle once and for all if her lost husband walked out there in the storm this night...was doomed from the start. Almost all the male figures wore dark suits that appeared identical in the night time downpour, and without faces there was nothing else to go by...just a chorus line of stick figures with leering skulls and hanging suits, anonymous in their shared mutilation.

He could have been any one of them...or none o them.

It was almost a relief.

Maybe he wasn't out there. Maybe this nightmare had nothing to do with Matt at all. Just maybe these things came from some military or government vehicle that had crashed nearby, or was parked behind the truck stop right now with its back gate forced open. Seriously, who knew what cargo any eighteen wheeler out on the road might be carrying? Hell, this was already like some kind of bad movie...was there any certainty where these things really came from?

"Oh, no."

Marisa's soft gasp jarred Rachel out of her reverie and back into the room with the hellish view.

The waitress had dropped the bat and covered her mouth with both hands. A single tear started down her cheek as she stared at the window.

Rachel tracked her horrified gaze to a wraithlike figure in a pale dress. It was hard to see much through the streaming window, but the older woman could tell even in the rain it had a full head of thick black hair very much like the girl staring at it, and its garment looked like some kind of formal gown...or perhaps a prom dress.

"Vicky?" Marisa choked out. "*Madre de dios! Vicki?*"

The girl took a halting step towards the window.

"Doc!" Harley called while coming off his stool, "Grab her! Don't let her do that!"

Rachel recovered and moved towards the girl just as she stumbled toward the window.

"Vicki!" the tears now flowed. "*Soy yo, Marisa! No te recuardas de mi?*"

Rachel caught her just as the thing in the window came alive.

The two women shrieked as the dead woman gaped her jaws in what was becoming a familiar prelude to attack and slammed herself against the window. The whole pane shook as the monster now focused in on them, withered hands splayed against the glass. For one heart stopping second Rachel thought the horror would come crashing through the weak barrier and land on them both. And if that window broke there would be more of those things piling through in a heartbeat.

The sound of the pane creaking in its frame sounded like imminent death in her ears.

But evidently it was made of sterner stuff than she realized. The window held...for the moment...and the veterinarian grabbed Marisa as the girl cried out at the specter.

"*Vicki! So yo! Marisa! Tu hermana, Marisa! Lo siento! No hagas esto!*"

Not knowing what else to do, Rachel put herself between the young woman and the window and embraced her tightly. She couldn't understand what the girl was saying, but from the sound of her voice she was bordering on hysterics. She could also hear more hands thumping and squeaking on the glass behind her and feared all their luck would soon run out. A look to her left revealed Harley had halted on his way over, obviously not wanting to add any more motion to the scene.

It was up to her.

With gentle care, Rachel eased herself and the girl two small steps away from the glass. A glance back revealed the dead woman to be pressed up against the window...her teeth and cheekbone making an audible "scritch" as they slid across the pane's surface...but at least she wasn't slamming up against it anymore...much. The distraught waitress must have seen enough, because she felt Marisa bury her face into her shoulder and start to cry.

"*Lo siento, Vicki!*" she sobbed into Rachel's shoulder, "*Lo siento! No sabia! Por favor, lo siento! No sabia!*"

"Easy," Rachel soothed, and hugged the girl tighter. "Easy, Marisa. We're not out of this yet."

She could still hear the scratching on the glass behind her, and could see Harley staring at it with hair trigger intensity. Behind him, she spotted Deke and Stacey standing frozen behind the counter and Gerald and Holly in the kitchen door. Nobody moved, and another series of thumps from the window told her that the thing was still focused on her back. The tension hung thick in the air, and Rachel knew their luck couldn't hold out much longer.

"Marisa," she breathed into the crying girl's ear, "we need to take another couple of steps away from the window. Okay?"

For a moment she didn't know if the girl didn't hear her, or if she was simply having to much trouble catching her breath to talk. Then, just before she intended to repeat herself, Marisa nodded her head.

"Okay, good," Rachel continued, still holding the young woman for all she was worth, "We're just going to take a couple of really slow steps backwards, and then I want you to tell me who that was. Okay?"

No answer.

"Okay?"

"Okay," came the muffled reply.

"Alright then," Rachel murmured as she gently guided the waitress backwards. "Just one sloooowww step."

The two moved in unison, almost as if dancing.

"Now another."

The sounds behind her faded.

"And one more."

The two stopped, still embraced, beside a booth on the far wall from the windows. Neither moved for a moment, and Rachel maintained her tight grip on the girl. The tall waitress had not shown one ounce of fear during this whole ordeal, but the sobs escaping her now were those of a deep and reawakened grief.

She didn't know what else to do but continue to hold her until sounds behind them ceased. It took a few minutes but, as Harley had mentioned, the dead didn't seem to see through the window well, and once they lost sight of their prey it wasn't too long until they reverted back to their still vigil at the streaming glass.

Another flash of lightning cast their shadows on the diner wall, revealing them to be once again standing in their grim cordon.

The danger had passed.

"It's okay, now," she murmured and tried to get a look at the young woman's face. "They've gone quiet again. Are you alright?"

It surprised her, but Marisa actually straightened up and wiped her eyes.

"Yeah," she sniffled, seeming to struggle between embarrassment and the grief that had gripped her earlier. She sat down in the booth behind her and took a shaky breath. "Yeah...just give me a second. I'm a little messed up."

Rachel slid into the bench across the table from her. She watched quietly as the young Latina brought herself back under control, before gently asking the obvious question.

"Who was it, Marisa? Who was she?"

143

Marisa closed her eyes for a second, then opened them and stared at the now still wraith in the window. The pain in her face hurt for Rachel to see. She had been seeing that look in her own mirror for longer than she cared to remember.

"That," she swallowed, then continued, "is my big sister, Vicki...Victoria."

"Are you sure?" Rachel looked from the girl to the dim, death-faced figure in the window. "Can you really be certain?"

"Oh yeah," Marisa whispered and gave another wipe at her eyes. "My mom and I helped her make that dress for prom. You see, Vicki and I weren't just sisters, we were best friends. I was going to wear it for my prom too, when I was old enough. But instead, I ended up taking it to the funeral home for Vicki. She died a week before the prom, and never got to wear it...so I didn't want it anymore. At least this way she got..."

The girl swallowed and wiped her eyes again, unable to finish the thought.

"Marisa?" Rachel reached across the table and took her hand, "What happened to her? Why did she die so young?"

The waitress swallowed and took another deep, shuddering breath. She stared somewhere into the darkness past Rachel's shoulder, and the doctor knew she was looking at a scene somewhere in the past.

"School was almost over for the year," the girl continued, "and we were at a swimming pool. Everybody was laughing and cutting up, and having a good time. It was just a bunch of kids having a party, we weren't doing anything wrong. We were just having fun. But sometime during all that," Marisa closed her eyes and took a deep breath, "Vicki jumped off the high diving board...and didn't come back up."

"Oh, God..." Rachel started, then faltered. She didn't know what else to say, other than to hold the girls hand and let her finish.

"Nobody noticed," the waitress buried her face in her other hand, "and by the time one of our friends got up on the diving board and saw her laying on the bottom of the pool, it was too late. She was dead. She had drowned right beneath our feet, and none...and none of us..."

"Easy," the older woman stopped her, "I get the picture. You don't have to say anything more."

"Yeah. Yeah, I do," Marisa raised her head and turned her tear stained face back towards the window. "*Te extrano, Vicki,*" she sobbed, "*Lo siento! Te extrano mucho! Perdoname!*"

"Marisa," the older woman now grasped her by the shoulder, "that's not your sister. It's not Vicki."

As soon as Rachel said it, she knew it was true.

Those *were* dead people out there. There was no way around it. And yes, those *were* the corpses of their loved ones standing outside in the driving storm, waiting for a chance to rip them to pieces...there was no denying that either. But it wasn't *them.*

"Doc...I know her dress..."

"No, listen to me." Rachel scowled at the windows herself, "It isn't *her.* And my Matt isn't out there either. Those are their bodies, and something...something obscene...has happened and has them doing this. But it isn't *them.* Those aren't our people out there."

"Doc, are you sure? Are you completely sure about that?"

The desperation in Marisa's eyes almost broke her heart.

Damn, Rachel, she realized with a shock, *Here you've been feeling sorry for yourself and this girl has been living with the grief and guilt of thinking she let her sister die...and now that dead sister is staring in the window at her. Guess what, you don't have a monopoly on grief in this world.*

"Yes, I am sure," Rachel slowly stood up and stepped out of the booth. "Yes I am...and I think I can prove it."

###

Rachel stood up from the booth and faced the windows.

Behind her, Deke moved in and sat down in her place. Across the table, Stacey slid in next to Marisa and embraced her without saying a word. That was a bit of a relief, as Rachel figured the girl's friends would probably be a lot more comfort to her right now.

She looked down the long line of dead faces that stared in to the diner, and for the first time that evening...hell, in two years...she felt something other than depressed, scared, or confused about life.

For the first time in years, Dr. Rachel Sutherland got mad.

Whether her clients were human or animal, it didn't change one very core fact that defined who she was. The one thing she had always dreamed of, and worked hard to be, long before she had ever met Matt. She was a doctor of medicine...a woman of science, by God...and it was about damn time she started to try and understand what was going on here. If this was something new, something outside all prior experience and wasn't in the books, then it was her job to figure out what it was.

It was about damn time for the world to start making sense.

But where to start?

She raked her memory of the past hour for clues. She called to mind her encounter with the creatures in the back door, and then what she witnessed of the fight in the back hallway. She compared those to the actions of Marisa's dead sister at the window, seeking any commonality that might give her an insight into these things. It didn't take long.

What first came to mind was the posture these things assumed, almost without fail, right before they attacked. The gaping jaws, the clawlike position of the hands...a posture bearing no resemblance to the stance a normal man or woman would assume in a fight or flight situation.

146

Stacey had said they were like animals. Rachel was starting to think the girl might be more right than she knew.

"Stacey," she called softly over her shoulder, "is there a way to turn off the lights in here?"

"Sure," came the doubtful reply. "You want to turn off the lights?"

"Just here in the diner," Rachel answered, "Not in the kitchen or the store. Can you do that?"

"Yeah, no problem. Deke, stay here with Marisa a second. I'll be right back."

The little waitress got up and moved briskly towards the back. Rachel watched her go, then glanced over at where Harley once again lounged on a bar stool. He watched her intently and she got the definite feeling this guy didn't miss a single thing going on around him, but at the same time he seemed relaxed almost to the point of being irritating. He was pouring himself another coffee as she watched, and gave a reassuring grin at her over the cup.

A second later, the lights went out.

"Whatcha got in mind, Doc?" Harley's drawl cut through the dark.

Hell, Rachel grumbled to herself, the guy even *sounded* relaxed. Everybody else was in different degrees of panic, fear, or despair, and the only thing she could pick up from this guy was mild curiosity about what she was doing. At the same time she realized she might be being a bit churlish, and should probably be grateful there was at least one cool head in the place.

"Something you said earlier got me thinking," she replied "How the water running down the windows seems to blind them."

"Yeah?"

"Well, I think that means something." She cautiously approached a window. "And I intend to find out if I'm right."

"Be careful, Doc. We just got them calmed down again, remember?"

147

"I remember," Rachel murmured as she fished her keys out of her pocket and found the little LED flashlight attached to her keyring. "But I'm betting it's going to be different this time."

She considered her choices. She found herself faced with the decision of sliding into a booth next to a window, or going over to the fire door where she would be right in front of one of these horrors with nothing but a glass door between them. The veterinarian looked from one option to another.

"I know I'm right," she muttered and set her jaw.

Squaring her shoulders, she approached the fire door.

It was filled with the hulking silhouette of what must have once been a very large man. It towered over six feet, and the desiccated hands that hung down on each side could have easily palmed a basketball in life...now they were talons that could quite likely gut her with one powerful slash.

"Doc," Harley's voice sounded a little tight now, "Be careful. You're getting awful close."

"It's okay," Rachel murmured as she edged in even closer. She concentrated on the large deaths-head that stared blankly at the door. "It can't see me yet. And even if it could, I'm not sure it would make sense of what it sees."

"Pardon?"

"Just watch," she shushed...and clicked her little flashlight on directly in the dead man's face.

The powerful little light illuminated the dripping skull. A terrified shriek and a suppressed yip of fear came from behind her as the horrible face jerked downwards to peer at the light source. The monster shifted stance, and leaned to bring its awful face down level with her little light.

Rachel didn't budge.

Instead, she leaned forward herself, careful to stay behind her light, until she was only inches from the monsters face."

"See the pretty light?" she muttered at the thing while giving the light a little shake. "Suuurrre you do. And that's all you see, isn't it."

"Doc?" Harley warned.

"It's okay," she snapped, "Just watch."

Rachel slowly moved the light to the right, concentrating on making the motion smooth and steady. The skull turned just as slowly to track it. She brought the flashlight to a stop and held it motionless. As she suspected, the monster didn't move for a second, then shifted once again to bring its face near the light.

"Lizard brain," she muttered, "that's what I thought."

"Doc?"

"It can't reason," she spoke a little louder. "It can't make the simple leap that there must be somebody behind this light. If I were to move it fast and make it act like prey, it might attack, but it would be attacking the light. This thing is running on pure hindbrain."

"Say again?" Deke spoke up.

"Hindbrain," Rachel repeated, now drawing the monster back across the door with the little light, "or Lizard brain. It's a small part of our brain near the back, that's a leftover from before the time our ancestors came down from the treetops. Hell it's from before the time they went up the trees in the first place." She hoped she wasn't stepping on any religious toes here but decided to press on. "It's not very smart...as a matter of fact it's pretty much just pure instinct."

"So they're like wolves?" Stacey's voice meant she must have returned from the kitchen.

Rachel frowned and stared at the dead man only inches away.

"I don't think so," she mused while watching its shriveled eyes follow the light. "Not wolves. I'm betting they're on a lower level, somewhere between piranhas and sharks...which in its own way is worse."

"Worse?"

"Yeah," the doctor muttered. "You can scare off a wolf. Not these things. I'm betting once one of these spots prey, it doesn't stop attacking until it either kills or is distracted by other prey."

"Christ," Deke growled, "that sounds just like the one that jumped on me."

"Yep, I remember." Rachel snapped off the little flashlight.

Taking what she was now sure was unnecessary care, she backed a couple of steps away from the door. She didn't move again until the dead thing in the doorway resumed the same waiting stance of its brethren, then she turned and returned to the booth with Stacey, Deke, and Marisa. Their faces could just be made out in the dim yellow light that filtered in through the windows from the sodium vapor lamps in the parking lot.

"But the important thing is," she nudged Deke over and eased into the booth beside him, "is that those *aren't* human beings."

"They're not?"

"No," Rachel emphasized, "Not even close. As a matter of fact, think of them as what the dork in the kitchen called them...zombies." She ignored Gerald's outraged exclamation from the direction of the kitchen door and continued. "It doesn't matter who they were when they were alive, these things are just the bodies that have somehow had their basic nervous system jumpstarted and are running on some kind of killer instinct. Most of the brain, especially all the higher parts that make a person who they are, or even a person at all, doesn't seem to be functioning. They don't even have the frontal brain power to put a coherent picture together when it's being distorted by running water on glass...at least not until it moves and gets close. They barely qualify as animals.

"So then..." Marisa haltingly started. "You mean..."

"That's not Vicki," Rachel finished for her. "It's the body she left behind, and now it has been taken over by something else. And if she loved you half as much as you love her, and I can tell she did, then wherever she is she would be horrified to see it's become a threat to you. So don't confuse that thing out there with your sister...don't give it that edge. It's a zombie, and all it wants to do is kill

150

and eat. It doesn't matter what dress it's wearing. Understand?"

She could see the girl staring at her in the dim light, needing to believe this with every fiber of her being.

"It's not her," Rachel repeated. "Vicki is at peace...that thing is just a monster that stole her dress."

That seemed to settle it.

Marisa looked at her a moment longer, her dark eyes huge in the dim light. Then slowly, she began to nod. She brushed the hair back from her face, continuing to nod to herself, then pushed up from the table and turned towards the window. The girl wobbled slightly, steadied herself against the table, then made her halting way towards the center of the room...where she once again faced the nightmare looking in through the glass.

This time her tear stained face bore no expression whatsoever.

The figure outside didn't move. It just stood there like a grisly statue, with the wind driven rain splattering off of it with such force it had a slight halo of mist around it. Another flash of lightning revealed the gruesome face beneath the drenched matt of black hair, then darkness fell, returning the dead woman to just another silhouette against the parking lot lights..

Marisa didn't flinch. She just stared at it a moment longer, her face a wooden mask.

"*Usted no es Vicki,*" she spoke at last. Her voice was soft and even, "*y si te pones en aquí te voy a matar.*"

Without another word she turned and headed back for the kitchen. She brushed by the dark forms of Gerald and Holly, then slammed open the swinging door with the palm of her hand before marching through. The light from the kitchen rose and fell in the darkened diner as the door swung open and shut in a declining pattern.

All eyes in the diner stayed on the door till it stopped swinging.

Then everybody seemed to exhale at once.

"You did good, Doc." Stacey turned back to face the older woman with a look of pure awe. "You did damn good."

"I just told her the truth," Rachel sighed. "I hope she is going to be okay."

"She will," the elfish girl beamed at her, "She just needs to be left alone for a while. I'll go check on her later once she's had time to settle. She's been carrying that for a long time."

"Hell of a way to have to deal with it," the doctor muttered.

Hell of a way for me to have to deal with it, too.

She looked back at the windows, and their deathly rank of watchers. As her eyes swept the dreadful line, she understood one of the true horrors of what these things were. They weren't just monsters...they were the past, made present. And if you didn't get away from them, they would eat you alive...just like her past had been doing to her for the last two years.

The time had come for that to end.

Under the cover of darkness, Rachel wiped a tear of her own that threatened to fall.

Goodbye Matt, her heart whispered out into the darkness. *I will love you forever, but I have to let go now. I want to live.*

CHAPTER SEVEN: RISING WATERS

Rising Waters - Marisa

The time clock read half past midnight when she eased open the kitchen door and slipped back into the gloomy diner.

"Marisa?" Harley's soft voice in the dark indicated he still sat in the same place at the counter he had before.

"Yeah. Just me."

As her eyes adjusted, she saw he still leaned against the counter next to the coffee machine. She also noted the pot was empty and automatically reached under the counter to grab a new filter and bag.

"Hey, you don't have to do that," Harley protested. "I was just being lazy and hadn't got around to doing it myself."

"It's alright," she replaced the filter with practiced ease and dumped in the premeasured bag of coffee. "It's my job."

Grabbing the pot, she gave it a quick rinse at the nearby sink before filling it with more water and pouring that into the top of the machine. Then out of sheer force of habit, she grabbed a rag from under the sink and started wiping off the counter.

Harley watched without comment.

Marisa cleaned in silence, scrubbing the rag in small circles. It was a chore repeated so often she could have done it with her eyes closed. The waitress made her way down the counter, picking up and moving shakers and paper towel holders with automatic efficiency, while running the rag beneath them. The only sound in the darkened room came from the rain drumming against the windows and the rhythmic squeak of her rag on the countertop.

She never once glanced at the black figures in the windows.

It was something to do...something mechanical, requiring no thought...but in about a minute the inevitable happened and she reached the end of the table.

Marisa leaned forward and rested her weight on both hands gripping the edge of the counter. She stared at the polished surface, feeling six kinds of fool, before straightening and turning to face the shadowy man in the battered hat. She could barely make out his face in the dim yellow light filtering in, but it didn't take a genius to know he had been watching her throughout this entire little performance.

Putting her hands on her hips, she stared back at him for ten long seconds before finally speaking.

"Thank you," she spoke it like a challenge, "for saving my life in the store earlier. I guess I owe you one."

"You're welcome," Harley pushed his hat back, and his almost ever-present grin cut through the darkness. "But you already evened that score when you thought of the keys and saw to it they got out here before I got tired and let those things in. You saved all of our asses."

Marisa thought that one over for a second.

"That's not really the same thing," she replied.

"We were in trouble and you found a solution. Then you acted decisively once you knew what needed to be done."

"Maybe," she conceded, "But a lot of it was your friend. He did most of the hard stuff while I was mainly bossing him around."

Harley laughed softly in the dark..

"That sounds like Deke," he chuckled. "He's a good kid. He just needs somebody to point him in the right direction and light a fire under him from time to time. How's he doing back there anyway?"

"Oh he's doing great," she snorted. "Stacey is sleeping under his arm and he's got this big goofy look on his face like he's stoned stupid. You wouldn't know to look at him that he was injured and surrounded by killer dead people."

That brought another chuckle from the shadowy figure.

"I'm glad to hear it. He's been worshiping her from afar for almost as long as I've known him."

"Hmph. Well, he's got her. She thinks he's 'nice', and Stacey likes nice."

"Good." Harley turned back towards the coffee pot as it started to fill. "So how about the others? How are they doing back there?"

Marisa rubbed her arms and looked at the kitchen door.

"Benny is still out," she sighed, "but the doc is looking after him. She thinks he'll make it if he gets time to recover. She won't say so, but I think she's more worried about Grandpa Tom."

"Grandpa Tom?"

"The old trucker back there. He isn't injured or anything, but he doesn't look so good."

"Okay."

"I guess that leaves the jackass and his dishrag of a girlfriend."

"Gerald and Holly."

"Whatever." Marisa pulled a tray out from under the counter and started refilling the square sugar bowls with little packets of sugar. "They're alright too...unless he mouths off to the doc again. I think she's about ready to neuter him. So that's where things sit."

Finishing her self-imposed chore with the sugar packets, she returned the tray under the counter. She stood back up to see Harley's dim figure reaching for the now full pot.

"You're forgetting somebody," he replied mildly as he poured himself some more coffee. The sound of the hot liquid filling the cup could barely be heard over the storm, yet at the same time it seemed to thunder in the silence that fell between the two of them.

Marisa stiffened, then took a deep breath and forced herself to unclench her jaw. It wasn't like she hadn't been expecting this.

"You mean me."

"You're the only somebody left."

She gathered up the plates that had belonged to Grandpa Tom and Leaping Larry. Remembering the kitchen sink to be full of bloody rags at the moment, she headed for the little sink behind the counter instead.

"I'm not injured," she replied. Her voice sounded flat even to her own ears.

Harley said nothing.

Pulling a cabinet door under the sink open with her toe, Marisa dumped the contents of the plates into a small wastebasket within. She could feel the man watching her...evaluating... and stood up again with gritted teeth before dropping the dishes into the small sink with forceful emphasis. The second she did it the girl knew she had messed up and clenched her eyes shut.

The crash of broken platters added fresh new edges to the humiliation that already cut through her.

"Look, Harley," Marisa turned and tapped her breastbone with a finger. "I'm hurting, okay? But that's not why I came out here. I came out to say 'thank you.' That's all. I wasn't hunting a shoulder to cry on."

"Understood." He watched her over the brim of his cup as he took a drink. "But that really wasn't why I asked."

"No?" She eyed him doubtfully. She had to concede, at least to herself, that he hadn't shown the slightest hint of anything but concern...but on the other hand, the next man she met without an ulterior motive would be the first.

"No."

"Okay, then," she sighed and leaned back against the sink behind her, "you were just being nice. So that's one 'thank you' and now one apology I owe you. I'm running up a score tonight."

"Hey," Harley set down the cup and spread his hands. "I didn't say I didn't have my reasons for wanting to know. Actually, I do. I just wasn't trying to hit on you."

"Oh, really."

"Yes, really," he continued. "I'm looking for backup."

That caught her by surprise, and she tilted her head in curiosity.

"Backup? What do you mean?"

"I mean," he picked up the cup again and took another drink, "sooner or later, this situation is going to go fluid again...probably in the morning, once the rain stops and they can see inside the windows...and I've got to start working on a way to get us out of this. If things get ugly, and I need to take chances, then I'm going to need a 'wingman'...somebody to watch my back. My first choice would be Deke, but he's hurt."

"So you want *me* instead?

"Well," he started ticking off his fingers, "outside of Deke, there are only three other men here. One is unconscious. One is old and apparently sick. And the last one is Gerald."

"You don't have any confidence in Gerald?" her sarcasm dripped in the darkness.

"I need somebody who can move fast, think fast, act decisively, and who can think of other people besides themselves."

"Oh well," Marisa rolled her eyes, "so much for Gerald."

"Yeah," Harley's easy smile widened, "It's not personal, but I don't think I'm brave enough to have him watch my back."

"That wouldn't be brave," she scoffed. "It would be suicide."

"Can't argue with the truth," he poured himself another cup of coffee, "but it don't change the fact, come morning, I'm gonna have to find a way to get us out of here...and that means trying to get to one of those vehicles in the parking lot."

Marisa gasped and stared at him.

"What? Are you crazy? They're too fast!" She surprised herself with the intensity of her objection, and quickly toned it down. "Look, even if you somehow got past those things and outran them to a car, you probably couldn't get it open before they were on top of you. And you want me out there with you?"

"No," Harley stated firmly. "If I make a run for my truck, then it will be by myself. But even then I would like to have somebody I can trust manning the door, in case I can't make it but still have a chance to turn back."

Marisa considered that for a moment.

"I can do that," she nodded. "But then what? How does that help us?"

"I've got a .45 automatic and a box of ammo under the seat of my truck. Maybe I could draw these things away and thin them out a little bit at the same time."

"They're dead, Harley. I don't think getting shot is going to bother them all that much."

"Maybe," he shrugged, "but I'm remembering the one I tangled with in the store. If breaking their neck paralyzes them, then their brain still runs things...even if it's that lizard brain the doc was talking about. So I'm bettin' blowing their head off will drop them."

Marisa winced at the memory.

"I guess," she agreed doubtfully, "but it still sounds like one of those plans you rednecks come up with right before you yell 'Hey guys, watch this!' and die horribly."

"Thanks a lot!" Harley laughed again as he leaned back in the stool and against the rear wall with his hands behind his head. "You're just a bundle of optimism, aren't you."

"I just don't want to watch somebody else die, okay?"

The memory of those monsters feeding in the store, and the whimpering wreck in front of the counter, rose in her mind again. That image, alongside the one of the monstrosity that was once her sister, caused her to swallow hard and suppress a shudder. It was all still so fresh.

"Are you sure you're okay?"

He hadn't changed position, but his face was dead serious.

"I'm okay," she snapped, recovering with an effort. "I'll be your 'wingman', if you want. I'll hold the door for you if you try that stupid stunt, and I'll cover your back if I can otherwise. But I want you to promise me you haven't already settled on this dumb idea, and stopped trying to come up with something else."

"No problem. I promise. I'm considering a lot of contingencies and there are some things I'm going to check out and get straight before I do anything. At the moment, I'm just figuring out what we're up against and who I...waitaminute.."

Harley came to his feet so fast it made her jump.

"What is it?" She whirled, half expecting to see one of the monsters had somehow found its way inside.

"They moved."

"What?" She followed his gaze to the front windows. The line of cadavers still loomed outside the large windows. "Where? They're still there."

"They've turned their heads." He glided forward through the dark room on cat feet. "They're watching something...something towards town."

Now that he pointed it out, Marisa could see many of the skulls were now in profile. Several others were slowly turning their heads to match them.

"What is it?" Despite Doc Sutherlands demonstration of how these things couldn't see into the restaurant when it was dark, she still didn't feel comfortable approaching the windows. "What's going on?"

Harley slowed as he approached the front window, and eased forward. Careful not to put a hand on the glass, he leaned against a window sill and looked in the same direction as the cadavers.

"Police lights!"

"Really!" Hope leaped in her chest. "They're coming?"

"Three cars with lights flashing...no...four of them! The police are coming!"

Rising Waters - Rachel

"Hey, everybody! The police are coming! They'll be here in a minute!"

159

Rachel jerked herself out of a semi-doze and looked up just in time to see Marisa fly back through the door and into the restaurant.

The kitchen around her came to life as the waitress's words sank in. Gerald and Holly tumbled off the counter and rushed for the door. Deke was already in the process of gently attempting to wake the sleeping girl under his arm, and even Grandpa Tom had started to his feet.

Hope gave an energy to the air that only seconds before had been heavy with despair.

Rachel headed for the door, then hesitated. She glanced back at the form of the janitor on the floor and bit her lip. Over the past couple of hours the man seemed to have stabilized, and there were signs he might even regain consciousness in the future, but the idea of leaving him back here unattended still didn't sit right with her. At the same time she desperately wanted to see what was going on out front.

Indecision tore at her.

"Hey, Doc?"

She looked up to see the old truck driver giving her a knowing smile.

"Why don't you go on out there," he nodded towards the door as he sat back down on his crate. "I'll watch our friend here and let you know if anything changes. He'll be okay."

Rachel considered this proposition with reluctance.

"Are *you* okay?" She eyed the man doubtfully. His color and demeanor had improved over the past two hours, but she still worried. The last thing she wanted would be for him to suddenly drop with a heart attack with nothing but an unconscious man for company.

"I'm fine," Grandpa Tom insisted, "I'm just old and a little out of shape. On the other hand, you're the only one with any medical knowledge and it might be necessary for you to be up there where the action is going to be."

"Are you sure?"

"I'm sure." He crossed his legs and made a big show of being at ease.

Rachel wasn't convinced, but she really did want to see what was happening out front. The man *did* look better, and she certainly wasn't going to call him a liar. Not to mention he also had a point of her possibly being needed up front as well.

Another three seconds of thought decided the matter.

"Okay," she relented after giving him another dubious look. "But if you so much as feel funny, you call me back right then. Understand?"

"Understood," the old man gave an exasperated sigh, "I will. Now shoo!"

Rachel "shooed."

She pushed her way through the door, barely pausing to give her eyes time to adjust to the darkened restaurant. Once again, it felt like being on the wrong side of the glass in a darkened aquarium. The sound of rain drumming against the windows created a white noise that added a hushing effect to the atmosphere of the room.

The silhouettes of the dead still lined the perimeter outside.

Rachel made out the rest of the survivors standing in a knot in the middle of the room and moved to join them. They were watching the front windows, where she could see Harley standing close to the pane and peering out to the north up the highway. The tall young man squinted through the streaming windows with a calculating look on his face.

"They've stopped," he announced, just as Rachel reached the group.

This brought a few noises of dismay from the small crowd.

"They've stopped?" Gerald demanded. "What do you mean they've stopped?"

Harley didn't answer right away, but continued to stare out to the north. He reached down and picked up a toothpick from the table next to him and stuck it in his mouth as he studied the situation.

"They're about a quarter mile out," he reported, "sitting in the middle of the highway."

"What! Why?"

"Maybe they're waiting for backup," Stacey offered while rubbing the sleep from her eyes. "Four squad cars don't seem enough for this."

Rachel saw the others nod at this, but the look on Harley's face worried her. She had the feeling that he knew something, or had noticed something, that he hadn't shared with the rest of them. She had already noticed the way he paid attention to everything going on around him despite his laid back geniality.

"Maybe," Harley chewed his toothpick with a thoughtful expression. He didn't sound very convinced.

"Maybe?" Gerald echoed. "C'mon, the chick is right. They're not stupid. They're just waiting for more firepower."

"That's assuming they know what's going on here," the man at the window muttered.

"Of course they know what's going on here. Why else would they have stopped?"

"I wonder..."

"You wonder what?" Exasperation filled Gerald's voice.

Harley ignored the question.

"Holly?" he asked instead. "Did you ever manage to actually get somebody on the line when you called for help?"

All eyes turned to the thin blonde.

"No," she swallowed. "I did manage to leave them three different messages though...before all my bars disappeared and I lost service. I told them there were a lot of these things."

Harley nodded again, but kept his eyes fixed up the highway. Outside the storm thundered, and almost impossibly seemed to intensify.

As Rachel watched the man at the window, she started to get the sinking feeling that something was wrong...badly wrong. A quick glance at the other dimly lit faces in the diner confirmed she wasn't the only one. And after the initial surge of hope from just a minute ago, this new injection of doubt was more than she could stand.

"Okay, Harley," Rachel spoke up, "tell us what's wrong. What aren't you saying? We're all in this together, so how about you share what you think you know with the rest of us."

Once again, the man went silent.

He frowned down at the floor, chewing the toothpick, and Rachel could tell he was struggling to decide what to say. At any other time she would have waited for him to come to his own way of saying things, but her nerves were beginning to wear thin.

"Just spit it out, Harley."

Harley straightened and turned from the window to face them.

"Okay, Doc," he favored them all with a sad grin. "You win. The truth is, I don't think this is a rescue at all."

"What? What do you..."

"Not a rescue!" Gerald interrupted. "That's ridiculous! If it's not a rescue, what is it then? You don't think they're just parked out there enjoying the storm, do you? Of course it's a rescue! What else could it be?"

Harley shook his head, pulled the toothpick from his mouth

"I think it's a retreat," he answered.

The entire group stared at him in stunned disbelief.

"I think," he continued, "they are pulling out from Masonfield."

"But..." Rachel struggled for words.

Once again, Gerald stepped up in her place.

"Because of a fight at a football game!?" he bellowed. "What kind of candy ass cops do you guys have out here!"

"There was no fight at the football game," Harley replied, "at least not the type of fight you are talking about."

The bad feeling Rachel felt earlier began to become a sick certainty. She did a quick recall of the football field and its surrounding area, and it only took a few seconds for her to realize what Harley had to be talking about. The picture that rose in her mind almost made her choke with horror.

"Oh no," she whispered. "Masonfield Cemetery!"

She heard Stacey gasp beside her and knew the girl had come to the same conclusion. She looked over to see the small waitress covering her hands with her mouth, her eyes wide with realization. Beside her, Deke went visibly pale in the dim light, his lips silently mouthing one word... "Mom."

Ten seconds ago, Rachel had thought things were about as bad as things could get. Now she realized they were worse. Much, much worse.

And she could see that realization spread in the faces of the others.

"Wait! What do you mean?" Holly looked from her to Harley, and back again. The out-of-town girl looked both terrified and confused. "What are you talking about? I thought *these* things were from the cemetery! How could they get all the way over there? They can't be in two places at once!"

"No," Rachel forced herself to regain control. "These things are from Mazon County Cemetery. Masonfield Cemetery is in town, next to the Lutheran Church. It's only two blocks from the football field and...and it's...and it's several times larger than the one we're dealing with out here."

"Oh Christ!" Holly gasped. "You think they would attack a football field full of people?"

"Without hesitation," the doctor replied. The mental image of hundreds of death-faced monsters attacking a bleacher full of helpless families made her stomach turn. "I think they would have been drawn to the field by the stadium lights, or at least most of them would have been. Come to think of it, the lights are probably what brought the ones from the county cemetery here. The rest would have fanned out through town, attacking anybody they came across."

"Causing a mass panic and the overwhelming of the 911 system," Harley concluded. "Most of the officers who answered the initial calls probably died fast because they had no idea what they were stepping into...which would have added to the confusion."

"ORrrrr...." Geralds nasal voice cut in, "there was a big fight at the football game, just like somebody suggested earlier. And when the storm messed up the cell tower behind your phone company it also messed up the lines causing the 911 system to fail. And now that they have the fight stopped and finished processing their jail full of football addled yokels, somebody has finally noticed their 911 lines were down and listened to the messages...and now here they are."

Despite his snotty presentation, Rachel had to admit Gerald's scenario was appealing. It offered a lifeline of hope in a situation that looked bleaker by the second.

"Couldn't he be right, Harley?" she queried.

"Of course I'm right," Gerald huffed. "Occam's Razor...the simplest solution that fits the facts is almost always the correct one."

"I hope he is," Harley answered with a doubtful shrug, "I really do."

"But you don't believe it."

"I don't know," the tall young man tilted back his hat and turned to the window. "I think the existence of these things has already redefined what the 'simplest solution' may be. I guess we'll find out in another few minutes."

"What do you mean?" Rachel pressed.

"Well," Harley moved close to the glass and squinted out into the storm again, "if he's right, then they will sit there until reinforcements arrive...either from Houston or San Antonio."

"And if he's wrong?"

"Then they are sitting out there trying to figure out what's going on here, and weighing the risk of stopping for gas. The fact they're parked out there tells me that one or more of them must be running low. They'll have to decide one way or the other soon and move because the next available stop for gas is thirty five miles down the road."

"If that's the case," Deke asked, "why not just double up in the cars that still have gas in the tanks and leave the empty ones behind?"

"Because," Harley bent closer to window, "they won't have the...Aw shit...I was afraid of this. Here they come! We've got to warn them off!"

The last small flame of hope Rachel had been holding on to flickered and dimmed. The one time she had hoped Gerald would be right, and it looked like Harley's doomsday scenario was turning out to be the case.

"Wait, warn them off?" Gerald's voice went up an octave.

Harley ignored him.

"Stacey," he spoke urgently, "I need you to run back into the kitchen and start flashing the lights in here. They might see it and know not to stop."

"Sure, Harley." The little waitress disengaged from Deke.

"Harley," Rachel warned, "that will make the zombies refocus on us in here. It may excite them as well."

Stacey hesitated in the act of turning for the kitchen.

"I know, but..."

"Wait a minute!" Gerald broke in. "Warn them off? That will leave us here alone!"

"They can't help us," Harley tried to explain, "Stacey go on. At least this way..."

"You don't know that!" Gerald yelled as he reached out and laid a hand on Stacey's shoulder. She stopped once again in the act of heading for the kitchen and looked pointedly down at his hand.

"Hey!" Deke started to come around the girl towards Gerald. "Hands off, Buddy!"

"Gerald," Rachel soothed, "I think Harley's right..."

Gerald wasn't hearing it.

"No! Wait!" He cried as Stacey started for the kitchen again, and this time grabbed her arm.

And that's when things went to hell.

Rachel realized as soon as he did it what would happen. She saw Gerald's hand close in a tight grip right on the spot where the monsters at the back door had torn Stacey's arm. He probably had no intention of hurting her, for that matter he most likely had no idea what he had just done, but that didn't change the outcome. The small waitress cried out in pain and clutched at his hand over her arm.

A split second later Deke punched him dead in the face.

This had one intended, and two unintended consequences. First, Gerald fell over backwards with a bleating wail. Second, Deke also choked back a whimper of pain and grabbed his shoulder which had likely been torn open again from the exertion. Even worse, Gerald hadn't released Stacey, which resulted in her being pulled to the floor by her injured arm. And then things escalated from there...

"*Pinche pendejo!*" Marisa snarled and snatched the baseball bat she had been carrying earlier from a nearby table.

"No!" Holly tried to either grab Gerald or get between him and Marisa; it was hard to tell in the dim light. Either way, she had put herself in serious jeopardy of getting brained. Meanwhile, Deke looked like he had just figured out that the good hand he had used to grab his wounded shoulder could just as effectively be employed to continue beating on the downed redhead. He looked enormously pleased with the discovery and appeared to be readying himself to put that plan into action.

Rachel saw that things were about one second away from descending into a brawl...

...with her right in the middle of it.

"GODDAMMIT!" she bellowed at the top of her lungs. "KNOCK IT OFF!"

Everybody froze... and as all eyes settled on her, Rachel became suddenly aware of how much older she was than the rest of this bunch. Hell, with the possible exception of Harley, these were all kids. Some of them were only fresh out of high school. No wonder Grandpa Tom had decided to have her come up here...he hadn't wanted to be the only grownup in the room.

"Okay," she took a deep breath. "First...Gerald, let go of Stacey's arm."

"But..." Gerald gasped, his eyes wide in what Rachel realized was the prelude to hysterics.

"Now!" she snapped, and was gratified to see him comply. She had a sudden hunch that he had never been punched in the face before, and in his little world Deke, Harley, her, and the rest of them were all almost as alien and threatening as the monsters outside. At another time she might have felt sorry for him, but at the moment he could damn well have his little breakdown on his own time. "Now go over there and let Holly tend your nose. I'll come check on you in a minute." She gestured towards a booth by the fire door.

Then Rachel turned her attention to the young redneck who still looked at Gerald with blood in his eyes. She decided a little redirection might be the order of the day here.

"Deke, I need you to take Stacey over to the counter there, and both of you wait for me to come look at your bandages and see if they need to be redone," She said it gently, but with the same firmness she would have used in directing a tech to help her with a patient.

"Yes, ma'am," Deke nodded and helped the girl to her feet.

Rachel found the "ma'am" somewhat mortifying under these circumstances but chose to say nothing. Apparently Harley was content to let her be the only adult in the room so the doctor figured she might as well start assuming the role. She turned to address Marisa but the girl was already walking past her towards the kitchen.

"I'll go flash the lights," the taller waitress growled as she passed.

She didn't make it.

"Marisa, stop," Harley's voice brought her up short. "It's too late for that now. It's time to go with plan B."

"Plan B?" she frowned.

"Yeah," Harley peered out the window as it began to brighten with the reflected beam of headlights. "Can you turn off the lights in the store from back there?"

"Yes. Why?"

"Because," the tall man sighed, "something very bad is about to happen, but at least it may give us an opportunity I can take advantage of. I'm afraid it's 'wingman' time, but I need those lights out in the store."

Plan B? Wingman? Rachel wondered to herself as she watched Marisa nod and rush for the back. *What's going on with these two?*

Whatever it was, Marisa didn't look terribly happy about it.

Rachel didn't have time to puzzle over it because things started to happen at a rapid fire pace.

The windows flared with light that she could just make out being the result of several police cars turning off the highway and pulling into the gas pumps. Their beams sliced through the downpour and hit the streaming windows, fragmenting into thousands of brilliant points of light. The shadows of the dead were cast in sharp relief against the running glass. Unfortunately, they were the only clear shapes she could make out through all the light and distortion. Adding to the confusion, the red and blue strobes from the cruiser's light bars caused the rain jeweled windows to pulse in a disorienting cadence.

The crack of thunder only made matters worse.

"Can you see what's going on out there?" She stood on her tiptoes and squinted at the windows from her place in the middle of the room. "What are they doing? What's happening?"

"It's hard to tell," Harley called back. He had one hand up trying to shield his eyes from the glare. "I think two have hung back at the road, and the other two have pulled into the pumps. Hold it, there might be another car or two out there that's not cop cars. Yep, there are definitely more cars out there. I didn't see them because they don't have lights on their roof."

"Harley, be careful!" Deke called from his place at the bar. "Those headlights coming through the windows are going to make you visible to the outside!"

Rachel cursed herself for not thinking of that. The fact that Harley hadn't either surprised her.

"It's okay," the tall redneck answered, but took a couple of steps back from the windows anyway. "They've all turned around and are looking at the cars. I wonder why they haven't attacked yet?"

"They're probably confused by all the lights," Rachel answered, still craning to see, "and this rain is probably making it worse." She saw Marisa return from the back and noticed the doorway to the store had gone dark. "I doubt it's going to last, so you might want to take that into account with whatever you and Marisa are up to."

"Actually, I'm counting on it." Harley continued to stare at the window.

"Believe me, this ain't my idea," Marisa muttered. "I was hoping he would forget this little plan of his."

"What are you talking ab..."

"They SEE them!" Harley called, "Here we go!"

Rachel looked back at the front window to see the silhouettes had already assumed that attack crouch they favored, with the shadows of their spread claws magnified on the wet glass behind them. Something...some movement at the gas pumps they recognized as human...must have triggered them.

Everything from this point on was inevitable.

"And there they go," Harley said as the monsters at the front window charged off into the storm. He rushed back to the window and faced to the north again. "One...two...three..."

"What are you doing?" Marisa demanded, her hands knotted around the handle of the bat in a tight grip.

"Four...fivesix..." he held up one hand to ward of interruption.

"Hey!" Holly called from her and Gerald's side of the diner, "They're all leaving from over here too!"

Rachel looked over to see cadaverous shapes running past the windows and towards the gas pumps from that side of the truck stop as well. Everything seemed to be happening at once. The dead were staging a mass attack on the gas pumps.

"Seven...eight..." Harley waited a second or two longer then turned back to the room. "Hey, Holly? How many zombies did you count in the store again?"

"Ten?" the blond recalled, trying to keep track of the action going on outside while answering the question. "That's right, isn't it?"

"Yep, that's what I recall too. Okay, eight just ran out the front door and one is cooling her heels in the freezer...so unless something has changed, that leaves one."

A gunshot cracked outside, and the shadows cast into the room split and veered as one of the cars out at the pumps must have started to move. Faint screams could be heard through the din of the storm and Rachel understood people were running and fighting for their lives out there...and some weren't going to make it.

"What are you thinking, Harley?" she yelled as she ducked under a table.

It occurred to her that bullets flying around came with dangers of their own. Especially since the only thing separating them from the monsters outside were large sheets of glass.

"I'm going to try and improve our position," he replied. "Marisa, I need you to come over here and get ready to unlock the door. Stay low."

"Tell me you aren't making a run for your truck," the waitress grouched as she scuttled over to the restaurant door. "There's too many of those things out there...even if they *are* distracted."

"Run for his truck? Harley, are you insane?" Rachel hissed from under her table.

More gunshots sounded from out in the storm, and shadows slid across the walls as another car pulled away from the truck stop. Any second she anticipated the sound of a window shattering, heralding their collective doom.

"I'm not going for the truck," Harley crab walked over to the door next to Marisa. "I'm thinking if there is only one of these things left in the store then now is our chance to get all of them out of the building. That would give us a second area to retreat to in case something happens to one of these windows. If nothing else, it will give us more options and also a large supply of junk food if we end up having to stay here for a while."

"Harley," Rachel warned, "I don't think this is a good idea. I know you beat one of these things once, but do you really want to square off against another one? They may be stronger than they look, and you can't be sure there isn't more than one of them over there."

She winced at the sound of another scream from outside but held his gaze.

"Doc," he replied, "the last thing I want to do is go over there...but it needs to be done. This situation ain't gonna get better by itself. And now that we know there ain't gonna be any help coming, it's up to us to get out of this alive. I *have* to do this."

"Are you sure?" Marisa challenged him, "Are you absolutely sure we're on our own?"

"Marisa," Harley's tone took on a quiet urgency, "those cop cars out there have radios. They know what's going on in the world, and they just acted on it. They could have chosen to park and wait between here and town until help arrived...but they didn't. And the only possible reason for that is they knew help wasn't coming. That means it's down to us."

Rachel's stomach plunged as she followed Harley's logic and could find no flaw in it. She realized that while Harley had been "lounging" up here drinking coffee, he had actually been putting all kinds of pieces together about the situation as a whole while the rest of them had been fighting different personal demons and trying to come to grips with the situation right in front of them. She began to wonder just what all he had figured out.

What the hell was going on out in the world? How widespread was this thing?

"Right now," he continued, "the zombies have all been pulled away and their attention is elsewhere. That

172

isn't going to last, and we aren't going to get this chance again. I have to try this while it's still possible."

Marisa looked from Harley, to Rachel, and back to Harley again with a tight face. The doctor could tell the girl was struggling with what he had told her, and not liking it any better than she did. At the same time, she appeared to come to the same conclusions. Like it or not, there was no other way.

"Okay." She fished the keys out of her pants and started hunting the one to the door. "If we're going to do this then let's get it over with. I don't want to have to think about it too long."

"Hey wait," Harley objected, "I said *I* would go..."

"No! *You* wait." Marisa cut him off. "I'm your 'wingman', remember? Face it, you're our best chance of getting out of this alive and we can't risk losing you because you decided to be a hero and go do this without somebody watching your back." She pointed the key to the door at his nose. "So you think about that when you make these plans of yours. If it's too stupid for you to have me along as backup, then it's probably too stupid for you to be doing in the first place. *Comprende?*"

Rachel could tell the girl was scared right down to her socks, but that she didn't intend to back down on this. Whatever understanding these two had come to earlier, it looked like she meant to make him stick to it.

Harley must have seen that too.

"Okay," he gave in with an unhappy sigh, "if you insist. But let me handle things over there. This is what I do...what I need *you* to do is stay clear and watch my back, okay?"

The waitress nodded, her jaw set tight. Even in the dim light, Rachel could see how white her knuckles were from clutching her bat.

"Okay, then," Harley indicated the lock, "the clock is running. Let's do this thing."

"You two be careful."

Rachel almost jumped out of her skin at the sound of Deke's voice right behind her.

She turned to see him and Stacey hunched under the table behind her. The look on Deke's face, and the fact he hadn't even offered to go in with Harley, told her volumes about the shape his shoulder must be in. She knew the young man's pride must be killing him, but the hold Stacey had on his arm told her the girl had already explained to him that pride was no substitute for common sense. The fresh blood on both of their bandages made her want to go over and kick Gerald in the ass.

"We will," Harley nodded, "we should be done and back within five minutes at the longest...probably a lot less. You guys just keep your heads down till this is over."

Having said that, he moved over and crouched on the other side of the doorway while Marisa slipped the key into the lock. They all watched as she turned the key with silent care. Harley then eased the door open, did a quick peek inside, and slipped through into the darkness beyond. A second later the waitress followed.

The tips of Marisa's fingers were visible near the bottom of the door as she took care to make sure it closed in slow silence.

Then she and Harley were gone.

Another crack of thunder shook the building, making the three of them jump. For a second, Rachel thought it might be another gunshot. A quick scan of the windows revealed them all to be whole, and she realized the sounds of battle from the direction of the gas pumps had stopped. Headlights from at least one car still sparkled against the glass, telling her that some people hadn't managed to escape the onslaught.

Everybody who could had already left.

They were now alone.

"Ooookaaayyy..." Rachel breathed after a few more seconds of silence.

She turned to the young couple behind her, noting the looks of worry and guilt on both their faces.

They want to help Harley and Marisa, she realized. *Those are both of their best friends who just went into a dark place with monsters, and even though they know better, they think they ought to be in there with*

174

them. They're both hurt and scared out of their minds, but they would step up in a heartbeat if asked.

Rachel realized she really wanted to keep these two as friends...if they lived through this. Some people, no matter their station in life, were just good people. She had a feeling she would like Marisa and Harley too, if she got a chance to know them better.

"They're going to be okay," she assured them. "Harley seems like a pretty capable guy, and Marisa is smart. They can handle this."

And if they don't, I'm the last uninjured adult capable of doing much other than maybe Holly. Don't make a liar out of me, you two. I've had enough unpleasant surprises tonight.

Of course, that was when the fire alarm went off.

Rising Waters - Marisa

Marisa barely dared to breathe as she eased the door shut behind her. She squatted on the floor, directly behind Harley, trying to peek over his shoulder at the darkened room beyond. To her right, light filtered in through the tinted front windows in an angled beam that cut off sharply at waist level. It didn't illuminate much, and left the floor near the front shrouded in blackness. The shelves loomed like dim mountains to her left, cutting off almost all view of most of the store.

The air reeked of scorched coffee pot, and a smoky haze made visibility in the dim light even worse.

This is me, following a 200 lb redneck into a dark store full of killer dead people...armed only with my good looks and a baseball bat. I've been watching way too many Michelle Rodriguez movies. Next time, I'll just throw a wig on Stacey and she can play the gutsy Latina chick.

She froze as Harley reached back and tapped her on the knee.

175

He pointed at the nearby front entrance, and made a twisty motion with his hand that Marisa understood to be directions to lock the door. That made sense. The girl nodded, crept in silent, slow motion over to the lock and inserted the key. She noticed him shift position as she moved and realized he was doing it to keep himself between her and the rest of the room.

Normally such a move would have struck her as tedious male posturing or an overwrought gesture of chivalry, but since there were real man-eating monsters out there in the dark she decided she could be a little more generous in her evaluation of the action. Besides, it didn't *feel* like he was making some kind of gesture...it felt like he was simply covering her back while she did her job.

The key turned in the lock and the mechanism snapped home with an uncomfortably loud *"clack."*

Marisa winced at the noise, and peeked back to see if a hoard of skull-faced monsters was descending on her with gaping jaws.

Nothing.

Nothing but Harley crouched behind her, scanning the darkness.

"Got it," she whispered, then winced again as she realized the only way he couldn't have known it was if he were deaf as a post.

He didn't seem inclined to give her grief about it, instead gesturing at her and then at a spot at the end of the first row of shelves. Again, his meaning was obvious and she moved to the indicated location. Once there, she stopped and watched him for further instruction.

Harley started a complicated series of gestures that made absolutely no sense to her whatsoever. He must have seen the confusion on her face for he stopped before she could cut him off and held up a hand to signal her to wait and not move. Keeping his eyes focused somewhere down at the other end of the store, he did a careful crawl over to her and put a cupped hand to her ear.

"There is one down there behind where the cash register used to be," he whispered. "I think it's the last one in here, but I can't be totally sure."

Marisa squinted at the dark corner in question, but couldn't see anything. If it was there, it wasn't standing up or it would be silhouetted against the window. For a second she wondered what it would be doing on the floor, then remembered that was where Gladys had died. Then she didn't want to think about it.

"I'm going to sneak down there and try and surprise it," Harley continued. He put a finger to her lips as she started to object. "I need you to stay here and make sure nothing comes out of one of these aisles behind me. Understand?"

She favored him with a suspicious look but he shook his head.

"I'm not just trying to keep you out of harm's way. If something comes out of an aisle after I pass it, I need you to scream to catch its attention. Get it to come after you. Then you jump back through the door so I can try to either get it from behind or at least avoid getting caught between them."

Marisa pictured that in her head, and realized it made good sense. She nodded her assent at Harley, who wasted no time in turning back to face the far end of the store.

The man moved in a smooth crouch, staying just under the level of the light coming in the window. This had the effect of him disappearing in the darkness under the smoke filled shaft. She tried to keep track of his position and marveled at how he could move so quietly in boots.

And given the outcome of his last fight with one of these things, the girl now allowed herself the hope that maybe...just maybe...he could take this one out by surprise before it knew what was happening. She didn't know how he planned to do it but had every confidence he had a plan in mind.

Unfortunately, she never got to find out what that plan might be.

A piercing electronic shriek cut through the store without warning, causing her to squeak in surprise, and the security lights in the back corner of the store came on. While not as bright as the overhead fluorescents, they were still sufficient to fill the store with light...revealing Harley to be halfway towards a monster that had just finished tearing a large strip of skin from Gladys's body.

Oh shit! Marisa gaped up at the security lights. *The fire alarm! What the hell? All the stoves are off so... so somebody just opened the fire door in the restaurant!*

She didn't have time to think beyond that.

The dead thing rose to its feet, the long strip of skin still hanging from its jaws, and Marisa tried not to look at the bloody wreck of her coworker at its feet. At the same time, Harley started to run towards the ghoul.

"Marisa!" he yelled, "The side door! You're going to have to close it!"

The monster charged, and Harley met it in a flying tackle just as it started to come over the wreckage of the counter. His greater mass drove the dead thing backwards and the two of them tumbled back over the mess, gripping and tearing at each other.

This left Marisa with a straight shot at the side door...other than for the savaged body of the store's last customer...the door still blocked open where Gladys used to enjoy her smokes.

She hesitated, torn between running for the door or rushing over to help the man fighting the dead thing on the floor. She knew he hadn't originally intended to get into a clinch with the horror. It had been forced on him by circumstances. Whatever advantages his fighting skills gave him on his feet might not translate into a wrestling match on the ground...especially with an unnaturally strong monster that bit, clawed, and didn't feel pain.

She raised her bat and took a couple of steps towards the struggling pair.

"No, Marisa! The door! The things outside are going to hear this noise and come back! Hurry!"

A quick glance at the front window confirmed this. Several snarling shapes were already visible coming between the cars of the parking lot in a headlong run towards the store. They would be there in seconds.

"Shit!" Marisa sprinted for the open door.

It stood propped open by a cracked cinder block Gladys used to prop her foot on while taking her breaks. She could see it swing away from the block even further at times as the wind caught it and pushed it wider. The driving rain flooded in, creating a reddened puddle that surrounded the corpse of Gladys's last customer and covered about a third of the store.

Marisa didn't dare take the time to negotiate around the body so she jumped it while at a dead run in the puddle. That didn't end up working out very well. She landed skidding towards the door, completely out of control. The tall girl fought to maintain her balance, then had her feet fly out from under her just as her hand closed on the metal handle.

"Goddammit!" she shrieked as she grasped the handle in a death grip and flailed to get her legs back under her as she continued to slide forward. Her momentum threatened to carry her out the door, and she realized there now existed the very real danger of the monsters coming around the corner of the store to find her sitting on her ass outside waiting for them.

No. She absolutely refused to die like that.

Water flew from where she splashed and slid in the open door. A heavy blast of rain hit her in the face, blinding her as she fought to stand. Things were getting worse by the second. Time was running out and if she didn't get this done fast then both her and Harley were dead. The struggling waitress realized she needed to forget about regaining her feet and just focus on getting the damn door closed.

Marisa lashed out in an effort to kick away Gladys's door prop and her sneakered foot flared with pain as it connected badly, but with enough force to knock the heavy brick over. It felt like she had broken at least one toe...maybe more. She pulled herself to her knees, biting back tears, then leaned backwards in a final effort to use her weight to drag the door shut.

It shut with a squeaky hiss, cutting off the noise of the storm outside.

She was safe...almost.

Marisa rammed the key into the lock and twisted it, just as the faint sounds of splashing footsteps announced the arrival of the predators outside. The bedraggled young woman didn't even look up, not wanting to see what would be glaring in through the door at her. Besides, she realized her problems weren't over yet.

A thunderous crash announced that Harley and the monster still fought behind the broken counter. At the same time, the slap of dead palms against glass drove home the fact that both her and the battle were visible to the monsters outside, and it was exciting the hell out of them. If she didn't do something damn quick, they were going to be in here...door or no door.

Marisa pulled herself to her feet with a whimper.

Her foot hurt like the devil itself, and in the process of getting up she discovered her hip hurt as well. She had no doubt she was going to be sporting a major league bruise there, probably acquired when she initially slipped and hit the floor. The fact her clothes were now sopping wet was just icing on the cake.

She scooped the bat up from where she had dropped it when she lost her balance, and tried to use it as a makeshift cane as she tottered away from the door. It wasn't really the right size for the job and she decided it would be faster to just hobble in misery.

"Hang on, Harley," she groaned, "I've got to knock those lights out and then I'll be back."

"Good idea," he gasped. "I'll be right here."

He and his opponent came into view as she limped further into the store. Harley had solved the biting problem by somehow stuffing a leather bank pouch from the busted cash register into the creature's mouth while holding its head against the floor with one forearm. He had his legs wrapped around its middle and one arm, and was struggling to keep the other from grabbing him. A ragged gash ran down his forearm and blood covered his shirt.

"The doc wasn't kidding," he continued through gritted teeth. "These bastards are hellaciously strong! I'll hold this guy, but you might want to make it quick."

180

Marisa nodded and turned to head up the aisle towards the lights...

...when the store went dark again.

"What the hell?" Harley's strained voice cut through the dark.

"*Mierde!*" Marisa snapped. "Now what?"

Then the obvious explanation hit her...Stacey must have turned off the alarm. The main control panel for it was in the back hallway next to the storeroom. Both of them knew how to reset it since at least once a month a kid or some drunk would push open the fire door by mistake. It was just another exciting feature of the job.

This time, the surprising new development wasn't a disaster in the making.

On the other hand, that meant it was time for her to join the fight with the man-eating, killer corpse.

The question was, what could she do?

Marisa was no wilting wallflower, but her mother had not raised an idiot. She had no illusions of jumping into a fracas between a deadly monster and a trained fighter.

She had done it with Deke because she hadn't had time to think about it, and Deke was losing the fight anyway. But this was different. Harley had fought the thing to a standstill, and she was scared of doing anything that might put him at a disadvantage again. At the same time, she remembered Deke and Stacey both talking about how these things didn't tire and realized a standstill already put Harley in trouble. She needed to do something, but she didn't know what.

In the end, she opted on asking the expert.

"Harley?" She squinted at the dark shape of the two combatants struggling on the floor. Without the light, she didn't dare swing for fear of hitting him instead of the creature. "How can I help? Just tell me what to do. Should I go get the others?"

"Nope," he grunted. "That wouldn't do much but risk getting the others hurt...and it ain't necessary."

"You sure?"

"Yep. I'm sure. You still got the bat?"

"Yeah, but it's hard for me to see. I'm scared of hitting you by mistake."

"Good," he gasped. "You're using your head. What I need you to do is lean the bat against the end of the shelves right there, and then step away."

"Right here?" She wondered what in the hell he could be planning.

"Yes. Right there. Just lean it, handle up, against the end of the shelf. Then I want you to go back over to the door to the restaurant."

"Harley..."

"I need you by the door." The strain in his voice left no room for argument. "I'm going to try something but I'm going to need room to maneuver. And if it doesn't work I'm going to need you holding the door for me."

"Got it," she replied. She carefully leaned the bat where he said and took a step back. "Is that good?"

"That's fine. Now go ahead and get clear."

Marisa understood he was about to attempt something extremely risky. At the same time, she also knew he didn't have a choice.

When you had a tiger by the tail, the most dangerous part was letting go.

"Harley, be careful."

There just wasn't anything else left to say.

The waitress turned and hobbled for the doorway as fast as she could. She figured it was just as well he sent her all the way to the door before doing whatever it was he was going to do. In her current shape, she wasn't going to be outrunning anything. It only occurred to her as she reached for the handle that he had probably been thinking exactly along those lines.

"Okay, I'm here," She grasped the handle. "Whatever you're goi..."

There was a grunt and a crash from the darkened area.

It was hard to tell what was happening, but she detected a flurry of motion on the floor. Then the awful figure of the walking corpse rose up against the window. Its ghastly head turned to focus on her, where she stood visible in the light from the parking lot. A split second later Harley came up out of the darkness at the end of the shelves where she had laid the bat.

He didn't hesitate.

The weapon blurred in the dim light as the big man closed and attacked in one fast, viciously savage motion. The monster had just started its attack posture when the bat connected against the side of its head with a sickening *crack*. It staggered and fell back against the little counter behind the register. Harley didn't wait to see if it would recover. He spun the bat and brought it straight down on the monster's head in three powerful, consecutive swings.

He hammered the thing to the floor...each impact marked by a sodden crunch that left little to the imagination. It was violent, brutish, and the last blow sounded with a meaty finality that convinced Marisa the monster would not be rising again.

She gave silent thanks she hadn't seen much but silhouettes.

Harley's figure stood there, breathing heavily, then stooped down into the darkness of the floor. A couple of seconds later a small flare of yellow light came to life. She realized he must have grabbed a loose cigarette lighter from the debris of the wrecked counter. Now he had bent down to examine the corpse.

"Harley? Are you okay?"

"Yeah, I'm a little scratched up, but I'll be okay. You?"

She had seen the blood on his shirt earlier, and knew the thing had at least clawed him pretty good a couple of times. Still, he didn't seem very concerned about it so she figured that was between him and the doc.

"I hurt my toe, but I'll live. What are you doing?"

"I'm looking at something," he muttered, then spoke up. "Something weird."

"Something weird?" her laugh had no humor in it whatsoever. "What could possibly be weird on a night like this?"

"Something you probably don't want to see," Harley replied in a bemused tone. "As a matter of fact, it's something you definitely don't want to see...but the doc definitely should."

Rising Waters - Holly

Damn you, Gerald! Damn you! Damn you! And damn me too!

They hadn't thought of the fire alarm.

Only two minutes earlier she had been sitting in an enclosed building with all the bad things that wanted to eat her outside.

Only two minutes earlier she had been at least somewhat safe, comfortably dry, and of all the things she had been questioning...none of them had been her sanity.

Only two minutes earlier.

Then Gerald had raised his pale, blood smeared face from the table, and stood up in an effort to see the carnage outside. He squinted at the retreating figures in the storm, looked over at the small group of locals huddled under the tables near the doorway, then brought his now wide-eyed gaze back to her.

His eyes locked with hers, yet he didn't really seem to see her because the half grin that spread across his face was in response to some thought within. His hand emerged from beneath the table with his car keys. He pointed the electronic door opener at the window beside them and pushed the button.

"Look, Holly." He nodded out the window, and she followed his gesture to see the parking lights on his BMW flash in the rain. "The big yahoo was right. They've all run for the gas pumps."

"Gerald, what are you thinking?" She didn't trust where this observation was leading. Gerald wasn't exactly the risk taking sort, especially if discomfort or actual bodily harm was a potential outcome. But something was different here. She noticed something about his eyes were off.

His pupils were contracted to pinpoints, and when he refocused on her she got the chilling suspicion that the Gerald she knew had taken a back seat to something else for the moment. This was Gerald "distilled."

"It's a straight shot," he smiled. "Nothing between it and us but rain."

Was he kidding? There were people *dying* out there.

"Gerald," she whispered, "that's insane. Just drop it."

"No." He didn't even take umbrage at her disagreement. "It's not. I knew parking away from these clod kickers was a good idea at the time, and now it just worked in our favor. The beamer is at an angle away from the gas pumps, so we wouldn't be running straight at those monsters."

"Gerald, stop it."

He didn't even slow down...just kept speaking in a low, intense monotone.

"We can make it to the car in five seconds. And those things won't even know we're out there until we're safe in the beamer. Then we can wave bye-bye to these filthy creatures and be back in Austin in three hours."

In a depressing flash of intuition, she understood that the "filthy creatures" he referred to weren't just the ones out in the storm. She may not have been "small town" but she still came from way out on the country edge of South Houston. It made her wonder how much higher on the "evolutionary scale" she rated in his eyes. At least he was still talking in terms of "we" in his current state."

"Gerald, we can't," she pleaded. "It's suicide. Besides, you'll ruin your beret out there in the rain."

Holly knew how stupid that sounded, but it was exactly the kind of trivial thing that Gerald usually cared about when more important matters were at hand. It was a forlorn hope, but she prayed it might get through to him.

It didn't.

"We can," he continued in an eerily calm voice, "and I will. On the count of five, I'm getting out of here and going home. You are free to come with me. Five..."

"Gerald, no!" she hissed. This was completely unlike him.

"Four."

What the hell was she going to do? This was lunacy! Between the stress of being out of his element, the horror of the past few hours, and now the punch in the face from the smaller local boy, Gerald had apparently snapped.

"Three."

She regarded him with despair.

He meant it. He was going to do this, and now she had to make a choice. Either go with him, or get left behind.

"Two"

It was safe in here...but was it? Harley had said there wasn't going to be any help coming, and if he was right, then sooner or later they were going to have to make a run for it anyway. Once daylight came, and the storm ended, the dead were going to be able to see inside...and then these windows would only last so long.

"One"

And she understood on a gut level that if she remained here, they were through. Gerald wouldn't look back. He would take it as her choosing the people here over him and would wash his hands of her. That would have consequences of its own.

"Go," he stated in the same calm voice, stepped out of the booth, and rushed around the seat for the fire door.

In the end, habit made her decision for her.

Something inside, some lost voice, wailed for her to stop as she found herself taking off after him. She shut it out, sick with the knowledge it was the fading voice of who she had been two years ago. The voice of the girl who had real friends, real passions, and real opinions...the girl who hadn't met Gerald yet, and all the opportunities that came with him.

Now was not the time to indulge in going over past choices, she told herself.

Now it was time to run.

Gerald hit the door ahead of her at full speed, and she followed right at his back. An ear splitting, electronic shriek assaulted her ears as the door flew open and she understood they had just made a critical mistake. They had forgotten that opening the fire door would set off an alarm. Now, instead of making their run for safety with the advantage of the monsters not knowing they were coming, they had just announced their presence outside to the entire countryside.

As she staggered out into the blinding chaos of the downpour, she realized they were committed. Any attempt to stop and turn back would cost valuable seconds, allowing the zombies to react and attack. Besides, a flicker of motion to her right caused her to turn and see several wasted, loping figures coming from behind the truck stop towards her.

The monsters had been closer than she realized! They must have been back there, out of sight of the action up front, and only now drawn around the building by the sound of the alarm. There were at least a good half dozen of them. Even worse, they had already spotted her and were well into the process of running them down. Lightning flared, bringing their gaping jaws into stark relief in the wild storm. Then something came around the building behind them...

...something truly awful.

C'mon, don't look back, just run! Don't look back, just run! Just run, just run, just run!

Gerald began to widen the gap between them, and she had a sudden image of him leaping into the car and hitting the electronic lock switch as soon as he slammed the door, leaving her outside to be ripped to pieces. It wouldn't be malicious on his part. He simply wouldn't think to wait for her until it was too late.

And she would be just as dead.

Holly fled through the rain with desperate eyes fixed on the approaching car and a grinning pack of the living dead snapping at her heels. Ahead of her, the dark shape of Gerald ran into the hood of the car then fumbled his way around to the driver's door. The sight of him grabbing for the handle prompted a burst of even greater speed.

"Geralllldddd!" she wailed as he yanked the door open and jumped inside. "Waiiiittt!"

The slam of his door shook the car as she grasped the handle of her own. She yanked on the handle with a ragged cry, ripping her own door open, and saw his finger punch the lock button at the very same instant.

You son of a bitch! You would have actually done it!

Holly didn't have the breath to scream at him as she dove into the car and snatched the door shut behind her. She could wait till later. When they reached Austin, she fully intended to inform Mr. Gerald Plimpton that they were through...while he lay clutching his thrice kicked balls on the ground. But until that glorious moment, getting out of here would do.

Holly made a silent promise to send help back to the Textro as she wrestled on her seat belt. At least she could do that much for them. She knew she had done it for all the wrong reasons, but maybe turning this last act of submission into something useful would help her face the girl in the mirror a little better. Assuming she made it out of here...

The smack on the window caused her to look over and directly into the eyes of the nightmare only inches away.

It must have once been somebody's little girl.

Like all the others, the face was now gone...but the pigtails still remained. The smallish claws slapping the glass had bone tipped fingers, and Holly realized that even this little thing had ripped its way up through wood and earth to the world above. Its child-sized skull was level with Holly's own, and it snapped and scrabbled at the glass like a maddened animal.

Other hands started smacking the windows around her.

"Gerald! Get us the hell out of here!"

Gerald finally managed to slam home the keys, and the engine roared to life. Holly gave silent thanks that he had just had the BMW overhauled. A second later he found the headlights and turned them on.

She almost wished he hadn't.

"Holy shit! Look at that!" Gerald breathed and pointed out the windshield, "I was right! That ignorant yokel animal doctor had the nerve to lecture me and I was *right*! *HE* sure as hell didn't come from no graveyard! I wonder what that backwoods bitch has to say about *this*!"

His finger shook in triumphal justification as it pointed at the cause of his outburst.

Outside, the enormous, ravaged corpse of Buddha Boy Norville stood bathed in the headlights.

Unlike the other dead things roaming the parking lot this night, he still had most of his face. Only one section that included a cheek and part of his neck was missing, giving him a strangely bulldog-like appearance. But the damage didn't stop there.

Massive tears ran down the sides and front of his vast torso, giving his once great belly the appearance of pleated cloth. Large gobs of fat and meat protruded from the bottom of most of the ripped sections, and a two foot length of colon hung from his left side. His pleated flesh wobbled and swayed like a skirt as he lumbered around to the side of the car.

"Geralllld" Holly moaned. "Get us ooouuut of heeeerrrrree..."

"Shhhhh...." Gerald's head swiveled to track the huge monstrosity. "Just don't move and let them settle down. Remember, they can't really make sense of what they see through wet glass. Pretty quick they'll lose track of us and go back over to where the action is."

"Goddammit, Gerald..."

"Just hush!" He turned towards her with a finger to his lips. "And relax. This glass is a lot tougher than the stuff in those windows anyway. Now be still. Everything is okay."

"I don't think so." She frowned through the rain pebbled windshield. The pale monster swatted one of its skeletal companions out of the way as it reached the driver's door. "I think this one is different. I'm serious! I think you need to hit the gas right now!"

189

"I just had this thing refurbished. I'm not panicking and plowing over a bunch of these things and wrecking the front end. Not when..."

She saw the huge zombie lean down and peer through the glass at the back of Gerald's head. The bloated white face almost filled the window. Its milky eyes zeroed straight in on the oblivious redhead, and Holly had no doubt it knew exactly what it was looking at.

"Dammit, Gerald!" she shrieked. "Floor it! Now!"

Too late.

The man turned back to the window just as it exploded inwards in a shower of fractured glass. Holly screamed and threw up her hands to keep the flying fragments out of her face. A split second later Gerald's flailing elbow caught her in the side of the head, causing her to see stars. She could feel him thrashing in the seat beside her, as she tried to clear her vision and get a grip on what was happening.

Holly shook her throbbing head and looked over to see Gerald dying.

The monster had driven its fist through the window and now it's massive hand clenched most of her boyfriend's face, with its fingers hooked under his jawline. She could hear the bones of Gerald's face crack under the thing's grip, and knew the thrashing was due to him suffocating. It seemed to be trying to drag him headfirst out the window. Holly realized the only reason it hadn't already succeeded was due to the seatbelt holding the man in.

Not that it helped him much.

He made a strangled gurgle behind the massive hand as it tightened further, causing more popping noises. Blood began to squeeze out between its thick fingers. Gerald flopped in the seat like a dying fish, the visible portions of his head now blue from oxygen deprivation. Holly knew he was going to die if she didn't do something, and do it damn quick.

The girl grabbed the gear shift and ground the transmission into gear. Then she unsnapped her seatbelt, threw her leg over the gear shift and stomped the gas pedal. Beside her, Gerald twitched and spasmed, his head now twisted up and back as the monster continued to pull. The engine roared and the tortured squeal of rubber on slick asphalt cut through the din of the storm.

For a moment, the car didn't move.

Then the wheels found their purchase and the BMW leapt forward. Unfortunately, physics were not to be denied and that meant something had to give. In this case it was Gerald's neck...

...as his head tore loose in one wet, gristle popping, rip.

Holly shrieked anew as the headless corpse geysered blood and fell over against her. Gore fountained from the severed neck, drenching the girl as she fought to get the grisly thing off of her. It wasn't easy due to the reclining position she was forced into by having her foot on the gas pedal. She kept it jammed to the floor, barely noticing the multiple thuds against the car's bumper as it rocketed blindly past the truck stop towards the rear of the parking lot.

With a howl of despair, Holly pushed the corpse back upright...only to have it slump forward now that it had slipped free of the shoulder restraint, and fall forward onto the steering wheel. It turned under the cadaver's weight, and she felt the car veer sharply to the left.

Even dead, the jackass was still doing all the driving that mattered.

Holly fought to push herself up so her head would be above the level of the dashboard and she could see. At the same time her foot groped for the brake pedal, but Gerald's legs were in the way. In the end it didn't matter, for she got her head up just in time to see it was too late.

A wall of corn stalks filled the headlight beams outside the windshield.

The BMW went off the asphalt and into the soft, deep mud of the plowed furrows at over sixty miles per hour. It was almost like hitting a wall.

Out of her own shoulder strap due to her efforts with the gas pedal, Holly slammed against the dashboard with bone crunching force as the vehicle smashed into the drenched soil, bounced out, then plowed another long trench into the mud. The airbag deployed after the bounce, almost smacking the slight girl unconscious while sparing her a second impact during the final collision with the soft earth. After another couple of seconds the heavy car bulldozed to a stop...buried up to its axles in the streaming ground.

Nothing moved for a moment, the hissing of the rain in the corn stalks closing back in as a substitute for silence.

Holly became aware of the storm hammering the roof in the darkness, unsure if minutes or mere seconds had passed since the crash. She lay, half slid down the seat to the floor. Every part of her body hurt, and she didn't want to think about the weight now leaning against her from the driver's side. She knew what it had to be, but this time she felt pretty sure the blood on her face belonged to her...

...along with assorted fractures, contusions, and god only knew what other damage.

A feeble attempt to raise one arm sent jagged shards of crystal sharp agony through her back and side. She was hurt...hurt bad. The only reason the girl didn't scream was because the pain from inhaling almost caused her to black out. She barely clung to consciousness, and the effort to do even that drained her by the second. Her grip on the world was fading. It felt as if her mind circled a black hole at the back of her head, soon to be sucked in by its inexorable pull.

Some small part of Holly realized with a remote sense of sadness that when that happened there would be no coming back. It would be her final exit. The big goodbye.

She was dying.

And she wasn't even scared.

Holly lay there in the dark wreckage, barely moved by it all. The thought of dying in a half sunk BMW in the middle of a soggy Texas cornfield only generated a mild sense of bemusement. It sure didn't live up to the dramatic passings performed by many of the actresses she had aspired to follow. It didn't appear she would even get the benefit of an audience.

Then a flare of lightning lit the night, and she saw she wasn't alone.

Not even the skeletal face peering in over the edge of the driver's side window alarmed her. Her only response was to think the pigtails were a sad touch.

You were somebody's baby, weren't you. Her mind did another shallow orbit of that black pit, and she understood the next one would be its last. *You know what? When I was your age I wore pigtails, too. I guess compared to you, I got bonus time. No point in complaining...you get what you get. And once you're dead, what difference does it make?" You just sleep the Big Sleep, not caring about the nastiness of how you died or where you fell." Right?*

Paraphrasing the line of Raymond Chandler's reminded her of Humphrey Bogart, and Holly smiled at the thought she still had control over one last thing in this life. One last thing...even though it would be unwitnessed by any audience that would appreciate it, it would still be hers.

Her exit line.

The dim outline of the thing shifted position, as if trying to discern whether somebody inhabited the car or not. In silhouette, it looked like a child peeking over a candy counter. Holly supposed in its own grisly way, it was. She gave it a feeble smile, and summoned the last of her strength.

"Here's lookin' at you, kid."

It was barely more than a whisper, but it was enough.

The small horror locked its gaze on the source of her voice, and scrabbled frantically at the edge of the window. The scratch of its claws and shoeless feet made a loud, frenzied staccato against the metal of the door. After a few seconds, the little monster's struggles pulled it over into the car and it immediately launched itself without at the still form in the far seat.

But Holly wasn't there anymore.

Behind the gentle smile, the girl had made her final orbit and fallen down that endless hole into nowhere.

Back at the truck stop, three horrified pair of eyes stared out the windows at the monster that used to be Buddha Boy Norville. It calmly tore a chunk out of Gerald's fleshy head with its teeth as it lumbered towards the gas pumps.

"Oh my God," Rachel breathed aloud in open disbelief, "the poor little bastard was right."

CHAPTER EIGHT: STORMBREAK

Stormbreak - Rachel

"Marisa," Rachel carefully used one of the last strips of cloth available to wrap the end of the girls foot, "I can't tell if you have a broken toe or not...not without an X-ray. Truthfully, I don't think it is. But I can definitely say you aren't going to be winning any footraces for a while, so keep that in mind. Okay?"

The dark haired waitress hugged herself and nodded, not bothering to reply. That worried Rachel more than the injury to the girl's foot.

It's getting to us, the doctor reflected as she glanced around the kitchen. *We're all tired, scared, and starting to wear down. And it just keeps getting worse. Every time something happens, it ends up being worse than before.*

"Hey." She gently shook Marisa's uninjured foot to catch her attention. "You still with us?"

"I'm okay," the girl responded in a distracted voice. "I'm just trying to figure a couple of things out. Have you talked to Harley yet?"

"Not yet." She gently worked Marisa's sock back over her injured foot. "I know he wants to show me something, but first things first. So I've got him doing something for me until I'm done here. Somebody's got to keep you two tough guys patched up, you know."

That elicited just the hint of a smile at the corner of the young woman's mouth.

"Thanks, Doc. So I'm still good to go?"

Rachel eyed the girl judiciously.

"Well, I suppose so." She handed the waitress her shoe, then held up a warning finger as the girl reached to take it. "But you're going to have to use your own judgment, depending on what you're doing. I would recommend you avoid situations that require you to run. Even if you can force yourself to do it, you won't be as fast and you won't be able to keep it up long. And of course, it's going to be sore as hell."

"Yeah, I noticed."

"Just remember," Rachel held her gaze, "we can be as tough as the guys...or at least some of us can...but we have to be smarter about it."

"I know."

I bet you do, Rachel surveyed her patient. *You've been through hell tonight, in more ways than one, but you're still ticking. And if you're willing to do what it takes to get us out of this alive, I guess I shouldn't complain and get on with doing my part.*

"Then you're 'good to go.'" She patted the girl on the leg and turned towards the back hallway. "I guess I better go look at what Harley wants to show me."

"But you don't want to see it, do you."

Rachel stopped and looked back to see Marisa favoring her with an evaluating look of her own.

"No," she admitted. "I'm a veterinarian, not a human doctor. I'm used to the sight of dead animals. But I'm no different about dead human bodies than anybody else. I don't want to see this. Actually, I'm a little scared."

"But what about you at the fire door with your little light?" Marisa cocked her head in curiosity. "You didn't seem bothered at all then."

"Because I stopped viewing those things out there as bodies," Rachel pursed her lips and thought aloud. "Whatever they were...and no matter what they look like...they aren't really corpses anymore. They're...something else."

"Something else?"

"I don't know!" Rachel looked at the ceiling in despair. "It's like they're organisms of some kind now. But they don't make any sense! Gerald said it might be something contagious, but I mocked him for it and treated him like an ass. Now it turns out he was right! And he got killed by something I promised him couldn't happen."

Marisa pulled herself to her feet and gripped Rachel's shoulder.

"Gerald *was* an ass," her voice was low and fierce. "He wasn't right about anything, Doc. He just shot off his mouth without knowing what he was talking about, and things happened to turn out that way. You may know science, but I know people. Gerald was an idiot who got *himself* killed, and even worse he killed the only person who stuck up for him at the same time. On the other hand, you're actually trying to understand this thing. And when you told him that, it was because you believed it. That's *different.*"

"I know," she conceded. "It just doesn't make it feel much better."

"That's because you're not Gerald. Hey, look...believe me, I know what it's like to be scared. Do you want me to come with you?"

Yeah, and even scared you followed Harley into a store with a killer corpse and did what needed doing. This is starting to get embarrassing.

"No, it's okay," Rachel assured her. "I'll be fine. Besides, I won't be alone."

"You sure?" Marisa queried, "I don't mind. After all, I already cried all over *your* shoulder tonight. And since I'm sure I look like a drowned raccoon now, it's not like you're going to be doing me any damage."

"Thanks, Marisa," Rachel laughed. "I won't forget it. But I'll be fine. Besides, now that the bathrooms are open, I think Stacey wants a little company so she can go before she pops."

"Seriously!" the little waitress chimed in while carefully pulling herself up from her place beside Deke, "And while we're there, we'll see if we can de-raccoonify you."

"That bad, huh?" Marisa groaned and fell in step beside her fellow waitress as they headed down the back hallway towards the door to the store.

"Actually, it sort of gives you that wild and tousled look so many guys seem to find sexy."

"Really?"

"Nope, not really. Sorry, but you pretty much look like a rabid raccoon."

Marisa gave a long suffering sigh as she pulled the door open, and rolled her eyes at Rachel who had been following behind. She gave Stacey a friendly shove through the door before making a mock throttling motion behind her back, then followed the smaller girl into the darkened store beyond. The pair of them laughed about something before pushing their way into the girl's bathroom.

This left Rachel standing at the hallway door, trying to see into the gloom of the unlighted store.

All alone.

She knew it was supposedly empty and safe now, yet couldn't help but feel vulnerable while standing at the edge of the darkened area. Tonight just wasn't the night for dark rooms. Harley had come back in here earlier to make sure everything was still dead, but the gloomy store still filled her with unease.

"Harley?" she called in a soft voice. "Hey, Harley? You in here?"

The door to the men's bathroom cracked open, spilling light into the short back hallway of the store.

"I'm in here, Doc."

Now it was Rachel's turn to roll her eyes.

"You want to 'show me something' in the men's bathroom?"

"Yeah." The irony of her remark seemed to be lost on him. "I drug the thing in here so you would have light to see by."

Well, that made sense.

She knew she might as well get it over with. Steeling her nerve, Rachel took a deep breath and marched over to the door. She pushed through with firm resolve, then stopped and sized up the scene in front of her.

Harley knelt on the tile floor by what must have been the creature in question. It wasn't immediately obvious since he had covered it with a vinyl tarp he must have found somewhere in the store. It appeared she would be spared her encounter with a corpse for a moment longer. Still, her eyes were drawn to the blue square of

198

vinyl like reluctant magnets. The tarp was a considerate idea on his part, but it just meant there was one more grisly "reveal" she had to get through.

"Let's just get this over with." She nodded at the covered figure.

"You sure?" Harley asked. "Marisa told you how I killed this thing, right?"

"Yes, she did. She said you beat its brains out with her bat. I understand this won't be pretty, so let's get on with it."

"Well, that's just it." He stared down at the covered form and readjusted his hat. "I beat *something* out of it, but a lot of it wasn't brains."

"What?" Rachel frowned at the man, then down at the figure under the tarp, "What do you mean?"

"Okay, I'll show you. Maybe you can tell me what this stuff is. By the way, there's a trash can under the sink there if you get sick."

Rachel waved the suggestion off with a grimace and bent to look as he slowly pulled the tarp back.

It wasn't pretty.

The thing lay there with what was left of its skull turned to the side. Its head had been beaten down, almost flat, to a level about even with where its ears used to be. Shards of stained bone stuck up through shreds of flaking grey scalp, and a large section of skull had split off from the back and now hung loose by a flap of leathery skin. If it had been dead before...it was deader than dead now.

It was at the hole created by the loose piece of skull that Harley pointed.

"See that?" He indicated a fibrous white material protruding from the wound. "That's not brain. What is it?"

"Well," she winced at the intensified smell caused by him lifting the tarp, "it's an old corpse, Harley. It could be a lot of things...like a product of plain old ordinary decay."

"I don't think so," he muttered. "I finished off the other zombie I had disabled earlier tonight. Its head is full of the same stuff. Two bodies, that must have come from different coffins, and yet the same stuff in both of their heads. What are the odds of that?"

She thought about it for a second and realized he had a point.

"Hmmm," Rachel scowled and bent lower for a better look. "I can't argue with that. It's still probably nothing, but let's see what we have here. You have a stick, or screwdriver, or something?"

"I've got my pocket knife."

"Even better," the veterinarian grunted and got down on her knees beside the body. She pulled the tarp from the rest of it while Harley fished in his pocket for the knife. The sight of the full cadaver didn't bother her as much as she feared. As a matter of fact, the doctor started to feel that the filthy clothes hanging off the thing were the only reminders of its former humanity. She gave it a long slow look from head to foot and realized she had just started the same type of cursory examination she would give if about to perform a necropsy.

And why not? Like you told Marisa, this isn't a person and it isn't exactly a corpse anymore either. It's like some kind of organism, and here is your chance to figure this thing out.

"Okay then," She took the proffered knife and bent to the task, "I guess I get to be the first person in history to perform an autopsy to figure out why something *wasn't* dead. We might as well start with the area in question."

"We?"

"Yep, you killed it, Mister...you get to help me cut it up." Rachel severed the flap of skin holding the hanging piece of skull. "You aren't going to go squeamish on me now, are you? Oh, and get me a roll of toilet paper, please. My operating gloves are out in the truck so I'm going to have to improvise."

"Nah, it ain't squeamishness." Harley stood and went into the nearest of the toilet stalls. "I just don't like staying where I can't see what's going on outside."

He returned with the requested roll, which she took and set beside her. Tearing off a piece, Rachel used it to move the piece of cranium aside. She considered the ruined skull before her then used another piece of tissue to hold a bone fragment as she began to cut that free as well.

The pieces came off easier than she expected.

"Well," she continued talking while she worked; the monster's head was a wreck and pieces came off easily, "I don't think this thing is going to get back up, but I'm not confident enough in that to sit here in a bathroom all alone with it. So I'd appreciate it if you hung around till I'm done. You can stand over there and look out the door if you want but...well, well, well, check this out."

"What is it?" Harley leaned over to look at her handiwork.

Rachel had now removed the side of the cadaver's skull facing upwards, revealing a side view of the brainpan's contents.

"This," she indicated a squashed, grayish area in the rear half of the head, "is brain." It filled about half to two thirds of the skull. "This..." she now indicated the white fibers filling the rest of the cranium, "isn't brain. But you knew that. Have you had medical training, Harley?"

"Nah, not exactly," he followed her demonstration with intent interest, "just some fairly basic field first aid. Stuff like that. So show me what I didn't know."

"Uh huh." She eyed him doubtfully then continued. "Well, notice how these threads seem to flow towards the back of the skull and then downwards. I'm betting..." She used the knife to cut out a piece of the brain and then set it aside. "Yep...looky here."

"What am I looking at, Doc?"

"It's not just on the outside of the brain, it's penetrating into it. And mainly into the hindbrain areas, which are the most intact." she tilted her head, concentrating, then cut deeper and lifted another piece out of the way. "Interesting."

"What do you mean?"

"Well, it seems to continue on down the brain stem to the *foramen magnum.*"

"The whozit?"

"The hole at the bottom of the skull." She frowned at the indicated area. "It's especially thick here, and now

it's back on the outside again too. Hmmm...I wonder..."
She inserted the knife into the mass.

The corpse thrashed, causing Rachel to scream and
both of them to dive away from it.

Suddenly, the bathroom seemed a very small place.
The veterinarian scrambled backwards in a blind panic,
trying to put as much distance as possible between her and
the flailing body. That resulted in her smacking into the
wall and clanging the back of her head against the bottom
of a urinal hard enough to see stars. The pain blinded her,
filling her vision with exploding fireworks...but it didn't
slow her down from scrabbling under the nearby divider
into a toilet stall.

Any shelter in a storm.

Rachel struggled to her feet, and immediately
clambered up onto the john. She put her hands against
each side of the stall for balance and froze in place. Her
heart hammered in her ears. She took a few seconds to get
her breath back under control, and for her vision to clear,
then tried listening...

Nothing.

No sounds of fighting, screaming, or even feet
shuffling to indicate what could be happening on the other
side of that divider. Just the soft sound of the fan. Rachel
strained her hearing for any clue of what might be going
on.

Still nothing.

After a couple more seconds of silence she decided
to risk making noise of her own.

"Harley?" she called softly.

"Yeah, Doc?"

He couldn't have sounded more nonchalant if he
tried. She already had a pretty good idea what had
happened...as impossible as it seemed...but the idea of him
just waiting out there grinning about the event really ticked
her off.

"I'm guessing you're okay?" she asked sweetly
through clenched teeth.

"Other than a mild heart attack, yeah." At least it
didn't sound like he was laughing. "It looks like you hit a

nerve on that thing. It ain't doing nothing now. I think it's safe."

"No," she retorted. "Actually, it may not be safe. Here, take this."

Rachel climbed down and slid the pocket knife under the divider and back into the room. She heard the sound of his boots approach, and then stop.

"Okay," he answered. "But it ain't doing nothing. Besides, I've still got the bat."

"Harley, listen to me."

"Okay."

"I want you to cut its head off."

"You want me to what?! Seriously?"

"Yes." She felt foolish as hell talking from inside the stall, but if the inkling of a theory she had forming was even near correct...if those threads were doing what she thought they were... "Can you do that?"

"Sure...I guess," she could hear the shrug in his voice. "If that's what you want."

"That's what I want."

"Okay, just a minute."

She heard him approach the body, then stop again. The tarp rustled, and she realized he was imitating her trick with the tissues and using it as a way to hold its head still without touching it. There came a surprisingly short period of rhythmic rustling of the tarp she knew had to be caused by him holding it against the things head while he sawed on the neck, then the clomp of his boots returning to the stall.

"Okay, Doc. All done."

"Tell me you aren't standing out there with the head in your hands."

"I'm not." Now he laughed. "It's down by the thing's feet. What the *hell*, Doc?"

"Sorry," she grouched and came out the door of the stall. "I'm just rattled and jumpy. And I've got a real bad feeling about what I've seen so far."

"Fair enough." Harley didn't seem insulted and followed her back over to the now headless body.

Rachel noted the head laying down between its feet and thought about asking Harley to move it so she could roll the corpse over and dissect the spine. Then a second idea occurred and she decided there was no need to bother. Retrieving Harley's knife she pulled the thing's arm out to the side and rolled up its sleeve. Making sure it's hand laid palm down on the floor, the veterinarian then cut a long, slow incision down the back of the forearm. Once finished, she spread the dead skin apart and immediately spotted what she was looking for.

"See that?" She pointed to thin grey and white line running between two blackened muscles.

"Yeah." His brow knitted as he stared into the incision. "What is it?"

"That's the radial nerve. But now it has a companion."

"The same stuff?"

"Yeah," she sighed. "The same stuff."

"So what does it mean?"

"Well, it means my first theory was correct. When I told Marisa earlier that something had hijacked these things nervous systems, I didn't know how right I was. This stuff has both taken it over and replaced it at the same time."

"What do you mean?"

"I mean whatever this material is, it operates independent of the host at the same time it's fusing with it. I'm afraid what it means to you is that you're going to have to go behead all the other bodies in this store. This stuff can heal independent of injury done to the body, which means you're probably lucky the thing you disabled earlier didn't get back up when you and Marisa went into the store. I guarantee it would have at some point. "

"Aw, hell. Gladys and the other guy too?"

"I'm afraid so," She laid a sympathetic hand on his arm. "You saw the trucker Stacey calls Buddha Boy outside."

"Yeah," Harley sighed. "Crap..."

"I know, I'm sorry." She patted his arm then pulled back her hand and turned her attention back to the corpse.

"But now it's time to solve mystery number two. Why the hell are these things eating at all?"

"Because they're zombies and they woke up hungry? What do you mean?"

"I mean," she muttered as she ripped open the corpse's shirt, exposing a grey chest and abdomen, "that outside of Hollywood, 'zombies' don't make sense. The pancreas deteriorates into a puddle of digestive enzymes not long after death, and literally digests the rest of the organs in the lower abdomen. Embalming only slows the process, not stops it. There's a reason the ancient Egyptians used to pull the organs out of their dead before mummifying them."

"Damn," Harley looked at her with respect. "How do you know all this?"

"Believe it or not," Rachel chuckled, "they teach us 'animal doctors' a thing or two in college as well. Heck, sometimes they even let us read books."

"Sorry. I didn't mean it like that."

"I know, no problem. The point is, the corpses we've seen tonight shouldn't have any internal organs to speak of...at least not below the diaphragm. So there should be no point in them eating anything...yet they do. I wonder why that is?"

Harley shrugged and said nothing.

"Well," she muttered and placed the knife at the bottom of the corpse's sternum, "it's time to find out. This might not smell very good.."

She braced herself for the stench, and pushed the blade into the corpse's belly. The embalmed muscles were stiff, and it took a surprising amount of effort on her part to force it all the way in. Then using two hands on the handle, she braced herself and pulled downward, slowly slicing through the cadaver's abdominal muscles until she reached its groin.

"Whew!" Rachel wiped her brow then starting folding herself two large pads of toilet paper. "That was harder than it looked. Now, let's see if we can figure out what makes these things tick."

Taking a pad of tissue in each hand and holding them like potholders, she pushed them into the incision and pulled it wide. It opened with a wet, viscous ripping sound magnified by the tiled walls.

A second later both Rachel and Harley peered into the exposed cavity.

"What the hell?" Harley muttered. "It's just more of the same stuff! Only it's not white."

The body's abdomen appeared to be stuffed with pink cotton candy.

"Actually, this is beginning to make an ugly kind of sense," Rachel murmured and used the knife to probe into the mass. A few seconds later, she retracted the tool with a dark lump impaled on its blade. She examined it for a couple of seconds, then closed her eyes and scraped it off against the monsters leg.

"What was that?"

"That," she took a deep breath, then exhaled slowly, "was a piece of Gladys. It was being directly absorbed through the cell walls of the biomass, which is why the stuff is pink. And that pretty much tells me what it is..."

"It does?" the tall young man leaned back and looked at her in surprise. "What is it, Doc?"

Rachel looked down at the dissected corpse for a second, her face a mask of incredulity, then looked back at him.

"It's a fungus, Harley," she said it as if she could barely believe it herself. "It's a goddamned fungus!"

"A fungus?" Deke frowned. "You mean like a mushroom?"

"Not exactly." Rachel leaned back against the sink, ruefully aware that once again all eyes in the kitchen were on her. "A mushroom is a fungus, but most funguses aren't mushrooms. They can look like a lot of things...from mushrooms, to furry patches of bark...microscopic cells...or like this stuff....cotton or hairlike roots. There are all kinds of them. And now it seems we've discovered a new type. One that can animate a corpse, and can also be passed from killer to victim."

"Lucky us," Grandpa Tom growled. "So not only do we have to worry about all the dead people from the cemetery up the road, but everybody they killed too. Christ! How many have they killed here so far?"

"I have no idea," the doctor sighed, "but it's probably safe to assume the big monster who killed Gerald ain't the only one out there."

"So who all do we know is dead or missing?" Harley asked as he watched out the diamond shaped window of the kitchen door. "Maybe we can build a rough idea from that. We can exclude Gladys and the customer in the store...I don't want to go into it, but I made sure they won't be getting back up. And we can be pretty sure Gerald ain't going to be either. Holly is a possibility, but since that just happened it will be a while."

The room went quiet as people turned the question over in their heads.

"There was Arnold, Leon, and Tomas working out back," Marisa stared at the ceiling, "and we saw Lizzie...err Libby...walking back there too." The raven haired waitress winced at using the nickname on the prostitute when she realized the woman must have died horribly back there. "And there were five or six rigs lined up."

"So, about ten." Harley nodded. "I've been counting and I keep coming up with a count of around forty of these bastards, so we're talking about a twenty five percent increase in their numbers if all those people get up. So far, we've only seen one though."

"Well, you aren't going to see Arnold, Tomas, or Leon," Stacey said in a quiet voice. Once again her face took on the tight look from earlier and Deke pulled her in close beside him. "They were...all over the garage back there. Those things tore them to pieces."

Rachel considered that and realized she had been missing the obvious.

"You know, now that you mention it, I might have been wrong. You're probably not going to see any of the initial victims," she mused aloud. "These things woke up hungry, and there are a lot of them. They probably pretty much devoured all the people they first ran into. But by the time they got to the big guy, they must have already eaten a bunch of people and weren't so hungry. They still chewed a pretty good bit out of him too...but he might be the only one."

"Let's hope so," Harley replied. "Because he bothers me. He's not just bigger and stronger; I think he operates on a different level than the others as well. I don't like the way he occasionally looks around. None of the others do it, only him."

Rachel thought about that for a moment too.

"It may be due to him having a fresher nervous system for this stuff to work with," she theorized. "He might be more advanced than the rest of them. The way he acted when he attacked Gerald and Holly would certainly suggest it. He went right to the driver's side door and smashed in the window instead of scrabbling at it like the others."

"Okay then," Harley looked around the kitchen, "in that case I think we need to find a way to block this door. The one to the store locks, but this one doesn't. Somebody might want to think about organizing a quiet run up front to the store while it's still dark and pulling all the food they can get back here."

"Is that safe?"

"We don't have a lot of choice. We also need to knock out this hallway light so it doesn't shine through every time the door is opened and catch something's attention. I also recommend no more trips out of here unless it's to the bathroom, and be sure and go before dawn. I think the rain is already starting to ease up as it is so these things are going to be able to see inside soon."

"How long is it till dawn anyway?" Rachel rubbed her eyes and stifled a yawn.

In the last few hours she had been in a fight for survival at the back door with man-eating monsters, raced to stop one man from bleeding to death, tended four other wounded people, consoled one half hysterical young woman, and performed her first autopsy on the body of a human being. She was exhausted. And the truly frightening part was the knowledge she was one of the last uninjured and healthy people in the room.

The cuts on Harley's forearms were superficial, the result of grappling with the monster in the store, and he ignored them. Marisa's foot injury seemed minor, but Rachel knew it hurt and could be a problem if the girl had to move fast. Deke's shoulder was worse from punching Gerald, and the doctor knew the muscle probably needed to be stitched up to prevent it from tearing even further. Stacey's arm lacerations were painful but not debilitating, but the massive bruise on her ribs had to hurt. And Grandpa Tom...

...she was way over her head with that situation. Whatever happened to the old trucker was probably going to happen, and she could do damn little for him. He looked a lot better, but she noticed he still hadn't found a reason to get up off his crate yet. He needed a hospital...now. The same held true for the little janitor, lying bundled on the floor.

So if something happened to Harley or Marisa...it would be time for Dr. Rachel Sutherland, DVM to put on her action hero cape.

But until then, she could really use a nap.

"It's four in the morning, Doc." Stacey pointed over at a time clock on the back wall. "It will start to lighten up in about two hours. Sunrise won't be for almost another hour afterwards though."

"Okay then," Rachel realized Harley had just left the delegation of chores to her, "then we better make the most of it. Stacey, can you and Deke sneak up to the store and start bringing food back here?"

"Sure. C'mon, Deke." The two headed down the back hallway, hand in hand.

"Tom?" she turned to the old trucker on the crate, "I don't want you to push yourself, but I could use some of that male handiness with mechanical stuff I'm sure you're just brimming with. Everything big in this kitchen looks bolted down, and I would appreciate it if you would just kind of look stuff over and see which you think would be the easiest to get loose and be used to block the door. Can you do that?"

"No problem, Doc."

"Well Harley, that leaves...hey! Where are you two going?"

Harley had already started down the hallway towards the store, escorted by Marisa and her bat.

"I'm...err..." he spared a quick glance at Marisa, "...*we're* going to get a better look at things. There is a storeroom next to the coolers on the store side, and I wanted to check it for tools and stuff. Then I intend to find out more about what we're up against. When I was dragging those bodies into the store cooler I noticed some rungs set in the wall going up to a hatch in the roof."

"Is this wise?" She folded her arms and fixed a level look at him.

"It's actually my specialty, Doc. I know what I'm doing. Besides, I've got Marisa watching my back."

"Fine," Rachel sighed, "if you're going to be out there then put some extra effort in looking for a way out of this place. There's something I didn't say earlier because I didn't want Deke and Stacey to hear it, but I think you two need to know this.

"Oookaayyyy..." Harley and Marisa stopped and looked at each other, then back at her.

"Gerald may have been right about something else, too," the veterinarian continued. "This stuff may infect living people as well."

"*Mierde*!" Marisa hissed, "Are you serious!?"

"Yeah," Rachel looked from one to the other, "It would be slower, because we have something dead people don't...an immune system. And it would probably depend on the seriousness of the initial exposure, such as being wounded by one of these things. But there is a good chance we've all been exposed to one degree or another."

"But you're saying," Harley frowned in concentration, "that those of us who were actually clawed by those things have the greatest risk."

"Yes. And bites are likely even worse. While I've tried to clean all the wounds, those are the injuries where people are actually getting infected tissue come into contact with internal tissue of their own. And the deeper the injury, the greater the risk of infection since I can only clean so deep."

The two chewed that one over a second before Marisa put her free hand to her forehead.

"Oh no...Benny."

"And Deke," Rachel whispered. "Those two have the worst exposure. There is no way I got everything out of their wounds. But Harley, you and Stacey aren't out of the woods by a long shot. You guys are a close second on the danger list. And if these things have been releasing any kind of spores, then we may all be infected. The truth is, we would have been better off if Gerald's virus theory had been the case. This could end up being a lot worse."

"So we're screwed." Marisa dropped her hand and met Rachel's eyes with a level glare. "Nothing we do really matters because we're all going to turn into these things anyway. Or at least some of us are."

"Maybe. I still think it's going to depend on the severity of the exposure. We need to keep a close eye on Benny."

"Keep an eye on Benny? Why? Nobody is doing anything to Benny!"

"Easy," Rachel soothed, recognizing the flash of protective anger in the waitress's eyes. "It's nothing like that. I'm a doctor, remember? I don't hurt people. Besides, there is another reason I'm bringing this up."

"What's that?" Harley cut off whatever Marisa was about to say.

"I may have a solution to this problem...if we can just get to it."

"What do you mean, 'get to it?'"

"Well, the one bit of hope in all this," Rachel continued, "is now that I know what I'm dealing with I can start approaching it as something to be treated. I have an anti-fungal medication out in my truck that may go a long way towards protecting us, if we can get it before being infected too long."

"You mean you can cure this stuff?" Marisa brightened visibly. "Holy hell, Doc! That changes everything!"

"No, I didn't say that," Rachel cautioned. "I said I could fight it. The medicine in my truck would need to be administered early in the infection. Fungal infections can be real bastards to beat once their deeply entrenched, and this stuff appears aggressive. I've got other medicine at my office which would work a lot better, but you let this crap go on too long and I don't know if even it would work. Once it has taken over the nervous system, I doubt anything could save a person then."

"So our priorities have changed," Harley nodded, "Got it."

"We need to get to my truck or somewhere else I can get some medicine. Either way, we have to get out of here."

"What am I looking for, if I make it to your truck, Doc?"

"Harley..." Marisa warned but the tall man held up his hand.

"It's in a red tackle box with a white lid," Rachel answered. "You'll find it in the large toolbox in the back of my truck. Just lift the lid and it should be right on top to the right. The toolbox is locked, though. If you come up with a way to go for it, be sure and get the key from me first."

"Right. Anything else?"

"Not really," the veterinarian sighed, "other than to emphasize that time is not our friend here. Having Deke and Stacey get supplies keeps them busy, and gives them something constructive to keep their spirits up, but holing up and trying to wait these things out is probably not a realistic option."

"Understood." Harley changed direction and headed back towards the kitchen. "I had been thinking we would spend today hiding out back here and try something tomorrow night, but if we are running out of time then I'll go straight to Plan B."

Rachel watched the tall man go back into the kitchen and head for the restaurant door.

"Plan B?" She caught Marisa's arm as the girl started to follow after him.

"Beats me," the girl grouched, "I didn't even know what Plan A was. He never tells me anything. We're gonna have to work on that."

Stormbreak - Marisa

"Harley!"

Marisa pushed through the door into the restaurant and used a convenient flare of lightning to locate the man standing at the other end of the room.

He peered with folded arms out the last side window towards the diesel pumps. She noticed he had already pulled a toothpick from his hat brim and now chewed it as he stared out into the storm.

"So," She marched over to him and faced him with hands on hips. "Plan B?"

"Yeah," he exhaled around the toothpick, his mind obviously elsewhere.

Marisa stared at him for a moment, and when he didn't speak again reached out and tapped him firmly on the shoulder.

"Harley," she growled, "I don't want to complain or anything, but being your wingman seems to involve an awful lot of standing around wondering what the hell you're up to. You want to help me out with that?"

"Huh?" He seemed to come back to himself and turned to her.

"I said," She folded her arms and glared at him, "Doc was sort of wondering about Plan B. But I thought instead of just telling her it was something crazy that would most likely get you killed, I would come in and get all the juicy details first. That way it looks like you at least trust your wingman enough to tell her what's up before you run off and get eaten. You do trust me, right?"

"Trust you?" He looked confused at the direction the conversation had taken. "Of course I trust you."

"Oh good!" she snapped. "Because me being a silly girl and all, I got this crazy idea you might be holding out on me there for a second. But then I realized you surely wouldn't do that because I told you before, I've got your back...even if I don't like what you're about to do. Right?"

Marisa could feel her temper begin to rise and reined it back in. She wasn't really looking for a fight, but this needed to be settled.

"Right," he agreed, still looking nonplussed.

"Good, because what I am NOT, is a sidekick. *Comprende*? That's Deke. What I am is the person who needs to know what you're thinking so I can do my part right. Who knows, I might even come up with an angle or two that will give whatever plan you're cooking up a better chance of working."

"Marisa, I..."

"No," She surprised him by putting a finger to his lips. "Hear me out, okay?"

He stopped, then nodded in the dark.

"Like I told Doc, she may know science but I know people. I can tell you've been trying to protect us, and I don't mean by just fighting these things when you got the chance. You've been cool as ice through this whole thing. You had already figured out what was going on in town earlier tonight, and you didn't say anything until you didn't have a choice. You knew how freaked out we all already were, and you wanted to spare us that while you could. You had probably already figured out where these...things...were coming from as well..."

His lack of reply was all the answer she needed on that one.

"Yeah," she set her jaw and nodded. "I thought so. And the worst part is, you're still doing it."

The ever present grin on his face grew decidedly pained, and she knew she had scored again.

"So here's the deal, Harley." She stepped up and looked at him with solemn eyes. "We're just going to start over and try again, okay? Only instead of me being your 'wingman,' we'll be partners in this thing. I've still got your back, but no more secrets, and no hiding things from your partner. I know we barely know each other, but I really need to trust you. *Comprende?* And I know the only way that is going to happen is if you trust me too...so let's start over. I'll go first..."

"First?" Harley's smile took on a confused look.

Instead of answering right away, Marisa took a step back, squared her shoulders, then fixed the taller man with a serious look.

"*Hola.*" she said with grave formality. "My name is Marisa Odalys Jacinta Valdez, and I am your new partner. I work here at the Textro while saving up for school. I know I'm a girl, but I am not a china doll. The thing with Vicki caught me by surprise, and it hurt me, but I'll be okay. My toe is sore, but I used to be an athlete and I've played hurt before...so I'm okay there too. I am tougher than I look, but I'm not an idiot and I won't do anything stupid just to prove myself. I like chocolates, drive-in movies, and men who respect me enough to tell me the truth. My turn-offs are politics, professional wrestling, and dead people who are trying to eat me. Okay, now you go..." She folded her arms and looked at him expectantly.

The man stared at her, his face a mask of surprise.

"Your turn," she prompted. "Go ahead."

Harley looked at her a couple of seconds more, then recovered.

"Okay, you win," he sighed, then met her with the same serious look she had assumed earlier.

"Hi. I'm Sergeant Harley Wayne Daughtry. I was a scout in the US Army and assigned to a sniper squad in Afghanistan, where I served two tours of duty. My primary assignments were penetrating into hostile territory, gathering and assessing intelligence, and the hunting and neutralization of Taliban fighters. I got out a few months back, and now I'm just kind of easing back into life here in the states. My main, overriding objective tonight is to get everybody out of here alive, and somewhere safe."

He paused a second, then continued in a slightly lighter tone. "I like chicken fried steaks, fishing, and people who don't give up. I haven't really made a list of turn-offs yet. Should I?"

"It helps."

"Okay, I'll try and work on that." He tilted back his hat, and looked at her with unconcealed curiosity. "So now what?"

"Now we see if you mean it." Marisa slid into the booth beside them and indicated the bench across the table from her. "So tell me, how bad do you think it really is out there."

Harley appeared to think about it a second, then eased himself into the seat.

"Well, if Houston or San Antonio had sent any kind of help, we should have seen something by now. The fact they haven't can mean several different things. Either they don't know enough about what's going on here to respond, or this is going on in several places and they can't respond to all of them at once, or they have the same problem we have. Without more information, I can't tell more than that. Masonfield, is a different matter though."

"What about Masonfield, Harley?"

His face tightened, as if he regretted mentioning it, and the look he gave her was both somber and grim. She realized immediately what he was thinking.

"Yes, I have family in Masonfield," she answered his unspoken question. "But I need you to tell me anyway. That's the deal. That's the way this works. Besides, we already know they have trouble over there."

Harley nodded and folded his arms on the table. Taking the toothpick out of his mouth, he examined it for a second before tossing it into the ashtray. Then he turned his head and looked out into the storm as he continued.

"By this time," he spoke softly, "all the people who were killed at the football game have gotten up and joined the zombies from the cemetery. Actually, enough time has now passed that their initial victims may have gotten up as

216

well. There would be hundreds of them, maybe over a thousand. And these new ones tend to wander around more, so all those who got up probably spread out through town as well. By now I estimate the only survivors are probably a few people who went to bed early and have slept through this entire thing. They'll die as soon as they get up and go outside tomorrow."

"You're sure about that?" Marisa closed her eyes and took a deep shuddering breath. She had half expected something like this, but hearing it confirmed with such finality still felt like a punch to the heart.

"Yeah...I'm sure," His voice sounded flat. "It's already over. That's not guesswork, but simple mathematics. Losing their police and having all those people die at the same time created the perfect storm of events. Even if some people holed up, they would have been overwhelmed. I'm sorry, Marisa, but Masonfield is dead."

The two sat unspeaking, the rain thrumming against the windows

I'm not going to cry, Marisa swallowed and clenched her jaw. *I am NOT going to cry. If I do, I might not be able to stop...and Stacey and Benny need me. There will be a time for crying later.*

She opened her eyes to see Harley looking at her with obvious concern. It didn't take a genius to realize he must be wondering if this latest news, on top of the shock of encountering her dead sister, was going to be the straw that brought her down.

And the thought of that pissed her off.

She had told him to stop protecting her and to be honest. Now that he had, she would be damned if his doing so would break her. She had told him she was strong, and Marisa meant to live up to it. She had to. Benny and Stacey needed her, and she refused to collapse and let them down.

She would hang on to that, if nothing else. Until her friends were out of here and safe, she was going to keep it together. After that...well, to hell with after that.

For now, she would deal with now.

217

"Okay, Harley," she took another deep breath, then met his eyes with a level gaze of her own, "Now tell me about Plan B."

His eyes searched her face for a few seconds before he leaned back in his chair, apparently satisfied with what he saw. The brief look of respect that crossed his features gratified her enormously.

"Yeah, Plan B..." He reached up and pulled another toothpick from his hat brim. "Plan B is how I'm going to get all of us out of here in the next thirty minutes. But I don't think you're going to like it. It has what you would call 'Hey guys, watch this," written all over it."

Stormbreak – Deke

Deke leaned against the back wall of the darkened store, holding Stacey tightly in his arms.

The storm of emotions whirling through him matched the one outside. He was injured, his mom was either in danger or dead, and the girl who sat firmly at the center of his universe was hurt both in body and psyche. He couldn't do anything about the first two situations, and the last one confused the boy and made him feel hopelessly ineffectual. The little waitress would perk up from time to time and put on a good show, but then quickly revert to just wanting him to hold her. She said it made her feel safe.

He didn't know whether to believe her or not.

She would cling to him tightly, not crying, and not saying a thing. But from time to time a shudder would run through her small frame and he would worry. It pained Deke to admit it, but he felt helpless and over his head here. He almost wished Marisa was more available to talk to the girl. She had been Stacey's first choice to run to when this nightmare had first started. He felt a small stab of jealousy about that, but had the honesty to admit the the other woman would have probably done a better job than he had so far.

218

So here he stood with the girl of his dreams wrapped in his arms, and him submerged in an agony of self doubt.

What would Harley do? Oh hell, who am I kidding? If I was Harley I wouldn't even be worried about this because she really would feel "safe" with me. He's already taken out two of these things single handedly. So far I've managed to climb a wall, break a desk, and get my ass kicked by a little old lady zombie. And Stacey had to rescue ME from IT! I gotta step it up here. But how? Now I'm hurt and more useless than before.

Stacey shivered again and tightened her grip on him. He returned the gesture with his uninjured arm, not knowing what else to do. Having the amazingly built little waitress press so tight against him should have been a fantasy come true, but right now those kind of thoughts were a million miles away. Right now, he just wanted her to be alright.

"Stacey?" he whispered. "Are you okay?"

She didn't say anything, but he felt her nod her head against his chest.

"What are you thinking?" he probed, hunting anything to give him an idea what to do.

"I'm not."

He sighed, not knowing where to go with that.

"I wish there was something I could do for you. If there is, anything at all, just tell me."

"You're doing it."

Deke resisted the impulse to sigh again and stared at the ceiling. The frustration in him mounted. Part of him understood this was what he needed to be doing right now, but another rebelled at the idea of Harley taking care of business without him helping. Hell, worse than that, he'd been replaced by a girl...even if it was by a scary girl like Marisa. As much as he adored the feel of Stacey in his arms, he should have been with Harley fighting these things. He exhaled in exasperation at this turn of events.

A soft chuckle from the girl in his arms brought him back into the present.

"I must be slipping," Stacey looked up at him with surprisingly merry eyes. "Because I get the definite feeling you want to be doing something else. Dumping me so soon?"

"No!" Deke hugged her tight. Suddenly Harley could take care of himself again. "Hey, I will stand here and hold you all night if you want. That's my job, and I'm glad to have it."

She continued to look up at him a moment more, then that famous smile spread into existence and seemed to light up her face in the dark.

"MmHmm," she nodded to herself with a pleased expression. "Definitely nice. But I can see it's my turn to take care of you for a little bit."

"Huh?"

"You're a guy, and I can tell you're dying to do something...useful. You don't know what yet, but if I don't figure something out you'll come up with it yourself. At least this way I'll have some input and can limit the damage."

"I'm that obvious, huh? I'm sorry. I meant it about holding you all night."

"I know," she smiled at him. "And you'll get your chance, because it really does help me. But this is a two way relationship, which means I help you too."

Relationship? Holy shit! When did that happen?! Not that I'm bitching or anything!

"So," Stacey continued, "we've already got all the chips and junk food moved into the back. What else would be a good idea to grab while we're in here?"

Deke's eyes roved the darkened store, trying to imagine anything that might make a difference. Something Doc might have forgotten about. Other than food and drinks, what did they really need? He racked his brains, trying to come up with an answer, when his gaze settled on the spot where Gladys met her end. The dark mounds of rubble marked where the cigarette rack had crashed down on the glass counter display. His stomach got a bit queasy, but an idea started to form.

"Hey Stacey? Who's got the store keys?"

"I think Marisa does. Why?"

"Well," Deke pondered aloud. "I remember her saying Gladys had the other set, but I don't remember them turning up when Harley moved all the bodies to the cooler."

"No," Stacey frowned. "But I do remember him coming back with the car keys from the customer who died up there with her."

"Yeah, so he must have gone through their pockets when he put them back there. That would only make sense."

"True. But," Stacey held up a finger, "that would also be why he didn't find Gladys's keys. She kept hers in a purse."

"And her purse," Deke continued the thought, "must have gotten knocked to the floor or buried under the rubble when they attacked Gladys. So Gladys's keys are still in here, and it might be a good idea to find them so we have a spare."

Deke finished on a triumphant note. He could still do something important that would help everybody else. Not to mention, showing up in the back with the spare set of keys would make him feel more like a contributing member in this little group of survivors. He might be "rear echelon" now, but he was still a functioning member who was making a difference.

The boy started towards the front, then realized he was alone. He turned to see Stacey had only taken a couple half steps before going pale and somber.

"Yeaaahhhh..." the girl hesitated. "Uh, Deke? I don't mean to be a downer, but Gladys *died* over there, and I'm not really crazy about the idea of crawling around in her blood."

That brought his enthusiasm to a lurching halt.

Now that she mentioned it, the thought didn't really appeal to him either. He had never particularly liked Gladys, but he did know her. The woman had been a bit of a grouch in his direction, yet she had also been a part of his world since he was a little kid. The realization she had been standing there a mere nine hours earlier when her world came to a violent end was a bit unsettling.

"Right," he agreed. "I hear that. I guess I got excited and I wasn't thinking."

He came back and started to lean back against the wall again but Stacey caught his arm. The pained look on her face caught his attention even more.

"No, Deke," she sighed. "You were right. It's an excellent idea. Somebody really should have thought of it earlier. It might even be a lifesaver if we get separated, or if the zombies get into one side of the truck stop when Marisa isn't near the inside door. I just let the idea of Gladys dying there rattle me for a second."

"Hey, it's okay." He put a hand on her shoulder. "You've already had a hell of a night. I'll tell you what...I'll go see if I can find the purse while you just hang back on this one."

"Hell of a night?" she echoed with a hollow laugh. "*Everybody* has had a hell of a night. It's not right for me to suddenly pull a dainty princess routine while you carry the load."

"I don't mind. Besides, I don't think you're being a 'dainty princess,' Stacey."

"Really? What would you call it?"

Deke studied her for a second, realizing she was trying to work herself up to doing this. Yet one look at her face told him it was the last thing she should be trying to do. She had been tough as hell tonight, but it had taken its toll and she wasn't ready for this.

"I call it not wanting to tromp around in your coworker's blood," he answered with a shrug. "Besides, you saved my butt tonight so you're entitled to three 'dainty princess' moments. This will be number one. Okay?"

Stacey didn't answer right away.

"Okay?" Deke pressed.

"I guess." The girl managed to look doubtful but grateful all at the same time. "Are you sure about this?"

"Yep," the boy said over his shoulder as he started back towards the front. "Besides, it's still standing in water up there and I'm the one wearing boots. So this really counts as just being practical."

Stacey didn't reply, but Deke was gratified to see she remained behind.

Now he could focus on getting something done.

###

Stormbreak - Marisa

Still reeling inside from his revelation about Masonfield, Marisa struggled to digest this latest statement. Normally, she would have probably said something disbelieving or sarcastic, but right now she just didn't have it in her.

"That bad, huh? This plan of yours must really be something."

"Well, it's elegant." He put the toothpick in his mouth and nodded towards the window. "But it has a couple of doozies for kinks. First things first, though...you wouldn't happen to know the owner of that truck out there, would you?"

Marisa looked out the window, grateful that this particular pane didn't feature a corpse staring back in at her. The diesel pumps shimmered in the distance under their awning lights. The lone Peterbilt parked beside them seemed like a relic from a bygone world...a world that ended nine distant hours ago.

"Yeah. That's Grandpa Tom's truck."

She looked over to see Harley exhale in obvious relief.

"Good," he murmured. "At least we have the keys to it. There's one less problem to deal with."

"Okay," she pressed, "but it's no different than our cars. We can't get to it. Especially now that that jackass managed to draw the rest of those *putos* up here before getting his stupid ass killed."

"Actually," Harley chewed the toothpick as he stared through the running glass, "that may end up working in our favor. I wonder how many are left around back."

Marisa tried to figure out where he was going with this.

"Who knows?" she shrugged. "I guess we could go up to the roof and count them. But why?"

"Because," he answered while peering up at the black sky, "I seem to remember there is a power line running from the roof of this building over to the awning over the diesel pumps. I can't see it right now due to the darkness and the storm, but I'm pretty sure it's there."

"It is," Marisa confirmed, now looking up into the blackness herself. "Every so often some trucker frets about hitting it, but it's too high."

She stopped a second, as the implication hit her.

"Harley, I know what you're thinking," she turned back from the window towards him. "But it won't work. That's a power cable. You try to climb out on it and you're just going to get electrocuted. Especially in the rain!"

He glanced back over at her, his grin now back in place, even if it did look a little tight.

"As it is now, yeah," he agreed. "That's one of the main reasons this wasn't Plan A. But if we cut the power, everything changes."

She looked out at the distant pumps, then back at the man.

"Maybe," she conceded. Personally, she thought it looked like a hell of a long climb, even for a guy in Harley's shape. "But how do we knock out the power?"

"Well, right there is where this starts to get kind of hairy. The only way to do that will be to cut it off at the breaker box. You wouldn't happen to know where those are, would you?"

"Sure," she frowned, "They're in the back hall. You've passed them a bunch of times."

"No, those are the internal breakers. Those would be for the stoves, coolers, and other stuff inside. What I'm talking about will be outside, probably on the back wall somewhere. They'll be big metal boxes, maybe with handles on the sides...and they'll have padlocks."

She stared at him wide-eyed.

"Harley, you can't be thinking of going out there."

"I'm sort of out of choices," he shrugged. "So, do you know where they are?"

"Yes, they're on the back wall near the corner on the left as you go out the door. But what are you going to do? Go out there and start going through keys till you find the right one? I don't think those evil bastards are going to stand around and let you do that."

"No, you're right," he conceded, "I won't have time for that. My only chance will be to sneak down there real fast, clip the wire on the meter collar, and pull the electric meter out. That'll cut the power to everything, but if Doc's right then we can't stay here anyway."

"Harley, this is *loco*. You can't go out there! You'll get killed and that won't help us. Besides, even if you do make it, then what? Can you really make a climb like that? Can you? That's a hell of a long way, and it's raining." She reached over and gently tapped the bandages on his forearm. "I know you're tough, Harley, but those have to hurt."

"They won't be an issue," he replied.

She studied him for a second, understanding what he said wasn't braggadocio, but just a simple assertion. At the same time, she understood this had been "Plan B" for a reason. Harley had his doubts, even if he wasn't voicing them.

"Fine, but even if they don't bother you...and even if you do make the climb...then what? None of the rest of us could make it, or would have any other way of getting out there to join you."

"That's the easy part," he grinned. "I'll just pull the truck over by the store, and everybody can use a table or something to climb over to the top of the trailer from the roof. Then I'll take a nice leisurely cruise down to the rest area a couple of miles down the road and ya'll can get off there. Everybody gets wet, but nobody else gets eaten. What do you think?"

Marisa stared across the dim table at Harley as she turned this new scenario over in her mind.

The simplicity of the solution stunned her.

And it *was* a solution. It would work...it would actually work. After all the blood, death, terror, and tears over the past nine hours, the whole lot of them could be saved by something as simple as hopping onto the back of a parked truck from the roof.

Assuming Harley could reach that truck.

She fought down the surge of excitement and refocused on the problem of the power cable. She didn't really share Harley's confidence in this plan. Hell, she didn't even share his pretended confidence in this plan. The idea of any one of them stepping back outside filled her with dread.

"I don't know," Marisa muttered as she struggled between the hope of all of them riding off to safety on the roof of the truck...and the mental image of Harley being caught and torn to pieces at the breaker boxes out back. "I don't like this. There has to be another way."

"Well if there is," Harley sighed as he scooted his way back out of the booth and stood up, "you're gonna have to come up with it in the next ten minutes. We're running out of time, and I need to get moving."

"Where to?" Marisa stood up to follow him.

"First the roof," he answered as they started for the door. "I'll need to get a count and position on every zombie out back of the truck stop. When I go out there, I don't feel like running into any nasty surprises."

"I'm right behind you."

Harley stopped a second and looked at her.

"You know it's going to be wet out there, right?"

"No kidding." She folded her arms and lifted an eyebrow at him. "I hear it gets like that when it rains."

He looked up at the ceiling with a grin and shook his head.

"Well, yeah," Harley chuckled. "If you put it that way. But I always thought Stacey was the comedian of you two."

"She is," Marisa replied without missing a beat. "I'm the smart one who listens to weather reports and brings her raincoat and umbrella."

That brought a bark of laughter and the man held up his hands in mock surrender.

"Okay, you win," he conceded good-naturedly. "I just thought you might prefer to try and think of other options down here where it's dry while I'm up top scouting things out in the storm. It's not like there's any zombies on the roof, you know."

"We'll see," she indicated the direction of the kitchen door with the bat. "But I'm not taking any chances, 'partner.' *Bien?*"

"Good enough, partner. Let's go get wet."

The two turned towards the end of the counter that marked the path to the kitchen door, but they barely made it two steps.

The loud bang of the restaurant door being slammed open sounded behind them. It was done with enough force to rattle the glass in the rest of the room.

They whirled to see Deke fly into the diner, his eyes wide with fear...

...and that was when disaster struck.

Stormbreak – Deke

Turning his attention forward again, Deke moved in what he hoped was catlike silence down the aisle. He sized up the situation in front of him as he went. Several wasted silhouettes had returned to their stations outside the windows, but with the lights out they really didn't concern him. Besides, he was going to be squatting on the floor below their level of sight.

But it also meant he was going to be operating below the level of what little light came in through the windows. And the visibility was poor enough as it was.

The youngster crouched as he reached the end of the aisle and moved slowly forward towards the dark mounds of rubble. Water sloshed around his boots, as he carefully made his way into the puddle. He moved in a three point stance, one hand on the floor for extra balance. Moving like this made his shoulder hurt, so he slipped his injured arm back into the sling. He wasn't going to need two hands to do this job anyway.

As expected, he could see almost nothing.

He felt his way around in the mess, trying to find anything that might feel like a purse. It wasn't easy because the puddle was full of objects. A few he could make out by feel...lighters, cigarette packs, cans of snuff. Others were more mysterious. And everything was soaked. He fumbled through the debris, trying to put mental pictures to everything he handled.

He kept finding long, plastic wrapped objects that confused him. They seemed out of place in an area mainly featuring tobacco products. After the fifth or sixth one, he stopped and tried to imagine what they could be. If they weren't cigarettes or snuff, they had to be something that had been on display on top of the counter. The problem was, the counter displays changed regularly.

But that was the clue that gave Deke the mystery object's identity. Halloween was right around the corner, and the store display had been featuring stuff for trick or treaters. Things like Halloween stickers, reflective tape...

...and glow sticks.

"Yes!" Deke fished the next one he found out of the puddle. "Perfect!"

It took a little effort in the dark, but he managed to tear the foil wrapper open and snap the plastic tube. Instantly, a soft green glow illuminated the floor around him.

"Now we're cooking with gas," the boy muttered as he started scanning the debris. "Now where are you?"

"Deke?" Stacey's voice came from the darkness at the back of the store. "What are you doing?"

"Hunting the purse," he called back softly. "What color is it?"

"Umm...it's tan, I think. Or maybe beige."

Deke chuckled to himself as he searched, realizing that was the type of distinction only a girl would make. In the past few hours he had started seeing Stacey as the human being she was, instead of the fantasy he imagined. Yet somehow that was making him fall for her all the harder.

"Wait a minute," he murmured as he spied the very edge of something in the blackness under the rear counter. It was a pale blotch, barely visible in the light of the glowstick.

Excitement built as he leaned down to get a better look at the thing. It was definitely a purse or handbag of some sort. Harley would have never noticed it when moving the bodies, especially since he wasn't looking for it in the first place. One of the creatures must have kicked it under the counter when it attacked Gladys. Deke had only spotted it because he was crouched so low to begin with.

Being essentially one handed, Deke reached under the counter with the hand holding the glow stick and fished the object out.

It was what he thought it was.

"Got it!" he yelled and stood up, holding the purse aloft in triumph.

And then everything went to hell.

"Cool..." Stacey began, but then her voice rose to a shriek. "DEKE! LOOK OUT! BEHIND YOU!"

As soon as she screamed, Deke understood his mistake.

The hand holding the purse also held the glow stick. And he was waving it right in front of the window. Sick with realization, he pulled down his hand and turned to face the inevitable...and in the process turned a serious mistake into a catastrophic one.

Now he held the glow stick in front of him, and between him and the window...fully illuminating him for the benefit of the two horrors on the other side of the glass. There would be no going back now. Both had already spread their talons and crouched for the attack, their deathly black sockets fixed firmly on his face.

Reality slowed to a series of split seconds, and Deke thought faster than he ever had in his entire life.

It was too late to stop the attack. If he stayed where he was they would be coming through the glass after him.

If he backed away, the result would be the same. Even if he dropped the glow stick, the light coming in from the front gas pumps was enough for them to keep a fix on him and attack. Which meant he was screwed. He couldn't hope to fight even one of these things in his current shape, and there were two of them.

And Stacey was somewhere behind him, trapped against a door that only opened from the other side.

In the tiny fraction of time he had left, it was the last realization that dictated his course of action. He knew he was probably dead, but perhaps he could see to it she didn't die with him.

"Stacey! Get in the men's bathroom and block the door!"

Remembering the doc and her performance with her little flashlight, Deke slapped the end of the glow stick against the glass and ran for the restaurant. He hadn't really formulated a plan, other than to get away from Stacey before the monsters crashed through the glass upon him. It was just the first thing that came to mind.

Yet it appeared to be working. He could see the twin predators following the glow stick and chasing along beside him out of the corner of his eye, Even as he looked, a third one joined the pursuit.

Deke shot across the entrance of the store and reached the doorway to the restaurant at a dead run. The sound of the monsters slapping and sliding against the glass as they pursued filled him with both hope and dread. They were taking the bait, but the inevitable outcome had only been forestalled by a few seconds. When he turned to run away from the glass, they would be coming through the windows after him. In his current shape he might, or might not, be able to outrun them to the kitchen.

But if he was going to die, he could at least see to it that it happened with a firewall between the monsters and Stacey.

He slammed open the door to the restaurant, preparing to yell for the people in the kitchen to get ready to block the door. Instead he almost stumbled to a halt at the sight of Harley and Marisa staring at him with shock in the middle of the darkened diner.

What the hell? Weren't they supposed to be on the roof or something?

Realizing his split second of free time was up, he shouted a warning and ran towards them.

"Incoming!" he screamed, and an instant later the crash of the window shattering sounded behind him.

The roar of the storm filled the diner, and along with it he heard the scrabbling of the monsters as they poured into the breach after him.

The dead were now inside restaurant.

DEAD STOP

CHAPTER NINE: RESURGENCE

Resurgence – Rachel

"Incoming!"

Rachel jerked her head up in the process of helping Grandpa Tom unbolt a small steel table from the adjoining grill. The aged trucker had figured out the table was just long enough that if they pushed it against the swinging door, it would wedge against the broken down old dishwasher and jam the door shut. She hoped he was right because it sounded like they were about to need to put his idea into practice.

Her heart seized up at the unmistakable sound of one of the large windows in the restaurant shattering. The glass had been breached, and the dead were now about to be inside with them! Somewhere in the diner Marisa shrieked and cursed all in one breath. She thought she made out Harley yelling something, but then another sound jerked her attention away.

"Doc!" Stacey's scream floated down the hall amid the sudden pounding on the employee door. "Let me IN! Hurry!"

Rachel stood up, torn in confusion. What was going on? What should she do? What the hell was Deke doing in the diner? Why was Stacey still in the store? The chaos was coming from the diner, but if Deke was in the diner didn't that mean Stacey was alone in the store? With only a split second to decide, and nothing else to go on, Rachel made her choice and dashed down the hallway towards the employee door.

"Tom!" she called over her shoulder. "Do whatever you can! I'll be right back!" She saw the old man rise from his work and pull the hunting knife he carried in the sheath at his back before refocusing on the door ahead.

Things would just have to hold together without her for a few seconds.

With the zombies all outside, they had unlocked the door between the store and diner earlier. It was a decision she had not been crazy about at the time, but had gone along with in the name of quick retreat in case somebody got cut off from the kitchen. But now, even if the zombies were currently in the diner, leaving one of them alone in the store with nothing but an unlocked swinging door between them and the horde was not her idea of an option.

She reached the metal door, where it literally vibrated from the pounding of the girl on the other side.

"I'm here, Stacey!"

She grasped the door handle, praying the girl didn't fall in on her with a bunch of death-headed horrors ripping her to pieces. On the other hand, sounds of crashing and struggle now came from the kitchen so things might not be any safer back here. Part of her wondered if she wasn't about to let the girl in just so she could die with the rest of them here in the back.

She pulled open the door, only to have the waitress almost knock her over on her way inside.

"Deke!" the girl screamed as she barreled past the vet and towards the kitchen. "The purse!"

It seemed Stacey was still hale and hearty.

"You're welcome!" Rachel shouted after her while shutting the door.

For a brief second she wondered if she were the only woman here who actually ran *away* from fights. At the same time, she knew there was strength in numbers and their odds of survival improved markedly with each of them that were willing to work or fight together. So the only real choice was to get back there and add two more hands to their side of the fray. If nothing else, she could help whoever was trying to hold the door shut.

Then she stopped in horror as she realized she wasn't going to get the choice. A knot of combatants slammed against the rear wall of the kitchen, and proceeded to roll along the wall in her direction. The fight was coming to her. And it was a nasty one.

The thing must have died in a fire.

It was charred and blackened from head to toe. And since a corpse like this would have required a closed coffin for the funeral, they hadn't bothered dressing the body. It really didn't matter. Only its height gave her reason to believe it might have once been male, since the monstrosity fighting with Harley and Deke looked more like a burnt scarecrow than anything else. Its teeth showed a startling white against the rest of the seared skull, but other than that it was almost impossible to make features out.

At the moment those teeth were also stained red because they had just closed over one of Harley's hands. He fought to free himself by slamming the thing against one side of the hall and then the other. Blood ran down the man's shoulder and back where the monster clawed with its free hand.

Deke hung on to its other arm with grim tenacity, using his weight to try and keep that hand out of the fight. He was bleeding again as well. His shoulder punctures had reopened, and a fresh line of blood ran down the side of his face from what must have been a head wound under his hair.

Rachel didn't know how much longer he was going to manage it since the monster was slamming him back and forth with the same ferocity Harley was unleashing on it. She could also just make out Stacey on the other side of the thrashing combatants. The veterinarian wondered if the little waitress had lost her mind because it looked like she was trying to find a way to get into the fight.

Harley grunted in pain as the monster bit down, and used his trapped hand to momentarily pin its head against the wall. He hurled three ferocious forearm smashes against its cranium, each one obviously intended to crush it's brainpan against the cinder bricks. But the blackened skull held and the monster slammed the man back against the opposite side of the hallway instead.

If it hadn't already had Harley's hand in its jaws, it could have bitten his face off at that very moment.

But now that its back was away from the wall, Rachel could also see the thing must have encountered

Grandpa Tom at one point. The handle of the old man's knife protruded from its ribcage near the spine. The monster showed no sign the weapon bothered it in the least, which Rachel knew better than anybody else that it wouldn't. The vulnerable areas on this monster were small, and most were well protected.

Most of them.

"Deke, Harley, hang on..." she gasped, then stumbled as Deke was slammed into her.

Rachel managed to recover and move back in as the monster swung the boy the other way and into Stacey on the other side. The little waitress clutched him as if to add her own weight to the pull on the things arm, but at the same time seemed to be grabbing at something hanging from Deke's shoulder. The doctor ignored them and started to reach for the knife.

Unfortunately, her timing was off.

Harley now slammed the thing back across the hallway. Using his body to pin the monster's loose arm against the wall he used his free hand to try and pry the skull's jaws open. His face was red from the effort he was expending. This only lasted for a few seconds before the mass of bodies crashed back against the other wall again.

"Dammit, Doc!" he gritted out. "How the hell is this bastard so strong!?"

Rachel ignored the question and tried to stay focused on her objective. A second later she saw her opportunity and darted forward to grab the handle of the old man's knife. Her hand closed on the weapon and she fought to pull it free. But that was when Harley managed to push the thing off of him again and up against the opposite wall.

Or it would have been up against the opposite wall if Rachel hadn't been trapped behind it.

"Oof! No!" She gagged, and struggled to get free. The smell of burnt flesh and formaldehyde filled her nose and caused her to retch. With the knife trapped against the wall with her, she decided she could at least help by using her other hand to try and snag the arm the monster was using to claw at Harley.

236

It was like grabbing a steel bar.

The power of the thing as it ripped the woman from behind it astonished her.

They've been feeding, and they're getting stronger, the clinical side of her brain observed with a detachment utterly unsuited to the current circumstance. *These things are getting deadlier by the hour.*

Then the matter at hand took up her full attention as the five of them now toppled over onto the floor in a thrashing heap.

For a moment, Rachel just concentrated on not getting squashed. This was pretty much impossible since the entire group had fallen in her direction. All of their clothes were blackened from wrestling with the vile thing, and the situation kept getting worse by the second. People were tiring, but this monster wasn't.

At the same time, Rachel realized she now had the hunting knife free in her hand. She wasted no time into putting it to use. She might not be a fighter, but she was a surgeon...and by God she knew how to cut where it counted.

Bringing the knife up alongside the monster's head, she inserted the blade behind the masseter muscle and started to saw. It was tough work. The corpse continued to struggle, and the muscle seemed to be almost some flexible form of wood. But Rachel gritted her teeth and held on, pulling on the blade for all she was worth. She had dissected things before, but never had they put up such a fight.

Then the muscle parted and the knife suddenly came free.

Deke gave a gasp as the point of the blade jumped and cut his forehead, and Rachel remembered with embarrassment how the old man had warned of that very thing before cutting the other monster earlier. But at the same time, the monster's jaw unhinged and Harley managed to pull his hand free of its teeth.

Yet that was also when the horror lashed out again, this time throwing Deke and Stacey clear of it. Harley pushed back himself, getting his feet between himself and the creature and using them to shove it away from him and Rachel. Having all their combined weight off of her was a relief. At the same time, she realized they may have just made a terrible mistake.

The zombie lurched to its feet, now free of her and Harley and loomed over the four of them on the floor. Its jaw now hung at an odd angle from her impromptu surgery. But despite giving the monster an even more ghastly appearance, the damage hadn't made it any less dangerous. Especially not now.

With them lying all around it, it had its pick of targets...and it wasted no time in making a choice.

The charred abomination turned and faced in the direction of the younger two, and once again spread it's talons to attack. Rachel couldn't see the pair for Harley laying half on top of her. She screamed a warning, knowing it was useless, and watched in horror as the grisly creature lunged downward in their direction.

Then a thunderous bang blasted through the tiny area, almost deafening her.

Bits of skull and brain splattered across the ceiling, and the corpse stiffened and stood straight up. Rachel watched in shock as the horrid corpse teetered there for a second. Then, as if in slow motion, the thing fell backwards. Rachel and Harley just managed to role away from each other in time for the monster to land between them...with most of the back of its skull missing.

Rachel scrambled to her hands and knees and looked over to see Stacey lying on her back with a snub nosed pistol still pointed where the monster stood a few seconds earlier. The girl's eyes were wide and showing lots of whites, and her breathing came in short gasps.

"Is it dead?" Stacey panted. "Doc, is it dead? Make sure it's dead!"

All it took was a glance over at the cavity in the back of the thing's skull for Rachel to know this monster wouldn't be getting up again. What little brain it once had to work with now clung to the ceiling in clumps. This particular cadaver had rejoined the dearly departed in a very final way.

"Oh, it's dead," she reported.

Rachel pulled herself over against the wall and leaned against it with a sigh. She glanced across at Harley who had done the same on the opposite side of the hall. Blood smeared on the wall behind him, and he held his hand protectively under his arm. She realized she would be playing doctor again shortly.

"Are you sure?"

A glance back over revealed the little waitress to still be holding up the gun. Deke was just starting the process of laying his hand on the girl's arm and trying to get her to lower the weapon. He looked as surprised by the firearm's appearance as the rest of them.

"I'm sure," Rachel soothed. "It won't be getting up again. So, tell me...where have you been hiding *that* little gem all evening?"

"Oh, this?" The girl refocused on the gun in her hand, then handed it over to Deke. "Deke found Gladys's purse in the store, and I just remembered that Gladys carried a gun in it. I've never shot a pistol before."

They all looked at the girl in astonishment.

"Well," Harley groaned as he started to struggle to his feet, "you sure made that first shot count. You blew this bastard's brains everywhere."

"Yeah," Stacey's pale face matched her shaky voice. "I sorta noticed that. Yay me...and now we're going to celebrate by Deke taking me to the little girl's room, because I'm about to be really, really sick."

That motivated them to move.

The three of them managed to get up and hustle the small waitress down the hall, before sending her and Deke into the darkened store beyond. Then, shutting the door again so no light would show into the store beyond and attract unwanted attention, they slumped once more against the walls. But only for a second...

"*Que paso?*"

They both looked over to see Marisa standing at the end of the hallway, regarding them with folded arms and a dour expression. Rachel realized with a guilty start she must have been dealing with the door, with nothing but a sick old man for help. She must have done a good job of it, because they were all still alive.

"Grandpa and I have the door blocked, so we're okay," Marisa answered her unasked question. "But there's about a dozen of them in the restaurant."

The girl walked over and prodded the dead monster with her bat.

"So, who's back here shooting up the place?"

***

Treating Harley was as distracting as it was a relief.

On the one hand, the man never made so much as a sound while she cleaned the long lacerations on his back. On the other, she couldn't help but notice the physique that went along with the handsome face and felt an uncharitable stab of resentment towards the two other women in the room. Being the odd woman out in this little group was beginning to bug her, and Rachel decided if she survived this it was time for her to get back out into the world.

The time for mourning was definitely over. When she found civilization again, she intended to hit the first dance floor that crossed her path.

At the same time she couldn't help but chuckle inside at the way the taller waitress studiously ignored the process. Marisa was in the act of removing her raincoat from an excursion to the roof, and gave every sign of being absorbed in doing that and finding a place to put her wet umbrella. But to Rachel's experienced eye the girl may as well have been wearing a sign that read, "I am sooo not paying attention to the gorgeous hunk of man in the room."

"Okay, Harley." She refocused on the task at hand. "Let's pull that hand out so I can take a look at it."

He lifted his hand from where it had been soaking in a sink full of hot soapy water, and she took it and held it up to the light.

Fortunately, during the fight he had forced the hand deep into the monster's jaws where the molars had been doing most of the damage. Otherwise he would have most likely lost half his hand. As it was, a deep semi-circular bite mark stood out in bloody relief, and the last two fingers on his hand had swollen up like sausages.

"Can you feel this?" she asked as she gently pinched the end of each finger.

He nodded in affirmation, which relieved her. At least the nerve hadn't been severed. The bite was just in the right place to do that kind of damage.

"Okay," she instructed. "Now make a fist."

He complied, but she noticed he wasn't able to fully close the last two fingers. Which was exactly what she had feared. The hand would heal with time, but for now its use was limited.

"Harley," she spoke up and looked him firmly in the eye. "I'm going to get straight to the bad news. Your plan to climb that power cable is now out of the question."

Harley had filled them in on the plan while Marisa locked the doors between the diner and the store, before heading up to the roof. Rachel thought the overall scheme had been a little crazy in the first place, but admitted the idea of using Grandpa Tom's truck to get them all out of here had been inspired.

The man grimaced and tried to clench his fist tighter.

"Forget it," Rachel snapped. "I don't care how tough you are, your hand won't have the grip to support you. That bastard chewed it up good, and you're lucky the damn thing is still attached."

The tall redneck obviously didn't want to hear it, but she could tell he was too smart to argue with reality. Another experimental flex of his hand, and she could see the resignation in his face.

"Yeah," Harley sighed. "I suppose you're right."

"That's the spirit. We doctor types love hearing that."

"Okay," he grinned ruefully, "you win. So tell me something, Doc."

"What?" Rachel studied the fingers, trying to decide if a splint was in order.

"How the hell are they so strong?" He frowned in obvious memory of the fight. "I remember you warning they might be. Then I remembered how the first one I fought was tough but I never really gave it a chance to show its stuff. But the second was definitely in my league power wise. And this last one...Holy shit! I thought I was fighting a bear or something."

"Yeah," she nodded and decided to settle for just wrapping the two fingers together. "I've got a theory about that. Since this stuff is hijacking these corpse's nervous systems, the usual safeguards aren't in place."

"Usual safeguards?"

"Uh huh." Rachel picked a strip of rag and started to wrap the two fingers. "We only use a certain percentage of our muscles potential strength. It's like a throttle built in to our endocrine and nervous systems to keep us from injuring our muscles and joints. But I don't think these things have that. I think they are using what muscle they have left at close to a hundred percent. And the percentage probably gets closer to a hundred percent as they feed."

"Damn," Harley breathed in dismay.

"Yeah," she warned, "and if the same holds true for that monster that used to be Buddha Boy—and I'm betting it does—then you absolutely do *not* want to get into a tussle with it. It tore Gerald's head off with one hand."

"Right," He watched her wrap his fingers for a second then turned his head towards Marisa. "Marisa, did you happen to get a fix on where Buddha Boy was."

"You told me to, didn't you," she replied shortly. "At the moment he's over on the store side of the parking lot."

"At the moment?"

"Yeah," she finally settled for hanging her umbrella from a hook above the grill. "All the others have pretty much gone to just standing around out there. But that one walks around."

"Yeah," he sighed, "I noticed."

"I also did it like you told me to for out back," she continued. "There are four of them back there, all just standing there too. One of them is standing only a few feet from the breakers, so he's going to be a problem. Or at least he was. One is out past him between the cornfield and the diner. One is by the light pole off to the right between here and the trucks. And one is standing back there near the shower rooms. Oh, and there is one crawling around in front of the trucks. I'm not sure what's up with it, but its legs don't seem to work and it doesn't look like a threat."

Harley started to speak but she held up a hand and continued.

"I checked from both ends of the roof, like you said, so I would have different angles and there would be less area out of my view. And also like you said, I made note of any areas outside my view. The one area I couldn't totally make out was behind the dumpster enclosure. There could be a zombie behind it, but if there is, it is either right up against the fence or really short."

Rachel watched Harley nod as he took all this in, and remembered him coaching the girl before sending her up there. The veterinarian had insisted on treating his wounds before letting him run off up to the roof, so he had instructed Marisa in what he wanted done and sent her ahead.

It was just as well he did because an ugly situation had been brewing and Marisa had been right in the middle of it.

Marisa had been furious at Deke about the glow stick incident and had been dressing him down righteously over it. The boy took it in hang dog fashion, but it got to the point Stacey had come to his defense. Then, when Harley's plan and the reason behind it had been revealed, it was Stacey's turn to get mad about being kept in the dark. She pointed out Deke wouldn't have even been trying to find Gladys's purse if they hadn't been sent on an errand just to keep them busy.

And everybody remembered whose decision that had been.

Since that had resulted in all of them looking at her, Rachel had chosen to try and cut the impending fracas short. She could tell everybody was exhausted and reaching their snapping point. With tempers fraying, she decided to take no chance of making things worse by offering a defense that might be taken the wrong way.

Instead of attempting to explain how she had been worried about dumping more stress on Stacey, she simply went straight to taking complete blame for the fiasco, offering a full on apology for underestimating them both and promising she would not leave them out of anything again.

The unqualified apology had surprised and mollified Stacey and Deke, but she could still see Marisa fuming and sending dire looks in Deke's direction.

That's when Harley told Marisa he needed her to cover for him and go to the roof while he got tended to. The volcanic glare the raven-haired waitress had fixed on him left no doubt she suspected she was being sent out to cool down, but since it really needed to be done she hadn't objected. Rachel also had a hunch the girl didn't protest because it gave her a graceful way to de-escalate in her own way.

Now as Marisa made her report, it was obvious her main focus was on it being understood that she had done the job right as opposed to carrying on a grudge with Deke.

"Thanks, Marisa," Harley winced as he started to pull his shirt back on. "It's important to get good info on what's going on out there even if Plan B is cancelled."

"Good. It was a stupid plan. It would have only gotten you killed," the waitress grouched. Her mood mustn't have improved all that much, even if she weren't directing her ire at the younger redneck.

Still, Rachel found herself forced to agree with the young woman's blunt assessment. It had been a plan borne of desperation, and it was probably just as well it hadn't been attempted.

But it also left them back at square one...in a truck stop that the dead had now breached, and some or all of them possibly infected with the fungus. Up the creek without a single paddle in sight. So although the plan had probably not been practical in the first place, it still felt like a blow to have lost the ability to even attempt it.

Apparently Stacey hadn't gotten the memo.

"But, the truck part..." she looked at Harley. "That part would have worked, right?"

"What do you mean?"

"I mean, if you could have gotten to the truck you would have actually been able to drive it, and we would have really been able to get on it from the roof?"

"Yeah. Tom says it has a ten speed manual. I can handle one of those. I would just have to be careful to remember the length of the trailer. The roof part would be a cinch. There's a couple of long folding tables in the storeroom, and they would make easy bridges."

"But it doesn't matter," Marisa cut in. "That truck may as well be a thousand miles away. Harley can't get to it. Even if his hand wasn't hurt, and he didn't get killed trying to cut the power to the line, I don't think he could have made it."

"Well, no," the smaller waitress agreed. "But what if somebody drove him up to the truck? He could get into it then before the zombies got him, right?"

"Sure!" Marisa snorted. "And since we're daydreaming here, they can serve him coffee and waffles on the trip!"

"I like coffee and waffles," Harley mused aloud.

"Well be sure and order them with your dream car," Marisa snapped, "because all the real ones are surrounded by zombies, remember?"

"Not all of them."

Now all eyes really did turn on Stacey.

"What do you mean, Stacey?" Harley leaned forward intently, "I've studied all the cars. The only one that was even possible to get to was Gerald's, and now it's gone. We're cut off from all of them."

"What about the one in the shop?"

For a second they all looked at her blankly. Then Marisa gasped and Harley did a quick look from Stacey to her.

"The shop?" he asked.

"Yes!" Marisa came alive, "Oh shit, yes! Arnold was working on a car in the shop! And there's almost no zombies between us and there! Stacey, you're a genius!"

245

The room came alive with excited chatter.

Rachel felt a surge of excitement as well, but she also remembered the haunted look Stacey had assumed earlier when the topic of the shop came up. Whatever the situation was back there, it couldn't be good.

"Okay," the veterinarian cautioned. "Hold on a second. Stacey? If they were working on the car, how do you know it would be running?"

"Because they were done, Doc. I know because the car was off the rack, and the hood was closed. And..." the girl went slightly pale again, "...Arnold's red toolbox was closed. I remember because...because Leon's head was lying right next to it."

That calmed things down a bit.

"*Mierde*," Marisa closed her eyes. "They must have been cleaning up to go home when these damn things hit."

"Probably," Stacey started to look tearful. "Oh God, those poor guys. They were almost out of there."

"But, the keys." Harley interrupted. "What about the keys to this car? Where would they be?"

Stacey and Marisa looked at each other, and Rachel could tell they both knew the answer and didn't really like it.

"They would be in Arnold's pocket," Marisa answered. "He always pulled whatever car he was working on out into the parking lot before leaving, just in case a truck came in needing repairs later."

"So the keys are there," Harley pulled a toothpick and started chewing it, "that's good. That's very good."

Rachel worried that desperation might still be forcing his hand, and tried to bring things back down to earth.

"Okay," she reminded them, "but even if they're there, there's also enough zombies to kill and devour three men in there with them. I don't see how this is any better than the cars out front."

"No," Stacey replied, emphatically shaking her head. "Most of them chased me. When I looked back I saw them pouring out both doors...from the mechanic's shop and the showers. All the ones from the trucks went to

Gladys's side of the building. If there's any left in there, it's probably only one or two."

"Just like the ones in the store when those cops showed up," Harley muttered. "They go for the kill even when they've got a dead victim right at their feet."

"That's not a surprise," Rachel mused. "It's a hunting strategy that makes sense at their level. Their victims aren't going anywhere, so chase the fresh meat.

"And we've got a gun now!" Marisa chimed in. "So if there is one or two left...no problem! I'm betting you're a pretty good shot, aren't you, Harley?"

"Pretty good," the man nodded absently, still chewing the toothpick, "but there's only five bullets left. And it's a snub nose. Not good for the kind of accurate shooting these things require unless they're close. So we can't afford to get too cocky."

"Right," the waitress nodded, all business now. "You carry the gun, I'll go with the bat."

Harley didn't look happy about that last part, but didn't object. Rachel guessed he had finally given up on dissuading Marisa from accompanying him on these kinds of things. He just sighed and then gestured at her rain gear.

"You're going to have to leave that stuff behind," he said. "It's too brightly colored, and it will slow you down. I guess you can loan them to Doc and Stacey while they're up on the roof."

"Right."

Rachel looked at the two in dismay, shocked at how fast this was developing.

"Wait a minute!" she interjected. "You two aren't seriously talking about going out there."

"Yep," Harley readjusted the hat on his head and nodded towards the time clock. "And we're going to do it real soon. It's five thirty, Doc. We're running out of darkness, and we don't know how much longer it will rain. We need to get everybody and everything ready and up on the roof. I'll go get those tables up through the hatch. Get your patient here...err, Benny...ready to move, and I'll be back to help you guys with him in a minute. Oh, one other thing..."

"What's that?" Rachel asked.

"We're not going to be able to get to your truck...and for reasons I won't go into right now, getting to your office in Masonfield is pretty much out of the question too. Is there anywhere...*anywhere*...else we can get this medicine you want? Remember, under these circumstances anything goes, so breaking in to get it is fine. Think hard."

Rachel nodded, and desperately searched her memory of the area. A few seconds later the answer came.

"Yeah!" she nodded. "If you go about fifteen miles up the highway, right over the county line and take a right at the cutoff to Lake Cowell, there's a large rural vet clinic and feed store about three miles further down the road. Doc Cummings place. He has a large practice so he's probably even better stocked than I am."

"Good, we now have a destination. We'll stop at the rest area to get ya'll off the trailer and into the car with Marisa, then we'll head straight there. Deke, I want you to run back into the store and scrounge up some cigarette lighters, flashlights, and all the batteries you can throw into a shopping bag. We don't know how much longer the power is going to hold, wherever we go. Let's go."

"Now?" Deke asked as he stood up.

"Now," Harley confirmed. "And while you're at it, grab some more of those glow sticks real quick. When you're up on the roof, I want you to light them and toss them out towards the corner of the highway and the county road. Try and make them skip a time or two. Maybe you can draw these bastards further away from both the truck and the back, and give us a better head start."

"You got it."

Deke and Stacey hustled out of the room.

"Hey," Grandpa Tom pulled himself to his feet, then tossed Harley a set of keys. He still looked pale, but had definitely improved over the past couple of hours. "It's the key with the big plastic head. It has power locks, so just push the button on the key ring before getting out of the car to unlock the doors."

"Thanks," Harley caught them out of the air and pushed them into his pocket. "Anything else?"

"Yeah. Don't scratch my truck."

"Right."

The old man gave him the eye for a second, then gave an approving nod.

"Good luck, son. Don't get eaten."

Rachel watched the sick trucker hobble down the hall, leaving her alone with Harley and Marisa. Things were happening too fast for her. Just a couple of minutes ago they had been getting ready to accept having to spend the day hiding out in the kitchen and hoping for the best. Now they were about to be going up on the roof to wait for rescue...

...or watch Harley and Marisa die horribly in the parking lot below them.

Suddenly the pair looked very young to her. Every instinct she had screamed they shouldn't be doing this.

Yet she knew they were right. They just couldn't spend the day sitting back here and waiting to see if they would die or not. Holing up might be a legitimate survival strategy, but it required them finding a viable place to do so and preferably after obtaining the antifungal medication. The Textro, with its plate glass windows and zombie infested diner simply wasn't it. Besides, sooner or later the utilities were going to die and they would be trapped in pitch blackness amid spoiling food and no running water.

They had to do this. And the only way she could help was do her job as well.

"Okay," she sighed. "Marisa, Stacey told me there were some plastic tablecloths somewhere the Textro used for special dinners and such. Let's get one of those and wrap Benny here in it. That way we can at least keep him mostly dry up there. Then I guess you two can go save the day."

***

Resurgence – Marisa

"Are you okay?"

Marisa nodded her head in the now darkened hallway, fully aware of how silly it was. She didn't trust herself to speak yet. Stacey and Deke's footsteps still sounded on the ladder up to the roof. Only after hearing the thud of the roof hatch closing, did the young woman finally allow herself a vocal exhale. She felt sure it's shakiness wasn't lost on Harley's ears.

She had been okay, and working herself up to slide out the back door after Harley once they opened it, but had gotten interrupted. Stacey had come rushing tearfully back down from the roof to hug her and wish her luck. The anguish in the gesture affected the young woman deeply, and almost brought her to tears herself. Marisa would have just preferred that Stacey's "wishing her luck" didn't feel so much like her saying goodbye. All she could do was hug the smaller girl back, promise her she would be fine, and not tell her what she was really thinking.

You're my best friend, Stacey, and I love you like the sister I once lost. I'll be damned before I do nothing and let you die too.

Instead she had finally handed the weeping girl back to Deke with the stern warning to look after her, and sent the two back to the roof. Knowing the boy had endured the agony of climbing down the ladder again with his injured shoulder to accompany her reassured Marisa his feelings for Stacey were genuine. She just hoped he got his act together fast enough to live up to the rest of the job.

Now she had to work herself up to doing this crazy stunt all over again.

At least Harley had the decency not to try and talk her out of it.

"Okay," he prompted softly in the dark, "let's go over it one more time. First of all, where are they?"

Marisa refocused on the question and the matter at hand.

"One near the breaker box. One between that one and the corn field. One was by the light post but Deke said

250

it went chasing a glow stick. So that just leaves the one back there near the showers, and whatever might have been concealed by the dumpster enclosure."

"Good, now what's the plan?"

"The plan is," she repeated, "I will ease open the door, and you will go out first. I am to watch how you do it and then do it the same way. If something out there makes a move for you, you *will* dive back through this door, slam it shut, and not worry about apologizing for knocking me down until later."

"Um, I don't remember that last part."

"I added it," she growled. "Deal with it. Now, if we both make it out there alive, then we are to move slowly towards the shop, hoping the rain and darkness will disguise us from the zombies for long enough to give us a head start. Once anything does react, we run for the shop. You will lead, and focus on taking the zombie out near the showers if it gets in our way. I will run to the shop door, but not go in unless I have to until you get there. From that point on we make it up as we go along."

"Right."

Marisa nodded to herself, grateful to have the opportunity to settle herself by going over things again. Having a plan to recite helped. Now there just remained one more thing. She hadn't intended to bring it up, but her brief session with Stacey had made her reconsider.

"Uh, partner?"

"Yeah?"

"There's just one other piece of information," she sighed. "I didn't mention it earlier because I didn't think it mattered, but I guess this partner thing means I shouldn't hold anything out from you either. Sorry about that."

"Forgiven. What is it?"

"Umm...the second one...the one out between the breaker boxes and the cornfield...I'm pretty sure that one is Vicki."

Harley didn't reply right away.

Marisa could feel him studying her in the dark, knowing what he must be wondering. She kicked herself for not bringing it up earlier. After all, trust was a two way street.

"Is it going to be a problem?" he asked, his voice betraying nothing.

Was it? Would it cause her to hesitate at a crucial moment, possibly endangering both her and Harley?

No.

She wouldn't let it.

"Absolutely not," she stated with flat finality. "It's a zombie. All it wants to do is kill and eat. Vicki is dead."

Apparently that satisfied him.

"Good enough."

He moved around her in the dark and took the same position at the door he had held before Stacey had interrupted things. It was go time. Marisa fought to ignore the pool of acid forming in her stomach. This time it was going to happen. This time they were going to go through with it, and there would be no further reprieves.

"You ready?" Harley whispered.

"Hell no," She grouched back. "So let's do this before I come to my senses and change my mind." She briefly wondered if that ought to be her battle cry.

"Right."

With just the tiniest of clicks, Harley turned the knob and eased the back door open.

A dim yellow light spilled in, and the splatter of rain hitting the asphalt filled the hallway. A rumble of thunder rolled in from the night sky, but it sounded nothing like the cracking booms of before. The storm had abated somewhat. What had been wind driven sheets now fell as a steady downpour. Having been on the roof earlier, the cold didn't surprise her when it came rushing in. But it reminded her how miserable the others must be, now huddled under plastic tablecloths on the roof. She had loaned Doc her raincoat, and Stacey her umbrella, yet she knew they were scant protection from the elements tonight.

But it was a lot more than she had. Unfortunately for her, the dark red of her uniform was much more suited to this venture than the bright pink of her raincoat.

Marisa watched as Harley eased out the door. He took an agonizingly long time to do it, but she understood why. Due to the arrangement of the parking lot lights, the back of the building was in shadow. Only the distant lights toward the rear of the parking lot shed any illumination back here, and that was reduced further by the rain.

Which was a good thing.

Harley had explained the most likely thing to give them away at this stage was motion. So he crept slowly out the door, he eyes focused down the back wall where she knew the zombie near the breakers stood. After another moment, he slid out of sight and she knew his back must be against the wall beside the door.

Now it was her turn.

Following his example, Marisa moved in very slow motion. She eased at a glacial pace out into the storm. Water falling from the roof above splattered on her hair and down her collar, soaking her in seconds. The shock of the frigid water almost took her breath away. It was so cold...icy cold. But ignoring all of that was easy.

All it took was looking down the length of the back wall and seeing the haggard silhouette near the breaker boxes. She froze as a distant flash of lightning dimly revealed the skull and grinning jaws. It seemed to stare towards the back and slightly away from them. Then the light faded and the thing's shadow stood down there, motionless. Its black outline framed against the yellow glow of the light around the corner, it was a silent death machine waiting for something to trigger it.

And beyond that, there waited something even worse.

Marisa forced herself not to look at the figure in the pale dress about thirty feet further away.

The young waitress swallowed and fought to keep her breathing slow and steady. Better to concentrate on the matter at hand. She carefully slid the last few inches to her place beside the back entranceway, pulling the door almost closed behind her. Once she felt the slick painted cinder bricks pressed against her back, she held her breath and squinted across the doorway at Harley.

He simply looked back at her, his face almost invisible under the shadow of his hat.

She knew what he was waiting for.

Her hand gripped the doorknob with knuckles almost white with tension. Now came the hardest part of all. Her job was to close the door. She and Harley had agreed that if they didn't make it, they needed to leave behind a place for the others to retreat to in case they needed to leave the roof. And the only way to do that was to close the door behind them...thus cutting off their only means of return.

Other than Doc, the rest had been too injured to leave downstairs alone. They wouldn't have been able to move and climb the ladder fast enough if the dead got in. And Rachel needed to be on the roof with the others in case something unexpected happened.

So this was the way it had to be.

Marisa felt like punching Harley for making this her job. Mainly because she suspected he did it so she would have one last chance to change her mind and bail out. And dear God how she wanted to...

Every instinct she had screamed for her to get her ass back inside and put the metal door between her and the monsters where it belonged. This was all or nothing. This was insane. She stared at that crack of blackness made by the last inch of space between the door and the jamb. Whatever she did next, it was what she would have to live or die with.

Marisa closed her eyes and took a deep breath.

Hey guys, watch this!

With silent care, she pulled the door shut.

The small jolt of the lock catching felt like the closing of a coffin lid under her hand. Now there was no going back.

Marisa looked back up from the knob to see Harley still looking at her. Unable to talk under the current circumstances, she settled for giving him a fatalistic half smile. It probably came off as more of a grimace than anything, but he must have gotten the meaning. He gave a conspiratorial wink back before indicating the direction of the mechanic's shop with the faintest nod of his head. They had business to take care of.

It was time to take a walk.

Resurgence – Rachel

Ignoring the lightning, Rachel clutched a pipe leading from the air conditioning unit for balance.

The roof was every bit as bad as she feared it would be. Up here, they were fully exposed to the storm with absolutely no cover. Especially here at the back edge. And the rain still fell in buckets. She wiped her eyes to clear them of the wet hair plastering her forehead.

Marisa's raincoat hung a little long on her, and the hot pink was definitely not her style, but she knew she was probably the driest one up here. Stacey and Deke huddled under Marisa's umbrella nearby, and Grandpa Tom stood beside her with nothing but a plastic tablecloth slung over his shoulders while he acted as a tent pole to keep the injured janitor's head dry. They were a drenched and sorry looking lot, but that didn't concern her right now.

Right now, she held her breath as the two shadows moved away from the back door below.

They moved slowly, using the odd gait of the zombies as they went. It turned out that Harley had also been paying attention to the way the things moved while drinking coffee earlier in the night. He said he had done so in order to better recognize the things at a distance under bad visibility. Instead, he ended up putting the observation to use in mimicking their movement, and teaching Marisa to do the same.

But would it work?

Rachel had no idea how the dead identified each other as "not prey" or if that were even the way they functioned. Their behavior had a decidedly animalistic feel to it, but she had so little to go on.

What triggered these things to attack?

What senses were functioning, and at what capacity?

Why did they consider humans food yet ignore the food on the store shelves?

These questions now badgered her in a relentless stream. The answer to any one of them might give them an advantage they didn't have before. Now that she had an answer to what actually caused these monstrosities, it almost drove her crazy to think how little she understood them...mainly because she suspected that understanding them was going to be the difference between life and death in the long run.

These things had a logic of their own, and knowing that both relieved Rachel and drove her crazy. They made sense, in their own ghastly way. She just needed time and opportunity to figure out how they really worked. If she ever got the chance.

For now, all she could do was watch in helpless silence as two kids risked everything to buy her a few more days on the planet.

"Good," she murmured as she watched the pair advance unmolested another ten feet. "Goooood..."

Yet something was wrong.

She could tell it just by watching them. They were doing the gait right, but somehow it wasn't quite *right*. Something was different. Something she couldn't quite put her finger on, but whatever it was made them just ever so subtly different than the creatures they imitated. Rachel got an ugly premonition as she continued to watch, and a quick glance down at the two nearest corpses confirmed her fears.

The dead were watching them too.

Neither had moved, or assumed an attack stance, but both had now turned their heads to face them. Grinning jaws and hollow sockets pivoted ever so slightly as they tracked the pair.

Rachel didn't dare make a sound to warn them. A scream on her part might rouse the zombies to a higher state of alertness, causing them to attack just on instinct.

Even worse, it might bring more from around the side of the building to investigate the noise.

A desperate look back at the two showed their advance to be agonizingly slow. She couldn't imagine how hard it must be for them not to break out into a run. Death smiled at them from all directions. Yet somehow they kept the same steady pace as they moved together towards the back.

Moved together...

Oh shit! That's what they're doing wrong. They're working together. Moving as a team. The zombies don't really do that. Not in that fashion.

It was a subtle difference, but now that she knew what it was it stood out in a way that seemed to scream "different." And she wasn't the only one noticing.

Rachel looked back down and detected a definite new alertness on the part of the two nearest zombies. They had now shifted their stances so their bodies faced the pair as well. Worse yet, the distant one at the showers ahead also tracked them with its gaze. Even the one drawn a ways off by Deke's glow sticks now followed their progress.

She could sense the countdown starting, and knew it was only a matter of time. With this much attention on them they couldn't hope to get there without doing something "unzombie-like" enough to provoke an attack. That one single mistake announcing them as prey.

As it turned out, they never got a chance to even make the mistake.

"Marisa! RUN!"

Stacey's scream almost caused Rachel to jump out of her raincoat.

She whirled to see the girl pointing off to the right, towards the store side of the parking lot. A sick feeling of certainty gathered in her gut as she followed the waitress's gesture to the asphalt below. There was one other zombie that had to be accounted for...one that functioned on a higher level than the others...and it was him.

Buddha Boy.

The mangled giant lumbered into Rachel's view from the right, still taking bites from something she didn't want to identify as it went. Even from its greater distance it had spotted the two, and recognized them as not zombies. The detached, clinical side of her mind immediately drew the conclusion that, if nothing else, this monster had superior eyesight compared to the others.

At least it didn't seem in a terrible hurry.

But that didn't matter now, either...because she turned her head back in time to see all the other corpses had gone into their attack postures and were starting to charge as well. The race was now on.

Harley and Marisa must have either heard Stacey's scream or figured it out for themselves for they had started to run as well.

"Go!" Rachel whispered as she watched the pair flee.

In the distance, she could see Harley sprint out ahead of Marisa. Only the knowledge this was part of the plan helped her fight down the urge to yell at him to wait for her. Even knowing that, she still felt relief when she saw him veer off to intercept the predator running at them from the direction of the showers. Now she clutched the AC pipe and prayed he could pull off what he planned.

The distance between the man and the monster disappeared by the second.

Then, at what seemed the very last instant, Harley brought himself to a controlled stop. The distance and lighting made seeing his face impossible, but Rachel noted he pulled off the next maneuver with the same degree of near nonchalance she found so irritating earlier in the store. It looked like something out of a movie. The man calmly raised the pistol, aimed, and blew the monster's head to pieces as it closed the last of the space between them. They couldn't have been more than three feet apart.

At least that left them an unobstructed path to the shop door. But they weren't out of trouble yet. The creatures were still racing up from behind...

...and Marisa was struggling.

Although the young woman still ran at a good clip, she had also developed a noticeable limp. And the horrors chasing her looked even faster than they were earlier tonight. Rachel realized to her dismay they were actually gaining.

Dammit, Marisa! I warned you about that toe! I told you to be smart!

Rachel raged in despair at the stubbornness of the girl. Whether broke or not, Marisa's toe hadn't been up to this kind of punishment. The veterinarian had to admire the determination that allowed the other woman to push herself through what must now be real agony, but the sheer foolhardiness of it pissed her off. Now the dead closed in behind her and she lost ground by the second.

Still, she had nearly reached the door. It was going to be close, but it looked like Marisa had enough of a head start to make it.

Then things got worse.

Another horror joined the chase.

And this one had an angle on the waitress.

Small and quick, it darted out from the gap in the cornfield on the left where Gerald's car had plowed into the tall stalks. Tiny jaws gaped and pigtails flew as the feral shape raced across the front of the mechanics shop on a collision course with Marisa. The girl must have seen it at the last second for she tried to raise her bat at a dead run.

But it was too late.

The filthy thing leapt and landed on her just as she reached the door.

Rachel and the others could only watch in horror as Marisa struggled with the monster in the shop entrance. The two were silhouetted against the light from inside the shop, with the little atrocity practically up on the tall girl's shoulders. She tumbled against the doorframe under its ferocious onslaught. Then Harley slammed into the pair of them, knocking them both inside, before rushing inside himself.

A second later the door slammed shut and the shooting began.

Rachel held her breath, praying to any higher power listening to make everything work out okay. One look at the others showed they were doing the same. But only the thunder answered from above.

The night fell silent, other than the hiss of the rain falling on the asphalt.

Then the sound of Marisa's scream reached them from clear across the flooding parking lot.

CHAPTER TEN: MAELSTROM

Maelstrom – Marisa

"*Pinche puta!* Get *off* me!"

The moment Marisa had feared all night had finally come.

A monster had caught her.

One of its filthy talons clawed her side while the other tangled in her hair. The horrid little skull snapped in her face, and only the bat she had up under its chin kept it away from her. It dripped with mud, it stank like roadkill, and the ferocity of its assault threatened to unbalance her. Her foot hurt horribly, and after the impact with Harley it was all she could do to keep from falling as she struggled with the little demon.

All around them crows flapped and squawked, creating a maelstrom of black feathered bodies that filled the air of the mechanic's shop.

Marisa and the child-sized horror whirled through the feathery chaos. Despite its size, the little monster's strength was terrifying. The frenzied relentlessness of its attacks gave her no chance to do anything but struggle to keep it off her face. Only its light weight gave her any advantage at all.

With a strangled snarl of desperation the tall young woman slammed the creature against the wall, trying to pin it against the cinder blocks with her bat. If she could just free herself from the little monster's clutches for a full second she intended to beat its brains out all over the concrete floor. At least she hoped she could bring herself to do it if the opportunity presented itself.

A gunshot blasted somewhere to her left, and she knew Harley must have his own hands full at the moment. She had caught sight of a couple of red drenched skulls rising from the other side of the car when she stumbled into the building. Another shot almost deafened her, and the faint sound of Harley cursing caused her to look over to see what danger loomed from his direction.

That was when the monster managed to bite her.

As Marisa turned her face to see what the problem was, the rotting imp yanked her head closer by her hair. She reacted in an instant, pulling back hard enough to lose almost a handful of the ebony strands, but it was too late. The vile thing had also managed to work the bat a little lower down its throat and lean its head towards her...and a split second later its teeth sank into the top of her ear.

Marisa's scream cut through the garage like a ripsaw.

White blazing agony exploded as the horror bit down. Blinded by both pain and panic, instinct took over and Marisa pulled her head back with all her strength. This elevated her anguish to a searing new level as the monster bit harder and pulled back as well. Things held for one long, torturous second. Then the inevitable happened. Skin severed, cartilage tore, and a hot torrent of blood gushed as she tore her head free.

For a frozen moment in time, the girl stared in mute astonishment at the creature. The thing briefly stopped its struggle to focus on the piece of flesh between its teeth. Its staring eyes remained fixed on her face, but the little monster's attention appeared to relocate onto its new meal. It almost seemed to leer as it gnashed the small piece of her between its bloody teeth. Then, after a few seconds, it gulped the grisly morsel down.

That was when something inside Marisa went *sproing*.

Her coworkers were dead. All of her friends were either hurt or dead. Her family was most likely dead. Her dead sister was waiting outside to kill her. Hell, she had been living with the knowledge she could die horribly any minute for the entire night. And now this. Now she had been bitten. Now some half-pint, stinking, little pigtailed punk of a zombie had maimed her.

Somewhere within her...somewhere deep inside...a psychic gate rattled and something looked out between the bars. Something that wanted to have its own say about this new development. And that something had feral eyes and grinning teeth of its own.

Red tinged her vision, a rushing filled her ears, and the bloody waitress let loose an inarticulate howl announcing the current battle for survival had reached its conclusion...

...and an operation of a completely different sort would now commence.

Releasing the top of the bat with her right hand, she grabbed the little monster by the throat. The thing clawed at her arm and side with renewed gusto as she did. It tore her blouse and drew blood, but Marisa ignored it as she turned with the creature and slammed it down on workbench. The pain didn't matter anymore. The blood didn't matter anymore. The only thing that mattered was what was coming next. Pinning it again by putting her weight on the bat, she reached across to the shop vice and spun it open. Then she yanked the thing up in one vicious motion and slammed its head back down between the jaws of the device.

A few twists of the handle later and the creature was trapped. Breathing heavily, Marisa stood up before the struggling creature and surveyed her handiwork. Then she stared at the thing with a strange, almost puzzled expression. Her hand went to her ruined ear. It gingerly explored the damage and came back covered in her blood. Somewhere behind her a third gunshot went off but she ignored it. The girl stared at her bloodied hand for a second, then gazed back at the zombie again.

"You bit my ear off." she said in disbelief. "You bit my god damned ear off!"

Somewhere deep inside her, the lock on that gate went *click*.

The zombie thrashed but the vice held firm. Its mad eyes stared undaunted up at the bloody waitress, yet this time its gaze met one that stared back with something just as chilling. Something that grinned back with the knowledge that things had just come unhinged, and it was completely cool with that.

263

"And you know what?" Marisa added as she hefted her weapon of choice. "Mr. Bat doesn't like it when you bite my ear off! No, ma'am! No MA'AM! Mr. Bat doesn't like that one goddamned little bit!"

"Mr. Bat" then proceeded to demonstrate his displeasure in long overhand swings. Several of them, in fact. Unfortunately, their little conversation got interrupted a few seconds later.

"Marisa!" Harley shouted. "Look out! Behind you!"

The fear in his voice tore her attention away from the trapped zombie.

Marisa whirled to see another skull-faced horror coming around the end of the car near the garage door and heading her way. More crows scattered at its approach. Glancing to her right, she saw Harley stomping on something on the other side of the vehicle. He obviously had his hands full and wasn't going to be able to help.

And that suited her just fine.

A few minutes earlier this would have been a nightmare come true. But the primal thing now riding inside her was its own form of nightmare and it didn't waste one second before engaging this new opponent. With a rage filled howl she took three long strides towards the monster, and drew back her bat for a home run swing. The skeletal creature lurched towards her with eager talons outstretched, and the two closed like gladiators in an arena. Then, right before they met, the tall girl sidestepped and slammed the weapon with all her might into the dead things kneecap.

It was a direct hit.

The knee gave with an audible snap, and the corpse's leg buckled and folded the wrong way. It hit the floor in a thrashing heap. A split second later the same hard length of maple met the back of the monster's cranium as Marisa hammered its face into the concrete floor. This time the crunch of bone didn't bother her at all. An ecstasy of bloodlust swept through her and she screamed in rapturous triumph as she lifted the bat for another blow.

Four brutal swings later and the monster's skull lay in pieces. Its brains were splattered everywhere, covering both the nearby floor and Marisa herself. On the fifth swing, the end of the bat struck the concrete floor just past the ruined head and the weapon finally shattered.

Well, that sucked.

The girl held the broken handle up before her and gave it a disgusted glare before tossing it away and stalking back to the workbench. Oh well, that zombie was broken anyway...and she still had a conversation with a certain pig-tailed zombie-nugget to finish. Marisa hummed and scanned the line of tools on the bench in exasperation. Nope...nope... none of this would do. Then her eyes lit up at the sight of the large implement hanging on a wall hook at the end of the work area.

Perfect.

She snatched it off the wall, then returned to her previous spot in front of the trapped zombie and held up her new prize.

"I'm baa-aack!" She sing-songed brightly, her too wide grin almost glowing against her gore spattered face. "And looky! I brought my new friend! It's Mr. Pipewrench! Can you say hi to Mr. Pipewrench? Sure you can! Now wherrrrrre were we?"

Marisa looked up at the ceiling and tapped her chin thoughtfully.

"Oh yes!" she chirped cheerfully and held up her finger. "That's right! *You bit my goddamned ear off!!*"

At that point, Mr. Pipewrench resumed the conversation previously initiated by Mr. Bat. Being ten pounds of solid iron, he spoke slower but with great authority.

She got in at least fifteen full swings before Harley finally stepped in to stop her.

"Hey! Hey! Easy!" He caught her arm as she wound up for another big swing. "You got it! It's dead already! Holy shit, is it ever dead!"

Marisa heard him speak, heard what he said, but somehow the words and their meaning weren't connecting. Not that she really wanted them too. She still occupied that

265

happy place where she was the one dealing out all the death and destruction for a change, and she wasn't quite ready to come home yet.

But Harley seemed determined to be a spoilsport and make her.

"Easy!" he soothed as she struggled to take another swing. "C'mon, Marisa, let it go. It's over...it's all over. They're dead. We're still alive. We made it. Eeeeaaassssyyy..."

Part of her didn't want it to be over. Part of her wanted to feel the crunch of bone under the impact of the pipe wrench a few more times. Okay, maybe a whole lot of more times. But the other part of her...the part that understood one cooks a cow before eating it...finally began to reassert control.

It really was over.

They had made it.

Her arm trembled, and then fell to her side. As it did, the pipe wrench became surprisingly heavy. It slipped from her grasp and fell to the floor with a dull clank.

And deep inside that gate swung shut and locked.

Marisa stared at the smashed mass that had somehow slipped from the vise and onto the floor. It was just a shapeless pile of rotten gobs and broken bones. Other than the tatters of cloth, nothing remained to suggest it had once been human...or even formerly human.

And she had done that.

The bloody young woman heard the rafters above rustle with feathers as the crows evaluated this new offering. It occurred to her the crows were having one hell of a great night. Their buffet just kept getting bigger and bigger. And now they even had Textro waitresses serving up their next meal. She briefly wondered if that was funny, or if the thought ought to make her sick. The former felt a little too much like hysteria, so she leaned towards the latter.

Marisa swayed, but then rallied even as Harley reached out to steady her.

No! I will not pass out! She railed at herself. *I will not faint! I will not throw up! I will not cry! I will not lose control! Not until this is over...and not then either.*

The list kept getting longer and longer.

"Marisa?"

"I'm okay!" she gasped. "I'm okay. I just had a bit of a moment there, but I'm okay now." She actually wondered if she would ever be okay again.

"A bit of a moment?"

Harley now held her with a hand on each shoulder and looked her searchingly in the eyes.

The concern on his face touched her. He actually cared. The man was actually worried about her.

But it was the feel of his hands on her shoulders that demanded her attention the most. She could feel the strength in them. Not just the mechanical power that came with hard muscle, but the controlled and tempered grip of a man who understood that real strength was as much a matter of heart as it was brawn. And that strength felt good. As a matter of fact, it felt damn good, and a rebellious part of her mind noted that all she had to do now was take one step forward and that grip would turn into an embrace.

She had an idea that would feel pretty damn good too.

And if you do that right now, her practical side noted, *you will lose it. It will take precisely ten seconds for you to turn into a useless, blubbering mess.*

Marisa suspected this was probably true. But at the same time she couldn't help but wonder if it wasn't about time for her practical side to shut the hell up. After all, enough was enough.

She was tired, filthy, wet, scared, hurting, bleeding, apparently half crazy, and now missing a chunk of her ear. By god, she had *earned* this.

But even as she stared back into Harley's worried eyes, and struggled over whether to take the step or not, the matter was decided for her.

A thunderous boom reverberated through the building.

Marisa jumped and Harley spun towards the door. What the hell?

Another powerful boom sounded, and the door shook in its frame. Crows squawked and flapped overhead as the sound thundered through the building. Then another tremendous blow landed and this time a large dent appeared in the metal door.

A dent she recognized as the size of a certain massive fist. A second later another dent showed up beside the first. Is sounded like the very building shook around them. Marisa grasped the situation in horrifying clarity, and choked back a cry.

Harley had been wrong. It wasn't all over. It wasn't even close

As a matter of fact, things were now worse.

"*Ay Dios*," she whispered. "It's Buddha Boy."

Maelstrom – Buddha Boy

Thoom!

The carnivorous giant that had once been Gary Norville drove its massive fist into the door again. It couldn't see the prey anymore, but that didn't matter. It knew they were there. Unlike its lesser brethren, Buddha Boy transcended the "out of sight, out of mind" level. As a matter of fact, it transcended the others in a number of ways.

It hardly rated as intelligent in most ways the term is understood. But in many ways that mattered, it did a good simulation. Rachel Sutherland's trick with the LED light would not have worked on this monster.

Its ravaged but relatively fresh neural system simply outclassed its comrades.

Death is not kind to the human brain, especially the delicate frontal lobes where most of the higher functions are housed. So anything like true reasoning still lay beyond this creature's abilities. But where the children of the graveyard dealt with the world on a "recognition" basis, this colossus "understood" things. Fundamental memories, stripped of all reason, identity, or self-association, gave the titan the benefit of many concepts without it ever truly using them. It simply grasped the basics of situations confronting it.

It understood it didn't have to wait for hunger to drive it in order to start wandering for food. It understood glass didn't make a wall. It understood that things didn't simply disappear when the lights went out. It certainly understood when something shut a door it wasn't just gone. And it understood if it knocked hard enough, that door would open.

And Buddha Boy could knock very, very hard.

Gary Norville had been no athlete, but the muscle mass necessary for carrying around his three hundred and fifty pound bulk was more than most people might think. And while this was not the honed or hardened muscle of a weight lifter, a great deal of it lay buried under the layers of fat and it now operated at a level it had never been close to before. While its skeletal companions ranged in strength from that of a normal person to the power of an extremely strong adult, Buddha Boy was another matter entirely.

The monster drove its fist into the metal door again, feeling the steel warp under its assault. It understood the door would give soon, and anticipation drove it to strike even harder. It had already fed on the morsel torn from Gerald, and one of the bodies from the assault on the gas pumps, but Buddha Boy had a large capacity and a desire to fill it.

The pair of lesser dead picked up on that anticipation, flexing their jaws and hands and moving in close. The giant only heeded them long enough to swat one hard enough to send it tumbling back across the asphalt, while crushing the skull of the other that actually got between it and the door.

It also understood it didn't have to share, at least not until it had satisfied itself.

And satisfaction lay only seconds away.

DEAD STOP

Maelstrom - Marisa

Another tremendous boom thundered through the garage, sending the crows swirling though the rafters. The sheet metal roof shivered, and a couple of tools clattered to the floor from the shelves.

"Oh shit, Harley! We've got to get out of here! Please tell me you've got the keys to the car."

Marisa looked at the man in desperation. Not a remnant remained of the madness that had overtaken her earlier. Sanity now returned in full force, and it told her in no uncertain terms what odds they faced against the monstrosity now beating its way through the steel door.

"I haven't had a chance to," came his tight reply. "I had just finished the last zombie off and came to see if you needed help. Besides, if Stacey is right then they're in that pile of body parts in the corner...and I noticed those aren't exactly dead anymore. I think the fungus has connected it all and the whole mass is alive now."

"Oh Jesus...."

Marisa looked over into the corner, then clenched her eyes shut and swallowed. That "mass" had been three of her friends. Leon, Tomas, and even old Arnold in his grouchy way. And now they were reduced to one more sight she would be spending the rest of her life trying to forget. She could only pray the squirming mess had no memory or intelligence.

It was almost too much. This nightmare just kept evolving and didn't show any sign of stopping. Every time she thought they had finally seen the extent of this night's horror, something even worse reared its head.

Another earthshaking slam jerked her attention back to the present, and the reality of their situation. They had bigger fish to fry.

What writhed in the corner might be an abomination of the highest order, but right now Death was knocking at the door. And he would be coming in any minute.

Buddha Boy was here.

Harley must have seen the despair in her eyes, for he summoned a grin that at least tried to be reassuring. Unfortunately, it looked more desperate than anything else.

"It's okay," he said, and moved towards the door. "I got this. I just need you to be brave one more time."

Not trusting herself to speak, she only nodded. She couldn't think of anything to say now anyway. It was time to get back into action. She doubted he would be able to hold the door closed for long and moved to find something to help him brace it shut.

"No, don't move," Harley waved her back as he reached towards the door handle. "I need you to just stand there, where he will be sure to see you when I open the door…"

On second thought, there might be something that needed saying, after all.

"When you *WHAT*???"

"I gotta open the door Marisa," he spoke in a low voice as he leaned against the buckling structure. "If I don't, he's going to break it and they'll all get in. Better to let him in and face him alone."

"And he's going to just waltz right in while you hold the door for him? That's awful nice of the big guy!"

"Well, that's where we get to the 'you being brave' part."

Of course it was.

"Annnnnnd my job is to be bait." She sighed.

"I just need you to catch his attention and draw him past me. I'll be behind the door. Then you run around behind the car when he comes in. I've still got one shot left, so I'll just step out and put a bullet in his head. It'll be easy. Then I'll get the keys, we'll hop in the car, and it will all be downhill from there."

"Right," Marisa nodded and faced the door again. If Harley said it would be easy then it was probably going to be difficult as hell, but that was just the way her evening was going. The gore splattered girl figured she was getting used to it. Hell, she had already done two or three death defying stunts tonight anyway. What was one more?

"Remember, run. Don't even try to mix it up with this thing."

That brought a hollow laugh from her.

"Don't worry, Harley. Miss Crazypants is gone for the evening. It's just me now. Don't you feel lucky?"

"Actually, yes." He replied with a sober look. "*Your* judgment, I trust."

Well, that was always good to know.

"Aw... thanks, partner," she smiled weakly. "I'll be good and run away. Now please don't die, okay?"

As if on cue, another thunderous crash shook the door.

"Not planning on it," he winked back.

Then Harley's grin tightened and he held up one finger while grabbing the doorknob with the other hand. It was go time.

"Okay..." He lifted his hand higher like somebody getting ready to drop the flag at a drag race. "Get ready...annnnnd...here we go."

Marisa watched him jerk the door open and step behind it in one smooth motion. And even though she had prepared herself for this, the sight of this new threat took her breath away.

The monster literally filled the doorway.

Buddha Boy's pale bulk spanned the entire breadth of the door frame. The great body was swollen and off color, a monstrous corpse that dominated the entranceway. And at well over six foot, its bald head almost reached the top as well. There could have been an entire horde of ravenous dead behind the creature and Marisa wouldn't have been able to tell. Whatever possible remnant that may have remained of her former berserker self melted away in the presence of this behemoth.

Its dead white eyes practically glowed in its mottled face. They scanned the room, then stopped as they came to rest on her. Their pearly surface seemed to take on an unholy sheen at the sight of the lone girl.

Oh looky! She swallowed. *He's taking the bait. Lucky me! Harley, you better not miss.*

"Hey, Buddha Boy!" she stammered out in mock good cheer. "You want your usual? No prob...HOLY SHIT!"

The monster exploded in her direction.

And in one split second she realized they had made a terrible mistake.

They should have known that if the skeletal monsters from the cemetery could move quick, then something with fresh new muscles would be just as fast...or faster. But they had underestimated this thing. Its bulk had thrown them off, making them think it could only move like Buddha Boy in life. Now it stampeded towards her like a juggernaut of mortified flesh.

Marisa was a split second away from being torn limb from limb.

Realizing she didn't have time to run around the end of the car, Marisa whipped around and began a desperate attempt to dive across the hood instead. She started from about eight or nine feet from the car, knowing the putrefying giant was already almost right on top of her. Her long legs closed the gap in three rapid strides. This was going to be close. Hearing the slap of his naked feet right behind her, the terrified young woman gathered her strength and leapt for all she was worth.

She didn't make it.

The rancid titan landed on her like an avalanche.

His mass smashed her down onto the car in mid leap, buckling the metal of the hood and driving the air out of her lungs. It felt like somebody had dropped a dead elephant on her. The girl's spine bowed and her ribs threatened to snap under the titanic pressure. Marisa gagged and her vision became ringed in red as she struggled to get her breath back under the immense weight. The monster had her pinned like a bug. She was starting to suffocate and a whole new order of panic set in.

Worse yet, she could feel the thing turn its head against the back of her own, and realized it was preparing to bite...and there wasn't a damn thing she could do about it. She couldn't even wriggle under the crushing load.

Marisa clenched her eyes shut, steeling herself for the agony of its teeth cutting into her neck or shoulder.

Benny...Stacey...I'm sorry. I almost made it back for you guys. I really tried.

Then a thunderous explosion went off right behind her ear.

Gladys's gun.

Even before the blast faded, Marisa realized what had happened. Harley must have been running behind the monster, chasing it as it charged, but not daring to take the shot until he could get close and make sure it counted. When it had caught her, he had caught it a scant second later. Then he must have put the gun against the creatures head, right behind her, and pulled the trigger.

Her head rang from the guns report, and if felt like she wasn't going to be hearing anything out of her right ear for a while...at least what was left of it...but the crushing weight suddenly eased. A second later it disappeared entirely.

Marisa slid off the hood of the car in a boneless heap. It felt like she had been squashed flat. Now, instead of just her toe, ear, and hip, every bone in her body hurt. Even her chest ached as she drew in her first gasping breath. Once she got her air and vision back, she fully intended to give Harley an earful about this particular plan. Next time, *he* could damn well be the bait.

"Marisa!" She dimly heard Harley yell through the ringing of her ears. "If you can hear me, slide under the car! Hurry!"

Huh?

What the hell?

Marisa cracked open a blurry eye to see Harley standing about seven or eight feet away. The man crouched in a fighter's stance, his face tight with tension. He tossed the empty pistol to the floor nearby, and she instinctively understood it was to free his uninjured hand for combat. For a second, the move confused her. Then her vision cleared further to reveal the awful truth.

She was seeing Harley from between Buddha Boys legs.

The giant corpse still stood.

It must have been getting ready to go after Harley when her labored attempts to breathe had recaptured its attention. Now it twisted to turn its pearly white eyes back down to where she lay. Looking up at a naked fat man from the floor already gave her a picture she would rather not see, but the sight of the monster's grisly cranium only made things worse. Almost half of the top of its head was missing, exposing brain matter and some strange cottony fuzz.

Harley hadn't missed...he just hadn't killed it. And now he was out of bullets and facing a monster that didn't feel pain, didn't get tired, and could punch its way through a steel door. For a second, Marisa tried to understand how this could have happened, and then the answer hit her.

Oh shit! The doc called it hindbrain, and Harley shot it in the side of the head! He must have missed the part of the brain this thing is using!

Now the corpulent horror looked like it intended to renew its previous hood-top acquaintance with her. And with it staring straight at her, she knew she had no chance to slide under the car in time. It shifted its feet and started to reach for her...

"Hey! Big guy!" Harley shouted and clapped his hands together. "Over here! I'm your dance partner now! C'mon, look at me!"

The monster paused and glared back at the man.

Marisa held her breath and forced herself not to move. The behemoth's meaty hand hovered less than a foot from her face. Her eyes almost crossed as they focused in on the blood crusted paw. Each finger was as thick as a sausage, and she knew they combined to form a grip capable of crushing her skull like an eggshell.

Every fiber of her being wanted to try and scramble away. But she understood the motion would only ensure an attack, and it could grab her before she had a chance to escape. Still, it was the hardest thing she had ever done. She just hoped Harley knew what he was doing, because she doubted he would have much more chance in a hand to hand struggle with this monster than she did.

"C'mon!" Harley clapped his hands again. "C'MON! I'm right here! Come get me!"

The giant seemed to consider him a moment.

"Yeah, that's right! Come get some, fat boy!"

CLAP!

"C'mon! What's the matter with you! Come get me!"

CLAP!

"C'mon, damn you! I'm right here!"

Harley spread his hands, as if offering himself to the monster.

Marisa tried to convince herself that he wasn't just doing this for her. She wanted to believe he had some higher strategy behind this crazy move, but this time she knew better. This time he wasn't just doing his job. If he were being ruthless and practical, then his best shot of killing this thing and saving the others was to attack it from the rear while it attacked her. But he wasn't doing that.

Instead, he was openly inviting a killer behemoth to close with him, just to get it away from her.

Yet while she stared at that massive, gore-smeared hand so close to her face, she found she really couldn't hold it against him. He was being stupid as hell but she could let that slide until later. Assuming there *was* a later. Right now he was welcome to play hero to his heart's content.

The three of them stared at each other a second longer.

Then the monster made its choice.

Marisa couldn't help but yell a warning as it bolted towards Harley. It closed on the man in a flash, once again showing that astonishing acceleration to full speed in almost no time flat. She knew its momentum had to be enormous, and the man's only hope was to find a way to dodge its charge.

But Harley didn't do that.

Instead he braced himself, and drew back one hand now curled into a two pronged claw. A split second later the giant slammed into him, driving him backwards...but not before Harley lashed out and drove his hooked thumb and fingers into the monster's eyes and buried them up to their last knuckles in its sockets.

276

The effect wasn't immediate. The monster still plowed forward, now with Harley in its grasp. The pair of them hurtled on and smashed into the cinder brick wall with tremendous force.

Marisa heard Harley grunt from the impact and knew it must have hurt terribly. The memory of being crushed under the titan's weight still loomed fresh in her memory. She knew being smashed against unyielding concrete by the thing had to be far worse. At the same time, she realized what Harley had just done and renewed hope caused her to scramble to her feet.

The monster was now blind.

And that meant it couldn't see her coming.

But it still had Harley against the wall with one of his arms clasped in its huge hand. He had slumped down till he almost hung from its grip, although she couldn't tell if it was because he was hurt or just trying to avoid the monster's other fist as it flailed wildly for a target to smash. Or maybe both. One of those blows impacted against the cinder bricks hard enough to leave cracks, and Marisa realized she needed to do something fast.

"Hey, *pendejo!*" she shouted, desperately searching for a weapon that would have some hope of hurting the thing. "I'm over here!"

She really didn't expect it to accomplish anything. Hell, she was just yelling while trying to figure out something else to do that might make a difference. So it caught her completely unprepared when the giant corpse turned and lunged in her direction.

Marisa jumped back with a scream as the monster stumbled blindly after her.

She backpedaled towards the car again, her gaze locked on the monster's mutilated face. It looked even more horrific than before. Its eyes were now torn sockets weeping tears of black ichor.

But its ears must have worked fine because it zeroed right in on her. It couldn't move near as fast like this, but the area wasn't very big. She wasn't anywhere near out of trouble yet. Even worse, the thing still held

Harley by the arm and dragged him along behind like a forgotten toy.

But realizing it tracked her by sound gave Marisa an idea.

"Buddha Boy!"

She shuffled sideways as she yelled, and noted with rising hope that it altered course to follow. The monster continued to drag Harley along behind it like a rag doll. She couldn't tell if he was dazed, unconscious, or dead. What she did know was she needed to keep the creature distracted or it might turn its attention back to the "bird in the hand." If Harley died there would be nobody to drive the truck. And that meant it was now all up to her.

She was going to have to kill this giant...

....all by herself.

But she had just figured out a way to do it.

It was going to be a gamble. And it would involve her doing something utterly awful. Even worse, it would mean getting back within reach of those huge hands. But Marisa had long since passed the point of caring about "awful" and gambles were all she had left. The monster did have one weak point, and she had just spotted the tool to apply to it.

Now she just needed to bring the horror within reach.

"Hey, *boboso!*" Marisa yelled as she backpedaled away. "Over here!"

The monster, who had just reached the car, now turned and lurched back towards Marisa's new position. That was exactly what she had counted on.

At her feet, right beside the red toolbox, lay the mechanic's dolly. The low, wheeled platform had allowed Arnold and Leon to lie on their backs and roll under cars to work on them. Now she intended to use if for something else. It took all of her courage to allow the thing to get closer, but she waited until it was where she needed it to be. Then putting her foot against the dolly, she pushed it out into the oncoming horror's path.

The results were spectacular, if not exactly what she intended.

Instead of stumbling forward with its head landing at her feet...like she hoped...the giant stepped directly on the dolly and had its foot fly out from beneath it. Its free arm flailed in the air while its foot went amazingly high for a creature with such a corpulent build. For one brief, suspended moment in time it reminded her of an old movie with a cartoon hippo playing at a ballerina.

Unfortunately, it appeared it wasn't going to go down. The foot started to lower as the gargantuan corpse somehow managed to regain its balance.

But that's when Harley struck.

The man must have been dazed and just instinctually taking advantage of the situation she created. He couldn't have really thought his actions through. Not unless he was trying to get himself killed.

In one lightning fast move he gripped the monsters hand where it held him by the upper arm. Then in the same motion he used it as a brace to swing both of his feet around and drive them into the back of its knee. His boots struck with the full weight and force of his entire body, and the nightmare came down like a ton of bricks...

...right on top of him.

Harley almost disappeared under the ghastly mass, and Marisa realized he only had seconds to live. He had recaptured the monster's attention. Now it had him pinned and could bring both hands to bear on him. Even as she grasped the situation she heard a muffled cry come from the man underneath the downed colossus.

But at the same time, she saw that Harley had gotten the creature into the position she needed, even if it had been by accident.

Grabbing the air impact wrench off the top of the nearby toolbox, Marisa charged into the fray. It was now or never. Given the thing's attention on Harley, she would have a clearer shot than her original plan provided. Now came the "doing something awful" part. She just hoped she pulled it off, and did it in time.

Dropping to her knees beside the blind giant's head, she drove the socket end of the air wrench into the section of exposed brain and pulled the trigger.

The wrench was a heavy duty tool, designed to tighten up lug nuts on eighteen wheelers, and with a torque of over twelve hundred pounds it revved up to seven thousand rpms in a second.

It was like turning the monster's skull into a blender.

Brain matter flew and Marisa gagged as the spinning socket sank into the grey mass. The worst part of the back spray caught her full force and added a coat of fungus and dead neural tissue on top of her previous layer of gore.

A split second later the giant spasmed and splayed out like a starfish. Unfortunately, that meant the arm it had underneath it in search of Harley now came flying out in the form of a monstrous backhand that caught her full in the chest.

It felt like being hit by a truck.

For the second time in as many minutes the air exploded from her lungs, and Marisa tumbled backwards like a puppet with its strings cut. Stars blasted across her vision as her head smacked against the hard floor. Her arm tangled in the air line as she rolled and the wrench came free of the monster's skull. It spun itself to a stop on the blood crusted concrete. The girl herself came to rest, face down on the cement, about five feet further away.

Then silence fell, with nothing but the crows to disturb it.

However it may have ended, the fight was over.

Marisa lay there hurting, barely caring whether she was dead or alive. Her body felt like a five thousand pound bruise. It would have probably been easier for her to pinpoint a place that *didn't* hurt, if she could find one. At the moment, she felt content to just lie on the bloody concrete and not think about anything. Not the dead, not the victims, not what might be going on in the rest of the country...nothing. She didn't even want to open her eyes, having seen enough of the bloody madness her world had descended into.

But she couldn't stop yet.

This wasn't over, and there were still people who needed her. Starting with the only man who could drive the truck out of here.

"Harley?"

Nothing.

"Harley?"

For another moment there was silence, then a faint grunt came from nearby. Since she never remembered any of the monsters making a vocal sound, she hoped for the best. To her surprise, even the effort of hoping seemed to hurt.

"Harley?" she groaned again. "Are you still alive?"

"I think so..." came the muffled reply.

"Oh, good," she murmured. "Just checking."

With that settled, Marisa considered the idea of simply laying there for a while. She knew she should get moving again, but the effort felt enormous. Besides, the others were safe on the truck stop roof, and there were a lot worse things than getting wet. Surely a little while longer wouldn't hurt them.

"Hey, partner?"

Now what...

"Yeah, Harley?"

"You remember that list of turnoffs you wanted me to work on back in the diner?"

"Yeah?"

"Well, I'm kinda stuck laying here under this fat naked dead guy, and it just occurred to me this would be a pretty good place to start."

"Really? You're stuck?"

"Oh yeah. And this definitely falls under the category of 'bad thing.'"

"Okay," she moaned, and stirred to rise. "Just give me a minute."

"Did I mention he's naked?" He sounded markedly unhappy about that.

"Okay, okay!" Marisa laughed and immediately regretted it. That hurt too. "I'll be there in a second. Keep your britches on."

"Oh, believe me...I will."

"Here you go."

Marisa took the offered keys as Harley slid in through the passenger door into the front seat beside her. They fairly gleamed from having been washed off by the man after he had fished them from the squirming mess of body parts in the corner. He really didn't need to do that since she was long past the point of being bothered by gore, but she decided it still counted as a decent gesture on his part.

The car was a refurbished Plymouth 4-door from the eighties, and she knew this thing was going to handle like a boat. Also, the last surviving shred of her vanity cringed at the vomit green color of the metal beast. Before tonight she wouldn't have been caught dead driving it.

But that was before tonight.

Tonight, she noted with relief there would be plenty of room for people once they got off the top of the truck at the rest area. Besides, the wild-haired, blood smeared, fright-fest she caught a glimpse of in the mirror didn't have any business being picky about anything.

"Okay," Harley started as she inserted the keys and buckled in. "Now comes the easy part. But I want you to recite the plan back to me, just one more time."

"Right," She rolled down the window just enough to get her arm out as she talked. "I turn on the headlights then open the door. That should draw the zombies by the truck back here toward us. I wait a few seconds to let them get away from the truck, then I back out fast, turn around, and drive straight through them. Then I pull up beside the truck, you hop out of the car and into the semi. After that, I drive on towards the rest area down the road. *Bien*?"

"Right," he nodded, obviously satisfied. Then he looked her way with a haggard grin. "We're almost out of here, you know. You ready to do this, partner?"

"I guess," Marisa sighed and turned on the headlights. "Let's get this show on the road."

She started the car and her taillights flooded the door behind them in red. Between those and all the light spilling out of the bay doors once they opened, it should be like waving a red flag in front of a bunch of bulls. Unwelcome recollections of the night's earlier charge on the gas pumps came to mind. She really had no desire to relive that.

At least a glance at the gas gauge showed a full tank.

Marisa reached a gory arm out through the window and snagged the hanging controls for the automatic bay doors. She stared in almost amused despair at the green button. Here she went again...once more opening the doors between her and the death faced horrors outside. This was threatening to become a habit with her. At least this time she had a car's body between her and the monsters. Hopefully it would be enough.

With a rueful shake of her head she stabbed the green button and withdrew her arm.

The electric gate motor hummed to life as she rolled up the window. Marisa gunned the engine, then twisted in her seat to see out the back window. Harley did the same beside her, something even easier for him since he wasn't wearing a seat belt. She started to protest, then remembered he needed to be unencumbered so he could make the jump to the truck as fast as possible.

Then all that was forgotten when the bay door rolled open to reveal the storm wracked night beyond...and the lone skeletal figure framed against the darkness.

"Oh no..." Marisa groaned in horror. "*Dios, por favor! No esto!*"

It was Vicki.

Probably blinded by the sudden lights of the mechanics shop flooding out over it, the wasted corpse stood unmoving in the entranceway. The taillights limned the pale figure in red. The image blurred in the slightly fogged rear window, and Marisa could almost imagine the gentle face those bones once formed...and in doing so, made what she had to do next almost impossible.

This thing had once been Vicki. The soft spoken girl who calmed her after Marisa got in those awful fights with her mother. The sister who comforted her while Papa spent his final weeks in the hospital fighting cancer. The best friend who helped her make a dress they were to share.

"That isn't her," Harley said softly beside her.

"I know," Marisa whispered and, despite what she had said earlier in the diner, fought to believe it.

Fungus or no fungus, that was Vicki's body out there. It was her brain. Could they be absolutely sure there was nothing left? Doc was sure, but Doc dealt only in science. Marisa believed in a lot more than that, even if she wasn't sure what all of it was.

"Marisa..."

"I know," she repeated, but her hand still hovered above the transmission.

And she did.

But whether or not Vicki still lived in there, that had once been an integral part of her...from the hands that once played the clarinet with such dexterity, to the full mane of hair, just like hers, that Marisa helped her brush every morning. Even the soggy remains of the dress they had so laughingly worked on together. Whatever that was out there, it had once been Vicki.

"Marisa..." Harley said in a calm voice. "The others are coming. They will be crowding in here with us in roughly eight seconds. There are a lot of them, and they are stronger than ever. We may not be able to push our way out of them from a dead stop."

"I *know*," she choked out as her hand closed on the transmission. She had threatened to kill this horror back in the diner. Now faced with the reality of doing just that, it was the last thing she wanted to do. But it was what everybody *needed* her to do...and it was what she was going to do. Right now.

She dropped the transmission into reverse.

This was going to hurt.

"I'm sorry, Vicki," the girl whispered. "Please forgive me."

Marisa stomped her foot on the gas and the large Plymouth shot backwards out of the garage.

It smashed into the wasted figure, causing it to fold over the trunk before whipping backward and disappearing under the car. The large sedan bounced and she could literally feel bone crunch and snap under her tires. It felt like pieces of her soul shattered along with them. The sound of it tumbling under the floorboards reverberated through the cab. Then it must have caught under the axle for a second before another jounce and crunch signaled its arrival at the front tires.

Jerking the wheel to the side, Marisa slid the large vehicle into a turn. She tried not to look at the broken heap of rags that emerged from under the front of the car. In the dim light of the parking lot, it looked so small, so trivial...just a piece of refuse discarded on the asphalt.

It lay there like a crumpled reminder that everything she loved was truly dead and gone.

Then the sight of it was mercifully blotted out as the monsters arrived.

Twisting the wheel again, Marisa slammed the transmission into gear and hit the gas. Her tires spun on the wet asphalt and the car threatened to fishtail. She didn't let up. Breathing in harsh gulps, she fought to keep the car on course as multiple thumps sounded off the front grill. Several skulls grinned in her headlights before gaping then disappearing under her hood. Withered claws slapped and scratched past the window beside her head. Once the car almost slowed to a stop as the rear tires caught and then spun out on a couple of corpses, but it regained traction and leapt forward through the grisly ranks.

Then they were through.

The Plymouth shot across the parking lot towards the diesel pumps, leaving the ranks of the dead behind. Marisa became aware of a pain in her jaw and realized she had been clenching it to the point of fracture. At the same time she caught herself looking in the rear view mirror. She refused to think what she had been looking for and forced herself to focus forward.

She had to let go.

She had to. Her friends needed her.

285

Marisa maintained speed then slowed the vehicle at the last moment. She did a rapid deceleration that allowed her to just barely bring the car to stop without skidding, but placed Harley's door almost perfectly across from the one on Grandpa Tom's truck. Out of the corner of her eye, she could see figures jumping on the roof of the truck stop and knew the celebration had begun.

Maybe someday she could join them.

"We're here," Harley confirmed and grabbed the handle of his door. "Your part is done. Now go ahead and get out of here. We'll meet you at the rest area."

He started to exit the car...

...and that's when Marisa surprised both him and herself by reaching out and catching his arm.

Halfway out the door, Harley stopped and looked back in at her with confusion.

"Marisa?"

The girl struggled to speak, to try and put the pain she was in into words. This wasn't the time, but she couldn't help it.

"Are you okay?" His eyes searched her face.

Was she? She struggled with that for a second and then decided to go with the truth.

"No," her voice quavered, and she discovered she didn't give one little damn about how pitiful it might have sounded. She was past all that now. "No I'm not. I need you to hurry up, *comprende*?"

"Marisa?"

"Partner," she smiled feebly but could feel the tears start to well, "I don't want you to take this wrong, but I'm going to need that shoulder to cry on pretty quick, okay? I'm sorry, but I think I'm going to need it in a big way. So please hurry up."

Harley didn't say a word.

The man took a quick glance out the rear window, then slid back in and pulled her into his arms. He crushed her to him with a fierce intensity that almost took her breath away...and even as sore as she was, it felt every bit as good as she thought it would.

286

"Fifteen minutes," he whispered hoarsely in her ear and held her tight. "Just get to that rest area and I promise I'll be there in fifteen minutes. And when I get there, I'm not going to let go again until you make me."

She clenched him back, her face buried against his shoulder. All she wanted at that moment was for time to give her a break and stop for a little bit. Just for an eternity or two...that would be fine.

But that couldn't be, because the horde was racing up behind them and Harley had to get to the truck.

"Fifteen minutes," he repeated. "I promise. Wait for me."

And then he was gone.

Marisa took a deep shuddering breath and recovered her composure as the man leapt out the door.

Harley covered the short distance to the truck in two quick strides. The eighteen wheeler's lights flashed as he used the automatic lock on the keychain as he moved. He leapt up onto the truck rail and yanked on the door. It didn't budge, and she realized the truck must have been unlocked earlier during Harley's struggles and now he had locked it again by mistake. She watched him fumble with the keys again just as a flicker of motion caught her eye in the rear window.

The dead were almost upon them...their grinning jaws becoming visible as they entered the diesel islands lights.

Marisa's hand hovered over the gear shift and she held her breath, ready to drop the big car into reverse. She had had enough violence and killing for one night, for the rest of her life even, but if these things came much closer before Harley got in the truck she wasn't going to hesitate to do some more.

Thankfully, the slam of the truck door informed her that Harley was in the cab and out of harm's way. She had now done all she could do.

It was time to go.

Fighting down the lump in her throat, Marisa shifted the car into drive and pressed the accelerator. The big car eased forward, past the restaurant and towards the front of the parking lot. In the mirror, the lights of the Textro fell behind her for the last time. She pulled the Plymouth up on the road, but hesitated before hitting the gas.

The highway stretched empty and dark into the rain. Marisa had no idea what kind of world lay at the end of it. She only knew it would be different, and wouldn't include most of the family and loved ones that had been part of her life. Even now, this still wasn't over. There still remained a lot of pain, heartache, and loss to deal with in the future.

But at least she wouldn't have to face it alone.

A glance back showed Harley had the eighteen wheeler's lights on and was just beginning to pull out and start his rescue. Marisa wiped her eye and watched as he swung out in front of the gas pumps in order to start a wide circle of the building. He was doing what he needed to do, and being there for the people who needed him now.

Her turn would come.

He had promised.

"Fifteen minutes, partner," she whispered as she pulled away into the darkness. "Don't keep me waiting."

EPILOGUE

Epilogue – Benny

"Benny? Can you hear me? Time to wake up!"

He didn't want to. He just wanted to sleep.

"Beeennnnniiieeeee. Wakey, wakey!"

Benny lay there, floating in the blackness, desperately wishing Stacey would go away. As fond as he was of the little waitress, she was annoying the hell out of him. Her voice threatened to pull him from the pain free oblivion he so wanted to sink back into.

"C'mon Benny. Wake up! The doc says you have to now."

The doctor?

His sluggish mind focused on the word and tried to build on the concept. The doctor? What doctor? Something wasn't right here.

Where was he? A hospital? Why was he in a hospital? And why would Stacey be there?

Benny struggled to understand. He fought to remember how he could have possibly ended up here. At first he drew a blank, then bits and pieces began to come back. A memory of arriving at work while listening to the radio about the approaching storm...a vision of a sky full of wheeling crows...Stacey dancing into the kitchen and swinging a towel...Marisa being angry...and...and...

He fought to bring it back out of the darkness.

...and looking out the back door to see a screaming Stacey being chased by demons! What the hell?

"Stacey?" he groaned and forced his eyes open. They felt like they weighed a ton. "*Que pasa?* What happened...wait...where are we?"

He wasn't lying in a hospital bed. He wasn't even in a hospital. Somebody had stretched him out on a couch in what looked like a feed store, or something very like it. He tried to move to sit up to get a better view but a restraining hand pressed him back down...something easily done since he felt weak as a kitten.

"Please don't move, Mr. Trujillo," the voice of another woman spoke from down around the vicinity of his legs. "I'm still stitching you up and we don't want me to have any accidents, now do we."

Stitches? He was hurt? Benny struggled to remember...

"It's okay, Benny," Stacey beamed at him. She sat in a folding chair beside the couch. "You're in good hands. Doc is a super genius at figuring things out. She got to spend a few hours online before the power went down and even figured out how to get people's blood types with the stuff they have here. Guess what? You and I are a match! Now you're getting a little of the good stuff...guaranteed to make you feel younger and look twice as cute in no time."

She grinned and held up a little plastic bag attached to a catheter that he realized was running to his arm. He also noticed a blood stained bandage wrapping the upper part of her arm as well.

"You're hurt..." he groaned. "What happened? Where are we? What were those demons chasing you?"

He watched Stacey look down towards the other woman, obviously for guidance, then face him again with a solemn expression.

Bennie guessed she had been given permission to tell him the truth.

"Those were dead people, Benny," she half whispered. "Zombies, Just like in the movies, only scarier."

"What? Zombies? But...how? Where?"

"They came from the county cemetery down the road," the girl closed her eyes and shuddered, "and they started killing everybody. Arnold, Tomas, Leon, Gladys...everybody. Only six of us got away. You, me, Marisa, Deke, Harley, and the doc. Well, there were seven, but Grandpa Tom died this morning. We're hiding out here at a vet clinic near Lake Cowell until we figure out what to do next."

Benny just lay there, trying to take it in.

"By the way," Stacey seemed to rally, and gave him a weak smile, "Doc has to give you a shot once this blood bag is empty. I gotta warn you, she's not as good at giving shots as she is at other things."

"I heard that," came the woman's voice down at his legs. "Just so you know, once I'm done with Mr. Trujillo, I'm coming after you're arm next. Be glad for the wonders of lidocaine."

Benny ignored the banter and tried to focus.

"Hiding out?" He fought to think. "Why are we hiding out? Shouldn't we go get help?"

"There's nowhere to go, Benny." The fear in her voice convinced him she was telling the truth. "According to the CB radio in the truck, these monsters are coming up all over the place...Texas, Louisiana, Oklahoma, and Arkansas mostly...and we're right in the middle of it. There were some people saying it could also be happening in Mexico. And the people they're killing are turning into monsters too! The government has called out the army, and there's been rumors of a quarantine. Somebody even said they bombed Killeen and Amarillo last night."

"Idiots!" the woman down at his legs hissed. "It's a soil based organism and they're blowing tons of dirt up in the air! *That's* helpful!"

"Yeah," Stacey winced, then continued. "Anyway, Harley said we should hide here until things settle down and we have a better idea what's going on. I think he's as scared of running into the army as he is of the dead things."

"But...but what about Masonfield?"

"We don't know...we know some people got away, but...we don't know. I'm sorry, Benny.

Benny could hear the lie in her voice. It landed on his heart like a wet sack of cement. He lay his head back and closed his eyes.

Masonfield dead? Probably his wife, Corina, as well? The dead rising from the grave? Entire states being quarantined? His mind reeled at having to wake up to all of this at once. He wouldn't have believed it, but he could remember the things chasing Stacey himself. This was real. It was catastrophic. It was....biblical.

"It's the end of the world, isn't it..." he breathed. "Judgement Day is finally here..."

"No!" Stacey whispered fiercely and gripped his arm. "It ain't like that! Doc says this is like a plague or a disease. It's bad, but we can fight this thing. Right, Doc?"

"Humans are notorious for coming through cataclysms," the other woman muttered while she worked on his legs. "Hell, I think we create our own from time to time just to stay in practice. Don't ever rule us out."

"What *she* said," the girl affirmed. "We ain't licked yet. Just hang in with us, Benny. We'll make it through this. You'll see."

Benny didn't respond, still trying to absorb the enormity of it all.

"Benny?" She took him by the hand. "I know you're hurting...we all are...but we're going to get through this. You just rest up and get better, okay? We made it through last night, and now the storm is over. We'll find our way from here."

He stared at the ceiling, not knowing what to say.

"We need you, Bennie," Stacey continued, her face solemn once more. "I need you, and so does Marisa. Of course she'll never admit it, but she does. Hang in there for us, okay? Please?"

Whether she knew it or not, she hit every button that mattered. Even if it was the end of the world, Bennie wouldn't dream of not being there for them. They were the daughters he had never had...even if both of them were huge pains in the ass. Somebody had to keep them out of trouble.

And he doubted the two young rednecks he barely remembered were even close to being up to the task. They were going to need his help.

Starting now.

"It's okay, *Chiquita*," he sighed and gave her a weak smile. "I'll be okay. Don't worry. Whatever happens, I'll be there."

###

Epilogue- Rachel

Rachel stepped out the front door of the country clinic and arched her weary back.

Benny Trujillo, Deke, and Stacey were now stitched up, and everybody had been given a shot of the antifungal medication. She had warned it might make them sick a day or two, but it was the most effective available. Now they all slept in the front office of the clinic. All in all, she allowed herself a small bit of self congratulation on a job well done.

Well, almost...

The sight of a small makeshift cross in the pasture across the barb wire fence caused her to wince in memory at her one "failure."

Grandpa Tom had made it. He had escaped with the rest of them. And when they had all staggered into the clinic after Harley jimmied the door, he had sank exhausted into the closest chair he could find. So had the others...except for Rachel, who had dragged herself back into the doctor's office to use the internet to post warnings about the nature of the threat and grab all the medical information she could while the power still lasted. She had been at it about an hour when Marisa had come back and quietly told her that Grandpa Tom was dead.

He had simply drifted away in his sleep, right there in the chair.

Rachel could only console herself with the knowledge she couldn't have done anything for him anyway, and that he got to pass peacefully. That had to count as some kind of victory, didn't it? Compared to what might be in store for them, he may have gotten off lucky.

Because in truth, Stacey was wrong...the storm wasn't over.

It was just beginning.

Now that she had the time to focus and think without the distraction of possibly dying any given minute, she started to realize the enormity of what they faced.

It has to be a soil based fungus, because it got in the coffins first. But now it's out, and spreading like wildfire. A five hour window between its host killing somebody, and then that somebody getting up to kill as well, is a ridiculously fast incubation period. And I don't even know if that's the only vector for transmission. Not to mention, the ground itself has been infected.

Marisa had told her earlier how Harley predicted the spread to have already killed Masonfield, and how fast he thought this stuff could expand. After listening to his reasoning, then applying her own knowledge of disease transmission, she realized he had actually underestimated it. The proliferation would be geometric, and if the rumored quarantine failed then Benny's concern might be more realistic than they realized.

This could be apocalyptic.

Rachel hoped not. Not just for herself, but for the new young friends she had made over the course of this ordeal. She really wanted to see Deke and Stacey get an honest chance to see if they had a future together. And Marisa and Harley...she wasn't quite sure what to make of that pair. They were something, but she couldn't quite figure out what it was.

A glance over at the feed store side of the building revealed the two of them had made impromptu recliner couches out of feed bags at the front corner of the building. Now they stretched out side by side, snoring in the afternoon sun. Rachel figured after all they did last night, and having to dig a grave this morning, they had earned it.

Rachel decided she could let them sleep and attend to their injuries later. She had already given them the antifungal shot and that was what really counted.

Until then, her job was done.

Now she just stood in the parking lot, soaking up the sunshine. The air fairly steamed with humidity after the storm from last night, but she didn't care. Just standing in daylight again felt glorious. The warmth helped drive the memory of last night's chill further from her mind, and gave her a sense of hope.

Rachel had instructed Deke to fill the four galvanized water troughs in the feed store full of water before the power cut out. So they had a supply that would last a good while. She also knew the hundreds of bags of animal feed were edible by humans, even if they tasted like crap. So they were covered on that score as well. Top that off with the fact they were surrounded by pastures and had an unobstructed view for at least half a mile in any direction, and they had what amounted to a secure and hopefully surprise free situation.

For the moment, they were safe.

Now it all depended on the rest of the world.

Hopefully the quarantine did its job. At least a line of heavily armed soldiers stood a much better chance against these things than the people of the Textro last night. She just hoped nobody did something stupid and tried to end this with some really big bombs.

But there was nothing she could do about that but wait and see.

Until then, the best she could do was plan and try to see they had everything they needed to get by until either help arrived, or they tried to reach the quarantine line themselves. Harley said they might try after things had settled down and he was sure the soldiers weren't just shooting at anything that approached.

Movement on the horizon caught her eye and Rachel turned her head. A flock of crows flew along the distant tree line on the other side of the pasture. She frowned at the aerial procession, and folded her arms as she tracked their progress.

She noted their current trajectory would take them to the east and away from the store, so that was a small relief. Besides, they were flying straight as opposed to wheeling like Stacey had described last night. So they weren't following a pack of zombies either. The grim side of her figured they had probably gorged enough lately anyway.

And then it hit her.

"Oh my god!" Rachel gasped. "The crows!"

"Doc?" Harley's soft voice came from the corner of the building. He must not have been as asleep as she thought. "Is everything okay?"

Rachel didn't answer, her throat locked tight as her mind desperately recalculated the spread with this new vector in the equation. It was the roughest of guesswork. Pure estimation. But even allowing for that, the answer she came up with dismayed her.

No. Everything wasn't okay.

The world was going to change. Whether civilization survived or not...whether man survived or not... nothing would ever be the same again.

The crows would see to that.

They had been walking and feeding in the bloody remains of all the zombie's victims. Now they were moving on in search of future feasts. And they were carrying the means of making those meals happen along with them.

Rachel watched in despair as they flapped their way over the horizon...

...their feathers dusted with a deadly cargo of spores.

ABOUT THE AUTHOR

D. Nathan Hilliard lives in Spring, Texas with his veterinarian wife, two children, and two cats. He draws his inspiration from a childhood living in different small Texas towns, accented by teen years spent in western New Mexico. He has experienced life through a diverse collection of jobs ranging from meter reading and being an assistant manager at a convenience store, to working at cotton gins, window factories, and uranium mills. After coming down with Charcot Marie Tooth (CMT) at the turn of the century, Mr. Hilliard now happily settles for tending house, raising his kids, and exploring the field of writing.

Made in the USA
San Bernardino, CA
04 September 2013